KARA STORTI

BACK BLUE

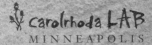

carolrhoda LAB

MINNEAPOLIS

Carolrhoda Lab™
An imprint of Carolrhoda Books
A division of Lerner Publishing Group, Inc.
241 First Avenue North
Minneapolis, MN 55401 USA

For reading levels and more information, look up this title at www.lernerbooks.com.

The images in this book are used with the permission of: © David Q. Cavagnaro/Photolibrary/ Getty Images (feathers); © Todd Strand/Independent Picture Service (letters, blade).

Main body text set in Janson Text LT Std 10.5/15.
Typeface provided by Linotype AG.

Library of Congress Cataloging-in-Publication Data

Names: Storti, Kara.
Title: Tripping Back Blue / by Kara Storti.
Description: Minneapolis : Carolrhoda Lab, [2016] | Summary: "Finn is a gentle, tortured dealer and addict whose life is slipping away. When he finds an almost magical drug called Indigo, he thinks it will let him break free, but he's dead wrong"— Provided by publisher.
Identifiers: LCCN 2015021012| ISBN 9781512403084 (lb : alk. paper) | ISBN 9781512404449 (eb pdf : alk. paper)
Subjects: | CYAC: Drug abuse—Fiction. | Drug dealers—Fiction.
Classification: LCC PZ7.1.S757 In 2016 | DDC [Fic]—dc23
LC record available at http://lccn.loc.gov/2015021012

Manufactured in the United States of America
1 – BP – 12/31/15

TO MOM WHO SHOWED ME CREATIVITY AND TO
DAD WHO TAUGHT ME PERSISTENCE.

CHAPTER ONE

MY CAR CRAPS OUT IN DAMMERTOWN. Here I am, it's two in the morning, stuck in front of what's probably a crack house, boarded up, spray-painted over, my cell doesn't work, the street lamp's flickering above me, and—

The light goes out.

I rest my forehead against the steering wheel.

It wouldn't be so bad if I didn't have ten thousand dollars in cash underneath my seat. It wouldn't be so bad if I weren't in the ghetto of ghettos, where just last week a little kid got shot. That's it. From now on, I'm sticking to slinging weed. I'm not doing this other sketchy nonsense, even as lucrative as it is, even as *exciting* as it is. I have to admit, begrudgingly, *I'm out.* Sweat is on the steering wheel from my palms. The window is fogging up from my hot and nervous breath. Okay, okay, okay. Finn, it could be worse, just play it cool, that usually gets you out of it every time. My twin sister, Faith, she'd say, *think bright.* I love my sister dearly, but her smiles are always real, and sometimes I want to tell her to wake the hell up.

All I've got to do is just get through this ordeal. Push through it; be a man. There's so much to look forward to.

Home. I'll feel the money in my hands. Dirty, gritty paper, thick stacks smelling funky and good.

Oxys. From my mom's stash. I'll take one and be loose, free, and in a warm bath of *I just don't give a fuck*. I'll smile. A real one. They don't come along often, for me, a salesman. That's what I am, like Pop—my father. Can't say that with any kind of pride, but there it is.

There are a few guys standing on a sagging front porch smoking and drinking from cans of beer. They haven't looked my way. Yet. What are my options? There's a gas station about a half mile down the road that gets robbed on the regular. And there's Jason Frye, my pot supplier's brother, whose place is around here, but he's the last person I want rescuing me today. Or ever. A couple of weeks ago he stole money from me, then I stole his girlfriend, then he slashed my tires, then I ratted him out to our high school principal for smoking weed in the bathroom. I'd say we're not on the best of terms.

I feel for the bag of money underneath my seat, just a simple L.L. Bean backpack, corners of the bills poking through the material, solid and reassuring. I can't leave it in my car, and I shouldn't have it on me while I go strolling through the projects. Either way, it's bad news. All I know is that it's mine (didn't even have to divvy it up this time), and I can't let *anything* happen to it. It's hard-earned cash that I've been dreaming about, putting myself to sleep at night by counting it like sheep.

These choices I have to make? It's not choosing what shirt to wear in the morning. It's choosing between what sucks and what blows, the epitome of a rock and a hard place. You can say that lately life hasn't been exactly generous.

The backpack is slung around one shoulder when I open the car door, the creak undeniable, it's like a burp in a library. The three guys on the porch, who are like, acre-big, take notice. Stupid car. Stupid neighborhood. It'd be one thing if I lived in New York City, where there's violence, sure, but tons of opportunity to become a better man. Not the case here. Instead I'm north of Albany, in rotten Dammer-fucking-town, where there is no other side, where no great life is waiting for me, where the earth threw up and walked away.

I start walking in the direction of the gas station, its light a pathetic, piss-yellow beacon in the night. Don't look back. Make it seem like I belong here. I kind of do. The trailer park I live in isn't much better than this, but it's home, and I would give my left nut to be there right now. I've been in this neighborhood plenty of times, but tonight it feels different, it feels meaner, and I feel small.

Though my footsteps are even and I've got me some swagger, I can hear the guys following right away and not even being shy about it. One of them says something, another one coughs.

Then, "Hey, where you goin'?"

Pretend I don't hear. Jason's place is up ahead to the right, and it looks like that's my best option. The sidewalk is uneven, wobbly ground, chunks missing from the blacktop. I try not to stumble. It's not even warm out, yet sweat is tracing lines down my back.

"You don't answer me? Why aren't you answering me?" His tough-guy voice echoes through the corridor of the street.

"What you got in the bag?" another asks.

Just one block to Jason's. I have to get there, like now, like *yesterday*, because the gas station is too far and probably closed. The money stacks are stabbing into my back through the L.L. Bean canvas, and the thought of it isn't comforting anymore; it feels dangerous, burden-heavy like everything else lately.

They're getting closer, hack-laughing, and I smell their late-night smell, beer, stale cologne, trouble. It's a white trash pot-pourri I know too well.

Jason's place is a few steps away now, thank God, because one of them is next to me. I can see his cigarette hanging from his mouth, his diamond earring glinting in the sickly, flickering street light.

"Is schoolboy scared?" The guy with the earring inclines his head, juts out his chin to showcase his fat face and pubic hair goatee. He's slurring his speech, and I think it's probably the norm and not the exception. His two friends are at his side, flank him, their shadowed faces are ominous and anonymous.

I walk up Jason's steps and bang on the door. I don't give a shit if I look desperate because I *am* desperate. *Please, Jason, be home, have a heart just this one time, I won't mess around with you anymore, I'll stay out of your way, truce. Please. Just please.*

One of them snickers, as if he can hear my thoughts. Jason's door is scratched and busted up, the half-moon glass window at the top covered with plywood. I cinch my backpack tighter against my shoulder and rap on the door again. And again, until my knuckles sing.

Nothing.

Jason's probably looking out his window and laughing.

So I turn and face them. Three against one. I'm six feet, got some muscle on me, but still, this is no fair fight. I feel for the Buck knife in my pocket that I know I don't have. I left it at home before the run, and sure enough they patted me down, before the drop. I do a quick glance around. There's a raggedy-ass shrub to the right of me and an iron railing of the cement steps to the left—nothing I can use as a weapon.

They're eyeing me hard, eyeing my bag even harder, and finally I say casually, "Hey, I'm gonna get going, all right?" Not the stupidest thing I've ever said, but not the smartest thing either. I make a move to leave but the one with the earring pushes me back.

"You look familiar," he says. "Don't he look familiar?" He turns to one of his buddies, who's wearing a tight white T-shirt with stains on the front, which draws attention to his muscular pecs. Pecs nods, and then spits on the steps in front of me. Of course I look familiar. I have blah brown hair and blah brown eyes (unless you look closer; I've been told they're golden-toned), but it's the scar on the side of my face and across my chin that distinguishes me from every other white dude in D-Town.

"He's that kid. Remember Andre talking about him? No business making this his territory," Pecs says. They don't have to nod or respond to know they agree. Then he says to me, "Stick to your *own* playground."

Earring guy cranes his neck to get a better view of my backpack. My heart is ramming against my ribcage as he jabs a finger at me. "What's that you got, schoolboy? The fruits of your labor? Might be your labor, but it's our fruit."

I smile a fake smile, because that's all I can do. Buys me some time. Relaxes them and me, slightly. Usually gets me out of a bind or two, gets me laid, gets me popular. Not sure what it's going to get me tonight, so I let the backpack strap fall from my shoulder, I shrug, and pretend to look resigned.

I jump—

Over the railing and take off, my bag bouncing against my side, as they sprint after me, sneakers slapping pavement, yelling, keys and lighters and whatever else jingling in their pockets, music to a race I don't want to be running. Good thing I'm fast and fit and see the brightness of the gas station, less than a quarter of a mile ahead.

I think I'm going to make it, I really do.

Then something sharp and hard hits the back of my head.

CHAPTER TWO

WHEN I COME TO, THE FIRST THING I FEEL IS A JAB TO MY SIDE. I open my eyes and see my sister, Faith, chomping on gum, grinding her three-inch heel into me.

"Get up, shithead," she says.

I sit up fast, too fast, as fast as my thoughts, which are spinning and starting to process. Broken-down car. Three guys. My—

"Where's my backpack?" I crank my head around, and all I see is pavement. Where are those assholes? They messed with me. You don't mess with Finn. I handle my shit.

"Where's my backpack?" Faith says in a mimicking tone, her earthy brown eye on a never-ending roll. "You're lucky you aren't dead, brother."

"What are you doing here?" I ask, dragging a palm over my face. My pulse is as loud as a boom box. Faith smiles tightly. She's been out dancing in Albany, I can tell; her face is all glittered up, and her eye patch is sequined and twinkling in the street light. "You shouldn't be here. This isn't a place for you to be."

"Uh-huh," Faith mutters, raised eyebrow saying, *You don't think I can take care of myself? Who's the one on his ass?* "Jason texted me and told me you got jacked. Good thing the punk's in love with me. He'd have left you for dead." Her voice is lower than most girls', quieter too, but she enunciates every word to make it count. Tonight this really drags on my nerves.

I get up. This is when I discover the brick that was used to take me out, and my head hurts like hell because of it. I'm only somewhat grateful that it didn't do more damage. I start scrambling around, running up the street, down the street, looking under porches, mailboxes, tipping over garbage cans, crawling underneath cars. Faith stands there, her hand on her hip, checking her cell phone. I'm dizzy, panicking, a crater of loss dug fast into my chest. Ten thousand dollars. More than I've ever had.

"Aren't you going to help me?" I yell. She crinkles her nose and looks up at the sky, then back down at whatever text she's composing. I wasn't expecting sympathy to ooze out of my sister, but still. I consider telling her she looks like a slut, short black dress, makeup-smudged eye, but I think better of it.

I sit down on the same spot of the pavement where I fell and put my head in my hands. My fingers graze a bump on the back of my skull. Damn it smarts, but there's no blood. The ringing in my ears isn't letting up, though.

"Do you realize how much money I just lost? And you won't even help me?"

Faith looks put off, like how dare I even address her. "Oh? So I'm supposed to help find your drug money? And be an accessory to a crime? Sure, bro, anything for *you*." Black fingernails to match her black dress and her black mood.

"Don't even be like that. I've given you some of that money to—"

"Nope," she says, plugging her ears, her phone still grasped in her hand. "We're not going to talk about that. I'm here to rescue your pathetic ass. Can we get going? Before we get shot or something?"

I groan, louder than I meant to. Faith is already getting into her car, a light gray rice burner that's a piece of shit on a good day. It's pointless to give another look around, but I do anyway, my breath ragged, going through the grater of my ribcage, coming out thin, barely there. When I collapse onto the seat of the car, Faith doesn't start it up right away, she's chomping and texting and playing with her earrings that dangle to her shoulders.

"So, we peacin' out or what?" I ask.

She looks up after a few moments, the glow of her phone a blush on her face. "I can't keep doing this for you, Phineas. It's constant damage control: bailing you out and watching you fall. It's getting old. I'm sick and tired of looking at your bloodshot eyes."

"Faith—"

"Listen, you smoke up, fine. Dealing weed, I've accepted that. Mom's valium you sold for twenty bucks a pop, great, she doesn't need that shit anyway. But running heroin, Finn? Seriously?"

She won't look at me. I didn't think she knew—it's not a fact I advertise like, oh hey, I just humped some H across three state lines, *cool*. Hid bricks of it in the hollow space behind my bumper, *sweet*. I try hard to keep our worlds separate.

I raise my finger. "One-time thing, I swear. The opportunity arose, and I had to take it." I'm not lying either, but she probably thinks I am. I pat my pockets down, check for cigarettes, but I know I left them in my car. Faith's glove box is empty. I would kill for a smoke right now. *Kill.*

"Why? So you can buy more coke? Pills? E? What's the flavor of the week?" Her voice is shrill, and I don't want to listen, don't want to listen at all. Don't want to admit to myself that she's on the edge too and that I put her there. I immediately say what comes to mind. I never said tact is my strong suit.

"Don't change the subject, sis. I just lost a shit ton of money. *Shit. Ton.* I'm legitimately freaking out right now, I was going to give it to you for school, for your business, 'cause seriously, what was I gonna do with it, you know? You could expand, have your own brand, a logo for chrissakes, I got ideas—"

"Shut the fuck up!" Faith yells, hitting the dashboard with her palm. And then I see something's happening. Blotchiness on the side of her face, mouth trembling, breath puffs out of her nose with force, shaking hands.

"Sister," I say, counting to five in my head, just like they told me to do. Steady myself before I can steady her. It's awful and hard, I'm not going to lie, it brings me back, every single time, to that moment right after her accident. "Look at me, okay?" She's not looking, she's focused on her fingers now clutching the steering wheel. "Hey, hey," I say quietly, putting my hand next to hers, careful not to make contact. "I'm going to come around to your side so you can get in the passenger's seat, all right? I'll drive us home."

She's frozen. This hasn't happened in a few months. I thought she was getting better because high school is almost over, and she'll be hearing back from colleges and on her way to a new life out of this hellhole.

It takes me some time to coax her out of the car, takes me even more time to get her to the passenger side. I push down on her shoulders to guide her into the seat, but she doesn't budge, her eyes are fixed straight ahead, past me like I don't exist. I can't break or bend her, that's why I can't help her. I'm getting frustrated, I want to slap her across the face. Her eye patch is askew. I fix it, she doesn't feel it. I get just a stare straight ahead into a beyond of nothing.

"Faith. *Please* let me help you," I say gently. "We're going home. We'll watch *The X-Files*. I'll make you a grilled cheese and tomato sandwich. Let's go do that, okay?"

For a second I think she hears me, her eye blinks, but then she's back into fortress mode. Usually she'd come out of it by now, usually she'd say my name, *Phineas*, in a slur like she's just awoken from a bad dream, and the recognition in her voice and eye would be a welcome home. My sister. My twin. We're not magical with each other, we don't read each other's minds or feel the scrape when one of us gets hurt, but she's the reason why I don't feel alone most of the time.

I take a deep breath. "Get into the fucking car, sis," I say, hoping the sternness in my voice will bring her back. Nothing. I decide to use some force, grabbing her waist, nudging her into the car, and that's what does it. She starts to scream.

"Aaaaaah owwww!" she yells, but it's not her snapping out of it, she's just sinking further into the depths of herself. I'm talking to her, telling her that this is how it's got to be, she's got to cooperate, but she's not, she's not leaving me any choice. Her hands grasp the car door, grab hold of anything so she doesn't have to do what I want her to do.

"Come on, Faith, I'm not hurting you, just please—" More screaming from her, she's hitting my face with her hands, there is no rationalizing, and boy, does it hurt, until she finally gives in and collapses into the seat of the car, but what happens next is worse. She immediately begins to shake, her eye half-closed, her hands stiff, her shoulders jerking, oh God, what do I do?

My cell phone. Still no service.

I do the only thing I can—hold onto her so she doesn't fall out of the car or hurt herself. I think I can hear bones creaking, the convulsing is lasting forever. How much time has passed? How much can her brain take? Why aren't her meds working? It's happened before, I remind myself. It just has to pass. I buckle her up, I'm in the driver's seat, start up the car, squealing out of the Dammertown projects. The car jars up and down; it's like the pavement we're driving on is more pothole than road and I'm scared I'm damaging her. Even though she's not shaking anymore, her stillness is as strong as an earthquake. I need someone else who can take over while I gather my thoughts, gather myself. I need that oxy more than ever; it's the one thing that would calm me down and give me the strength to deal. Without it, I drown.

When she opens her eye, we're halfway to the hospital. She's groggy, but I feel her power, her energy, return in a punch.

"Where the fuck are we?" she growls.

"I'm taking you to Ellis."

"Like hell you are. I'm not going in there. I told you that—unless I'm legitimately dying, I don't want to step foot in that hospital again. I'm fine. I feel *fine*. How would we pay for it anyway? You know Mom and Pop's insurance blows." She sits up straighter, pulls down the visor and checks herself out in the mirror. Combs her fingers through her hair. Reapplies lip-gloss she finds at the never-ending bottom of her purse.

"I'm taking you," I say, holding firm. I don't give a shit how much it costs. If I had more money this wouldn't be a problem, if I hadn't lost what was hers all along, our lives would be better.

"There's only one thing I need, Phineas," she says, quietly. I'm all ears, whatever she asks for, I'll deliver. I want her to know this, I want her to know that even though I'm only a few seconds older, I'm still her big brother. I wait for her to continue, but she doesn't right away. Faith looks okay, more than okay actually. As her state is improving, mine is swiftly deteriorating. The craving for oxys intensifies even more. I wish I could knock it out of my head, get my brain right, be a better brother.

"What do you need?" I ask finally. I turn my head to look at Faith who's staring straight ahead, a tear that hasn't dropped in the crook of her eye. You're killing me sister, you're killing me. She wipes her nose with the back of her hand, and the tear tadpoles down her cheek and disappears.

"I need to get the *fuck* out here. The fuck out of Dammertown."

"I know," I say at a red light, the longest ever.

Her sigh is miles long. "I have this terrible feeling that I won't. I'll get rejected everywhere. Harvard? What was I thinking? And I can't afford to go to college anyway. We're already in debt." She looks down at her lap. Her one eye, man, it holds more soul than a pair of ten.

I turn the car around at an empty intersection, away from the hospital, toward home. As far as I'm concerned, my mind is already made up. I need to get that money back, with surplus. *Need.* More than need, I would rather die, get a bullet to the head, than go without it. Not for me. For her, so she can get out of this place.

"No way you're giving up, sis. *Think bright*, Faith bomb." I crack a smile, and wait. Her face is slack and then she cracks one back. A sheath of wind cuts through the windows and ruffles our hair. The light turns green.

"Fuck you," she says, smiling full watt.

SATURDAY, MARCH 30

CHAPTER THREE

IT'S A COOL, DAFFODIL-BRIGHT DAY AT THE END OF MARCH, AND I'M WALKING UP A PATH WITH A PACK OF CIGARETTES, A BOTTLE OF SNAPPLE ICED TEA, AND MY POCKET-SIZED BINOCS. The episode in the D-Town projects was a few weeks ago, but every night in bed I think of Faith convulsing. It's not fair how her body betrays her. Like it's out to get her. My mind, damn, it's doing the same thing. The cravings are always *right there*, and I know they're wrong, and I know they're getting worse, but I manage to convince myself it's all good in the hood.

And maybe it is. Early Saturday morning is the perfect time for a Dammertown Cemetery visit, because I have the place to myself. I take my usual position at the top of the hill, overlooking the rolling landscape interrupted by granite and marble gravestones. I sit down on a dew-soaked wooden bench next to a pink mausoleum and a gated area of especially old graves. Look around to make sure no one sees me. Light up a Camel and let the nicotine run through. Pick up my binocs and wait.

Faith's doing all right, I tell myself. She'll be hearing from colleges soon, and there's no doubt she'll get in to at least a few. Yet I'm still dirt poor, because weed isn't selling like it used to.

Heroin's cheap and the high's like nothing else; however, dealing that is butting up against some dangerous territory. Plus I promised Faith I would stay away from H—dealing it, muling it, and whatever else I could be doing with it. No more scumbag moves. No more act first, think later.

Time doesn't pass when I'm at the cemetery. It just *is*. I wait and everything else around me waits too, and it's a good feeling to be alone. I've been bird-watching for years and nobody besides my family knows. It's not exactly a manly thing to do, and if my friends found out they'd be calling me Hello Kitty in an instant. But something about birds, *man*, they get to me. Even the big fat crows with their horror-movie caws make me want to become one. I imagine peering through their beady eyes as wings sprout from my shoulder blades and wind rumples my feathers. My travel-sized bird book feels good in my pocket and at night I consult it like a bible, reading the descriptions and Latin bird names like verse, but I know most of it by heart. That's one good thing about me: I've got a memory on steroids.

Egrets (*Ardea modesta*). They were once shot by the thousands so their feathers could be used to decorate women's hats.

Peregrine falcons (*Falco peregrinus*). They can reach speeds of 200 miles an hour when diving for prey. They use their balled-up talons to knock out their victim, then they catch the poor bastard before it hits the ground.

Barn owl (*Tyto alba*). They can swallow a large rat whole. After digesting its meal, the owl coughs up a pellet containing the rat's bones and fur.

I'm reciting fun facts in my head because it relaxes me when I spot the albino sparrow. I've been looking for that sucker for months, because the first time I saw it I nearly dropped dead because of its colors. The lightest of powdery yellows and the strangest kind of fluorescent white you've ever seen, an LSD trip of a color. Eyes gold-ish brown, like mine. Then it was gone, just like that, and I was embarrassed about how upset it made me. Wrenched my heart out good and quick. But now it's made an appearance again, even closer this time, only for me, I think, eyes just as gold, feathers prettier than I had remembered. My shoulders tense with excitement as I watch it sing on top of a gravestone.

Okay, my day is complete, and it isn't even seven a.m.

Then I notice something out of the corner of my eye but don't give it my full attention because of my crush on this stupid bird. It keeps trilling and my ears are eating it up and my eyes are full too. I could watch it, hear it, feel its presence for hours, but bird sightings never last long—you blink and there they go.

My bird flies away into a willow tree and is gone. I shut my eyes and swallow down disappointment, slightly embarrassed that I have to.

I see more movement in between a row of gravestones, just down the hill to the right. My mind registers that the thing I see is a person, a woman, hunched over, sniffing a tombstone.

What the hell?

I throw out the Snapple bottle in a nearby trash receptacle, and walk toward her. As I'm closing in, I see she's not smelling anything at all, she's *snorting*, Christ, she's doing a line right there—I've got to laugh because she's an old lady. I stop for a second, just watching with my hands in my pockets. She's got white puffy hair, the usual old lady 'fro, a hurricane could pass through and it would still be in place. I get closer. There's blush on her face and pink lipstick on her mouth, but it doesn't look bad on her, and she doesn't seem like those ladies who think makeup is the only thing standing between them and age. Late seventies, maybe eighty, I would guess. Not fat, but not that skinny either. When she comes up for air, she's smiling and smiling, not even noticing me, and her smile shines so bright I have to look away. Grinning at nothing in particular, eyes closed, and her hands clench up and release, clench up and release, in that way people do when their emotions are too big to contain, because the heart can only hold so much. I wouldn't describe what she's feeling as happiness. I've seen happiness on people's faces and this is something more. I'd describe it as bliss.

I take in the mirror with the drug remains on the top of the gravestone and my mouth waters. I don't even know what it is, and I'm craving it bad. The color is a brooding bluish-purple, a mysterious iridescent color you'd have to dive into the unexplored bottom of the ocean to find.

Her eyes open. She sees me. She screams.

I scream.

Probably all the birds on earth fly away.

I put my hands out, a gesture of peace, I'm not going to hurt you, crazy old bag, but she takes it to be the exact opposite. She starts to yell at me.

"What did I tell you about sneaking up on me like that? My heart's not like a cat, nine lives and whatnot. I'm sitting here, minding my own beeswax, and you decide to put another ten wrinkles on my face? Shame on you, Jimmy. You know better than that. Why don't you go set the table for dinner? Give me some space. Air to *breathe*." The woman's face softens. "Eggs tonight, again, sweetheart."

Her voice trails off and she starts to teeter, and my instinct kicks in and I move forward quickly. She falls against me, her coarse hair brushing against my cheeks, her perfume harsh against my nose. I scrunch up my face.

"Lady, are you okay?" I ask, trying to steady her. She's breathing hard. I'm breathing hard too. I can't help it; the drug is right there, a presence just as strong as that stupid albino bird. I hate myself for wanting it maybe even more than the birds, I hate myself for hating myself.

"Oh," she says. "Oh." She gently nudges me away. She's more anchored now. We stand apart.

"Are you okay?" I repeat.

"Course I'm okay, Jimmy. Why wouldn't I be? You know how I get sometimes."

"My name isn't Jimmy. It's Finn," I say as delicately as I can. She wipes her forehead with the back of her coat sleeve and looks around, the joy in her eyes sinking, sinking, falling, gone.

"No, you wouldn't be, would you." She pats her pockets, alarm crossing her face, and turns around like she's making sure that this Jimmy guy isn't here. Her lips tighten. "I'm sorry, young man, but things aren't like they used to be. *I'm* not what I used to be. If you can't understand that, then why would you be in a cemetery?"

I don't know what she's talking about. I don't know what to say. I'm going into default nervous mode—Latin bird names are scrambling up in my head . . . *Collumba livia* (dove), *Turdus merula* (common blackbird), *Carduelis tristis* (American gold-finch) . . . The reflection of the mirror shines on the gravestone.

"Well, now. What did you say your name was? Finnegan? Phineas?" She's examining me, head to toe, like she sees some-thing worth remembering. Stop looking at me, old woman, I want to say. She pauses on the burn scar. I bring my hand up self-consciously. No one in town looks at me that way anymore, they know me, they don't really see it, at least I think they don't. Actually, girls kind of dig it, gives me *character.*

"Yeah, it's Phineas, but everyone calls me Finn."

"Do you have a last name?"

"Do you want to mind your business?" I say, and immediately regret my tone. She's done nothing to me, but her looking at my scar doesn't sit well. Last time I checked, I wasn't a carnival sideshow.

She raises her eyebrows. "Boys your age. Such attitude. Where does it originate? Is it those baggy pants you're wearing? Is it those birds you're watching?" She gestures to the bird book that's only halfway concealed in my hoodie pocket. I press it against my stomach, pretending I can make it disappear.

"You don't have to be ashamed about it. I think it's sweet."

"Whatever, lady," I say. At this point I don't care if I'm being rude because I just want this encounter to be over. I'm glaring at her so hard she gets the point and starts to walk in the other direction. I'm relieved she's leaving.

I watch her walk for a little and notice the bottoms of her pants are wet from the grass. I wonder if she notices this too. I also notice that the mirror and the coke—or whatever it is—is so *close.* I pick the mirror up from the tombstone and it's heavier than I expected it to be, and there's more powder on it than I initially thought. Mouth's watering insanely now, the desperation for it is sad, then sadder, then saddest.

I take a passionate snort.

A jolt.

Combustion.

A memory.

It's so real it's a kick in the gut. I've never had a charge that feels so so so good, a warm cushion around me, safe and soft and familiar . . . a release. An orgasm, not sexual—spiritual—seeps under my toenails, *goddamn*, pumps into my blood stream, runs through my whole body, oh, oh *wow*, every molecule of my being juiced up, maxed out, the climax lasts for years and years and years, I just want to sigh and yawn and stretch and swim in the thickness of my content. It's not like weed or coke or pills, not even like heroin, it's something else altogether. It's pure, man, it's organic. I can taste it, touch it, be in it again. Hallelujah praise be.

My past. It swoops down and embraces me under its wing. One of the rare moments when I was completely, absolutely happy.

CHAPTER FOUR

**I'M IN THE WOODS BEHIND OUR TRAILER PARK, SECUR-
ING A FORT I MADE BETWEEN A TIGHT CIRCLE OF
TREES.** I nail four thick limbs between four birches, and make
a roof and walls with more branches I pick up. But that isn't
enough, no sir. I want more cover, in case of rain or another
threat, so I get the idea of placing a thick layer of evergreen
boughs over the branches. Finn, look at you go, I think, astro-
nauts and basketball stars have nothing to offer; mountain man
is my true calling. It's late afternoon, and Faith is hunting for
rocks for a fire pit next to the fort. We are eleven years old and
getting shit done.

Faith is very particular about the stones she selects. They
are either too big or too small, too rough or too smooth, too
dark or too pale. I pretend to mind, but I really don't. This is
before she lost her eye and we are happy. Her long, dark hair
curls up around her shoulders, mine is shaggy around the ears,
and our jeans have a constellation of holes in them. She mumbles to herself and chucks a rock off to the side.

"This is harder than it looks, you know," she says.

We hear a noise. A rustling. Probably a squirrel, but we
both turn toward the sound and wait. Thirty seconds pass and

it comes out from behind a fallen, moss-blanketed tree. A tiny kitten, a puff of fur, gray and white, meowing at us. My sister is immediately in love but she doesn't pounce, she doesn't squeal, she just stands there and lets the kitten come to us. Finally it does, padding its way through a patch of ferns and soggy leaves.

"Come here you little thing," Faith says, bending her knees slightly and leaning toward it. My throat clenches up. I'm not sure why. I swallow hard.

"It might have rabies," I say. "You don't know where it's been."

"Sure I do," Faith says softly, so not to scare it. "It's come to find us."

"Well, fine then. I'm not going to the hospital if it bites you and you start foaming at the mouth."

"I can take care of myself," she says. I shut up after that.

The kitten is in her arms in a matter of seconds. She brings it into our fort and sits down with it on her lap, talking to it like a baby, her vowels all high-pitched, each sentence a question. Are you hungry? Are you sleepy? Do you miss your mommy? Do you like your new home?

I continue to secure the fort. Each branch and bough and limb is one step closer to awesomeness and the idea that I've built a sturdy shelter is giving me a rush—I'm convinced that this afternoon I've become an inch taller, a pound heavier, and the hair on my chest is ahead of schedule. Once I'm done with my masterpiece, I pick up where Faith left off with the fire pit. I find myself being just as particular with the type of rocks I stack up. I see where she's coming from. They need to be just right.

"Phineas," Faith says from inside the fort. "Phineas. Come pet our new kitty."

"It's not our cat."

"It is *now*. Come on. She's just the most adorable little thing you'll ever see. She purrs nonstop. Will you come inside and see?" Her voice is muffled. I'm guessing it's because she's nestling her face against the cat's neck. I grab another rock and jam it into place. This is going to make for a great bonfire. I can picture my friends sitting around, roasting marshmallows, laughing, telling me how this place is all right.

She raises her voice. "Phineas, please?"

"Fine. Fine." My reply is overdramatically exasperated. "If that's what's going to get you off my back."

I go inside and sit down on the forest floor splotched with sunlight, sigh hard, dusting off my jeans, my T-shirt. The motion hurts all the bruises. Faith plops the kitten on my lap, which hurts them even more.

"Hey! Hey now. I didn't tell you to do that." I raise my hands and suck in my stomach so the creature is touching as little of me as possible.

"She won't bite," Faith says.

"How do you know she's a she? You're a pervert if you looked."

She scowls at me. "I didn't *look*. I just *know*."

The kitten is purring, nudging me in the stomach with its hard, tiny head. I surrender. I think it's going to fall off my lap, so I put my arms around it to keep it in place. It settles and rests against me.

"She likes you," Faith says, smiling. She traces her finger into the dirt to make a heart.

I look up at the ceiling of the fort, satisfied that there are no gaps. I barely see the trees above and know that the camp is fortified, ambush-ready. No leaks or weak spots. This will be my safe haven after school, my quiet place, my *escape*. Solid work, I think to myself. Faith is humming some stupid pop song, and the kitten is like a hot water bottle for an ache. We both lie back.

"I was thinking we need curtains," Faith says, suddenly.

"For what?" I ask, sleepiness slurring my speech. The drowsiness comes out of nowhere. I welcome it.

"For our home, silly. This would make a good one, don't you think? See that corner over there?" She points to a small gap in the boughs. "We could put up some light blue curtains. The kind where you can see through them." She leans over and whispers something to the kitten, probably sharing the idea, as if it's got great taste in interior design. Nevertheless, I go along with this. Faith likes to pretend a lot, which is fine with me. She talks about the house we're going to live in, the car we're going to drive, the places we'll see.

"The kitchen table would go over there. But you can't put anything on it unless we're eating dinner. I like it when things look neat," she says.

"Our room isn't neat," I say, lazily kneading the kitten's neck.

"It's because you're messy."

I let the comment slide. The kitten molds its body further against me. I rub it underneath its chin, and its head presses down on my fingers, as if to say, more, more, more. My sister chatters endlessly, and I stop listening to her words, but I like the sound of her voice. The fort smells like pinecones and Christmas trees, and the kitten is so soft and uncomplicated. On and on with Faith's babbling, on and on with the purring, the smells and sounds and my fingers busy petting fur, and I don't think I've ever been this comfortable and content in my life.

24

When there's a break in Faith's rambling, I say, "Did you know that a cat's heart beats twice as fast as a human heart?"

"No," Faith says. She turns on her side to face me, immediately drawn in. She likes it when I start spouting unusual information I learned from old encyclopedias Mom bought from the Home Shopping Network and never used. "Tell me more."

I don't skip a beat. "Sir Isaac Newton, who discovered the law of gravity, also invented the cat door."

"Really? He's so smart."

"There's a word for the love of cats. Ailurophilia."

"*You're* so smart." This comment startles me. I'm not sure she's said this before with such emphasis.

"Nah," I say.

"You are, Phineas. I wish I knew as much as you. You know *everything*, and it makes you so cool, like you're a superhero or something."

"Oh come on, that's just dumb." Claws knead the material of my shirt in the way that kittens do when they're content.

"No it's not. Someday you're going to be in the *Guinness Book of World Records* for the guy who knows the most facts. Which is funny, because it's a book all *about* facts."

"That is kind of funny," I say, my fingers full of fur. Faith's eyes are set on me, beaming with such adoration I'm partially embarrassed. Only partially, though. I would do anything for my sister. The only fact I need is that my twin feels the same for me. This fact has been confirmed and verified. We're each one-half of a pretty kick-ass whole.

The kitten twitches from a dream, opens its eyes, and then closes them again. My sister scooches closer to me and scratches it behind its ears. It doesn't wake up and its sleepiness is contagious. I fade into slumber thinking about how almost all calico cats are female, a cat's normal temperature is 101.5 degrees, a group of kittens is called a *kindle*, and their eyes come in three shapes: round, slanted, and almond. The knowledge is so powerful that I wonder if the kitten senses it. What does the kitten know? Does it feel at home as I do, in the forest, in the shade of boughs?

———

The fort fades away, and I'm leaning against the gravestone, my head tilted up toward the sky, mouth open. Jesus, I still feel on top of the world, so alive, every fiber of me. Hello world! Hello *me*! Put my hands up to my face to see if this is real, to see if *I'm* real, and when I do, I notice something that's got to be a mind trick. Surely a hallucination. My fingers smell like pine and Christmas trees, which all right, I'm outside, and there are evergreens around, but where did these little hairs come from? They're stuck between my sweaty fingers, gray, no longer than an inch. I rub my eyes, shake the fog out of my head, but that doesn't make them disappear. Is it the old lady's hair? Well, that doesn't make sense. There's an explanation for this. There has to be.

But no time for contemplation because ... *whoosh* ... a wave of euphoria wraps itself around me, around and around. I close my eyes and breathe in deep this new life, a life that isn't waiting for the cemetery but is running away from it. For the first time in a while, I'm alive. This is not the sleepy, unmotivated comedown of weed, or the hysterical anxiousness of coke withdrawal, or the soggy blue depression of postheroin. This feels natural. Muscles loose, mind more alert than before.

Before I know it, I'm running past every gravestone,

feeling untouchable, invincible, wings on my back snapping to their full span, feet barely touching the ground. I can do anything, and this second is lasting forever. I can ace the SATs and become a CEO and fix Pop and Mom, fix Faith's eye with a click of a button. I'm going to leave behind some incredible legacy that everyone will talk about for years, because it will be so magnificent.

I am magnificent.

I sprint, I go, going hasn't ever felt so right, racing over the dead, shouting their names, Betsy, Randall, and Carlyle, a monument to honor a goddamn dog named Ellie. Ellie! I scream, Ellie!

When I've raced around the whole cemetery I'm out of breath, but not so out of breath that I can't call everyone I know to make big plans for a party tonight—I want to get my peeps together, I want to celebrate us, celebrate living, celebrate—

Hope?

Then the idea comes to me, of course, it's genius. I'm going to start creating buzz around this drug at the party, this new thing, whatever it is. I'll get a hold of it, and it will change the landscape of the drug scene, and with my marketing brilliance, I could make a killing. Yes. This is *exactly* the answer to my problem. What needs to happen. I just need *her.* The old woman. I walk back to the gravestone where this all began.

In loving memory of
James Thorbor
May 5, 1925 to June 7, 1971
All we have is now

James Thorbor.

Jimmy.

Now I have some information to go on.

I've *got* to find this lady.

CHAPTER FIVE

WHEN I GET TO OUR TRAILER, MY BUZZ IS ON A STEADY, SLOW BURN, A FEELING THAT'S ALMOST AS GOOD AS THE INITIAL EUPHORIA. At least it's a Saturday, and I don't have to show up at my shitty job for another few hours. I work at the local sub shop and come home every day smelling like bread and cold cuts, but I guess there could be worse things. Mom's on the couch biting her nails and watching television, and Pop is who knows where. Faith's probably in our bedroom studying in the closet we don't use for clothes anymore. It's big enough for a tiny desk, a lamp, and if she wants total privacy, she can slide the door shut almost all the way. Our clothes are folded in plastic boxes underneath our beds and in the drawers of our dresser. We used to be slobs; now we're Spartans.

"Where've you been?" Mom asks, her bare legs tucked underneath her. She didn't do her hair today, and there's a stain on her "Keep Calm and Drink Coffee" T-shirt. The dark circles under her eyes are like muddy puddles.

"You know where."

Mom starts laughing. "My little birdie boy. Don't you got something better to do?"

I wave her away and walk around the piles of boxes. Towers

of them, some so high they are taller than my six feet. It's a bunch of Jenga stacks just waiting to collapse. A new shipment must have come in the mail today.

"You going to open these?" I say, touching the tape that's tight around one of the packages. The number of times that I've asked this question . . . but still, I'm not going to let it get to me today. I mean, who cares? We've all got our thing, right?

"Yeah, I'm going to open them. Just haven't gotten around to it." She slides a cigarette from the pack on the coffee table and lights it up. I give her the ashtray that's across the room on the kitchen table. People look older when they smoke and Mom's looking about eighty-five after five seconds of puff and exhale.

"Just like you haven't gotten around to those over there? Or those? Or those?" I ask, pointing.

This small living room is filled with boxes in various shapes and sizes, in various stages of being unpacked, ordered from QVC or those junk catalogues the average person would throw away. The battery-operated "Zen" water fountain that trickles so loud I can hear it from my bedroom. The blankets and comforters that are still in thick plastic, forgotten on the floor. The plaques and prints and pillows with sayings like "Live well. Laugh Often. Love Much" or "Shit Creek Survivor" or "Home is where your story begins." Brand-new pots and pans sticking out of a half-opened box and a juicer that has yet to see the kitchen.

"Don't give *me* those judging eyes," Mom says. "I could judge *you* all day."

I swipe my hand over my face. Usually a comment like this would rub me the wrong way, but I still feel calm, and the hope of my plan is still there.

"Sorry," I say. And I really mean it, I do.

"Hmmm." Mom studies me and then goes back to the television. She's been watching more and more every day. Reality television, soap operas when she's working the night shift, and of course, the Home Shopping Network. I make my way through the maze of boxes toward my room, knowing how to ease my body around without bumping into them, but then I stop.

"Hey, do you know the name Thorbor? Ever heard of it?" I ask over my shoulder.

Mom's barely listening. There's a hot chick on the television screen, lips shiny, boobs fake. "Hmm?" she says again.

"Thorbor."

"Oh." She bites her pinky nail, cig locked between her other fingers. "Sounds familiar. Maybe. I see so many people during the day that I can't keep track. Why? What have you done?"

The question isn't unreasonable, and I can't blame her for asking. There's always room for bad behavior, and I've done my fair share of it. All of a sudden I feel sad for Mom. D-Town is perpetually depressing. Our community runs on restaurants and car dealerships and Mom and Pop work there, respectively. Maybe I shouldn't criticize them for coming home exhausted and drunk, respectively. Yet what's the point of analyzing when I'm still riding the wave of my buzz?

"I haven't done anything," I say gently and go to my room.

———

Faith's sitting on her bed, holding a piece of paper in her hands, staring off into space. The window is open and the breeze flutters the pages of a notebook on the night table we share. Her long hair is in damp tangles, black nail polish chipped, nails bitten down. She's been crying and knowing that makes my stomach clench. The eye patch she wears is covered in cream-colored lace. These eye patches she's been making for years. She's developed an online business out of it called "Eye Love Hue," which sells fashion eye patches of all different fabrics and colors and textures, casual and fancy, sparkly and plain. Her customers aren't just women who've lost an eye—it's becoming a trend with women in general. I'm surprised Mom hasn't ordered boxes of them.

"What's wrong?" I ask. I sit on the floor, take off my Adidas sneakers, and slide them under my bed. The binoculars and pocket bird book I stow underneath my bed too, along with the mirror bagged up to save the powder. Wouldn't want that precious dust going to waste.

Faith doesn't answer me.

"I'm not going to ask you again," I say.

She sniffs and looks at me. "I got into fucking Harvard."

"Shit, Faith. That's awesome. It really is." I'm ecstatic for her, but I don't want her to see it. She gets pissed when I'm happy and she's sad—it disrupts the equilibrium of our twinship. Even though this is great news. Even though this is the best news.

"I didn't think they were going to accept me," she says, smacking the back of her hand against the piece of paper. *Thwack.* "I believed it when Oneonta sent me their acceptance letter. But this?"

"I told you they would. You're seventeen with your own business. You've got perfect grades, and you've got like, what, twenty articles published in entrepreneur magazines? They eat that shit up. They'd be stupid not to take you."

She nods and then wipes her nose on her sleeve.

"So what's the problem?" I ask, leaning against my bed. There's really no arguing; Harvard is for Faith and vice versa.

She looks at me, distraught replaced by annoyance. "What's the problem? What do you think's the problem?"

The splotch next to her mouth is starting to appear. She didn't tell Mom and Pop about her episode, and she probably wouldn't have told me if I hadn't been there. I know that when an attack happens, the likelihood of another one happening is pretty high. Once the floodgates open . . .

I try to stay calm. "Didn't they give you a scholarship or something?" Her aggravation is growing, and my anxiety is busting out of me.

"They're giving me five thousand a year. But that doesn't even put a dent in it. They do this thing for low-income families, but Mom and Pop aren't low income. Not on paper." She looks down at her hands. "I should have never applied there, Phineas. I don't know what I was thinking. They say the classes aren't that great at Harvard anyway. They're all taught by grad students. That's what I've heard."

Now *I'm* aggravated. "I thought you wanted to get the fuck out of Dammertown?"

She sighs. "I don't know, I've been thinking about it. It would be too much of a burden. For our family. For *me*." She stares me down, wanting me to acknowledge that her anxiety is there and she's losing the battle. Well it's okay, sis, because I've got my weapon sharpened and ready. It's in the form of a drug that transported me to my best memory and returned me smelling like pine, with fur between my fingers. Who wouldn't want the ability to time travel like that, or the illusion of it? Who wouldn't want a memento to remember it by?

"I'm going to get you the money," I say firmly.

"Phineas, come on. Stop that gallantry shit. You don't have to take care of this." The letter is shaking in her hands that have silver rings on almost every finger.

"You'll have it. I promise."

Her eye narrows. "You make good money selling weed, but not *that* good. And don't even think about muling heroin again, fuck face." I don't remind her that some of her medications and doctors' appointments have been funded from this fuck face's *efforts*, not to mention the startup money for her business.

"What if there's something else?" I say. I probably shouldn't have, but the hope of it is making me giddy yet scared, and my words come out wobbly and strained, because underneath that hope is hopelessness. The last time I tried to solve our financial problems, my sister lost her eye.

"No," she says, sharply. "Absolutely not."

"You don't even know what I'm talking about."

"I don't care what you're talking about. This conversation is over." She slices the air with a flat hand to emphasize *over*.

I jump up and yank the acceptance letter out of her grasp. "See this?" I hiss. "This is your ticket out of D-Town. Think about it: if you don't let me help you now, when you're old and gray, you're gonna look back at this moment and regret it. If you stay here, you'll end up in just another trailer, as just another waitress, wondering how everything got so shitty."

Faith yelps like she's just been bitten and lunges after me. I keep the letter away from her. She sobs, "You take that back. You take it back. I'll never end up like that. *Never*. If anyone's going to end up like that it's going to be *you*."

The words hang in the air. What she's said can't be unsaid, and there is just no response to it because we both know she's right. I place the letter on her bed. I don't look at her. This is not the girl in the fort anymore—that girl is long gone.

"Phineas," she says. "I'm—"

"Nah," I say, raising my hands between us, like there's a wall and I'm feeling for it. "I've got to get ready for work." I turn my back as I rummage through my drawers to find a clean shirt and a pair of jeans. I change in the bathroom, the muscles in my neck tight. I'll prove to her she's wrong, that I can help her get out of here. This time my plan will be so good, it won't create negative consequences for anyone but myself.

CHAPTER SIX

I SEARCH THE WHITE PAGES ON MY IPHONE IN BEN'S
SUBS AND GRUB AND CALL EVERY THORBOR LISTED IN
DAMMERTOWN, SCHENECTADY, ALBANY, AND BEYOND.
There aren't that many, so it only takes me ten minutes before
I realize I've hit a dead end. No one by the name of Thorbor
knows of the old woman with white puffy hair, and I feel dumb
that I didn't pick up on another distinguishing characteristic.

I wipe the counter down and a sliver of lettuce sticks to
my dishrag.

Maybe I'm making it too complicated. It could be as simple as me going back to the cemetery on Saturday morning
at the same time, assuming she makes a weekly pilgrimage
to visit her deceased hubby. All I need to do is ask her where
she got the drug and then go to the source. Surely the dealer
has heard of me, and I don't doubt my negotiation skills.
Though paying for Faith's tuition is the priority, I've been
thinking about expanding my business anyway, so this might
be the opportunity I need. People around here are getting
sick of brick weed, and the harder stuff is too expensive and
not my territory. As I'm running through possible scenarios
and persuasion tactics, someone walks through the door of

the sub shop. I look up and my heart stops.

This girl isn't from around here.

I know that because I know every girl in D-Town, and they don't look like this.

Her eyes grass green, her face without makeup, her wavy blonde hair cut short to her chin. Plain white T-shirt that looks everything but plain on her. She's got an air of simplicity, an aura of cool, calm, and strength.

She's the prettiest girl I've ever seen. Like, so pretty it hurts.

I nod at her, but play it cool, continue wiping down the counter, sneaking glances as she reads the menu above my head. There isn't much up there, just turkey, roast beef, Italian mix, chicken salad, and tuna salad, because Ben feels that classic choices are the best policy, even though I know his business is going to tank by the year's end. I make a prediction that she'll order turkey with a lot of vegetables on it, because she looks like a girl who cares about nutrition.

She's taking a long time to decide.

"Fascinating, isn't it?" I say, finally taking the plunge.

"What?" she asks, tucking a piece of hair behind her ear. She's wearing green stud earrings that match her eyes. I wonder if she did that on purpose.

"I read somewhere that it takes women longer to make a decision, but they're more likely to stick by their decision in comparison to men."

"Is that true?" Her smile kills me. "Did you know that all human brains start out as female brains?"

I step closer to the counter and stop cleaning. This new girl's got game. "No shit."

"Yeah shit." She nods, biting her lip. I get the urge to reach out and touch her face, and I'm sure I'd be able to swing it with a girl from around here, like Erica down the road who does my homework, or Diane who brings me lunch on most days. But this girl seems untouchable, so I'm going to have to earn this.

"You're new to Dammertown," I say, laying down all the confidence I got. Shoulders back, head cocked, a bounce in me even though I'm not moving.

"You must be old to it."

"Feels that way. So?"

She sighs. I like the way her breath sounds, like it's brand new to the world. I don't want to look away, don't want to miss a detail, but this is so unlike me to be nervous around chicks. Steady yourself, I think. You are Finn. You are *you*. Strong. Cool.

"I moved here a week ago. I don't like it," she says.

"I don't think anyone does. Why did you move?"

She hesitates. Part of her doesn't want to share. I see this. She likes her privacy, and I'm okay with that. Did I mention that I'm an ace at reading people? But I *really* want to know; I want to know everything about her.

"I've got family here and my dad wants a quieter life. New York City gets a little . . . distracting."

"Those are good reasons," I say. She nods. I bore my eyes into her because I know that *always* has impact. I wait for her to giggle or ask me my name or make some awkward comment about the day or the tattoo that covers the underside of my forearm. It's of a female cardinal in flight. I've always thought female cardinals were more beautiful than the males, because of their muted colors, those subtle tones of red, tan, and gray. I never pass up an opportunity to tell girls this.

I'm priming myself to drop some knowledge at a moment's notice: Female cardinals sing a longer and more complex melody than males. When cardinals are ready to get it on, the male finds food and feeds the female by putting the food into her mouth, which looks like they're kissing. Males will defend their breeding territory so ferociously, they have been known to attack their reflection for hours, believing that it's another intruding male.

She pinches her lips together, still scanning the menu. She hasn't looked at my scar once. "I guess I'll go with the Italian mix sub. Extra cheese. Extra dressing." She jams her hands into the pockets of her faded jean shorts.

My shoulders slump a little at the lost opportunity to share some cardinal wisdom. "Is that your final decision?" I soften my voice—I'm practically crooning—and give her my trademark smile. Crooked, just enough teeth, distracts from my scar. It works. Every. Single. Time.

"Yes," she says, digging through her purse for money, not even giving me a glance. Is it my scar? Do I smell too much like cigarettes? I make her sandwich in silence, trying to come up with another strange fact to share to get her attention.

At the cash register I hand over her wrapped-up sub, secured with masking tape, "IM" written on the top in my chicken scratch. I tell her the price; she gives me the money. Our fingers don't even touch. The register dings open.

"So, you'll be at D-Town High?" I ask. My last chance.

"I start on Monday."

"Maybe I'll see you around."

She shrugs. "Yeah, maybe." She turns to leave, her hair swinging as she moves. I slam the register drawer closed a little too aggressively. She looks at me over her shoulder. "Do you know your brain generates so much energy in a day that it can power a lightbulb?"

It takes all my effort to conceal my happiness over the fact that our conversation isn't over. There are crumbs on the counter; I swipe them off with my hand so I'm doing something other than ogling.

"How do you know?" I ask. I look at her but try to keep my face neutral.

"I want to be a doctor."

Whoa. There isn't *any* doubt in her voice. No hesitation. She walks out the door, the smoothness of her legs distracting, the disappointment of her leaving even more so. When the door shuts, I feel closed in, claustrophobic, and surprised at my missed opportunity. I didn't even ask her name.

Definitely not a girl who belongs in Dammertown.

Definitely not a girl who belongs with me.

Doesn't mean I'm not going to try.

CHAPTER SEVEN

IT'S NINE O'CLOCK ON THAT SAME NIGHT, AND PEOPLE ARE TRICKLING IN THE FRONT DOOR. I land the perfect spot for my party: Taylor Kinn's four-story suburban palace while her parents are out of town for the weekend. It's in the nicest neighborhood in Dammertown, next to a sprawling golf course with a view of the Mohawk River. The neighbors aren't too close, and there's tons of land. Everyone at D-Town High wants to go. I got my pitch prepared to incite intrigue around the new drug, which involves the words *miraculous, transcendent,* and *ethereal.*

Bryce, a friend from school, gets his older brother to buy the alcohol. Bryce is stoned twenty-four hours a day but is the friendliest guy you'll ever meet. My best friend, Peter, has put together a thoughtful playlist of songs that induces ecstasy and staves off bad trips (trust me, he did the research): a mix of rap, hip-hop, and several chick tunes that are guaranteed to get a few guys laid.

Peter is an important fixture at all my parties. Though he's quiet and reserved, he puts off a vibe that makes people feel comfortable. He's the perfect person to be around when you're having a bad day. Takes the demons out of everything. He's also been my buddy for years, more than years, we went to kindergarten together and bonded over finger painting and coloring books. It's not often that you find a brother who isn't blood.

Several girls bring the party snacks, and a few others bring lava lamps, strobe lights, and someone managed to scrounge up a disco ball, but Taylor won't allow them to hang it on the dining room chandelier.

"Finn, where should I put this?" Diane holds up a giant bowl of Cheez-Its. Her shirt rides up so high I can see her belly button ring sparkle in the dim blue light. I've been giving orders for the past hour. Put the dip on the coffee table, off center, to the left. What were you thinking with that lava lamp? Not on the *floor*, on the fireplace mantle. Start off the set with hip-hop and not rock, *duh*. As for Diane's Cheez-Its, I gesture over to the dining room table overflowing with bottles of vodka, cheap beer and wine, rum, and Frangelico, which Peter must have brought, because he knows it's Faith's favorite. She's not a huge party girl, but she's been known to hit up a kegger or two.

Taylor is sidling up to me. "Isn't this great?" she asks, looking around at the pre-party spectacle, handing me a shot of who knows what. I down it in a gulp. Diane gives Taylor the evil eye as she sets down the bowl.

"You know it. Thanks for offering up your house." I run my fingers down a strand of Taylor's brown hair; she covers her mouth as she giggles. Her face is kind of plain, but she's got a banging body and that's fine, because she doesn't realize how cute she is. She pours some more shots, and we take them at the same time. She thinks it's funny for some reason, our impeccable timing, so I laugh with her. My throat burns and the tension in my neck fades. Didn't know it was there in the first place.

"Hey, I was thinking—" I start to say to her, but Peter is

suddenly next to me, nudging me in the side.

"I've got something important to tell you." He sounds eager, effervescent.

He pulls me away from Taylor and pushes me into a corner. The music is loud, and the house is really starting to fill up. I'm feeling the body heat, smelling the warm beer. There are faces I don't recognize, and it's all turning somewhat blurry now. I shouldn't have started drinking the moment I stepped inside. I've got an agenda to fulfill, and I should have started off by telling Peter about the new drug I stumbled upon. He'd be all over it; he's helped me push weed before to make an extra buck. Like me, he comes from a family who isn't exactly rolling in it.

"What's up?" I say, punching him in the shoulder. Peter doesn't flinch but his glasses slide down his nose. He slides them back up.

"I got into Ithaca College, man," he says, beaming bright. "Full ride. Can you believe it? *Full ride.*"

A second or two goes by, and then I nod with a big, no, huge smile. My reaction feels forced, and I feel like a jerk for faking it. But this isn't Faith telling me she got accepted to Harvard. This is Peter, my bro for life. I'd thought we'd stick around D-Town and rule it to the end. I guess now isn't the time to strike up a conversation about drug dealing when Peter's got the dean's list and summa cum laude twinkling in his eyes.

"Well look at you. Big man on campus. Maybe you'll finally lose your virginity," I say.

"Dick." He runs his hand through his hair. "I can't believe it, like, I'm kind of freaking out right now. I haven't told my parents, I haven't told anyone, except for you."

I punch him in the shoulder again. My force is a bit too hard but he doesn't seem to notice.

"That's great," I say again, trying to put as much enthusiasm as I can into my voice. "That's really great. I'm proud of you. Little Peter. Going into the big scary world. Being smart and shit."

Someone has turned on the strobe light and it's going a million miles a minute. I feel dizzy. Why did they even bring it? I lean against the wall to balance myself.

Peter continues, "Yeah, well, I'm not exactly sure what I want to study. You can claim your major at the beginning, or you can do an exploratory curriculum. I think I'm going with exploratory because I want to try out some different things."

"I thought you wanted to be a psychiatrist," I say without looking at him—his excitement is overwhelming, maybe a little annoying. Two of my friends walk in—he waves and she blows me a kiss. I give them a quick nod. They make a beeline to the drinks table where Taylor is playing bartender, spilling cranberry juice and vodka everywhere. How rude would it be to ditch Peter right this second and join them?

"I did. I mean I do. I just want to leave my options open." Peter takes a sip from his red cup.

I just can't do any more cheerleading at this point, so I raise my own cup to him. I attempt to steady my hand. I wonder if he's picking up on my sourness toward him, toward the whole situation. We're boxed in by a group of girls who are screaming at each other. *What do you want to drink? Rum and Coke. What? Rum and Coke. What? You want me to what?* An eruption of laughter.

And then it comes, the question I knew he would inevitably ask. "What about you?" Peter says. "It's not too late to apply. You're too smart to not go. Imagine all the chicks you'll meet."

"Why are you up my ass about this?" I snap. I should have left him and joined Taylor. Parties aren't meant to be venues to discuss career paths; they are meant as a means to *forget* about them, to *forget* about the rules and the five-year plans, *Christ*, shoot me in the head.

Peter looks hurt. "I'm not trying to insult you, Finn. And I don't want to tell you what to do. I've just always thought that you'd see Faith doing awesome and want some awesomeness for yourself."

"Awesomeness? Shit, I'm telling you, brother, you'll be impressed with what I've got cooking right now. Once I tell you, you're going to be begging for a piece—"

"Honestly, I don't want to know," he interrupts. "I've been hearing about your plans most of my life. Can this wait?" He's looking around him, probably hoping to see a glimpse of Faith. I'm insulted—I know I've had my pipe dreams, but this one is legit. Now I get the brush-off? The holier-than-thou?

"Finn, I'm sorry, I just—" He tries to put his hand on my shoulder but I flinch back.

"You just what? You just want to celebrate *your* victory? I won't stop you." I say. That's my cue to walk the hell away. He's calling my name, but I can tell his heart isn't in it. Where did you take Peter, you college-bound prick?

Taylor is on top of the table, gyrating, hiking her skirt up to display pale yellow, lacy underwear. She's putting on quite the show, about five guys are gawking at her, yelling out stuff I don't want to repeat, gulping down warm beer with sly looks and slutty poses.

What right do Peter and Faith have to judge me? I'm not like them. I don't make choices like them. I never have. I'm in a mood, and though I'm not sure what kind, it's diving straight through me like a deep sea creature, squirming, never adjusting to the pressure, just moving deeper and deeper. Someone hands me a cup, don't know who, don't care, and I slug it down like it's nothing, and there it is, the burn that overrides my venomous mood. Taylor calls down to me.

"Finn, come up here and dance. I know you want to." Her fingers are beckoning me, long skinny fingers that pull at me as if she's got a string around my waist. Pull. Pulling. Dragging. That's quite a string, and I climb up on the table and sling my arm around her. She screams like she's at a concert and raises her cup in the air, eliciting yelps and whistles. A blue light on the floor goes around and around, not unlike a police light, just a little slower, enough to balance out the spins I have from drinking. Taylor is blue then dark, blue then dark, and her short hair tickles my neck as she slides up and down against me. Thank *God* for not a lot of light, because I'm getting turned on and to make matters worse, she starts biting my lips, so I grab her with my mouth, and then it's tongues from here on out. The music pumps into us, loud, the type of thumping that makes your brain throb. The light swoops and the whole room is filled to the brim, hands up in the air, the beer stench strong, Taylor's saliva running down my throat.

We're in a bathroom. The tile is cold against my bare feet. I'm not sure where my socks went. Taylor has her head bowed over a spoon, heating up the underside with a pink lighter, her hair rounded against the curve of her jaw. She's in just her pale yellow underwear and matching bra. I can't exactly remember how we got here and why there's no light except for a few candles that flicker and smell like cinnamon. After the syringe is full, Taylor takes a skinny belt, rhinestone-studded, from a drawer under the sink and cinches it tight around her arm. The vein swells almost instantly and it's grossly sexual, it grossly makes me want to put my mouth on her skin. There's so much concentration, focus behind the pin prick. The pushing down goes on forever. I shouldn't be here. *Get out, Finn, get out now.* Her grin is wide, mischievous, and then it loosens and melts into ecstasy. She tells me it's my turn.

I'm being dragged onto the dance floor, my feet still sockless, and now my shirt is gone. It seems like all of D-Town High is jammed into this room, a room that's without pain and so high, it's soaring up, up, up and I've forgotten about my agenda, I've forgotten the drama, everything is all right, it's good. Man, it's *good.* I want to tell Peter this. I want to pull him close and say that we're cool and that I've got nothing but love for him. Where's Faith? I want to tell her this too, I want to say, sister, I'm so proud of you, so you be you and let me be me. It's settled. We bounce. We crack up. We roar.

Taylor is curled on top of me, grazing her teeth along my jaw (the side without the scar), telling me that she's been waiting for this for a while. Posters on the wall. A Monet print, one I don't recognize. Andy Warhol's banana. Glow-in-the-dark stars on the ceiling; there's the Big Dipper and Orion's belt. My belt is gone. My pants are gone. I strain my neck up so she can have more of it. Can't keep my eyes off those stars. Her sheets are rough against my skin, sheets that have been overused and overwashed. Taylor is naked, and she tells me it's okay because she's on the pill.

"No," I say, slowly, it's the longest word ever. She's not listening to me tell her that I have a condom in my car, it would take just a second to get it. Finn the responsible. That's me. The distance between here and my car is like a trek across the state of Texas, but the H in my veins insists that anything is possible. Could move Texas if I wanted. Swallow it whole.

"I know you're clean. I know I'm clean," she says.

I shake my head, whisper, "You don't know anything, babe." This doesn't seem to offend her, and I'm not sure if I wanted to offend. Her giggles are bubbles, they tickle my nose. She straddles me, flicks her hair, and doesn't look me in the eye when her hand guides me in. I'll blame it on the drugs and the shots. I'll blame it on the brain cells I've lost and the blurriness in my eyes. I'm not in my right mind, and it's so dark.

I tell her no again, but my hands are doing nothing and she's persistent and ready, and I can't help but touch her, as she sinks down onto me, her breath coming out in puffs. Her hair slinks over her shoulders and curtains around my face. When she leans over to kiss me, her tongue is cool, but the rest of her is burning up so much that when I take my hand away from the small of her back, it's coated in sweat. Her sweat mixed with some girly lotion is what I feel more than *anything* else—the stickiness of it, the realness of it, the *now-ness*. She sighs and moans softly, but the noise is far away, somewhere out there with the constellations, her voice's echo bouncing off stars. Fake stars. Spread out on her low ceiling. The movements of her body speed up, more insistent now, and all I have to do is lie here and enjoy it. Forgetting can feel so un-freaking-believably good.

SUNDAY, MARCH 31

CHAPTER EIGHT

SUNLIGHT LIKE THUMBTACKS ON MY SKIN AND THE TASTE OF DEATH IN MY MOUTH. My eyes are crusted shut, and those rough sheets against my back are so itchy. How can anyone sleep here? Oh God, I think. Taylor. Sex. Unprotected. Jackass.

"Phineas."

My sister's voice stuns me into action, I sit upright to cover myself. That's when I realize that my clothes are on. That's when I realize that I'm in my front yard, dirt on my face because there's no grass, just a gritty, lumpy mess of land. I now vaguely remember someone giving me a lift home. I must have passed out before I reached the door. When I press my hands into the ground to hoist myself up, my palm digs into a jagged bottle cap. I run through every variation of the F-word. Faith pushes me back down with her arms. The force of her shove is unexpected, shocking, like cold water splashed in my face. Second time this month I've awoken from unconsciousness to the Faith monster.

"You're a fucking idiot," she says, kicking her foot into the dirt so that it sprays on me. I spit out the pebbles that are stuck to my mouth. A wave of nausea cascades through me and I'm fantasizing about taking a handful of pills and going to sleep, maybe forever. It wouldn't be so bad, death's just getting into another car—didn't John Lennon say that?

"I know, I know," I say, putting my hands up. "I royally screwed up."

"No, Phineas. You are beyond that. You are planets away *fucked*. Peter told me he found needles in the bathroom after you and Taylor were in there for hours . . . God, Phineas. I'm just so disappointed in you." She looks at me with her jaw clenched, tendons in her neck tight.

I shake my throbbing head. Yeah, well, you're not the only one who's disappointed around here. Peter. My wing man. My ally. What the hell is he doing telling on me to my sister? I'm worried about you, man, he tells me. Then just stop. Don't worry. Let me live my life. Let me have *fun*. Do you know what fun is, Peter? *Do you?*

"Jesus, I'm fine. I'm alive, aren't I? I'm just a little hungover—"

She snorts loudly. "Don't feed me that bullshit. I know you've got issues—I get it, brother, I do. But I think you need help. I think you need to talk to someone before it eats you up inside." She looks at my scar. She never looks at my scar.

She lets me stand up now. She's still in her pajamas; the bottoms have clouds on them. Our trailer appears so dingy during the day: rusty railings on the broken cement steps, beige siding bleached from the sun, a striped awning that is cracked and chipped. Faith and I both have stopped seeing these details (glaring as they are) and focus on keeping our bedroom nice. If you can't control one thing, try controlling another.

"Where were you last night?" I ask, deciding to go on the

offensive. "You said you were going to come. But you didn't. Thanks for that."

"Oh no you don't. You're not going to make this about me."

"I want to know," I say, louder, using my demanding parent tone, eyeing her down. "You should have been there. Maybe I wouldn't have—"

"Asshole," she says, kicking dirt at me again. "I'm not even going to try anymore. All the times we've had this conversation, and you never listen. You're just getting worse." Groaning out her frustration, she piles her long brown hair on top of her head, then lets it fall dramatically. Before she walks back into the trailer, I notice that the eye patch she wears is new. It's gunmetal gray—and right about now it feels more gun than metal.

MONDAY, APRIL 1

CHAPTER NINE

THE MONDAY AFTER THE PARTY, ALL I'M HEARING ABOUT IS THE GIRL WHO CAME INTO THE SUB SHOP. I find out her name within minutes of arriving at school: *That new girl, Stacey Braggs, is slammin' hot.* In route to the second class of the day—biology—I see her and her fly-looking self. She's wearing tight jeans and a loose top with butterflies on it. I raise my eyebrows at her while she passes, and tip my chin as an acknowledgment; she does the same. I wait for her to stop and chat but she walks right by, like she kind of remembers me but not really.

"Hey, new girl," I call out. She stops and only halfway turns around. "Did you know that butterflies taste with their feet?" I point to her shirt.

"Did you know that the world doesn't favor guys who try too hard?" Without a moment's hesitation, she walks on to her next class. It takes a second for me to register her comeback and then I'm every shade of flabbergasted. She just flattened me, and it's too late for a response. Is she putting up a front? Was she insulted I called her "new girl"? Did I see a playful smirk on her face? I'm gonna say yeah. I'm gonna say, you won round one, sweetheart, but the world *also* doesn't favor guys who give up.

In biology class, Peter is sitting next to me at one of the black-topped lab tables, folding an origami crane. This is an activity he's always enjoyed because he likes the quiet precision of it. Before homeroom this morning I bitched at him for ratting me out to Faith and he's choosing to act like it's not a big deal. He's doing it in the spirit of *brotherhood*. He wants to *protect* me. Yet his posture says, whatever, Finn, just whatever. This is fine, he can throw me some shade, I just hope it doesn't last too long.

Our teacher is explaining how to dissect a frog in the front of the room by drawing diagrams on the chalkboard. That's next week's joy of an assignment. I turn my attention to Bryce.

"Dude," I say to him. "What's the deal with this new girl?"

"Stacey?" he asks sleepily, stoned out of his mind. Incense and weed is his permanent smell.

"Yeah, her. Is she like a snob or what?"

Bryce scratches the scruff on his chin. "Nah, man. She seems really nice. I have English with her, and when I dropped my pencil she picked it up for me. It was really far away too, like two desks away from mine. She got up, bent over, handed it to me all smiley and shit. I'm thinking about dropping my pencil a few more times."

Peter flashes him a look. "Bro, you're totally weird." Bryce shrugs it off. I expect this zany kind of comment from Bryce but I also know that him saying she's nice means she is. Even though he's a stoner, he's got a good read on people. Well damn, maybe being curt to me is her way of flirting. A kid sitting across from me who I deal to on the regular looks interested in what we're talking about. When I mouth "mind your business," he looks away. I know my rudeness will only draw him in more and this is exactly what I want. I failed to spread the word about the new drug at Taylor's party, so biology class will have to do, and this guy's got one of the biggest mouths in school; he hears you taking a dump in the bathroom and in 2.5 seconds all of D-Town thinks you have dysentery.

"Anyway, I've got some news to drop," I say in a loud whisper to Bryce.

"Mr. Walt," our biology teacher says, stabbing a piece of chalk at me. "Are you going to join us today?"

I straighten up. "I'm with you, Ms. Patten. All ears. And absolutely *riveted* by your diagram of frog guts. I really am."

Ms. Patten is in her twenties, and she's wearing this floral dress that screams appropriateness. She tenses her mouth, but she can't hide the flush beginning to form around her collarbones. I lean my forehead against my hand and try to concentrate on the scribbling in my notebook.

"Seriously, there's this new stuff," I whisper to Bryce again after a few minutes. I can see from the corner of my eye that the dude who I deal to is listening hard, as predicted.

"New stuff?" Bryce adjusts his wool hat, straggly hair pressed to his ears. He doesn't care it's almost seventy degrees out; his drug-addled nerves are so shot he's bulletproof.

"Yeah. It will blow your mind." I fan out my fingers around my head and look at Peter, the one I really want to listen, to understand. "This is what I was trying to tell you at the party. I'm not messing around with this one—it's not one of my schemes you think is gonna fail."

"I don't see them as schemes, Finn. You misinterpreted me. I just don't want you to get too deep into something you can't get out of." He's got his finished origami crane in his cupped hands, holding it like a gerbil or something, making sure it doesn't escape.

"Just give me a chance on this one. If I fail, I'll never bother you with stuff like this again."

Peter shrugs but I can tell he's considering. There's my loyal compadre.

I look at Ms. Patten. She's got her back turned to the room and is writing up another diagram or something while she's lecturing. I've got a few minutes at least.

"I'm putting it on the market soon, so spread the word. I need a big return on this one, and if you help me, I might give you a cut of it. Or at least I'll get you free samples."

"What's new these days?" Bryce asks, biting his pencil eraser. "I've tried everything. Bath salts. Kroc . . ."

Peter scoffs. "You did *not* try kroc. You think you did, but you didn't. You were too hopped up on H to know. Stop wanting to sound cool."

"Whatever, dude. Go keep smoking your weed, you lame-ass mother fucker," Bryce says, smiling wide, just to piss him off.

"I'd rather be a pothead than some doped out fool with acid burns down to the bone." He throws the origami crane at Bryce's head, and it bounces so hard it lands at the end of the lab table. Bryce laughs, snorting in waves, fist up to his mouth to muffle himself. Peter's not laughing but shaking his head, eyes bright with amusement.

Ms. Patten, thank God, is oblivious, so into frog digestion or whatever.

"Would you dickheads stop flirting and listen to me?" I whisper roughly. "This shit is *clean*. Goes down *smooth*, you come off it even smoother. It's magic. Transformative. Transcendental." The passion is coming out of me as I think back to the fort in the woods.

"Magic, huh? You said that about the purple weed and it was good, but it wasn't *that* good," Peter says.

"This is different. It is legitimately *beautiful*. You know I don't use that word lightly." I pause for effect. "I had the most intense hallucination that made me whole again. I'm telling you, this is no joke, man. I got to relive the happiest memory of my life. And when I say hallucination, I don't really mean it because I swear, you guys, I was *transported* into another dimension. The memory was so real I came out of it with dirt on my hands, smelling like the woods—remnants of my greatest memory, left behind as a gift. Yeah, you heard. A *gift*. And I felt *whole*."

I accentuate my words by pressing a finger down on at my notebook several times. Bryce is interested, I see that glimmer, I see that my words have gone through him—touched down on an artery, on to his heart. Peter, on the other hand, is oozing suspicion.

"*Beautiful? Whole?* Who *are* you, man?" he asks, disbelief spread across his face. Good. I want him to see a change in me, to see this was different.

"I'm serious," I say.

I look deep into his eyes, give him my most piercing look that usually squelches arguments across the board. He doesn't respond, he puts his crane off to the side and goes about making an origami frog that has a moveable mouth. Those have always been my favorite. I hate how I have such a soft spot for my best friend.

"I'll believe it when I see it," Bryce says, as he crosses his arms over his chest.

"Oh, you'll see it all right," I say. I'm getting more and more amped. "You'll see it, taste it, smell it, feel it—"

"Phineas *Walt*," Ms. Patten says sternly, her hand on her hip. "Have you listened to a word I've said?"

Without skipping a beat I say, "Frogs form a new ring in their bones every year when they hibernate, just like trees do. That's how we can find out their age." I smile sweetly; she flushes a tiny bit again. I lean my elbow against the lab table. I'm practically batting my eyelashes at her.

"Here we go," Bryce says, under his breath.

"Well, aren't you just a well of knowledge?" Ms. Patten says, wiping her hands on her dress, leaving behind chalk stains. "Do you want to get up here and teach the class for me?"

"I would. I really would," I reply; my *confidence* has confidence. I revel in showing off this stuff. I stand up, swagger to the front of the room and pick up a piece of chalk. Ms. Patten is so stunned she does nothing to stop me.

"You're going to give us a lecture?" she asks a little nervously, having started something that has now gotten away from her.

I hike up my pants a little, feeling the weight of my wallet in my back pocket. I like how it feels; it reminds me of how it's only going to get heavier when I find this mysterious drug.

"I'm gonna do more than that. I'm gonna tell you kids why frogs are the shit. Okay, listen here, right?"

Ms. Patten winces and is about to say something, until she notices everyone leaning in toward me. She knows I'm one of those smart kids with a lot of promise who doesn't apply himself; she wants to give nonconformists like me a chance.

My memory unloads on them, and soon I'm on a rant about how there's a type of frog that carries its young around on its back until they become adults, how frogs absorb water through their skin so they don't need to drink, how some can jump up to twenty times their own body length in a single leap. Then I hit them with this: a substance two hundred times the power of morphine was recently found in the skin of a frog. *Yeah.* That blows their minds quick. I'm on such a roll that even the slacker students are listening intently, and Ms. Patten's uncertainty has morphed into an all-out smile. My hands are gesticulating, they've got minds of their own, I'm telling the classroom the story of when my pop and I tried to fry our own frog legs, and no, they didn't taste like chicken. I glance at the clock and am surprised to see it's almost time to go and then my attention is drawn to the door.

She's standing there.

Stacey.

Watching.

I accidently fling the chalk over to the doorway, a moment of nervousness on my part, after which there's a moment of silence, the clock ticking as loud as a bomb. She bends over, picks up the chalk, walks over, and places it in my hand. This time our fingers touch and suddenly I don't know what's up or down, left or right. The bell rings and the class collectively jumps up and Ms. Patten yells about a homework assignment.

"Here you go, wiseass," Stacey says, wiping her hand on her pants, leaving behind a dash of blue. She smells faintly of nice-smelling soap. I think about telling her that I meant to throw the chalk across the room, as a final statement, to really make my point. *For drama.* I bite my tongue.

"Thanks," I say. When she smiles, it immediately becomes a new favorite memory and I do feel weirdly whole. This is the beginning of a better version of me. A version that a girl like Stacey would be into.

Okay, maybe Peter is right. Who *are* you, man?

SATURDAY, APRIL 6

CHAPTER TEN

IT'S SATURDAY MORNING FINALLY, AND A WHOLE WEEK HAS PASSED SINCE I SAW THE OLD WOMAN. The sky is overcast and primed for rain. I'm sitting at my usual spot in the cemetery and praying that she'll show up in spite of the weather. My binoculars are glued to my eyes, and I've been watching Jimmy's gravestone for an hour straight, but she still hasn't shown. This is not good. Everyone's hassling me about the mysterious drug, I've been talking about it nonstop, even Peter's interested. To add to the stress, Taylor lost her shit in the school parking lot and slapped me across the face because she had to get the morning-after pill. I told her, that's great babe, I'm glad you're being responsible, and then she goes and blames *me* for not wearing protection, even though I'm good and sure *she* was the one who insisted I didn't. She's just all butt-hurt that I don't want to be her boyfriend. Everyone knows I'm not boyfriend material. I'm crazy busy, I got shit to do.

To distract myself, I start counting gravestones, only the pinkish ones. There aren't that many so I count the black ones, which takes a little longer. Usually a house or clothes or a car can tell you something about a personality, but can a grave-stone? Does a really elaborate one mean something? Or a really plain one? I make a mental note to find out if there are any studies on it. I've got nothing like that tucked away in my bank of knowledge. Might be a tidbit to impress someone.

The first raindrop falls, a big splat on the bench, like a bug flattened against a windshield. Great. Then I see her puffy hair before I see her. Her walk is slow and steady and her coat swells as it traps the wind. She's carrying a package under her arm. When she approaches Jimmy's gravestone, I make my way down the hill. It's now raining sheets of mist and I pull the hood of my sweatshirt tight around my head. She kneels on the grass in front of the grave, tilts her head up, and opens her mouth.

She's drinking the rain.

Mrs. Looney Tunes over here. Christ.

When I approach her she's still in the same position and hasn't given me any indication that she knows I'm standing there. Beads of water trail down her raincoat, some are caught in her puffy hair. Maybe this is a bad idea. Maybe I'm the crazy one. But I committed myself to doing this. There's no other way to make this kind of money.

"Yo," I say, leaning in, my hands wet inside my pockets. I check myself. "I mean, hello, Mrs. Thorbor."

"Yo yourself," she says, her head tilted up toward the sky. "And it's not Mrs. Thorbor. I kept my maiden name. It's Klaski." Her pink lipstick is the only bright thing around. I pull the mirror out of my pocket and hand it to her. It takes a beat or two for her to notice what I'm doing. She looks at it, looks at me, and then goes back to her previous position—head up, eyes closed, mouth open.

"You left this behind. I'm returning it." She doesn't respond. I don't think she cares. I stand there, a little unsettled, but I remind myself of what I'm good at, and set the mirror on top of the gravestone.

"That is one powerful drug," I say. "You got a prescription for that, or is it some off-the-grid stuff?"

Nothing. Not even a twitch of recognition on her damp, expressionless face. She holds the package tight against her chest, a posture of defense. Okay, I get it, come on Finn, lay it *down*.

"Listen, I'm not going to beat around the bush. That powder—I tried it, and it—was beautiful. I'm telling you this from the bottom of my heart. Beautiful and pure, like a work of art that you can consume, body, soul, and mind." I pause. She's staring at my chin. The side of my face. My scar. What's the deal? I want to tell her step off, but I hold myself straight, because this is my mission. My sister deserves Harvard. I deserve a win.

"Anyway, I'm not here to rat you out, I'm here because I want you to hear me out. Who's your supplier? I probably know him. In fact, I'm probably friends with him. I've got history in this town and I can help you if you can help me. I know a lot of people who would die for this drug."

The woman doesn't say anything, just gets up slowly from the grass. She's calling my bluff, she knows I don't have shit for an argument. At least now she's making somewhat of a face—the corners of her mouth have curved downward; her nose has scrunched up, producing wrinkles that have no sense of direction.

"Like I said, I'm not here to turn you in, but . . . I'm just saying, I saved a little of that powder, in case the police need some evidence." I point at the mirror on top of the gravestone.

A twinge of shame pinches me. I try to shake it off. Finn,

you've done this a million times before. Persuasion. But this is an old lady. She's not going to be swayed by your smile or desperation to help pay for your sister go to college. She's got nothing to gain from you. Yet she's not walking away—in fact, she's leaning in closer. The package against her crinkles as she moves.

I lean in too, cocking my head. "Look, I just need a name, that's all, and I'll leave you alone for the rest of your life. It could be just a name or . . . we could make another arrangement. I'm just saying, lots of money to be made here . . . and you could be a part of that. No more living off social security and meals-on-wheels. Did I tell you that you look like my grandmother? God, if I could have helped her out like I'm going to help you, man, things would be way different. *Way* different."

Still nothing but that scrunched-up, wrinkled-up face. I'm sweating, I'm overheating, good God. I can't lose my cool. The misting rain feels soft on my face and makes the gravestones a shade darker than their original color. Man, if anything, my *mood's* a shade darker, or off-color, or *something*.

"I got contacts from here to New York City. We're talking mad profits." I wince, hearing myself do this hard sell to a little old lady. "Lucrative profits."

The lady snaps her head in my direction. "Mad profits?" she asks, startling me with her strong tone.

"Yeah, you heard what I said. It could be a successful business."

She seems to consider this, shifting her weight. It's then that I realize that this little old lady is almost as the same height as me. I don't want to admit it, but it's intimidating because her old lady 'fro—which gives her another three inches at least—is matted down, yet she still looks tall and overwhelming.

"Mad profits," she repeats, nodding once. "Is that the term you use these days? Mad?"

I'm a little off balance. Off my game. Maybe I should lay off the hard stuff and just stick with weed for a while. I could have done without the heroin at the party, and the few tastes of it during the week. The hill of the cemetery is steep, dizzying, and this Klaski lady is so damn steady on her feet.

"Yeah, like mad profits, mad skills. Out of control. Amazing. Unexpected. Do you know how many definitions the *Oxford English Dictionary* has for the word mad? Like a hundred."

She scratches the corner of her mouth and some of the lipstick comes off on her nail.

"I don't like how you kids use words these days. You murder words. You don't treat them with respect. You're the acronym generation, and that's not something to be proud of. OMG I was like WTF LOL BRB."

I draw up straight, stung a little in spite of myself. "Hey, we like our technology. Nothing wrong with being fast-paced. Anyway—"

"You know what I say?" she says, leaning on the balls of her feet, closing the distance between us.

I jut my chin out. "What?"

"*F-U.*" She spits out the letters, then moves past me speedily, way too speedily, her shoes slapping the sodden ground. The mirror is still on the gravestone. I scramble after her, almost losing my sneaker in the mud.

"What—no. That's not what you say. That's not what you say *at all*." When I catch up, she wrenches around and throws something at me. The package. It whacks me against the stomach and knocks some air out of me. It's hard, with edges. Not the magic powder, but I knew it wouldn't really be.

"That's for you," she yells huffing, puffing, red-faced. Her gray pants are soaked up to her ankles. She's pretty much a mess, but then what does that say about sweaty, inarticulate, bumbling me?

I pick up the package. It's wrapped in pages of a newspaper; its black and gray washing out with the rain.

"I'm not sure why I'm giving this to you," she spits at me. "I thought you would appreciate it, I thought perhaps we could talk about it some time. A conversation piece. But now I see you may not deserve it and you may not care much about it, because you have your fancy technology and letters, and what can an old lady like myself offer you? Oh wait, I know." She glares at me with toughened eyes. "Drugs. You want *my drug*. You want to sell it so you can make mad money. You actually thought you could sell this idea to me? You actually *think* I'm that stupid to fall for it? Oh, don't even look at me like that, child, I know your tricks. I know them six ways to Sunday. Why? Because you remind me of my grandson." She stabs her finger at me.

"Oh?" I squeeze the package, not really knowing what else to do.

Then her demeanor switches, eyes welling up so fast it's like the tears were *that* close, crouching, always ready. "He's . . . gone," she says. It doesn't matter who she is, if I see a woman cry I'm on the verge of it too. I look away, concentrate on the flat, charcoal-colored sky, the hills and valleys in the distance. Figures a cemetery would be the only place in D-Town that's picturesque.

"I'm sorry," I say. "I mean, I sincerely am."

"You don't know what you are in any kind of sincere way, young man. Now, I'm tired and I want go home. You imposed on my time to visit with my husband and if that isn't disrespect, then I don't know what is." Suddenly she's empowered again, the tears are gone, and my blood is boiling or bubbling or doing somersaults over what she's said. Don't like her tone or her sour-ass face, she's reminding me a little bit of Pop, or maybe Peter, Faith, all high and mighty, all of them without reason to be. But I regret the words even before I say them.

"Hold up there. Are you for real? Disrespect?" I step back with a bounce, shaking my head. "How would Jimmy feel if he knew you were snorting up on his grave? No, no, scratch that, *on top* of his grave. How would he feel if he saw you bombed out of your mind? I mean, what's an old lady doing tripping balls in a cemetery? Are you trying to like, relive your youth or something? I guess what else are you going to do, huh? Eat Jell-O? Play bridge? I feel sorry for you. I bet Jimmy does too."

She stiffens in shock, but not as overcome as I'd expect because she's up in my face in one second, all charged up.

"Don't you *dare* say his name. So help me God—" She rips the present or whatever it is out of my hands and starts beating me over the head with it. I try to shield myself with my arms, but that package is hard, and man, is she *strong*.

"Hey, Mrs. Klaski, stop, I didn't mean it, okay?" She's pounding on me something serious and it's actually starting to hurt. I don't want to hit back, obviously, I don't want to run, and I don't want to cower, so I stand there, shut my eyes and take it. I've taken it before.

Slam.

Thwap.

Grunt.

Her knuckles graze my face. I don't know how it happens, but it's not her anymore, it's Pop, intent on beating me to a bloody pulp because of a failing grade or catching me smoking in the bathroom. Those fists were boulders when I was young, and I was too much of a coward to fight back. And here he is, and I'm seventeen goddammit, I got muscle on me, I got fight in me, yet I'm back to that scared little kid who doesn't want to cause a stir in the household, tip the fragile balance, one light vibration and it all comes tumbling down. Oh God, my eyes hurt from clenching them so tight. Please stop, I say, please stop, but he keeps wailing at my chest, at my legs, because he's smart like that, giving me secret bruises.

"Finn. Phineas." I'm looking up. Somehow I've ended up on my knees, cowering like a little kid. A cough-gasp escapes from my mouth and then another one. I've taken a beating so many times—at school, at a bar, on the street—and have come out on top for most of them. But this, *this* is what breaks me? Takes me back like that? She places her hand on the side of my head, tender as all hell, shit, and for a moment I allow it, and then I shrug her away and sit on my ass. My throat's so tight I can't swallow. We're staring each other down, chests heaving, water pooling up on our eyelashes and dripping down our faces. She places the present at my feet and walks away.

I really didn't picture this all ending so horribly.

Way to go, Finn.

You really knocked that one out of the park.

I try to get my shit together, but something is needling me, and I can't put my finger on it. I move to the nearest bench with the soggy and partway torn package in my hands, not feeling the rain anymore and not feeling right. I don't know if I should open the package or if I should leave it here, where I think it probably belongs. Who brings a gift to a cemetery? Why did I think she was my best bet? Stupid lady. Dumb old woman.

My finger picks the corner of the gift. What is bothering me so much about this? I check my phone. I have to go to work in a few hours, and the thought of being around deli meat makes me want to puke. Yet it's a job and it's good to have; it keeps me out of trouble. It's not like I can shoot up at work. Maybe I should put in more hours for that reason. Yeah. I'm going to figure this out. I'm Finn. And that's what Finn does.

I tear away what's left of the sopping newspaper pages taped around the present.

I hold in my hands a hardcover book.

Audubon's *The Birds of America*.

No fucking way.

I've been wanting a version of this book forever, but it's like three hundred dollars online. A first edition of the book was sold at an auction for eight million dollars. My fingers tremble, and I'm getting all teary, which I'm not proud of, not proud of at all, but the way it feels in my hands, I don't know, it's incredible, incredibly stunning.

This is the best gift I've gotten in a long time.

I don't deserve this.

And now she knows I don't deserve it. She said I reminded her of her grandson and that she wanted to talk about the book with me sometime—talk with me, really? Like hang out? Book club? Of course I blew that opportunity, along with the possibility of obtaining the drug. But here one of the coolest books lies in my hands, and it is heavy, like heav-*y*, and I'm surprised she didn't do more damage to me with it. The cover is a little worn, and there's a stain on the spine. I slide it underneath my hoodie as much as I can to protect it from the rain and walk to my car.

I'm warm inside my Honda, windows fogged up, air humid, when it dawns on me. What's biting at me. In one of her rants she said: *Drugs. You want my drug.* "My" drug? Like it's hers and hers alone. Am I just overanalyzing, or is there something more to this picture?

My instinct is telling me there's something more. I open the book to a random page. Audubon had this crazy method of using wires and threads to hold dead birds in lifelike poses while he drew them. So funny how the birds had to be dead to make them look so alive.

The picture I turn to is of two white falcons, spotted with black markings. One looks like it's about to attack the other, and they're both perched on top of a cliff that hangs over a gray, sullen sky, an exact replica of today's. Eyes locked, wings rigid and muscular. Is that hate in their eyes? Or are they laughing?

CHAPTER ELEVEN

WE'RE PILED INTO MY ROOM AT THE BACK OF THE TRAILER. It always surprises me how many people I can fit in here. There are eight of us, some are playing the guitar, badly, and some are using their knees and legs as drums. Cigarette and pot smoke draw over us like a blind. Saturday night at Finn's. It's the place to be.

We sit and lean and slouch. These are my best buddies, friends I've known for years. I'm not saying they're all good people, but they're *my* people. They're going to be given an assignment tonight. I smoke and stew, deciding upon my words. Haven't been so good with them lately. Starting to feel like I lost my touch. *The Birds of America* is underneath my bed, on which most of us sit, and I swear I can feel its presence, maybe its warmth, as it incubates underneath our bodies. It might be totally moronic, but knowing it's there gives me a boost of confidence. The book is so solid. Today it held up to the rain *and* a beating. Where, oh, where are you, dear Mrs. Klaski?

Peter showed up, bright-green bong in hand, yet to be lit up. When he smokes, his eyes disappear and his nose runs. I don't know if he's here because we've made our peace or if he just wants to get really baked. Penelope, an ex-girlfriend of mine who's still after it, holds my hand, and Diane, who brings me lunch every day, is kissing my neck so much it's numb, but I lean into it anyway. Music blaring, hacking on smoke, talking a lot of *dude did you hear this, dude did you hear that* . . . I'm home (this is home), but there's a tiny part of me that isn't. There's a crack widening inside me, and I wonder when it'll start to show. If anyone's going to see it first, it's going to be Faith. That's why I need this new venture. I really need it. It's going to make things right, going to take away the guilt, and maybe the craving—getting worse all the time—will go away.

Faith is getting ready to leave for a date, bursting in and out of the room, looking aggravated, changing eye patches every five minutes and asking our opinion about which one looks the best with her outfit. The red lace eye patch to go with the black pants? The iridescent one to go with the white skirt? She's modeling, they're ogling.

"They all look great to me," Peter says. Faith winks her approval at him. He blushes.

"Stop trying to get into her pants, dude. It's getting old," Bryce says, taking out his rolling papers and a baggie of weed. He used to be such a dork, walking around middle school in a Teenage Mutant Ninja Turtle T-shirt, hitting on girls with gusto, always failing to impress.

"So who is this guy anyway?" Peter asks.

She answers eagerly. "He goes to Scotia High, but he lives out by Berton's Farm in Charlton." She throws on some blush and expertly lines her one eye in front of the mirror on our closet door. Her joke about herself is, voilà! Makeup in half the time.

"Oh, you're getting yourself a country boy, huh?" Bryce says, snickering. Faith sighs, exasperated.

"No, not a country boy, you douche. He plays in a band called Junkhead. You heard of those guys? They play over at Pinhead Susan's all the time and do a wicked cover of Nirvana. They're like, kind of brilliant. I want to look hot, you know, but not too hot like I'm trying too hard."

"It takes a lot of effort to look effortless," I say.

"Kiss my ass, punk," she replies.

"Heard you got into Harvard," Bryce says, rolling up a joint. Deft hands, pretty much the only deft thing about him. The energy in the room changes; I can tell because of my spidey sense. Faith looks caught off guard but she plays it smooth, shrugging her shoulders. I didn't even know she told anyone besides me.

"I'm not going." Her head is uplifted in a show of confidence, but I see she's avoiding looking at anyone in the room. "Not worth the money. Dammertown Community College offers all the business-related courses I want, for way less."

Bryce nods like it's no big deal. It *is* a big deal, though.

"Are you fucking stupid?" I ask. Penelope takes a strong puff from the pipe and blows the smoke in my face and giggles. I almost slap her across the face. "I told you I'd take care of it."

Faith doesn't answer me, she isn't even bothered by my disgusted tone.

Then Peter steps in. "Faith, do you really think that's a good idea?"

"I do." She turns and says directly to me, "It's too much pressure. Not right now. I really can't deal right now." And surprise, there's shakiness in her voice, that same shakiness she had the night of her seizure. Her vulnerability almost quells my anger. Almost. She's stronger than this. She has to be, for both of us.

"Cheers to that," Penelope says, holding up her pipe as if she's giving a toast. "Life is hard enough. College is bullshit. Just another way of turning us all into robots."

Goddamn people don't get it. They just don't get it. I'm in a room full of losers, my sister included. Faith thinks that she has anxiety now? What about when she finds she's stuck in D-Town, pushing paper, or tables, what have you, on a rainy hopeless day, when regret and longing are boring into you like oncoming car headlights on bright? I swear, once you miss the window of opportunity to leave this place, you aren't ever leaving.

"Gimme that," I say to Penelope, snatching the bowl out of her hands. I take a long, hard puff like it's my last, blow the smoke out so thick it engulfs the room. I hope Faith feels how livid I am, hope that it's raising the hair on the back of her neck. But she doesn't seem to notice.

"Half the school is going to DCC anyway. It would be the best way to ease in—I could go for a semester and then maybe transfer. Who knows? I need to get my bearings, you know? Do you all really feel like you've got your bearings?" she asks, looking around at us, brush in hand. For some reason it feels theatrical, an actor asking the audience a question and not expecting an answer.

"I understand where you're coming from," Peter says. In his eyes, there's so much longing it's painful to watch. My body's rigid, my hands are twisting around and over each other, goddammit Faith, for someone so smart . . . The bowl goes round and round, and she takes a hit, blowing smoke straight up. She's the only one standing, towering above us, and the smoke cloud makes her look even taller. Then she leaves the room with the clack of her high heels. I go after her, grab her wrist in the hallway. She jerks her arm away from me and hisses menacingly, "Back. Off."

I throw my hands up in the air, surrendering for now. Screw her. She isn't going to stop me. I will do this thing for her, whatever she says.

When I return to the room I clap loudly and everyone jumps. "All right, you fools, we got work to do."

My friends have been helping me sell weed for years now. I get the stuff, I pass it around, we all get a cut of the profits. It's been going smoothly, besides your run-of-the-mill scares. There was one time I was almost arrested. This female cop pulled me over and found a bunch of dime bags squished in between my seats. Somehow I got her talking about making cookies because I told her my mother likes medical marijuana in baked goods. Found out the cop bakes a mean cupcake so I go asking her about the ingredients, yellow cake, chocolate frosting, sprinkles or no sprinkles, whatever, she was putty the moment I opened my mouth. My mouth, my *something*, saves me every time.

I signal to Peter to turn down the music. "You've heard about the new shit, right?" I say to the group.

"Yeah, I've heard about it, but I don't see it anywhere. I'm ready for it, man, I'm ready for something different. In case you haven't noticed, I'm bored." This is Max, who isn't the sharpest tool in the shed, but he's definitely loyal. Loyalty goes a long way. "So where the hell is it?"

"Haven't acquired it yet," I say, lighting a cigarette, shrugging Diane off me. "And that's the problem. We need to find the supplier. I want a piece of this pie. If I get a piece of the pie, then you do too. So this is what we do. We've got to *organize*."

"We're not your army, Finn." Peter's voice is a warning. I

love the guy, I do, but he's *really* testing my patience. We're on the same team, dude, remember?

Then I decide I don't really care how he's looking at me, because the rest of them are full-on enchanted. My pitch is pitch perfect. You want something life changing? Try this shit. You need a shot of absolute ecstasy? Try this shit. You need to feel good again, in a way that feels pure, that feels healthy, like a cleanse, a catharsis, an exorcism?

"Exorcism?" Diane says.

"Straight up," I say. "But first things first. *Organize*. I want your eyes and ears open. I want you sniffing things out. I don't care who you got to talk to, talk to them. I don't care where you got to go. New York City? Syracuse? Fucking Niagara Falls? Don't matter, don't care. We've got to find it, or else." I stare at them with my serious Finn eyes, my razor edge shark fin glare.

"Or else what?" Peter challenges.

"Or else we're losing our lives!" I exclaim. "Are you all really making bank at your jobs? I'm certainly *not*. I'm sick and tired of throwing around salami and cheese for a living. You hear me? Weed's only getting us so far."

"Hell yeah," Bryce and Max say at the same time. Peter is finally nodding too. Diane and Penelope are silent. They're in another world, riding off the wave of their buzz.

"Girls, are you in?" I snap. They both perk up and murmur *yes*. What did I say about loyalty?

"Well, okay then, class. I'll give you your assignments."

I do just that. I give a list of contacts and locations to the girls and another list to the guys. As their eyes scan the words, I know they're not happy with what they see.

"Dude. I'm not going into that part of Dammertown," Peter says, scowling.

"We *never* go into Dammertown Heights," Bryce says, shaking his head at the piece of paper. I was expecting this. The D-Town ghetto isn't a place where we go. It's where the hard stuff is, coke, heroin, meth, and I know better than to encroach upon this turf, especially after my run-in there a few weeks ago. But my boys' faces will be unfamiliar, and they'll be perceived as some dumbass, curious kids. I hope.

"Penelope, let me see your list." Bryce grabs it out of her hand. "Hey, man, they've got it easy."

"No, we don't. We got to visit that smelly, creepy retirement home on Birch Ave. Why you got us doing that, Finny?" I don't like it when she calls me that, but I let it slide, puff my chest out, wind myself up again.

"The way this drug works is that it induces memories so vivid they feel real." I hang my hand in the air above my head for a pause and then let it drop. "Hell, they are real. Good memories. The very *best*. What old person wouldn't want that?" If the Klaski lady has the drug, then maybe other old folks do too. Not that I want to say anything about her at this point. She's the wild card that doesn't need to be a part of the equation.

They all look at me doubtfully. "Listen, guys, just go do your jobs. If nothing shakes out in a few weeks, then that's that. I'm not asking you to go and convince anybody of anything; I'm just asking you to go play detective. Haven't you always wanted to do that? Go sleuthing? Nail the bad guy? Well, the bad guy is this drug, and it's going to do nothing but good for us to find it. What do you say?"

I slide my hand up Penelope's thigh and nuzzle against Diane's neck, kissing her slowly behind her ear. "Say yes," I whisper.

Max and Bryce look at each other, rolling their eyes. Peter reaches for the fresh bag of weed but I intercept it.

"No, no," I say. "Not until I have my answer."

"What are *you* going to do? What's *your* task?" Peter snaps.

"I've got the hardest one of all, you pricks. I'm talking to Mike Frye in Vermont."

"He just tried to kill you," Max says quietly.

I nod. Don't really want to reminisce on that memory. I push that out of my mind.

"We have a deal then? Everyone in favor say 'Aye.'"

There's a beat of silence before they all agree. I toss the bag of weed over to Peter, who's shaking his head.

"This better be worth it, man, this really better be worth it."

SATURDAY, APRIL 13

CHAPTER TWELVE

AS IF MY RELATIONSHIP WITH JASON FRYE ISN'T COMPLICATED ENOUGH, MY RELATIONSHIP WITH HIS BROTHER MIKE IS EVEN WORSE. After I had hooked up with Jason's girlfriend, ratted him out to the principal, *and* didn't give him free weed for his troubles, his big bad brother comes down to D-Town from Vermont to teach me a lesson. This was a few months ago. Somehow he gets me cornered at a drive-in movie theater where I'm minding my own business with some preppy girl who feels naughty to be on date with me. Then suddenly I'm being dragged out of my car, thrown into the field beyond by three guys who hold me down so Mike can wale away at me. I'm proud to say that yes, it did take all three guys to restrain me, but I ended up with a broken nose, a black eye, a broken rib, and gobs of spit in my face.

I remember it way too clearly. Mike's standing above me, the bright red of his shirt assaulting my eyes, his saggy jowls supersized. The power behind his punches is unrealistic. "I really hate to do this to you, man," he says calmly as he hits me. "We have a nice business arrangement going. I don't want this to strain it. But I got to say, you fuck with my brother again and I'm going all the way with it. I'll just say that some of my best friends are on the force—and they'll have no trouble looking the other direction."

Our business relationship I wouldn't exactly consider "nice," but it works. He has an associate in D-Town who supplies me with his homegrown marijuana, I sell it to my usual buyers, then I take my cut and he takes his. No problemo.

Course my mouth gets in the way. I remember saying something to the effect of, "Aw, that's swell you got boyfriends on your side. I see you got a lot of boyfriends. I should show your woman what a *real* man is."

This rubs him extra wrong because he's obsessed with his girlfriend—Victoria—loves her to death, shows everyone photos of her fat ass on the beach, her latest selfie she posted on Facebook. Mike steps on my junk and I scream beyond bloody murder until I black out.

Phineas, don't you think you should get some help? You can't carry this with you for the rest of your life, I hear my sister say when I wake up in the hospital. Come to find out, Mike is the one who dumped me there.

This is the stuff I'm thinking about on my way up to Vermont. It doesn't get to me too much because I'm riding off a good buzz from a joint I smoked earlier. I know the buzz won't last but I've got to enjoy the peace it brings. You have to practice being present, Faith's therapist told her way back when. It seems like a waste of time to me—like the present is a butterfly meant to be caught in a net. Forever chasing, always elusive. And once it's caught, what are you going to do? Pin it down on paper and call it yours?

Mike lives in northern Vermont where he's got the weed empire of the Northeast. His acres of pot grow in the middle of nowhere and are sprinkled in between abandoned cornfields.

I have only been up here once to see him when I first started dealing, just a wet-behind-the-ears type of kid. He was so nice to me back then because I was so stupid. It didn't take me long to call him out on my pathetic cut. I negotiated. I told him that D-Town is teeming with potheads, I know every single one of them, and they all love me—I can get them to buy bud like it's penny candy. Now I'm on his bad side, but I've come bearing gifts. I had the foresight to save the residue of Mrs. Klaski's drug that was on the mirror she left behind.

Pine trees everywhere, a blanket of blue above. It's the type of day where the smallest thing feels miraculous: a rabbit sniffing a dandelion on the side of the road, an old person walking with a cane to his mailbox. I even see a couple yellow finches flit across the road. Those acrobatic little suckers thrill me every time. They bounce and undulate and call out when they fly to make themselves known. Attention whores they are. I drive with the windows down all the way, and for once I'm not listening to music because the wind sounds just as good.

Here I am, already on my way to accomplishing my assignment. I wonder if those bums have even dragged their asses out of bed yet.

When I turn the corner of a forgotten country road though, the miracles disappear. He's got five junk cars crowding the driveway and part of his front yard where there used to be grass, and in spite of all the money he makes, you'd never guess it if you looked at the crap-hole he calls a home.

And goddam it, there's Mike in the window like he's waiting for me, even though I didn't tell him I was coming. One of the guys who beat me up at the drive-in movie theater—I think his name is Nelson—walks out from behind the side of the house, wearing a camo-printed vest and no shirt underneath.

His overfed McDonald's stomach jiggles with each step. I feel for the knife around my leg. It's just a precaution but possibly a necessary one. I hop out of the car.

I wave to the glowering Nelson like he's my best friend. Mike hasn't moved from the window and even from here I can see that he's fatter, unhealthier, and greased up to the heavens.

"I come in peace," I say, raising my hands.

"Sure you do, you piece of shit," Nelson says, slamming me up against my car. I groan, then chuckle softly. He searches me, finds the knife in my jeans pocket (yeah, I had the foresight to bring two) and shoves it in my face. "This don't look like peace."

"You blame me?" I ask. Then I say quietly, "I'm going to reach for a book in my car. What's in it is something you'll want to see." Nelson is dripping with sweat even though it's not that hot out. He motions for me to get on with it. I open the car door and reach into the backseat for my biology textbook. He grabs it without hesitation and comes upon the small baggie of drug residue I saved between the pages. He raises it to the sky.

In the bright light, the powder's color is even more beautiful. It dazzles like a blue diamond, morphs with the light— sometimes more blue than violet, sometimes the other way around, switching back and forth, like a hologram. Needless to say, it doesn't look like anything else out there. I'm pissed off for not realizing before how goddamn pretty it is.

"Well, lookie here," Nelson says. "Mike's heard there's something new in town." This comment catches me a little off guard. I guess I've been creating more buzz than I thought. Or is someone else out there distributing it?

"Yeah, I got something new, son," I say.

I'm taking a risk, I know that. There is no guarantee that I'm going to find it here, but now I've got a hunch that I'm on the right track. From the window, Mike motions for Nelson to bring it over.

"Let's go inside and have a conversation," I say. "This could potentially be very big for both of us." Nelson doesn't like me telling him what to do but Mike's waiting. Curiosity is coming off him like paint fumes.

Before I'm fully inside, Mike's blocking the doorway, keeping the screen door open against his meaty shoulder. He's a real class act, I tell you: wearing a red hoodie with the Adidas logo on the front and cut-off khaki shorts. Sandals with socks. Dragon tattoo on his calf. He lifts his eyebrows and examines the baggie filled with the gorgeous blue substance.

"What's this all about?" he asks. He can't pass this up. I know his business has been sliding downhill since dry weather has killed off a good chunk of his crop, and he doesn't have enough manpower for hydroponics.

"It's a game changer," I say. "There's nothing like this out on the market. Maybe you know about it."

"Maybe I do, maybe I don't." He opens the bag and smells the powder. Doesn't give it a taste. His eyes are slow moving—from me to the drug, the drug to me. I can't get a read on him.

"I'm just asking for a talk, man. You can keep it, it's yours. Just let me bend your ear for like, five minutes."

"Bend my ear? Bend my ear? Look at this kid," he says to Nelson, gesturing at me with his thumb. "Never know what to make of you, Flynn."

The way he says this, it's almost fatherly, *hardy har har*, we should both slap our knees and have a good laugh or something. Maybe he's high right now, but I know better than that. A good supplier is never an addict. A good supplier is a businessman, and though I don't respect Mike, I respect his business—he's been successful for a long time now. But what about me, as a dealer? Do I get respect? I've got to get a hold of myself, not get high, find my center and all that, be more like a businessman and not so much a user.

"It's *Finn*," I say. Ignoring me, he walks inside but leaves the door open. Nelson follows behind me, good little puppy he is.

Inside, the thick, cream-colored carpet is worn down and the only furniture in the room—couch, coffee table, television stand—is nicked and humble as hell. There is a Buddha statue on the window ledge, no bigger than a coffee pot and without a fleck of dust. Two bookshelves flank the fireplace with no books, just various figurines of dogs, cats, and horses: trinkets a kid would collect. Everyone knows that Mike doesn't have kids. God help those children if he did.

Someone's in the kitchen rummaging around, and that's where we're headed. Victoria is there making a cup of tea in a bathrobe so silky and short my imagination doesn't even have to *work*. I can tell she gets off on it a bit because she doesn't leave right away. Instead she bustles around, big hips swaying to their own rhythm, boobs bouncing on the downbeat, until she finds a mug to her liking and a tea bag to suit her tastes. When she reaches for the teapot on the stove, I can see the bottom of her ass, and Mike sees that I see, but he doesn't pound me to a pulp. Instead he stands there admiring her for a few seconds, then says, "Honey, we need to use the room."

Her brown hair swings cheerfully when she turns around—mug in hand—and stretches up on tiptoes to kiss him on the cheek. He pats her behind.

"You notice this pretty thing?" she twirls around to ask me, waggling the fingers on her left hand. The diamond engagement ring's so big, planets should be orbiting it.

"Damn," I say, reaching out to touch her fingers for a better look, but I think twice. Last thing I need to be doing is getting handsy with the missus. "Mike's an A-plus sugar daddy, isn't he?"

She shimmies her hips slightly, and her smile is a spotlight in the room. "My number one guy." Mike winks at her and shoos her along; her slippers scuff against the floor as she leaves.

Now that I can pay attention to my surroundings, I'm struck by the state-of-the-art stove, stainless steel appliances, the granite countertops. The cabinets are a dusty blue and antiqued to achieve that shabby chic look girls always talk about. I guess I see where Mike's money goes—in here and straight to his stomach.

"Nice kitchen," I say.

Mike looks around, surveying his kingdom. "Yeah, it's special to me. Put in the cabinets myself."

Luck must be on my side, because I've never seen Mike this chipper before. Got to be partly because of his engagement to Victoria . . . now that I'm thinking about it, she does have a nice appeal to her, she seems to be a decent person, good vibes, what have you, someone you wouldn't mind shooting the breeze with on a park bench. Nelson opens the refrigerator and grabs himself a beer, cracks it open on the edge of the counter. Oh, big mistake, buddy. Mike dagger-eyes him hard. Nelson raises his hands apologetically.

"Sit," Mike orders me, pointing to the huge oak kitchen table. It'd probably take up half the space in our trailer. When Mike settles into his chair, he says, *speak*, so I start telling him a fabricated story about how I found the drug at some party in Dammertown Heights, took a hit of it, and had an experience so real, so supernatural, that I'm a changed man.

"Is that right? A changed man? How do you know it's not acid?" Mike's lips twitch, and by that I know that I don't have much time with my sales pitch. As it stands right now, he's not kicking my ass because I'm entertaining his. But who knows how long that will last.

"This isn't acid," I say, shaking my head. "When I came out of it, I have never felt happier in my entire life. No withdrawal, just peace."

I let the story tell itself. I let it all out with conviction, describing every smell and sound, every sight and touch, and how content I was, how I reached a true state of nirvana. I really go crazy with some high-level Buddhist monk shit, motioning toward his Buddha statue in the living room, hoping that I'm not laying it on too thick. But I go on about it, in true Finn fashion, saying I wanted nothing more in that moment, nothing less. I go as far as telling him about the pine smell on my hands.

He cuts me off. "Why the fuck do I care?"

I'm not expecting this. I'm liking the weight of the knife around my calf right about now. "We could make a killing," I say. "I just wish I knew who was dealing it."

"We. I've never liked the sound of 'we.' Even if I knew, why would I tell you? If I knew, I could make a killing all by myself."

"You supply, I push. Our usual arrangement. If this stuff is organic, which I'm betting it is, you could learn how to grow it, green thumb you are. Plus, I know your crop isn't doing so swell this year. The potential is astronomical, and people are already champing at the bit for it—I'm telling you."

There's a woven place mat on the table, and he's tracing his finger along the edges of it contemplatively, though it's hard for me to decipher if he's considering my offer or if he's deciding the best way to beat me up.

"How about you try this miracle drug, then you can see for yourself."

Mike doesn't say anything, he just looks deep in thought.

I continue, to fill the silence. "With your connections—and mine—I have no doubt we can track this down and start making ourselves some sick dough. All of New York State is looking for something new to drop—"

Bam. Fist against the table, rattling the glass in the cabinets. Mike appears pleased that I recoil. I swear, it was like, the tiniest bit, but my nerves, man, they're not the soldiers they used to be. I don't want to admit that it might be me overusing, amping me up, turning me into a rubber band about to snap.

"Shut up, kid. What do you say, Nelson? Should I try this shit or what?" His hand is still in a fist, and he's looking at me instead of Nelson.

"I think you should," Nelson says, nodding, taking a pull from his beer.

"We both try it," Mike says. "Me and Flynn over here."

"*Finn*," I say automatically but with no real power behind it. Mike waves me away. I shift my weight in his antique wooden chair, sweating a little, not knowing where this is going to go. Sometimes I shoot before I aim, and I don't want to admit that this could be one of those situations. From one of the hand-built cabinet drawers, Mike takes out a coke spoon and shoves it in my face. It's rusty, cool, and heavier than I would have expected.

"You first," he says.

"It's all about you, my man," I say.

He shakes his head, smiling slyly. "No, no, no, you're not seeing how this works. *You*, then me. You're in my house, and you're going by *my* rules." He places his wide palm over his broad chest.

Something tells me I very well might end up dead in a ditch, but this is the risk I'm willing to take. Right? The spoon is shoved in my hand, so is the baggie. I search inside myself to find more excitement than fear—yeah, okay, I'm not going to argue against experiencing the best memory of my life again. In the name of this quest, I can let go and give in to its magic. Take me back, man, please take me back. I actually wouldn't mind just tripping out for the next three days on this. It'd be so much better than the poison of the other drugs I've been doing.

"What's this kid doing?" Mike asks, waving his hand over my eyes. "You already wasted?"

I snap out of it. "Nah, drug's that good—it starts hittin' before you even try it." Mike glares at me, and Nelson shrugs. Come on, I want to say, can't blame a guy for being eccentric.

I look up to the sky, murmur a prayer for Faith, and snort. I hand the coke spoon over to Mike who watches me carefully. As my mind is pulled backward, I try to resist the freefall to see his next move. *Got to scope out his next move* . . . but . . . but . . . blurred edges. Unmoving figures. Immediately I know I've made a stupid decision. I don't see him reaching for the spoon.

In my peripheral vision, something begins to take shape. My mind is swooping backward, tumbling, and there's nothing I can do but ride it out. I don't want to, I'm getting a bad feeling, a syrupy darkness to accompany my anxiety. I'm trying to swim back toward shore, but the undertow's got me, it's just under, under, and . . .

I'm outside in front of my trailer. Sunny day. My sister is smiling. I know this day so well. The past sprints back so hard it pounds me like a fist.

CHAPTER THIRTEEN

IT'S DEEP INTO THE SUMMER, WHEN THE WIND PUSHES AROUND HOT AIR, WHEN THE GRASS IS SO CRISP IT HURTS TO WALK ON. I'm carrying out giant boxes from the trailer, and my sister is helping, though she's mumbling under her breath that this isn't a good idea.

Mom's been spending so much money on junk that all we eat for two weeks straight is macaroni and cheese from a box, and a few nights we go without even that. Pop is never home, and I stop wondering where he is. Mom is calling in sick a lot, although today she's gone to work. The couch has holes, the microwave doesn't work, and our clothes are too small and too ratty. One day it hits me. All these boxes, all these new things, all these people in trailers around us who *need* new things and need them for cheap.

When I pitch the idea to my sister, she immediately says no, that Mom would flip and Pop would lose his temper, like he's been doing more and more. His drinking has reached all-star levels every day, and more often than not it's Jack Daniels straight from the bottle.

I don't listen to my sister. Big brother knows best. I tell her that if she helps me, I'll buy her French fries and an ice cream cone every Friday. That sold her because all her friends have parents who take them on routine excursions to Friendly's or McDonald's. The last time we went out for dinner was for Pop's birthday, and he got mad that Mom took us to a place where he couldn't drink a beer.

We set up a table and chairs and make a sign with bright magic markers that says YARD SALE. Unpacking the boxes is fun—it's Christmas and it's a surprise every time. Even Faith starts giggling and ooo-ing and aw-ing, I bet she's wanted to do this for a while now, I bet—like me—she's fantasized about this very moment. From the most boring looking package, I uncover a set of beautifully hand-painted Russian tea dolls, which I line up neatly across the table in front of a tackle box. More surprises appear—a blender that doubles as an ice cream maker. A miniature glass house that lights up from solar power. A life-size rooster you use as a tomato planter. I do see the appeal in all these things, but I also see how the appeal is short-lived.

Once I get some music pumping, it doesn't take long for the neighbors to come, and the trailer park twitches and comes alive with stay-at-home moms, unemployed husbands, bored kids, curious elderly. They touch and pick through all the crap on display, remarking at the price of this one, the quality of that one, like they know what they're talking about, like they're QVC experts. Maybe they are.

My salesmanship is in full throttle. I sell a twenty-dollar Crock-Pot for forty to a pale woman who tells me she wants to start cooking soup for her husband.

"You know you can use your Crock-Pot for things besides cooking," I say, setting my stance wide, my hands on my hips. I admit, I read the instructions that included alternate uses.

"Is that so?" She raises her eyebrows at me. She's not

expecting an articulate eleven-year-old in a trailer park. It satisfies me that I've impressed her, so I want to impress her even more.

"It is. You can use it as an air freshener. Just throw some water in there, turn it on, dump a couple cinnamon sticks in the water, and let the steam do its work. You can also use it to make lotion, but I'm unclear on how to do that." I hold up the Crock-Pot so that it hits the sunlight just right—good lighting really does go a long way.

When the Crock-Pot-loving woman traces her finger along the top of the lid, I know I have her. She hands me two twenties, and it's a done deal. The Crock-Pot looks so big in her arms, she's carrying it like a newborn, hoping it will—and I start imagining scenarios—make her husband love her more, make her feel like she loves being a housewife, make her eager to cook a well-balanced meal. I see the sadness in this, and for a moment I feel bad for being so convincing.

Faith is having success too, especially when it comes to anything that has to do with fabric. She can tell the exact thread count of brand-new sheets, she knows whether a quilt has been handmade, she figures out a way to turn an everyday shawl into a cool-looking skirt. We're quite the duo, and it comforts me to hear her voice next to my voice, even though we're talking about different things . . . *If you like this hand mitt, you're going to love the matching dish towels . . . I'm going to do you a favor today, and it's only because you're my favorite neighbor . . . with this night-light, your kids will never wake up crying again* . . . we're on a roll, our salesmanship becoming even more persuasive, and everyone who passes through is so charmed because we're smarter than we should be. By four o'clock, everything is sold except for my old bike without a seat. That was a long shot. We made one thousand dollars. *One thousand.* That's more money than I had ever seen in my life, and immediately Faith and I are talking about groceries and how we won't have to worry about having food to eat for a while.

We're knocking back the last root beers from the fridge with our feet up on the table, watching the shadows of the trailers lengthen, when Faith asks, "Mom and Pop are going to be happy, right?" Her uncertain smile is a warm spot over my heart.

"No doubt they'll be happy," I say, leaning into the chair, lacing my fingers together against the back of my head.

"We can buy some deli cheese—not the kind that comes individually packed. What about lemonade? That sounds good right now."

"Think bigger," I say.

"Cake." Faith pulls her sunglasses below her eyes. "I would *die* for some cake."

"Now you're talking." We clink our root beer bottles together, watch the day sigh into late afternoon. I took care of business today. I took care of my family. Now Faith can have cake, and I can buy it for her.

Pop is driving up the road toward us, his green truck kicking up dirt and dust. It's surprising that he's home early; actually it's surprising he's home at all. My heart starts pounding in my ears, and anxiety pinches my stomach uncomfortably. Immediately I know I've done something wrong. Faith does too.

"It was my idea," I say to her firmly, setting my bottle down.

"I went along with it." Her voice getting all panicky isn't doing much to help my own nervousness, which is quickly escalating to fear. Dad won't necessarily be angry with the fast cash; he'll be angry that I didn't ask his permission.

I grab her wrist. Hard. "You don't say *anything*. I'll do the talking. You had *nothing* to do with this."

"Phineas, we both—"

"What did I say?"

I stand up, broaden myself as much as possible and wait for him to approach. He jumps down from his truck and wipes his hands on his pants. He's been looking especially jacked lately, really hitting the gym hard, and it wouldn't surprise me if he was taking steroids or drinking alcohol-spiked protein shakes—other dads don't look *this* ready to fight.

Before he can speak I say, "Hey Pop, don't freak out, but I think you're going to be really happy about this." I open up the tackle box and show him the money, and when he reacts with icy silence, I motion to Faith to go inside. She shakes her head, sunglasses shielding her eyes, but I give her my meanest look that always forces her to listen and she leaves. It's just me and Pop now, looking at the dull green money in the bright-orange tackle box. Sweat stains are forming underneath his arms. He squeezes his lips together and then walks into the house, the back of his neck reddening. I follow. He's not even in the house all the way when he freezes. It's a shocker to see so much space in our trailer, so much room to move.

"One thousand dollars," I repeat, walking inside behind him. "Pretty good, right? That's almost what you make in a month."

I realize this was a stupid thing to say a second before Pop whips around and slaps me across the face. I hear Faith's gasp from across the room.

"You. Don't. *Think*," he says, breathing hard, vapors of nastiness coming off him. As I'm holding my cheek, I hold my breath so I don't have to smell him.

"I'm telling Mom you were at the bar. You promised us," I say, sounding too whiny, too much like a weakling.

"I had a long day. And it's gotten even longer." He wipes his forehead with the back of his hand, stumbling a little.

"You *promised* us," I say again. And he did. He had promised us so many times, me, Faith, and Mom, that he would only have one drink a night. There was a long stretch of time when he didn't drink at all, but he still hung out with his buddies until late, playing poker, returning home stinking of cigars. Mom would sometimes accuse him of other things, mostly related to women, but I didn't care about that. I just didn't want him to be drunk.

"You're a liar."

Pop lifts his hand again, back, back, back, and swings, this time with his fist. But something happens before the fist connects, something that throws me off balance, I'm being pushed sideways by Faith, what the hell is she doing? I hear the pound, the smack, the bone crack, but I don't *feel* the pound. I crash into the wall, and Faith screams. It's all way too fast for me to understand, to comprehend, to realize. I have to touch my mouth to know that it's not mine yelling, to know that it's not bleeding and that I haven't been hit.

I pull myself up straight, still confused. Pop is crouched down low, whimpering, moving his hands in the air above my sister . . . above her body. Crumpled and crushed boxes surround him, the packaging strewn all over the place, Styrofoam peanuts, Bubble Wrap.

Faith's still shrieking. Then I get it. He hit Faith. It was a massive punch that wasn't ever meant for her, but meant for *me* (it's always meant for me). She pushed me aside and took the hit as a savior, a sacrifice . . . all because of my big mouth.

I go to her, slipping on plastic, hearing the pop of Bubble Wrap.

My father is apologizing over and over and over. *It was an accident*, he's crying. I'd *never* hurt you, he's insisting. Faith's sunglasses are still on, she's cupping her hands over one eye, and she's screaming. I crouch down, I speak low and firm, telling her to breathe, saying let me see, let me see. Pop is repeating *no, no, no,* on his knees now and finally Faith quiets down because she's gone into shock, or at least that's what I think. I pull her hands away from her face and see that the force of his punch cracked the lens of her sunglasses into her left eye and there are pieces of it wedged in the skin of the eyelid, in the eye itself, and there is blood leaking down the bridge of her nose and speckled over her mouth and some on the carpet.

"I'm sorry, I'm sorry, I'm sorry," Pop says to her, weeping, mouth slick and wobbly. "You weren't supposed to . . . I didn't mean to . . ."

"What did you do?" I yell at him. Attack him. Pound him with my fists. He doesn't even react. I push him out of the way, and he collapses on his side, his knees tucked up so far they're touching his stomach, fetal position. Worthless. Little. Pathetic.

Faith starts screaming again.

"Call 9-1-1," I tell Pop. I shouldn't be the one managing the situation but I am, and he listens for once because *I'm* the man, I'm the man. Pop scrambles to the phone. I pick up my sister, she's so light, and tell her to shush, even though she's stopped screaming now. Her skin is white, and her lips are following suit. I try not to look at her eyes, I try not to hear my father slurring his speech into the phone. Her blood is sticky between my fingers.

I set my sister down on the couch and kneel next to her. I'm not sure if I should take what's left of her sunglasses off her face (God, the little screws are in her eye too) or if that would hurt her more, so I don't do anything. I grab her hand and tell her it's going to be okay, but she's staring straight up with her right eye—she doesn't even nod. I'm dizzy with panic and because I don't know what else to do, I start talking to her about birds, her limp hand in my shaky one.

"Do you know hummingbirds are the only birds that can fly backward and sideways? Have you ever seen one up close? You should. I'll take you with me to bird-watch. I promise I'll let you come with me from now on, okay? Okay?"

I'm stumbling over my words and my lips are so numb I can barely move them. I squeeze her hand, and thank God she squeezes back. I rest my forehead against the edge of the couch because I'm *so so so* relieved. She can communicate. She's still with me. The birds help. They always do.

"I bet you didn't know that there are poisonous birds. The pitohui has skin and feathers that contain poison that can kill you upon contact. Well, that's a lie, I don't think it would kill you, but it might make your skin numb or something. Interesting, right? Also, in case you were wondering, turkeys can have heart attacks. I'm serious. The air force was doing test runs and fields of turkeys dropped dead because their hearts gave out from fear."

I pray she doesn't hear the skittishness of my voice. At least I'm talking and she's listening. Ignore the blood. Ignore the pieces of plastic lodged in her eye. Birds, birds, birds until the ambulance arrives, which feels like forever and then some, and even after they put her on the stretcher, my mind is still running away with bird facts and images of them, different colors, wingspans, all of them flying so high, so far, that nothing else matters but clouds and blue and Faith.

Pop and I ride with Faith in the ambulance and watch the paramedics give her oxygen and wrap her in a blanket because she's shivering. I take her hand again, and it's lifeless for a few moments . . . one second . . . two seconds . . . three seconds . . . four . . . then she squeezes my hand five times, and for some reason I know that she's giving me five letters, B-I-R-D-S, so I'm at it again, going through another file of facts, eagles, egrets, and emus, and this time I don't care what Pop thinks about it, I don't care if he thinks I'm not a man, because I like feathers and beaks and chirps.

I don't care, because birds are freedom.

They're strength.

And though they fly, they anchor too. They anchor us both.

CHAPTER FOURTEEN

SOMEONE IS SHAKING ME, SAYING FLYNN, FLYNN, FLYNN. I get slapped across the face. I think I'm drooling. When I open my eyes, Mike is jostling me around, he's all agitated but I can't decide if he's agitated *pissed* or agitated *thrilled*. I'm trying to process the memory, the most painful of any . . . she was in the hospital for a week . . . she didn't want a glass eye . . . Mom didn't talk for seven straight days . . . this is *not* how the drug is supposed to work and what if Mike had a similar trip? His meaty fingers are digging into my shoulders.

"Where the hell did you get that shit? It can't be Early's. This is 110 percent pure, this . . . blue stuff. It's darker than what he has. He must have improved on it or something. That's gotta be it," he says, he's bubbly, energetic, bouncing off the walls. "You ain't kidding. You ain't kidding at all. I had the best . . ." he swipes his hand over his brow, and his lip starts trembling. Nelson, who's been sitting on the kitchen counter the whole time, I guess, is wide-eyed and anxious.

"Are you crying?" Nelson asks Mike.

Mike slams his fist on the table. "Fuck yeah, I'm crying. These are tears of joy. I have reached my paradise, my Buddha state, all because of this little dude." He's shaking his head, still not believing. I'm still out of it. My hands hurt. I look down. A tiny piece of hot pink plastic is stuck to my palm. I start breathing so hard I'm close to hyperventilating. I say my sister's name, I say bird names, all in Latin, it comes to me fast, and . . . what am I doing? *It can't be Early's* . . . That's what Mike said. What does that mean? Befuddlement, ten times over, the pink piece in my hand, I touch it, move it around because I'm too stunned to do anything else. It takes a bit for me to realize what it means, what I have in my possession, that it might be a part of Faith's sunglasses. But then again I could have grabbed something off the kitchen table, there has to be a rational explanation, there has to be . . .

I shake my hand and watch the piece fall to the floor. I let out a groan that has Nelson grabbing for something in his pocket. Mike isn't on earth for the time being and therefore isn't questioning my behavior at all, and this makes Nelson stand down. If he pulled out a gun, maybe I would have welcomed it, maybe I need it to shock me out of this . . . eeriness? I put my head on the table, covering myself with my arms. It's too much.

"So when do we start?" Mike asks.

My mind is foggy and the aftereffects don't feel *at all* like the first time I did the drug. There's no euphoria, no burst of energy. This is worse than a heroin comedown. I want to go away, I'll pull a Thoreau and let the woods take me, and I won't come back. I got Mike over here delirious and making no sense, rambling on about Victoria, a kiss, a night of perfection. I couldn't care less.

"I don't *have* the product. I told you," I say, trying to get my thoughts together but I can't, there are still too many flashes from that day. After we took Faith to the hospital, she had her first seizure, with pink plastic and metal still stuck in her eye. Doctors thought it was a one-time thing as a result of the trauma. Didn't put her on any medication—at first.

I come back to the present. I emphasize to Mike, "I'm trying to *find* the product. Thought you would have a tip on it. But now you're saying *Early*. Who's Early?"

"Whoa, whoa, whoa, what are you talking about? Find the product?" He frowns, disbelieving. Does he have amnesia or something?

"I told you from the beginning that I'm *looking* for it." I grasp the edge of the table out of frustration. Seriously? He's pulling this crap on me? He's really forgotten?

But Mike isn't listening. He's gazing at the ceiling like he sees the face of God up there. His fingers are tapping real fast on his knees. Something's not right. Mike's not right. Then he smiles and it seems genuine, brand new. He's never smiled like this before, and it surprises Nelson so much he flinches as if he's been slapped.

"I swear to you. Best I've ever tried. Best. Ever. The first time we met—me and Victoria. She made me feel smart. Loved. I took her out for ice cream, she kissed me." He holds his hand up to his face, one side of it marked with a pink smear. Nah, can't be what I think it is, nah, there's no possible way that's a lipstick smear, an actual remnant of his memory that appeared out of nowhere. It's got to be a trick of light, a splotch on his face. Mike's eyes are all dreamy. Probably the first and last time I'll see him *glow*. "We didn't even fuck on the first date. We talked. More than I had ever talked to a woman in my life."

Mike gets up and he's cheering her name, *Vic, Vic, Victoria!*

"Mike, you feeling okay?" Nelson asks.

"I don't think I could feel any better. Finn. Product. *Now*."
He gives me an accusatory but possibly desperate look.

"I'm not gonna keep repeating myself. I told you—" I get up to leave but he's too fast, he's got his hand around my neck, a huge clammy hand that squeezes, tighter and tighter.

"You're lying," he says.

"Am not," I croak.

He wrestles me out of the chair by my neck, and I feel the little tendons and muscles and whatever else is in me stretch to their limit, the floor is hard, tile, really nice tile, and he's dragging me further into the back of the house, I'm kicking, reaching, grabbing chairs, carpet, walls, anything I can.

"Nelson . . . Nelson, you gonna talk some sense into Mike here?" I holler. Nelson isn't processing fast enough for me. He hasn't even jumped down from the kitchen counter, he's probably still floored by Mike's behavior. Mike is babbling on and on about how I'm hiding the product from him, how I'm deceiving him, and how I've always been a manipulative little dickhole. And here I thought we were on better terms.

I bat my hands around so that he'll let up but I can't reach him and I swear he's stretching my neck out, it's getting longer, I'm telling you, and his hands are getting stronger by the second. My sight is fuzzing up around the edges. I reach. I miss. I reach. I miss again. Out of control flailing. Maybe the knife really isn't around my calf. Maybe I imagined that it was there.

One last chance before I black out.

Faith, I think. If I could go back to that day, *I would have saved you*. Maybe I could have done something different.

It takes my remaining pathetic strength to grasp for my knife on my leg and ram it into Mike's foot. I feel the bone push aside, it creaks, but it doesn't crack. Mike yelps and falls to the floor, holding onto his foot. It takes me a few seconds to get to my feet, I'm feeling dizzy, out of control. Nelson appears, but I'm already shoving, running past him and out the door, toward my car, man, my hooptie's never looked so good, trip over a bush, land on my knees but the adrenaline has me up in a hot second, in my car now, where are the keys, fuck, I'm patting down my pockets, no keys, no keys, shit, shit, shit. Nelson is tearing through the door, the keys are in the ignition, *dumbass*, turn quick, throw it in reverse, backing out of the driveway before the car door is even shut, Nelson yelling, raging, chucking rocks at my car as I zoom up the road.

There are no yellow finches on the way back to D-Town. There are just crows, crows, and more crows, pecking at nothing on the side of the road, their black marble eyes hostile and unblinking.

Who the fuck is Early? And what did Mike mean when he talked about my having darker blue stuff?

CHAPTER FIFTEEN

IT'S LATE AFTERNOON WHEN I GET HOME, AND I DON'T WANT TO TALK TO ANYONE, I JUST WANT TO TAKE AN OXY AND GO TO SLEEP. Peter has left five messages, Bryce has texted me twelve times, and the first thing my mother says to me when I get through the door is: "Some girl is waiting for you in your room. The one with the nose ring. Who doesn't wear underwear. She thinks I don't notice, but I do."

Mom is drinking wine, flipping through one of her home goods magazines. The peacefulness of the scene is actually soothing, how mundane and leisurely. Sometimes Mom has this effect on me—her state of surrender at times makes me jealous. If only I could accept the cards that I've been dealt, if only I didn't have such fight in me. There's a lot to process and who knows when Mike's crew will show up and exact revenge.

"Where's Pop?" I ask.

"Where do you think he is?" she says. I have no desire to see him after reliving that terrible memory, so I'm relieved to know he's not around. She pats the couch seat next to her. "Come sit by your old mom before you go in to see that girl."

I do, because I don't want to see Penelope. She's one those needy girls that gets on your nerves after three seconds, but she's easy and always there. From where we sit, Mom's packages are stacked up high; it didn't take her long after the yard sale to fill the trailer up again—even more so than before—but I know better than to say anything about it.

"I'm worried about you," she says, taking a big gulp of her wine. She stares at the bruises on my neck.

"Ditto."

We sit in silence. Why did I get that memory instead of the fort one? Why the worst memory of my life? What did I do to deserve this? Is the universe sending me some kind of message? Like, Finn, you're a shithead, you try to get people hooked so you can make money and we're punishing you, muahahaha!

I'm *so* jonesin' for a high. The need comes on so fast.

"You're going to stay around and take care of me, won't you? I know you will, you're the man of the family now, my little boy." She nods and rests her head on my shoulder. I don't shrug her off. On another day I would have, but tonight the heaviness of her head, the heaviness of *her* is better than mine, and I can take comfort in that, as douche-y as that may sound.

Oh, my surroundings. My *home*. There have been too many times I've tried convincing myself that there aren't *that* many boxes and they aren't stacked up *that* high, and my mother only has a mild problem with it. She didn't used to always be like this, or at least that's what I remember when I was really young, when I had an imaginary friend and believed in the tooth fairy. I have a memory of her fixing up the trailer when we first moved in—she spent hours organizing all the cabinets to determine the best arrangement of cups, plates, pots, and pans; it took her careful deliberation to pick out the yellow ruffled curtains for the living room and for the tiny window above the sink. Pop even complimented her on her decorating prowess, and the beam that ensued from Mom was enough to put the radiance of the yellow curtains to shame.

Then Dad got out of shape, lost his charisma, couldn't sell cars for shit anymore. The drinking began soon after that, and so did the cheating. Mom reacted by almost shopping herself to death; such a sad cry for attention barely heard over the growing walls of packages.

"When you going to get yourself a girlfriend?" she asks, smoothing my hair behind my ear. "I want me some grandchildren one day."

My mind goes straight to Stacey. Not that I'm itching to be her baby daddy, but I *could* picture her as my girlfriend, holding her hand, hanging out by her locker, and kissing her on the cheek before she heads to class. Something steady and simple would be nice for once.

"Aw, Mom, don't even go there. Besides, I have plenty of girlfriends. Penelope is in my room right now." I wave in that direction.

She squishes her face up in disgust. "She's just your little plaything." Her hand smacks my kneecap. "Not your girlfriend. You're just like your father."

Oh *hell* no. It's my turn for disgust. I sit up straight. "I'm not like him. I won't *ever* be like him."

There is power in my voice, power coursing through me, I'm fighting so hard to separate myself from him because he's nothing to me. He's made Mom this way, he's made Faith her way, and he's made me . . . he won't make me anything. I've got a lead on the drug and that's all that counts right now. Early is the key. No doubt I can track down this cat—my list of contacts is from here to the moon. Yes. Finally, a small break.

Mom sighs and leans away from me, knowing our moment has passed. She'll have to go to the restaurant soon to wait tables—a restaurant I make sure not to frequent no matter what. The last time I saw the inside of that place was when Pop dragged me and Faith there as little kids to ask Mom for some money. Probably to buy some liquor. Mom didn't look surprised.

"You and your declarations," she says as she gets up, pours herself another glass of wine, and turns on the television.

———

The door to my room is open a crack, smoke wafting through, the smell strong and inconsiderate. I have my peeps smoke up in my room all the time, but in this case, I wasn't there to give her permission. Faith will especially disapprove once she knows it was Penelope.

"Hey," Penelope says, putting her pipe down on the nightstand. Usually she'd greet me with more enthusiasm, but there is none of that today. "You just killed my high."

"I think you should leave. I want to be alone." I don't care that my tone is brusque. Her half-shut eyes smile but her mouth stays flat. She doesn't move. "Did you hear what I just said?"

"I've got something to tell you."

Where is it, I'm thinking, rummaging through my socks in the bureau, searching through the drawer of the nightstand my sister never uses. My hand brushes up against the plastic bottle of oxys. Ah, yes, thank *God*. My body is trembling for it—I won't be able to concentrate without it. I pop a few in my mouth, hold them against my hot tongue as they dissolve. The buzz slinks through my veins; their effect is holy.

"Sharing is caring," Penelope says, reaching for a pill. I give her one. I'm seeing nirvana around the bend, so I'll do what she wants. Makes no difference to me. I catch a glimpse of my face in the mirror on the closet door and it isn't pretty. Bruises and welts on my neck, shadows under my eyes. I can't believe I stabbed that bastard in the foot, shit, I'm kind of proud of myself for such a blatant display of testicular gumption. Maybe it will get around; people need to know I'm a force to reckoned be with.

"Thanks," she says. "We're both going to need it once I tell you what I gotta tell you."

I glance down at Penelope's Doc Martens. She didn't take off her shoes when she curled up on the bed. Unbelievable.

"What's going on?" I ask, already bored, wanting to be alone.

She takes a hit from her bowl, blows the smoke out slow. The cloud's so dense it's impressive. I guess the high of the oxy isn't enough for her, and for a moment I sympathize. I know how that feels.

"Bryce's in jail. The cops got him, Finny." I try to ignore her high-pitched almost baby voice and concentrate on what she's telling me. Keep your cool. Let the buzz do it for you.

"What do you mean he's in jail?" I say, and then when I realize what I'm asking, I yell before she can answer. So long unflappable me. "How the hell did he end up there? What did you do? How did you screw things up? You fools can't do *any-thing* right! I give you one assignment, one *single* assignment, and one of you already got busted. Dumbasses. That's what you all are. A bunch of dumbasses who will never graduate high school, who will never succeed. I should have known, I should have just done this myself . . ." On and on I go. It's just letting off steam, I tell myself, it's something I need to do, vent, and it's okay when you're surrounded by incompetency.

Penelope is on the verge of tears. She recounts how the East Avenue knock-spot got busted by some cops who got a lead, and Bryce (who had a couple joints on him) happened to be there at the wrong place at the wrong time, carrying out his assignment. Penelope managed to hit the road before she got caught. Five guys were cuffed and thrown in jail for marijuana and cocaine possession. They confiscated a ridiculous amount of heroin. I thought the po-po had given up on D-Town, a place that is and will always and forever be bloated with drugs. There's got to be a new cop in town or something.

"He's at D-Town County Jail?" I ask gently. I feel slightly bad that I reamed her out, feel even worse that Bryce landed in the clink.

"Yes," she says, sniffing, hugging herself with her arms wrapped around her waist. Most likely Bryce will pay a fine. Two joints isn't enough to buy you jail time. I've got some funds to bail him out, so this is not the main problem. The main problem is that this is not going according to plan. The bust at East Ave isn't the first incident that's leading me to believe they're buffing up law enforcement. Just the other day, I heard about another drug bust went down in Jiminy Park—a safe haven for users, until now.

"Go bail him out," I say, not making eye contact.

"With what?"

"Get in your car and wait. I'll come out with the cash."

She pouts; I look up. Her tears have done a real number on her made-up face. Why am I in such a rage? The oxys should have evened me out by now.

"I think we should drop the search. It's just not worth it,"

Penelope says, getting closer. "Too much heat." I drag my fingers through my hair, trying to ignore the warmth radiating off her body as she craves comfort and touch. I inch away and she notices, glowering at me.

"Fuck that, we're not dropping anything. Forget it, Pen—you can give up, miss out on the fat stacks, but *I'm* not giving up," I say, putting my hand over my heart.

Penelope squeezes her lips together. "What are *you* doing that's so great?" she yells. "You came back empty-handed too, right? I don't see you celebrating. You suck. I suck. *We. All. Suck.*" She bites her fingernails. I'm back to not hearing a thing she's saying. Thinking about how I'm going to make this up to Bryce—seems like all I'm doing for the rest of my life is damage control.

"I'll come out with the money. Just get in your car, okay?" I sigh. The money from my dealing is under my bed, under one of the floorboards. When she walks out the door I yell, "And the next time you set foot in my room, take off your damn shoes."

I press my fingers against my temples and lean back against the wall. It was so sunny the day of the yard sale—what if it hadn't been so bright out? What if it had rained instead? I take another oxy—it's the only answer that will suffice.

CHAPTER SIXTEEN

IT'S AN HOUR AFTER PENELOPE'S DEPARTURE WITH THE CASH TO BAIL BRYCE OUT WHEN FAITH COMES INTO OUR ROOM, WRINKLING HER NOSE. I sit up from the bed and gauge her mood. It's hard to tell her deeper emotions when she looks so put-together. There isn't a crease on her skirt, and her hair clip matches perfectly with her purple platform shoes, whereas I'm wearing ripped jeans and a T-shirt with a hole in the armpit (a look complemented by the bruises on my neck). Such a stark difference that won't change any time soon. No worries, girls dig my style.

"Smoking up with the window closed?" she asks.

"Penelope." That's all I need to say. Faith doesn't like her, says she's got no respect for humanity and no love for herself.

"She's yet another stain in your life."

I brace myself for another lecture, but she stays quiet. After she throws open the window, she picks up an envelope that I hadn't noticed because I was too busy rummaging around for an OC. Which, by the way, is smoothing me out nicely, finally. That extra one was all I needed.

"What the hell happened to your face?" she asks, sitting on the edge of her bed.

"Tiger pit. You should see the other tiger."

"I'm not even going to ask."

"Good," I say, leaning against my headboard.

When she opens the envelope, she barely glances at what's inside, then tucks it under a stack of books on the floor. I think I see the Harvard insignia on the header of the letter. I'll have to check this out when she's not around.

"I'm sorry I've been so hard on you lately," she says softly, sitting down on her bed.

I perk up a bit. This is new.

"I haven't exactly been a darling myself." Is my voice slurring? I hope it's not slurring. I'm glad she's not close enough to see my red-rimmed eyes and runny nose. I can just play it off as allergies if she asks.

"The pressure of everything, you know? This is the end of high school," she says.

"The end of an era." I let the statement hang. I think it's a good one. "You should stop worrying about me for a while. I'm worried about *you*." There is a hint of a sad smile on her face. I want to take care of my sister, give her back the shelter of the fort with the kitten, the quiet, and the comforting stream of cat facts.

"It's like that scrambler ride we went on as kids," she says.

"What do you mean?"

She laughs to herself. "You know, the one at the amusement park in Lake George?"

I can't believe I forgot. It was an actual family outing, one where we all had fun. You're in these two-person cars shaped like different kinds of animals, circling around the arena while other riders are circling around you. There are flashing lights, loud music, a projection of stars splashed across a domed ceiling—it's a great acid trip without the acid. Good ol' fashioned fun used to be enough.

"We're going to get off that chaotic, dizzying ride, Finn. We've been so used to everyone in D-Town circling around us for years. We know the pattern, we know what kind of crazy to expect. But once it's over, there's a whole new crazy to contend with. Are you ready for that? I'm not." Her fingers trace a seam on the patchwork quilt she made that covers her bed.

"Huh," I say, scratching my chin. "I never thought about it that way. How about this instead? We'll create an anti-tinamous clause."

"What in God's name is that?" A gentle breeze slips in through the window, whispering through the curtains, lifting wisps of her hair.

"I'll tell you what that means, sister." I sit up a little straighter. It never fails to amaze me: just mentioning birds makes me stronger, gives me that extra dose of *I know what I'm doing so listen up good.* "You cannot, under any circumstances, as stated by the clause, act like a tinamous. It's an insecure bird that panics. They creep about at ground level keeping out of everyone else's way. But once they think they've been spotted, they panic. They shoot upward in a manic, high-speed flight. Like super-duper-über fast. They don't look where they're going, so a lot of them die—crashing against trees, falling into water—and mind you, they can't swim. The danger they're trying to escape from becomes less of a problem than the danger they put themselves in." I let that sink in.

My sister looks down at her purple-polished toenails. "I know I can't panic. It's not like I don't know that."

"You're brilliant, sis, I get it. But hop on this next ride and let it carry you. Don't fight so hard against it. Don't think it's the enemy. Take your meds, keep talking to your therapist every once in a while. Talk to *me*. If you feel yourself tweaking out, I'll remind you of the anti-tinamous clause."

"Easier said than done."

I nod, agreeing with her. Yes, indeed. But I know I can help, I have to.

"I know I haven't been the best brother. But I'm telling you, if all else fails, I'll shield you from hitting the tree, I'll pull you out of the water. I got your back like nothing else."

Even in my oxy-induced stupor, I'm adamant and passionate about this—and it comes through. Her jaw clenches, and I know she's pushing back tears by the way she turns her head so I can't see her one good eye. She holds both of her kneecaps for a couple seconds, then stands up, self-assured. We exchange bright smiles, the brightest, but when she leaves, doubt slithers back in, its slime a dark trail on an otherwise pristine surface.

Once I hear Faith talking to Mom in the television room, I scramble for the envelope Faith shoved between her books. Sure enough, it's a packet from Harvard giving instructions on submitting Faith's acceptance of admission. You've got to ride the ride, Faith. We're tall enough for it.

As I feel around for my laptop underneath my bed, my fingers graze the dulled corners of the Audubon book. My bible. How did that Klaski woman understand the secret of my heart? It's disturbing, it's stirring, it's embarrassing—I barely know her, she's as old as dirt, yet somehow she feels close. Is she aware that the original *Birds of America* book was huge because Audubon wanted to paint his birds life-size? Does she know that many of the birds' poses are awkward in order to show off their best features? I bet she's familiar with *Phoenicopterus ruber*, Audubon's rendering of a pink flamingo: beak about to nip the water, neck bent impossibly, grotesquely, but just right.

The rightness of my decision is a warm palm against my cheek. I fire up my computer and type in the website the letter instructs Faith to visit.

The computer keys against the pads of my fingers are so connected to the future, every click is ticking out the hours until Faith can go to college and become somebody. I picture her in a large, amphitheater-style classroom—some shit that makes you want to get your Aristotle on—deep in discussion, arguments, analytical thinking, damn, it almost seems possible to make the world a better place. If anyone can, it's Faith. And there is no better place to start than at Harvard. Not at some community college where the campus is as big as a postage stamp and teachers go to AA meetings around their course schedules and know fuck-all about anything.

I enter all Faith's personal information. I know her social security number ever since that night at the hospital—seemed like something a twin should have memorized. I've never typed so fast, and for a moment I pretend that I'm the one going to Harvard and that I'm bursting with joy and anxiousness to study poli sci or philosophy or some shit that isn't applicable in the real world. The real world that tries to take a dump on me on the regular.

Faith is heading back down the short hallway now, toward our room, her heavy shoes announce themselves even on carpet. I scramble to put the envelope back where she left it. I return to my laptop and minimize the tab with Harvard's website. She bursts through the door.

"Forgot to change my eye patch," she says, rustling through her bureau. She pulls out a fancy one—purple with glitter around the edges. "I'm off to the movies. I'll see you later."

"Remember," I say. "Thou shalt not tinamous." I'm relieved she isn't aware of my plot.

"A-freaking-men, brother."

I do the sign of the cross over my chest, which causes her to laugh. It's like being blessed, that sound. Once her heels make a faint *thump thump*, I click my mouse toward Faith's destiny, toward my own. I have no choice but to find that miracle drug.

Welcome to Harvard! The computer screen announces.

TUESDAY, APRIL 16

CHAPTER SEVENTEEN

IT'S ONLY A FEW DAYS AFTER MY RUN-IN WITH MIKE.
The bruises around my neck are purple and yellow, and I'm
positive that some girl in class is going to ask me about it, is
going to secretly think it's sexy. In my car I do a couple quick
lines of coke in the school parking lot. There's a reason why
I tinted my windows extra dark. I sit for a moment listening
to some Led Zeppelin, as the chemicals do their dance in my
veins, maybe a foxtrot, something bouncy for sure. My hook-
up is giving me a good deal on cocaine lately. His price won't
go down on heroin, though. That's good. I wish he'd jack it up
even more to discourage me from buying it. Although to be
honest, it would probably wouldn't.

Commotion as soon as I step inside D-Town High.
Screeches. A few *oh my Gods*. Sneakers squeaking and the shrill
voices of girls. Students and teachers are rushing around this
way and that, it's bananas, it's not even time for the first class
of the day. An exposed fluorescent tube light flickers above my
head, a few lockers slam. I follow the hall down to the end,
where the crowd is the thickest. I see what's what.

Red. Everywhere.

On the lockers. On the floor. On the floor something else.

A body.

Stacey.

My response is immediate. I push through the crowd, pushing whoever, it doesn't matter, and see the school nurse, Ms. Caven, hunched over Stacey, my dream girl Stacey, and a teacher standing nearby, his face ashen and somber. Stacey has blood smeared over her arms and splotched all over her jeans. There's a streak of it across her face. My heart is a cannonball ready to launch.

"What happened?" I ask whoever is listening.

Ms. Caven is holding Stacey's hand. "She's okay. The blood isn't hers," she says. "It's from her locker." I look up. The locker door is closed. "Can you do me a favor, Finn? Will you get everyone away from here? They won't listen to me."

"She's okay?" My voice cracks. "She is?"

Ms. Caven nods.

Act first, questions later.

I'm on it in a flash, raising my voice, backing people up, telling them y'all need to bounce. Everything's okay, it's not her blood, go about your business, please and thank you . . . "Well, whose is it?" they ask. "Why's it here?" "What is happening?" I don't know, I say, this isn't CNN, I just got here, fools. I tell them they're only making the situation worse, poor girl, poor new girl, and they best be getting on their way. Someone says sarcastically, "Finn to the rescue," while a few of the others snicker and I have to amp it up a notch, so I all-out yell.

"Would you motherfuckers get the fuck out of here?"

"Language," Ms. Caven says half-heartedly.

I'm mean eyes, powerful voice. They finally listen. Force to be reckoned with? You bet. Look what I did to Mike's foot.

I'm back on the ground next to Ms. Caven as Stacey's

murmuring and coming to. Seems like the blood gushed down from the locker after it was open. The gummy feeling of it against my knees and sneakers isn't going to be a highlight of my day. Thankfully Ms. Caven used to be an army nurse, so I doubt this is the worst she's seen. We're both holding Stacey's hands now, and I'm ashamed of myself because I'm enjoying the feel of her skin against mine even though it's covered with blood. What's wrong with me? I'm no hero, but why do I feel like one? One of the teachers fetches some water, and Ms. Caven and I help Stacey sit up slowly, letting her touch the back of her head, watching her try to gather herself and find words.

"A head. My locker. In it." She starts to fall back again, but we catch her.

I look around. Something written out in red spray paint, on the door of her locker.

OINK OINK

I cover my hand up with my sleeve and pull her locker open. Someone yells at me, but it's too late. I gasp. I can't help it.

It's a head. A pig's head.

Holy all the swear words in the world.

I swallow the bile rising in my throat, which only makes more come up, but I get control of myself. I should rephrase that: I *somewhat* get control of myself. Waves of nausea toss through me.

"We need to get her out of here," Ms. Caven says. I close the locker and catch my breath. "Mr. Fitch, can you call the hospital? I think she's okay, but I just want to be sure she didn't hit her head on the way down. Then call the cops after that and her parents. Finn, let's bring her to my office, okay?"

We both try to get her to stand up, but she's resisting, she doesn't want to move, she's pushing us away, she's actually saying I'm fine, I'm fine, I'm fine, but then her hand slips on the blood as she tries to get up. She makes a noise in the back of her throat that breaks my heart, so I pick her up, cradling her in my arms, and bring her to the nurse's office. Though she's not verbally complaining, I feel her body complain, she doesn't want to be carried, like some princess who can't take care of herself. Well too bad, because this is happening, and don't kill me if I enjoy it a tiny bit.

In the nurse's office, Stacey doesn't lie back on the cot. Her hands are clutched over her knees, and her hair is sticking to the blood on her face. Ms. Caven hands her a cold compress, which she doesn't use.

"Come on, honey, it will feel good on your head." Stacey pushes her hands gently away.

"I'm fine. I don't want to be in these clothes anymore."

"When you get to the hospital you can change your clothes. Come with me and we'll fix you up the best we can in the bathroom." Her voice is safe, motherly.

"I'm not going to the hospital," Stacey says adamantly.

Ms. Caven lists about a hundred reasons why she should, but Stacey's just saying no, no, no, hospitals aren't for her, she's great, her head doesn't hurt, she's not dizzy, no big deal, she didn't hit the floor very hard when she fell.

"Wow, you're stubborn," I say, leaning against the wall next to the cot. It's a white painted concrete wall that's arctic cold against my sweaty back.

Stacey's eyes flick toward me. "I'm not stubborn."

"You should listen to the woman, you know. A medical expert. You could have a concussion and if you fall asleep you'll die. Lights out. That's what I've heard anyway. Isn't that right, Ms. Caven?"

She shoots me a *stop being a smartass* look, a look I've seen so many times before, but I don't care, I know that she kind of likes it, probably because I come by often just to shoot the bull. The time she spent in the army she likes talking about and I like listening. Twice divorced, one-bedroom apartment on the west side, the nice side. Some older ladies have important shit to say. Mrs. Klaski. I'm sure she has some gems. Imagine if I heard some of them? It'd be entertaining, I'm sure.

Stacey needs to go to the hospital and I'm going to do whatever I can to get her there. Even if it means dragging her there myself.

"I won't fall asleep," she says. "I just hate hospitals."

I hate hospitals too. I hated listening to the doctors say Faith's eye couldn't be reconstructed. I hated hearing the other sick patients moaning in pain, but most of all I hated hearing my sister cry. For some reason, I want to tell Stacey all of this. But maybe I'm overreacting. People have been through much worse: like finding a pig's head in their locker, which is clearly a threat, but what on earth would a girl like Stacey have done to merit such a heavy-duty threat?

"Nosocomephobia," I say.

"Pardon me?" Stacey asks. Her fingers are clamped around the edge of the cot where she sits. She is refusing to lie down.

"Excessive fear of hospitals. That's the term for it. I just diagnosed you. You're welcome." I give her a sharp nod.

"I don't have that." She sounds bratty, in fact, stubborn. She's got that fierceness in her eyes too, the type I think I have. Ms. Caven is still trying to give Stacey things—an ice pack, some Tylenol, but Stacey wants nothing to do with it. I think all she wants to do is argue, so I give her what she wants.

"You might have that *exact* phobia. And it's kind of lame if you do. No offense."

I flash her a smile. The color is leaking back into her cheeks, and it feels like a small victory.

Stacey narrows her eyes at me, and it kills me, because it's as if she's wondering what to do, and I might be the one with the answer. I shrug. Why do I already feel like there's a connection here, a connection that has been here for years and years and years? Faith went to a psychic once who told her that I was her son in a past life, which was actually pretty gross, and that our souls are old and have been together in different roles during many, many lives. Maybe Stacey and I knew each other in another life, in the great *before*. I won't be buying a crystal ball any time soon, just in case I found out I was her son too, but given the frequency of whack-ass events in the last couple of weeks, I'm questioning my whole belief system. The fabric of reality feels more like a thread that's ready to break in an easy snap.

"Fine. I'll go. But only because Finn is irritating, and I just want him to shut up." She looks at me briefly, then up at the ceiling.

Ms. Caven beams, I lean harder against the wall for support, because I think I'm in love. I mean, it's ridiculous, but in this moment, a rush of affection hits me so hard that it takes all my might not to fall over. Ms. Caven is pretending not to notice that I'm head over heels for this girl. Stacey is alone on the cot—she should *never* be alone—so I sit down next to her, but not too close.

"I'm going to be okay, right?" she says.

More cracks in my heart. "Of course you are." I think about patting her knee like a grandmother would do, but I decide against it. God, what is happening to me? Ms. Caven is speaking to someone on the phone in serious tones. "You just went through some hardcore shit," I say, "and here you are, all cool and calm. I'm impressed by you right now. I really am. Nosocomephobia and all."

She smiles slightly. I smile slightly. Strands of hair are stuck to her lips, but she doesn't seem to notice.

"You have—" I say, and before I know what I'm doing, my fingers are gently swiping her hair away from her mouth. She doesn't flinch. She lets me. Her skin is cool to the touch. I can tell she's about to say something, but the gesture is done, and I look away from her and feel the blood rise to my cheeks.

I don't blush. *Ever.*

But here I go.

There are a lot of words that could be said right now. She could say, thanks, Finn, for being here for me. I could say, I want to take care of you, I want to protect you, and if anyone *ever* thinks about hurting you again I'm going to . . .

A man steps through the doorway and pauses. He's in full police uniform with his hands on his hips. Stacey's face lights up.

"Daddy," she says, scrambling off the cot and making a dash toward him, collapsing into his arms. Oh, hold up. For real? He's a big guy, pocked, rough-looking skin on his face, he's been around the block or ten. His body swallows her up as they embrace. Something about him makes me immediately want to stand at attention, maybe it's the way he darts his eyes back and forth between me and Ms. Caven, even as he kisses the top of Stacey's head.

"Sweetheart," he says softly.

I swallow hard. Ms. Caven introduces herself, and says softly, "Nice to meet you, Sergeant Braggs," clearly a little awestruck by him. He's not bad-looking, I'll give him that. I'm no longer in the room. I know I don't really exist when it comes to fathers and daughters in the same space, so I try to make myself as small as possible. Stacey is crying a little, not overdramatically, but just enough to show that she was really scared, but she's trying to be brave. Her father calms her, in the way that fathers should, holding her, telling her to shush, saying that he's going to take care of it and everything's going to be okay. I mean, I believe him. Must be his air of authority, or how he looks precisely as a police officer should. I can't believe I snorted up this morning. I'm irrationally worried that he knows.

I put this aside. My mind shifts to overdrive as I connect the pieces. Maybe it's a long shot, maybe I'm over-hypothesizing.

Oink. Oink.

He's the new cop in town, trying to be a big man on campus, rehabilitate the community and all that. Her father must have been part of the big drug bust on East Ave that landed Bryce in jail, and someone must not be too thrilled about it.

I know someone who'd be capable of this.

———

I storm through the empty hallway, searching him out. *Mike*, only *he* would do something as screwed up as this, that sick, sick bastard. God, it must have taken a lot of effort to get a pig's head. Where does one get a pig's head anyway?

Vermont. Farm country. That's where. Guess it wasn't that hard after all.

Mike probably put Jason, his loyal, thickheaded brother, up to this. The crackdown on drug activity is affecting Mike's business, compounded by his failing crop. He's pretty much screwed. Jason must have given him the inside scoop of Stacey's dad being the new sheriff in town. So why not send a message in the most hick-ish way possible, signed with love from the backwoods of VT? While Mike's at it, he's probably planning something for me this very moment. Him *and* his gimp foot.

I'm popping my head into classrooms, disrupting lectures, teachers slam doors in my face, Finn, they say, get your act together, what *act*, I think, this isn't an *act*, and I keep going, that stupid motherf—

Bingo.

Jason's sitting in Mrs. Buckley's class, chewing on a pencil and scrolling through his iPhone. I raging-bull it through the classroom door and pounce, no one's expecting it, especially not poor Mrs. Buckley, who is frailer than frail. I tackle Jason in his chair to the ground, ringing of metal, ears ringing just as hard, punching and hitting everything, his face, his chest, the chair, the floor, I don't care if I'm missing my target, I just feel like hitting everything, so I do, and my knuckles are getting raw, and guys are pulling me off him, and old Mrs. Buckley is calling for help.

"You did this!" I yell. I go back for more because they can't hold me down. All I'm seeing is red. Crimson. Burgundy. Vermillion. Cardinal. *Cardinalis cardinalis.*

Peter's next to me suddenly. Didn't even see him. Calm down, he says, not too loud, clamping his hand on my forearm, you don't know the facts, Finn, you're not thinking this through . . . I push him off. It's too easy. It's flicking a bug.

"Admit it!" I roar. It takes four guys to finally keep me off him, but I've still got a Grand Canyon full of fight in me.

"Man, *what* are you talking about? I did *what*?" Jason asks.

Jason is cowering on the floor, and for a split second I feel bad for him because he looks like cornered prey, bloodied and bruised. But we're the same size, he can scuffle with the best of them, and oh, did I mention that *he's* the one to blame? I shouldn't be sorry at all. Punk-ass motherfucker. Peter's staying out of reach of me, and Mrs. Buckley is out the door, still calling for help in a scratchy voice that isn't used to yelling.

"The pig's head in Stacey's locker. That's fucked up, man. That's some Godfather shit."

I try ripping from the abundance of grasps, but they aren't letting me go. Peter tells me to cut it out, calling me by my full name, Phineas Alexander Walt, like he's my goddamn father, saying to me it's not worth it. Jason's lips are practically white.

"I didn't do it, cocksucker," he says. "I *wish* I was that creative. I'd want to take credit for that shit." He wipes his bloody nose with the back of his hand, and winces from the contact. Too much blood today.

"I don't believe you. Mike put you up to it." Can't get the ringing in my ears to stop. The cocaine, my anger, my almost insanity—it wouldn't be shocking if I dropped dead of a heart attack right here. Maybe that'd be a good thing.

"Believe what you want. I didn't do it," Jason says. "You are going to be *so* sorry for this, especially after what you did to my brother."

I pull a Scarlett O'Hara by telling myself I'll think about that tomorrow. As for now I want to know.

"It's Early, right?" I say. "What about Early?"

Jason's alarm is clear as a bell on his face.

"What do you know about him?" he practically squeaks.

Someone is shouting my name. I turn around. He's coming at me with cuffs.

Stacey's father. Perfect. He's so deft I'm handcuffed before I can protest. The metal is icy and not altogether unfamiliar. I've been cuffed a few times before for dealing, but it wasn't anything I couldn't talk my way out of. Just another occupational hazard. But this. I've got no words for it.

Everyone stares as the metal locks around my wrists, their eyes like locks too, they'll relate this image with me for a while. God, Finn, what were you thinking? I don't feel like myself. Where did I go? I'm spinning, spinning, spinning.

Then I look beyond Stacey's father and see Stacey herself, standing in the hallway with a friend, watching, blood streaking her jeans, and I can't figure out if she's upset, no, that's not it, or if she's disappointed, no, that's not it either.

Those pretty green eyes are registering my true colors, oh, lookie here, the bastard reveals himself, full monty. I decide the way she feels is something between sadness and disgust. No. Longing and regret. That sounds about right. And shit upon shit, I realize that the friend standing next to her is none other than my very own sister, Faith. Of course they're friends, Stacey the doctor, Faith the prodigious entrepreneur. I haven't told Faith that I'm into Stacey, and I definitely won't be telling her now.

Stacey's father shoves me down the hall. Faith's emotions are so dense it's like she's saying it out loud. *You could be so good, Finn. But you're kind of an asshole.* You're preaching to the choir, sister, you're preaching to the damn choir.

I lay low for the next few days, don't deal, barely talk, squeaky-clean Finn over here, a husk, a shell, an empty chrysalis, that's me. Peter, instead of my sister, was with my mom when she came to pick me up at the police station. He wouldn't really talk to me because of how I pushed him off me in the classroom, and it looks like I actually sprained his wrist or something, but at least it's a show of brotherly attention—my sister was so disgusted by my behavior she didn't want to see my face. She said to me afterward, "You think that tiger pit was bad? I'm growing claws the size of machetes for you and you alone. Anti-tinamous clause my ass." Now she won't talk to me. Mom says she is "appalled" at my behavior, but her scolding is half-hearted and ineffectual. "I don't know what to do anymore, Phineas. You've gone so far off the rails they'll find you in the Atlantic."

I heard Nurse Caven put up a solid case for me when the principal wanted to suspend me indefinitely. "He's a good kid at heart," I imagine her saying. "He's struggling, but we can't leave our struggling kids behind. That's how it gets worse for them." Whatever she said, it worked—I got slapped with a week of detention and that's it. I wrote her a sweet-ass thank-you note with a box of Godiva chocolates I know she likes.

It's nice to have one cheerleader in my corner, but it doesn't even begin to balance out all the people who think I'm a certi-fied dirtbag, starting with my own sister, my former best friend, and ending with Stacey and her police officer father—along with the twenty or so other people in between.

I need to find where that powder came from.

SATURDAY, APRIL 20

CHAPTER EIGHTEEN

SATURDAY CAN'T COME SOON ENOUGH, AND YOU BET YOUR ASS I'M AT THE CEMETERY FIRST THING IN THE EARLY MORNING, WAITING. Mrs. Klaski never arrives. Yes, I want to ask her about *Birds of America*. What's her favorite print? I'm still figuring out mine. And yes, of course, I want to ask her more about the drug. About Early. My plan for the next move isn't materializing, yet I'm still sniffing out this Early character and thinking maybe she's my best lead. If only I hadn't beaten the shit out of Jason, I could have pumped him for more information. If only, if only, if only. I'm tired of defaulting to this all the time. There's got to be another angle I can approach in finding this dude.

When I get home from the cemetery, I know I can't resist anymore. No one's talking to me, whatever I thought Stacey and I could be was for shit, and the oxys aren't going to do it. I dial Taylor's number.

"Please forgive me for my abominable behavior," I say with flourish when she answers, milking each syllable. There's no response from her. "I want to be in your good graces again. I'm begging you."

"Who said you were ever in my good graces?" Now that

she's speaking, I can tell she's high.

"What can I do to make it up to you? Why don't I come over tonight? Make amends. I want to see more of your pretty face, smell more of that vanilla scent you wear. Can you allow me that?" My voice is smooth, laying down my best game, I'm really Sinatra-ing it.

"Finn," she says. I enjoy the way she says my name, like it's an answer to an important question. "I don't think it's a good idea."

"It probably isn't." I lean in closer to the phone as if she can feel my body heat. "We need to chill. We'll talk. I want to hear about what colleges you've gotten into."

"I haven't gotten into any colleges," she snaps, irritated that I don't know the minutiae of her life. "I'm staying in D-Town."

"So am I," I say automatically. "That's good, we'll get to know each other more after we graduate." I deserve to be flogged, as I'm fully aware that this is the *last* thing I want. But I haven't shot up in a while, and tonight I need the needle—the direct hit, the instant satisfaction, the two-second pause and then, aaaah, who am I again?

My comment about getting to know each other softens her. She's not the only one who will be left behind.

"My parents won't be home tonight. I guess it'd be okay if you came over."

It's almost too easy, and I'm not proud of being an expert-level scumbag.

"I'll be there at five," I say.

When I get there, Taylor's not looking so fresh. She's wearing a pair of paisley printed boxers and practically swimming in a Red Sox T-shirt. No hello, no hey Finn, how are you, nice seeing you, just a gesture to come inside. Hostess of the year. In the kitchen, she hops up and sits on the granite counter-topped island in the middle of the room, a throne of sorts, expecting me to say something interesting, to entertain her, her own private court jester.

"You all right there, babe?" I ask.

"Yeah, I'm fine. Just not feeling great."

I walk over to her and slide my hands up her bare thighs, tuck a piece of hair behind her ear.

"I know what would make us feel better," I say. Heroin's a mood thing, only temporary, I reassure myself, connect to the phases of the moon, appropriate when the stars are aligned.

Taylor eyes me with hesitance, glances at the clock on the wall. I caress her face with my fingers, light touch, thumb stroking the bottom of her lip. She lets out a sigh, and I go in for a kiss that she receives passively, part of her isn't here. An absent ghost of a kiss.

"I got some," she says. "Let's go up to my room."

——— ———

Even the needle feels good going in, warmed up from Taylor's touch. Seconds of ecstasy feel like a year's worth, I've just kissed God himself, the world is exquisite, right *on*. Down, down, oh Lord, the free fall has never been so sweet, I could plummet forever, good-bye mind, see you never, you weren't that great anyway. Had a way of being a record that skips, the same part playing over and over again. All that exists is *now*, I've caught it in my hand, here you go Finn, a baseball-size *now* that I never want to throw to home plate.

The fact that we're sharing the needle seems sacred, we've made this pact, we're blood brothers and there is no going back.

I'm in her good graces again, dammit, I'm beyond her good graces, I've reached her pearly gates, though not in a sexual way. The gates are open where nirvana is attainable. We're in this together, and this billowing cloud of calm hugs us in a womb-like circle, to nourish, nurture, and rebirth. The ashen pallor of Taylor's skin disappears, revealing an awakened tone, a cotton candy pink that I want to lick off and have for myself. I get the urge to write a poem, compose a song, paint on a canvas.

We lie on her bed, feet dangling off the end, gazing up at the ceiling decorated with glow-in-the-dark stars. Our breathing is in sync, we touch each other's hands every other minute or so, just to make sure this is real and solid, that there's ground to land on once we come down.

Taylor turns her head and is staring at the side of my face. She reaches out to touch me but thinks better of it. Somehow we ended up stripped down—she in her pink underwear and matching bra, me in my black boxer briefs. But it's innocent; we just want to be free.

"Your scar," she says. "How did you get it?"

I freeze. Didn't know freezing was possible in the warm blanket state I'm in. I think about answering her, maybe it would be a release.

"Come on. Do we really want to get into this now? Let's ride this out."

"I'm already coming down," she says. With her finger, she traces a line from the top of my forehead down to the beginning of my scar, then she stops. I tighten up. I don't blame her for not wanting to caress me there. I know what that skin feels like: rumpled, raised, wrecked. Ugly-ass scar. War wound.

"Don't really want to talk about it," I say.

Taylor props herself up on her elbow, face now taking on a

greenish yellowish color, cotton candy gone, eyes glassy and all surface. "I've always wanted to know. Everyone's been curious, for like, years."

"Everyone should mind their own business. Do I ask *you* personal shit like that?" I stare up at the ceiling, not wanting to address her probing eyes. The high is beginning its descent.

"No. But you might want to start if we're going to continue to do this."

"Do what?"

"You know, this." She gestures between us. "Like, date."

I start laughing. "For real? You call this dating? I wanted to get high, have a good time, chill, you know? I thought we were cool like that. Casual."

Taylor takes a moment to collect herself.

"I can't believe this. I can't believe *you*," she says, sitting upright, putting her face in her hands. "Is that all you care about?"

"Baby," I say, rubbing her back, still lying down, "of course that's not all I care about. I want to be your friend. You're important to me."

She slaps her hands on the comforter of her bed, groaning. "You're *such* a liar, Finn, you know that?"

Ugh to it all. The nausea has caught up with me, dragging me into its wretched space. Can't see straight, my scar is burning up, like I'm being singed over again.

"Everyone knows that it probably has something to do with the fact that your dad's a drunk and your mom's a pill head."

My blood boils so fast—my surroundings speed up like a time-lapse movie. I feel my hand raising, flat, rigid, unforgiving, ready to strike. To *hit*. I see Taylor cowering, shielding her face. Oh my God, I say to myself, oh my God, this is me throwing my arm down before the damage is done, this is me squeezing it to my side, thoughts going at top speed, regret, regret, forget, forget, stomach about to spill its contents.

"Don't fucking touch me," she says, pointing to the door. "Get out. *Get out.* I don't want to see you again. Go find your own dope."

I scramble to put my clothes on, saying I'm sorry, I'm sorry, Taylor, I'm just not myself right now, I'm so screwed up, but it makes her yell even louder.

"Get out, you piece of shit!"

Hightail it to the bathroom down the hall, destroy her toilet with vomit, seems like gallons of it, clean up the best I can, wipe my face, water from the faucet I gurgle and spit out. Don't look at yourself, Finn, don't you *dare* look at yourself in the mirror. But I do.

Brown hair, mussed up, sticking out in different directions. Haunted house–worthy shadows under my eyes. Skin a terrible shade of sick. Bruises around my throat. And my scar. It eats up the side of my face and a section of my chin, engulfing me, disfigured and beyond repair, I can't stand it, not because of vanity, but because it's showcasing what's on the inside. A Coca Cola–level advertisement of who I really am.

CHAPTER NINETEEN

PHONE CALL ON OUR LANDLINE IN THE MIDDLE OF THE NIGHT. I look at the time: 2:45 a.m. Probably the wrong number, so I don't answer it, plus I don't think I'm physically capable of crawling out of bed. My body aches to the bone; no, scratch that, my body aches to the *marrow*. Sleep carries me away soon enough, I'm dreaming about Stacey, her hair, the curve of her neck, wearing Keds sneakers instead of the knock-off Louboutins girls flash around here. Even in my dream I'm aware that I want to stay in the dream forever, and there's a persistent ache that resides in my chest because I know I can't. The incident with Taylor earlier today seems so far away.

Ring, ring. The phone again. I let it go. *Ring, ring.* Christ almighty. Faith yells at me to get it and I hear my parents rustling around in bed.

"*Fine,*" I say, dramatically throwing the covers off, setting my feet on the ground, dragging my hands over my face. My skin is so sensitive from being sober it's screaming from the contact.

Ring, ring. "I'm coming, I'm coming," I yell.

I pick up the wall-mounted phone in the kitchen. "Hello?"

Dead space on the line, until I listen carefully. Breathing. Raspy. What is this, a goddamn horror movie?

"Hello?" I say again, scratching the back of my neck. I scoff loud enough so the person on the other end hears it. "Well, good-bye then."

Click.

It's got to be Mike. I knifed his foot and made Jason my punching bag and that's not going to go over well regardless of the amount of apologies and free weed I gave him this past week. *Jason, listen man, I'm sorry, shit be crazy, but I'm going to make this right . . . we'll all get a cut of the profit, once I get my hands on this candy . . . you understand . . . in the meantime, why don't you take this as an apology . . .* It took my angel of a sister to convince him not to press charges. Faith's persuasion tactics were so powerful, Jason didn't sic his brother and the state of Vermont after me. Maybe the stress of diminishing sales and increasing heat from the police are working in my favor—Mike is too preoccupied to immediately destroy me, or at least that's what I thought. Now my heart's punching over and over against my ribcage. The phone is still in my hands. Deep breaths, deep breaths. He's after my blood and it's just a matter of time. He's playing with me, making me wait and just when I forgot, there he is, pow.

"Who was that?" Pop asks, appearing in the kitchen, giving me a start. He's wearing a maroon bathrobe he's had since the beginning of time, rubs his glasses on the sleeve and puts them on. Pop's a smaller man than he was, all that muscle and verve diminished, he's just an echo of himself. The only weightlifting he does is picking up a bottle.

"Wrong number," I say, placing the phone back in its carriage.

"Sure."

He pushes past me and opens the fridge and starts taking

out the fixings for a bologna and cheese sandwich, beer stench wafting off him. Who the hell eats a bologna and cheese sandwich at 3:00 a.m.? He twists the lid off the jar of mayo and slaps it on two pieces of Wonder bread. As a little kid I'd get all tense when he was in a mood and gauge how bad it was by the size of his forehead vein. I still catch myself evaluating it now. I've seen it worse.

Bologna first, packaged cheese slice, slimy iceberg lettuce, squish down, slice of a knife. Pop's fading masculinity, if that's what you want to call it, isn't helping his sales at the car dealership. He's doing worse than when he was drunk and angry. Now he's just drunk. Mom's afraid they'll lay him off soon, with the economy in the shitter.

I make a move to leave. He sits down, leans back, stops me with his eyes.

"Heard you got detention. For beating up some kid," he says, not considerate enough to whisper.

My brain's stammering even before the words escape. "It was for a girl—kind of. I mean—"

"For a girl, huh?" he says, bobbing his head in acknowledgment, contemplating his sandwich. With a giant chomp down, he starts chewing.

"Yeah, well, she's the new girl, you know, she just arrived at school. Her father's a cop, somebody put a pig's head in her locker . . . but I took her to the nurse, I think she's going to be all right, she's one tough cookie . . ." I'm rambling on and on, feeling eleven years old again, explaining my way out of trouble.

"So when's it going to end, Finn?" He takes another bite of his sandwich and drops it on his plate in disgust. In the dim light over the stove I see the crumbs scatter across the table.

"When's what going to end?"

I hate how he nods, like I've already given him the answer. Tears off a piece of crust and shoves it in his mouth, and points at me. "You and your sister. Born from the same egg, but so different. Why's that, you think?"

The boxes around us block the view of the front windows of the trailer, yet despite that I still see the lights of a car driving by. Extra paranoid is what I'm going to be for the next few days. Trapped in this trailer, trapped in a conversation with Pop who keeps asking questions I don't know how to answer.

"Actually Pop, since we're *fraternal* twins, Faith and I came from two separate eggs. You must be thinking of *identical* twins. They develop from the same zygote that splits into two embryos." I don't realize I'm doing it, spitting out my worthless facts, I really don't, until he starts laughing with his mouth open, bits of soggy crust flying.

"You're a real trip, you know that? Telling me how it is. If you put that much effort into applying yourself in school, in *life*," he says, laying his hand flat on the table, "then maybe you'd be more like your sister."

I shrug; there's no answer to this. I wish for once I could be viewed as a separate person from Faith—people can't seem to think of me without thinking of her. As long as this happens, I'm always going to come up short.

"Right now the future's not looking so hot for you, son. You continue to sell drugs, do drugs, and you'll end up dead in a ditch somewhere."

"I'm sorry I'm not everything you hoped and dreamed," I say, knowing the sarcasm of my tone is more than childish.

He shrugs, tears off a slice of bologna and considers it, but doesn't eat it. "Hey, shit happens."

I've seen pictures of Pop and Mom when they were younger, doing things I could never imagine them doing today—going to a baseball game, playing Frisbee, setting up a picnic. One picture I came across is of a field of wildflowers. Mom is wearing a pink dress with short sleeves, and Pop is in jeans and a green T-shirt. The vibrancy of their youth blasts you in the face. Apparently this was during a time when Mom liked to bake Pop peanut butter cookies and Pop would sew up loose buttons on her blouses. Never seen them do either of these things, but the pictures don't lie.

"Shit sure does happen," I say, ready to take him on. "I don't think Mom signed up for a drunk like you."

He bunches up his napkin, chucks it on his plate, and pushes the chair out from the table. The metal upon linoleum elicits a screech like nothing else. I don't flinch, though. I *want* him to come at me.

But he doesn't. He hasn't in years. Instead, he goes to the kitchen sink and wipes his plate off with the back of his hand. Without turning around he says, "*I* didn't sign up for any of this. Yet I don't blame myself. I blame—"

"Just say it, Pop. I'd love to hear you say it. You blame *me*. Come on, it'll feel good."

With his back to me, he's deliberating as I wait. The thought is always there: if I was the male version of Faith, none of this would have happened. Pop would be in tip-top shape and Mom would still be excited about her pretty curtains and when Faith would smile, both eyes would light up instead of just one. This is where I run the risk: if I start thinking that it's all my fault, then I'll start believing it's true. Maybe I already do.

Pop faces me. Then he shuts the conversation down. "Going to go get more shut eye. God knows I need it."

"Sure." I force out a yawn to make sure I get nonchalance across loud and clear, even though every fiber in my body is screaming, every muscle is poised for a fight.

SUNDAY, APRIL 21

CHAPTER TWENTY

THE SUB SHOP IS DEAD. My apron is covered in every condiment known to man and I'm ready to go home, take a shower, wash this day off me. Wash this *month* off me. It's between lunch and dinner and a few guys are outside smoking butts, holding their skateboards upright. I wave, they wave back. I hear the roll of gritty wheels and they're off.

The Birds of America is opened up on the shelf underneath the cash register at the sub shop, so I can refer to it when I'm feeling antsy or bored. The page I'm on is a picture of hawks, red-tailed, showcasing their undeniable beauty and ruthlessness. Hawks are known to flap their wings as little as possible to conserve energy and their cry sounds like a steam whistle. When the door jingles open, I'm daydreaming about hawks circling around me, in a blur. The male plummets deeply and then climbs again, as the female soars and coasts with indifference.

I hear footsteps up to the counter. I look up reluctantly.

Stacey.

Blond hair swaying as she moves. Lord have mercy. I haven't seen her since the locker incident; she's been staying away from school to recover.

I blow air out of my mouth to calm down.

"Italian mix? Extra cheese extra dressing?" I say. Did my voice just crack? Christ.

She smiles tightly and runs her finger along the edge of the counter. She totally hates me. I'm a barbarian to her, club and all, she thinks I'm going to throw her over a shoulder and drag her to my cave. The menu doesn't seem to interest her, but my face does. Oh, okay. It's kind of electrifying, her taking me in. She takes in my eyes and the shape of my mouth. I wonder if she minds my scar, I wonder if it grosses her out.

"Thank you," she says simply.

I'm confused. "For what?"

She threads a thumb through her belt loop and releases a heavy exhale. "For taking care of me the other day. For making me go to the hospital. I know I was a pain in the ass. I'm fine, by the way."

"Oh—yeah, I meant to ask. Sorry." I clench my teeth in shame. Good job, Finn, real smooth and considerate, not inquiring about the lady's condition.

She laughs quietly. "No, it's fine. I wasn't—" She places her hand on her cheek and looks away, eyes bright.

"That's really good." I smile, and it's not forced like with other girls. "I'm glad you listened to me—going to the hospital and all. I know what I'm talking about."

Her grin is halfway there and then it fades. "My father knows who did it. Someone in NYC who doesn't like him cracking down on the drug problem around here. He wants to let my dad know he's still watching."

I'm nodding, trying not to burn her up with my eyes. Then I register what she's saying. "So it definitely wasn't Jason," I say, more to myself than to her, wanting her to confirm it to make sure I really understand.

She's narrowing her eyes at me, trying to gauge if I feel regret. Of course I feel regret. I went all WWF on his ass for no reason, no reason whatsoever.

"No, it wasn't Jason."

Okay, Finn, get into this conversation, get in. "Pretty personal watching. The pig's head, I mean. That's quite a message to send," I say.

She shrugs. "My dad's used to it." She pauses, then adds, "He thought that transferring here would get us away from the violence."

"I guess he was wrong," I say.

"Perhaps," she says, her gaze drifting toward the smeared window that I should have cleaned days ago. I can tell she doesn't want to get into it. "My father had a talk with the guy who did it. Hopefully things will be calmer now."

Who the hell is the guy? My curiosity is acid eating away at me, but I fight it, out of respect for her.

"You're not scared?" I ask. She has to be; I sense the tension in her energy and notice the tautness of her jaw.

"I was," she says. "Especially with the police detail parked outside my house for the past few nights. But my father's a good negotiator . . . and he knows how to handle crime—whether it comes from the city or this Podunk town."

I nod, liking how she says "Podunk," liking how the insignificant can become significant when it comes from her mouth. At the same time I'm desperate to know who her father was dealing with in the city. Could it have been Early? Could he be the one who called me, not Mike? Or both of them? My head is spinning, I want to ask questions, but I don't want to bring her in to this, know what she really thinks of me. I don't even want to know what Faith is thinking of me right now.

"I don't know why I'm telling you this, I just—"

"I'm a good listener," I can't resist saying. "You feel comfortable with me, admit it." She looks appalled and my spunk diminishes as I step away from the counter, mentally chastising myself for being so bold. "I'm sorry, that was—"

"Listen Finn, whatever. I'm not here to say that just because you helped me last week means that I've forgotten about you beating up Jason. Yeah, I get he's kind of an idiot, but what you did to him was terrifically screwed up."

"He'll be fine," I say. I gave him two black eyes, a split lip, and a limp that I know he's milking to get attention from girls. It's all temporary, I tell myself.

"What about *you*?" She lifts her chin in my direction.

"Oh—well . . . no, I can withstand a lot," I say. She doesn't answer. I'm not sure why she's just standing there, not saying anything, just looking at me looking at her, it's unnerving really, even though the eye contact is making me tipsy.

"Do you think what you did was wrong?" she finally asks. Oh, okay, shit's getting real. This is *not* the type of conversation I want to be having right now.

"If we're gonna have a dialogue about morality, hold up, I've got to go fetch my fresh tweed blazer with the elbow patches."

She doesn't laugh. "I'm serious, Finn. What do you think?"

I blurt, "I *wasn't* thinking, that's the problem." I look down at the hawks on the page. Their fierceness is admirable and so is their one-track mind. All they want to do is fly and hunt—this is their nature, their calling, and what a blessing to have life reduced to such simplicity.

"I wonder sometimes . . . what makes people do things like that? Like what's going through your head, right before, and during? Is it blank, white fury?"

"Red," I say, surprising myself with the quick response. "Different shades of it." My mind is shooting off names of red birds as I say this, *flame-colored tanager, pine grosbeak, vermillion flycatcher, red-faced warbler.* Can you imagine if they all darted by at once? What a brilliant display that would be. Avian sparklers. Winged fireworks brightening the sky.

"The amygdala is a part of the brain associated with emotion—and they did this study where the amygdala becomes overresponsive to pictures of angry faces, compared to people with calm faces," she explains.

"You're going to make a great doctor," I say, not even trying to quell the sarcasm in my voice. I should have known this was a lost cause, this as in *me and her, her and me.*

"I am," she says, ignoring my tone. "So what are you serious about?"

Is she for real? Did Faith put her up to this? "Hey listen, Stacey, I'd love to continue this scintillating discussion, but I've got work to do, you know?"

She takes my glare and holds it, makes me give her my full attention. "Finn," she says, her voice like honey. "I'm here because we were both part of a monumental thing—I mean, all that blood? And you're getting me to the nurse and persuading me to go to the hospital? And the fighting between you and Jason? I needed to acknowledge it with you. I wanted to know what was going on inside your brain." She doesn't sound mad at me, just genuinely curious, and it makes my heart twist that she sees we were both part of this thing, too.

"Trust me, Stacey, you don't want to know what's inside this brain of mine. But to be completely truthful, I was worried. About you. It's not every day you see a girl you kind of dig covered in blood. Does something to you, you know?"

She's a little startled, uncertain—but not altogether displeased.

I'm not punking her, this is for real, as real as I ever get. She leans into the space between us, picking through my weeds, digging into the dirt of my heart. I let her. She can see what's there. She can decide if it's worth salvaging. I'm leaning, she's leaning, we're magnets.

"Can I take you out to dinner tonight?" I ask. I can't believe I'm asking. Balls out, I say. Balls *out*. But my heart is thumping in my ears, everything racing, my pulse, blood, nerves, running the sprint of their lives.

"You're asking me out?" she says. "After my father handcuffs you for assault?"

Though I maintain a façade of confidence, I feel like crawling under the counter next to the day-old rolls of bread.

But she won't let me go. "Why should I? Convince me," she says.

She opened the door again and my confidence comes rushing back. "Because I will create a night for you that you'll always remember," I say enthusiastically. "You'll look back and think it's one of your best memories. You'll want to relive it over and over again. Nostalgia will hit as soon as the night is over." I snap my fingers. "Like that."

She smirks and crosses her arms against her chest. "Really? That's all you've got? That might work on your other—well, anyway, you're going to have to do better than that."

Tough crowd. I think hard. It's got to be good, what I say, the best I have.

"I went bird watching a little while ago." I can't believe I'm admitting this to her. "I saw this bird. Like no other. Its beauty was out of control."

"What was it?" she asks with what seems like real interest. Only Faith has ever gotten what I feel about birds. And maybe Mrs. Klaski.

"An albino sparrow. I wish you could have seen it. You know, it's a beauty worth sharing, like everyone needs to see it, and maybe the world would turn into a microscopically better place." I'm getting all emotional about the damn thing, my chest and throat are tightening. "The colors were crazy. White, gold, pale yellow wings. An iridescence that you see on a sunny day in a pool of oil? You know what I'm talking about? That shit can get pretty gorgeous if you forget what it is for a second. Anyway, the bird stayed in view just long enough for me to feel really sad when it was finally gone. I haven't seen it since. But you know what?"

Stacey is silent, but a listening silent.

"When I saw it, I knew that it was a sign of good things to come. And then, almost right after that, I'm talking *that day*, I met *you* for the first time."

Her head tips down. I can't see her eyes. Maybe I've said too much. I *always* say too much. I await the verdict.

"Pick me up at seven. I swear if you're late, I'm not answering the door."

Hallelujah doesn't even cover it. She tells me her street address as I hurriedly write it down in case she changes her mind. Please don't see that my hand is shaking, please don't see . . .

"Should I wear something fancy?" she asks. Her voice is even, but I'm sensing she might be looking forward to our date, at least as an experiment.

"Nah, what you got on is fine. It's perfect, actually. Just bring a sweatshirt. In case the night air gets chilly." Her outfit is perfect, in fact. Jeans, comfortable shoes, a girly colorful top that isn't too showy.

"The night air, huh?" Then she turns around and leaves without looking back, thank God, because I'm smiling like an idiot and blushing all-out. Until the panic starts because I have a lot of planning to do, maybe too much, but I can call in a few favors and get the job done right.

CHAPTER TWENTY-ONE

THE CRAVING FOR DOPE HITS ME HARD. I imagine myself showing up at Stacey's zonked out of my mind, trying to be charming, bloodshot eyes, rock bottom just around the corner.

No. I command myself.

Well, my argument isn't working, because I'm lighting up in my car before I take off. It's just weed. No biggie. I let the smoke roll through me and keep it in for one beat, two beats, three beats. Exhale. The cool air snatches the smoke out of my window, as I pull out of the trailer park. A red truck I don't recognize pulls in at the same time, so close to my car that it grazes my side view mirror. I pound the horn and flip the bird. Is this just a random event? Or is this one of Mike's thugs threatening me?

My buzz is nonexistent. Total fail.

I show up at Stacey's door at 6:58 p.m. I'm wearing khakis and a button-down T-shirt, untucked. Faith said it looks okay, so that means it is. I've never been this nervous for a date, nervous to the point where I'm discreetly sniffing my armpits because I'm sweating so much.

Stacey lives in an old farmhouse about fifteen minutes away from the trailer park, where there are cow fields that flood in the spring and housing developments that started but were never completed. Sagging work trailers, cottages that are really shacks, sheds that are used for outhouses. I can't tell what's more depressing: poverty in the city or poverty in the country. Poverty's poverty I guess, but out here, the air's a little freer, the cows twitch their ears and tails, and it seems like hope grows when it's got the room.

Not that Stacey lives in poverty. The house is old but nice, the yard is really kept up, with lots of flowers in the front, and there's a minivan parked in the driveway, coated in yellow pollen. I want to write my initials in the dust, but I restrain myself. Don't need to mark your territory wherever you go, do you Finn? Especially since this is her father's territory. The man of the house who I'm not ready to face again.

I grab the bunch of daisies lying on the passenger seat and go up to the front door, which is a dark orange color, and knock, and when I say knock, I mean I use the brass knocker because there's no doorbell. It's straight-up charming, I admit. I hear her footsteps coming, light, quick; I clench my jaw and try not to squeeze the Gerber daisies in my hand too hard. The door opens. I flash my best smile.

It's her.

The other her.

The *old lady* her.

I'm holy shitting all over the place. Here is the Klaski lady with the nostalgia drug or memory drug or whatever the heck you want to call it drug, she gave me the mirror, the bird book, a scolding, she may or may not ruin my life. Here she is, standing in the doorway, looking just as surprised as me.

"Um," I say. "Am I at the—"

She slams the door in my face.

If shock could achieve perfection, this would be it.

A robin flies past my head and perches on a branch of a Japanese maple. Robins like sweets, and are drawn to berries, fruits, and even pastry dough. The song of a male robin is often the last bird heard as the sun sets, like a desperate last call. Is this mine?

The door opens again.

It's Stacey this time, she's apologizing, grabbing my hand, Jesus her skin is soft, and pulling me inside a narrow hallway with an old worn-out rug.

She just touched me. We touched. God, Finn, would you shut up? But that lady . . . what is she doing here? I'm just about hyperventilating, and this is just about the wrong persona I want to be projecting.

I look around to calm myself. I'm not ready to say anything in case my voice comes out in a squeak. Paintings on every wall, paintings of birds and flowers, not cheesy art, this is real, meaningful stuff, I know right away. My observation is confirmed when I gaze upon it. Directly to the right of me is a print of a plate from *The Birds of America*—Audubon's indigo buntings. There are three of them in blue—the males are always showier—and one of them in brown—the lone female. The male buntings are a vivid blue, dark, brooding, matched for midnight. A few flowers are downturned around them like little bells, but the blue buntings are the true flowers of the painting, blooming from vines that wind and loop around themselves.

"I'm so sorry about my grandmother. I'm—" I've never seen Stacey embarrassed before—even when she came to during the pig's head incident, she was more shaken up than ashamed.

"Seems nice to me," I say, trying to keep my voice as even as possible. I give her the daisies, she accepts them with a bright smile. A dimple on one of her cheeks. Why didn't I notice that before?

"Yeah. Right."

"Is your father . . ."

"He's not here tonight." And that's all she says about that. Too bad I'm never going to be the guy you proudly bring home to your dad. The house phone rings; it startles me. Immediately it has me thinking about the hang-up call I received.

"Why don't you take a seat in the morning room?" She gestures to the space to my right, illuminated by the setting sun. The bottom of her tank top flutters gracefully.

"Morning room?"

Stacey laughs, and it sparkles. "That's what Mimi calls it. She's got a name for every room. It makes us feel elegant." The phone continues to ring; she disappears around the corner.

I sit down on a light-blue couch with dark wood lion's feet legs. Shelves overflowing with books are built into the walls, and the coffee table in front of me has been well-worn but well-loved.

When the old lady—Mrs. Klaski, Mimi—enters the room, I'm not sure what to do. I ready myself to speak, but my words come out as *ums, I-I-I, well, so* . . . shit, I'm a mess, might as well say *do re mi fa sol la ti* . . . God help me.

Without hesitating, she sits down next to me, smelling like lavender and lemons, folding her hands in her lap. White bony fingers against the black of her pants. Her hair is an unstoppable puffy cloud.

"You can call me Orah," she says, shaking my hand. "I had a feeling this was going to happen," she adds without inflection.

"Must be fate, Orah," I say.

"I suppose I can't argue with that. Suppose you're still after what you're after." She purses her lips, she may want to appear resigned, but I know a power play when I see one.

This is really happening. We're really having this conversation in her so-called morning room. Orah's looking real unflappable and nonchalant, yet I imagine lightning sparking in the cumulous cloud of her hair.

"Listen. I'm not doing it for me. Or for the money, or whatever . . . well, it *is* for the money, but it's for my sister," I say, squeezing my knees to keep them steady.

"College?" she asks.

"Right. That's right. How did you know?"

"That's the hot button issue for kids your age right now, isn't it?"

I nod. Endless thoughts are pinging back and forth, all conflicting, the drug, my sister, the money, this woman, Stacey, and buntings circling around it all like a constantly morphing frame.

"I'd like you to do something in return," she says.

I face her, my desperation visible, I know it. I'll do whatever. I don't care about the dangers, the roadblocks, the possibility of ending up dead in a ditch somewhere. Pop, you really know how to make an impression. As long as Faith is happy, and I can supply her with some of that happiness.

"I want you to spend time with me." Hands clasped, head up. Proud, proud, proud.

Wait, hold up now.

"You want me to what?"

She presses the tops of her legs with the heels of her hands—I can tell that this is not an indication of insecurity or nervousness—it is more a signal of irritation that I haven't already agreed to it.

"You heard me. I'm getting old, in case you haven't noticed. My husband's dead, my son-in-law is too busy cleaning up the streets, and my daughter passed away at an age way too young. My grandson is currently out of our lives." Her mouth straightens, looks out the room to where Stacey is still on the phone. "Stacey will be doing her pre-med at Stanford," she says. "She doesn't have time for me."

"And I do?" I blurt. I sound 110 percent asshole, I feel immediately bad, but I don't apologize.

She pats my knee. Holy patience. I'm surprised she isn't beating me with one of her five thousand books. "I'm not looking for much. I want to learn about you, hear your stories. I want someone to shoot the breeze with. I believe you have the disposition for that, don't you think?"

I'm stunsville, all the way. She wants to spend time with *me*? My own grandparents didn't want to spend time with me— so much that I never met them. Something about disowning my parents when they decided to make a life together.

"Come to the cemetery next Saturday, usual time. We're going to do this together," she says. She looks around. "In the meantime, here." She pulls something out from underneath her shirt, and places it in my lap.

It's the drug in a ziplock bag. Dark blue, iridescent, looking like a descendent of fairy dust. Jesus fucking Christ. And I mean that with the utmost respect. I shove it quickly into my back pocket, where it barely fits. Good thing my shirt covers it up.

"This should be enough for now."

Enough for now? This could trip out a small army for days. *Yes.* Here we go.

She grabs my arm. "I don't want Stacey to know. Of course

my son-in-law, a *cop*, can't know either—he wouldn't suspect anything, not yet anyway, just getting his bearings in this town. That's why this endeavor won't be a prolonged affair. I want this drug out of my life. It's done too much damage. We'll do a few quick harvests, you do what you have to do with it, and then *finito*."

She makes a fist and brings it to her heart. I nod, hard, and look her in the eye so she knows I understand. A slow smile spreads across her face. It makes her look twenty years younger—or maybe it's just the light streaming in from the setting sun.

"You remind me of him," she says. "My grandson." Her fingers touch my scar lightly, briefly, as if she's dabbing perfume on my neck. I wait for the angry tirade to launch from my mouth. But it doesn't. She returns her hands to her lap and smiles gently, saying with her eyes, *see, I knew you didn't bite.*

I should be more uncomfortable than I am. It's creepy, right? But I don't inch away from her, I don't make an excuse to leave the room, I don't fill the silence with worthless chatter. The drug is next to me, Orah looks satisfied, and the golden dust of dusk rests at our feet.

Stacey appears with a daisy tucked behind her ear.

"Did you two make amends?" she asks Orah. At first I think she knows exactly what went down, but then Orah says, "I didn't like the looks of him . . . at first."

She winks at me. Stacey grins.

"I'll have her home by ten," I say. She waves us away and we leave the house.

I open the door for Stacey to get into my car. The sun fires up her hair and the daisy's petals bounce when she sits down.

"Where are you taking me?" she asks, her hands clasped very ladylike in her lap.

"It's a surprise," I say.

Tonight is full of surprises. I don't even have to put any effort into naming the drug, it suddenly comes to me as I'm driving with Stacey. The color of the drug: majestic, trippy, but kind of elegant, a hue for royalty and their palaces. Its effects unpredictable and mysterious, its origins unknown and provided by an old lady who shares my love for birds and Audubon. His painting of the indigo buntings—I don't think it's a coincidence that the tone of the bunting feathers is much like the tone of the powder. There's something cosmic going on here, a synchronicity that I'd be stupid to overlook. Ladies and gentlemen, I present to you the official moniker of the new drug on the block: indigo.

CHAPTER TWENTY-TWO

I PULL OFF TO THE SIDE OF THE ROAD, NEXT TO A NOT-SO-OBVIOUS TRAIL, LEADING INTO MY FAVORITE PART OF THE WOODS, WHERE FAITH AND I BUILT A FORT AND NAPPED WITH A KITTEN. A good-sized pond sits in a clearing surrounded by wildflowers and tall grass, the perfect place for swimming in the summer. As Stacey hops out of the car, I quickly shove the bag of indigo underneath my car seat without her noticing.

"Where are you taking me, Finn?" Stacey asks as we walk to the designated spot.

I turn to her. "Trust me, okay?"

"Ha," she says. "Right." Her light footsteps follow behind me.

Tonight the area around the pond is a special place. Trees are strung up with battery-powered lights shaped like globes, all different colors, all different sizes. I'm expecting immediate wonder from Stacey, but I don't get it. Music that I don't recognize is playing from an iPhone, some mix that Faith put together for me, she promised that it makes all girls a little softer, a little more agreeable. Those are her words, not mine. If my sister was a dude, she'd be a lady-killer too. Plus, now that she knows Stacey a little better, she's aware of her taste in music. Faith's willingness to help me out with this event either shows that she's forgiven me or that she believes Stacey's ambitious personality and responsible nature will rub off on me. We'll see about that.

I'm holding a picnic basket, filled with food Diane cooked. I gave her some excuse about how I wanted to treat my family to a homemade dinner—a pleasing and gullible soul always falls under my spell. Bryce is lighting candles on a fold-up table set for two. You could say that we're on okay terms after I bailed him out and thanked him for his troubles by writing two English papers for him—one on *Hamlet*, the other on *To Kill a Mockingbird*; hello cakewalk. Don't even need to say I scored him A's on both. Funny how I have more motivation to write other people's papers than my own.

Stacey seems less than impressed by the spectacle: *candles, music, food oh my!* . . . all for her. Okay, I can work with a girl who's hard to please. Not going to get my panties in a bunch just yet.

I touch the small of her back (she doesn't lean in to it) and lead her to the table. Gentlemanly Finn pulls the chair out for her, and she sits down. I can't read her for shit. Bryce takes the picnic basket and starts covering the table with containers of food—cheese and fruit, pieces of rosemary chicken, red potatoes, green beans, and dessert for later. Bryce bows like a chump. The candlelight flickers, the light globes sway among the branches, and I can tell Bryce has something to say unrelated to this date that conquers all dates. I'm screaming with my eyes, dude, you'll never guess what just happened, *pay day*, that's what.

"Finn, can I talk to you for a minute?" Bryce asks.

"Um, no," I say, even though all I want to do is talk—I've got the drug, I've got my girl, but it's just not the right time.

"I gotta say it." He digs the toe of his sneaker into the ground.

"Can't it wait?" I hiss. I flick my eyes toward Stacey, who looks bored out of her skull. Bryce shakes his head no. I try not to curse, get up from my seat and pull him an adequate distance away from the table. The leaves from a weeping willow dangle over our heads.

He holds onto his arm and scowls. "I don't know, Finn. I have a bad feeling that this drug is gonna be interfering with someone else's turf. After my arrest? I don't want to go through that again. I'm just not as pumped as I was." I wasn't counting on Bryce's second-guessing—usually this guy is full speed ahead, and then some.

I clasp a reassuring hand on his shoulder. "What do you mean, bro? There's no risk here, trust me." I regret it as soon as it comes out of my mouth. Of course there's a risk. There always is. I think about my conversation with Stacey and how this ties to the drug circuit in the city. But I've got to put these negative vibes aside, I don't want them soiling the magical night I'm trying to create.

I glance over to where Stacey is sitting, her light blue shirt aglow in the LED light. Bryce looks down at his feet saying, "You're welcome, by the way."

I nod, feeling like a jerk for not being more grateful. Of course I'm grateful. I got the best friends in the world.

"Thanks, bud, for doing me a solid," I say. We shake hands, fist bump. "Parting words for you: once you taste the rainbow, you'll change your mind, *trust me.*"

"Sure," Bryce says, though I know he's not convinced. He puts on his hat, tugs it down below his ears, and walks away. I'll deal with this later.

Back at the table with Stacey, who's picking her nails, legs crossed, foot bouncing. I don't even know where to begin with her, and I'm only like 54 percent sure she's into me.

"Am I encroaching upon your time?" she asks, clearly irritated that I left her alone.

"Oh yeah, totally," I say, joking around. "What are you doing here again?" I flash a smile. She is *so* not amused.

Some country chick is beautifully crooning from the speakers of the iPhone and it feels off, too obvious. I'm about to pour Stacey some white wine when she puts her hand over the mouth of her glass.

"Is this the way you woo all your girlfriends?" she asks.

"Nah, this is a new tactic. Is it working?" I tilt my head to the side as she smirks, and the candlelight makes her dimples pop and her hair shimmer. No, I'm not swooning, no, I don't think she looks like a legitimate angel. I serve us chicken and potatoes and green beans, and even though the food isn't fancy, it's still pretty damn tasty. *Thank you*, Diane. Stacey's not saying anything, and the silence is starting to suffocate.

"So are we going to discuss moral quandaries, or what?" I ask. I realize that all we've been doing tonight is asking questions, kicking them up, letting them fall without consequence. She takes a bite of chicken and sets down her fork, wipes her hands with the napkin in her lap. To my dismay, I realize I haven't taken my own off the table, like some unsophisticated prick. At this point I'm not looking to score; if I get through the night without saying anything stupid, I'll be impressed.

Stacey rests her folded hands on the table. "You know, my grandmother worked as a psychiatric nurse when she was younger. Back in the day when they used to give lobotomies and shock therapy all the time," she says. For the first time since we sat down she sounds interested. "That old abandoned asylum, up Barnhouse Road? She did her residency there."

"I can't see her doing that," I say, wiping my mouth daintily and setting the napkin on my lap. I want to show her how amazingly proper I can be.

"How would you know?" she snaps back. "You just met her." I shrink. This is going so outrageously bad I can't even stand it.

"Yeah, that's true."

"Hmm. Well, the asylum up there was made up of big sprawling buildings on big sprawling farmland." She stretches out her arms to show how big. "It was supposed to give patients privacy and encourage them to get exercise at the same time. Mimi had to go through these underground tunnels that connected all the buildings to bring patients supplies, bed sheets, whatever. They were scary labyrinths. And really dark. Nothing ever happened to her down there, but it could have." She angles her body toward mine.

I'm not sure where she's going with all this, but I could listen to her talk all day. It's not like the usual crap the girls I know talk about—television shows, makeup, fashion, inane chatter that should be boxed up with a warning label. Nausea and vomiting may occur . . . but then again, they could say the same thing about guys . . . football, video games, sex . . . sex . . . did I mention sex?

"Mimi told me the other day that there was this one patient of hers—she can't remember his name," she says. "But part of his therapy was making clocks. That's all he did, night and day, to calm the voices in his head. Clocks. He made so many. He gave them to all the staff at the hospital, to his friends and family." She pauses, nodding. "So after she told me this, she brought me into the guest bedroom and pointed to the wall where there was a clock. It's beautiful: dark wood, ivory-colored face, very simple, still ticking away after fifty years."

"Amazing," I say, abandoning my food for the time being. I don't want the sound of my chewing to disrupt the moment. "Is this why you want to be a doctor?"

The question seems to dim her mood. "Mimi regrets that she never became one. It's not something women did back then. So yes, that's part of the reason why."

"What's the other part?"

She moves a green bean around on her plate with her fork, but doesn't eat it. Certain talk doesn't jive well with food, and this is not a chicken and beans kind of conversation we're dealing with here.

"I wish I could help people, you know, who are addicts," she says. There's a hair band around her wrist, which she pulls off, and ties her hair up in a ponytail. But because her hair's short, pieces of it fall and frame her face. She's a goddamn piece of art. "I wish I could figure out a way to cure drug addiction, any addiction really. My brother—he's wrapped up in some pretty bad stuff, with some pretty bad people. My mom . . . she died after my brother was born. She had a really aggressive virus, and when the symptoms started to show, it was too late. Serious health problems run in my family."

I pause before I say anything; I want to choose my words carefully. Life isn't fair for dumping all this tragedy on such a beautiful, sweet girl like her.

"That's terrible about your mom. I'm so sorry. And about your brother? People get lost so easily." Even as I say it I realize how idiotic is sounds, like from a pamphlet about drug addiction or something.

"Like you?" she asks, cupping her face in her hand.

I'm immediately defensive. "What do you mean?"

"Your sister told me some things—"

My blood is rushing, Niagara Falls–style, through my ears. "Whoa, wait a sec, hon," I say. "My sister did what now?"

"She told me that you're struggling . . . with certain things. She's worried about you and I thought—"

I let out a sharp, unamused laugh. "What? That I could be your charity case? Do your residency here and now, with Phineas Walt, subject number zero, zero, zero, who has a family history of alcoholism and drug abuse?"

I'm glad the darkness hides my face, hides the slide show of contempt, rage, shame, down-to-the-marrow sadness—

"That's not it at all," she says, shaking her head.

"Then what is it?" I snap, restraining myself from swearing. The table vibrates, my funny bone activates and so does my fight-or-flight. I struggle against both.

"I just want to help you."

I let out a scoff to end all scoffs. *I knew it.* I knew it. For having some intelligence, I can be so gullible. Put a pretty girl in front of me, and suddenly brain damage. It's okay, I think, I got what I wanted, I got indigo, I got a plan, I don't need jack from her.

I smirk. "Hey listen, I appreciate your concern, sweetheart, but in all honestly, who the *hell* do you think you are? *You* have no idea who *I* am," I say, pointing at my chest. "You don't know that I've got goals like you. You don't know that I'm just as motivated. Just as passionate. So don't get all up on your high horse because of your astronomical SAT scores and your full ride to Stanford. I'm up there with you, *babe*, I just show it in a different way."

She's tightening her posture, ready to launch an attack. Well bring it, darlin', because if you want a war, I'll give you one. And just because you're the most gorgeous thing I've ever seen, it doesn't mean I won't verbally massacre you.

"Prosophobia," she says.

I don't wait a second. "Oh please. I'm not scared of progress, of moving on. I'm all *about* moving on. Like I said, I got big plans—"

"And they are?"

I blink. Then I get up, start gathering up our plates, throwing everything, even the leftovers, into a trash bag, folding up my napkin, closing up the bottle of wine we barely drank. The light is fading, the wind is picking up, and all I want to do is go home, get high, and go to bed. Fuck this nonsense. I'll tolerate lectures about the trajectory of my life all over the place, but not here, not on a *date*.

"So that's that?" she says, irritated with some disappointment in her voice.

"Yeah. That's *that*." I slam a plate down. "I'm not gonna sit here and try to explain myself to you. I don't have any obligation to do that, and now it's pretty damn clear that Faith put you up to this." God, that stings, my twin, betraying me like this.

"Finn," she says softly, "I like you. Your sister has nothing to do with that."

As I'm standing, stacking Tupperware with exasperation, she gets up and moves around the table and places a warm hand on my forearm. I jerk away, and the hurt in her eyes is a machete to the heart. I open my mouth to apologize, but I don't. We finish packing in silence, and the car ride back is over-the-top awkward and not over soon enough. It's well before ten o'clock

when I drop her off, and she disappears into her house without
saying good-bye.

CHAPTER TWENTY-THREE

MY MOTIVATION IS LIT UP, WILDFIRE CRAZY, AND AFTER THE STACEY DINNER, I WANT TO PROVE WRONG EVERYONE AND THEIR BROTHER, ESPECIALLY STACEY AND FAITH. I got this. I *more than* got this. Monday is a flurry of drug activity, I'm banging out Orah's product so hard it's gone within several days. People are learning that the rumors are true—indigo is transcendental, some ethereal shit not of this planet, the truth of its superiority to other drugs is spreading quick. I hand it out to football players in the locker room; I pass a few baggies to preppy girls behind the school where nobody goes; I sneak a gram under the dumpster in the school parking lot for our valedictorian; even Peter wants to try it, in spite of all his self-righteousness. I tell them what to expect, and pray they don't have a traumatizing experience from indigo like mine. And I soon find out, it *is* just me. It's not fair—everyone benefiting from the euphoria but me. Am I being punished by cosmic forces because I didn't just say no to drugs? Punished because my sister is damaged and it's my fault?

Each hit I see people take—whether it's in the school parking lot, in someone's basement, or on one occasion at the D-Town Drive-In—I learn something new. The high happens right away after one snort. Their eyes roll back and close, and a smile spreads slow and lazy, like spilled honey. This is when they relive their favorite memory; this is when the true magic occurs. Then the person is alive, soaring, higher and higher, for a long time. People say it feels like heroin, but better, because it lasts much longer, and you come off it nice. They are amazed by it and are amazed by me. They want to know when they can get more. And more. And more.

This is just the first week.

I go to sleep comforted by the money accumulating under my bed and the knowledge that Faith's tossing and turning at night will settle down once I've given her the freedom to leave D-Town. Once she calls me out on my business venture—and I know eventually she will—I can explain to her that it's all going according to plan, and come on, this drug is so new it isn't even illegal.

Bryce has a small group of people at his house during this whirlwind of a week. Taylor is there, and she doesn't talk to me, doesn't look at me once. I don't blame her; what I did was unacceptable and scum-baggish and makes me feel like I'm my father's son. An apology is in order, which I attempt, but she doesn't want to hear anything from me, except indigo.

The party is chill and I want to chill out too, but I can't use what everyone else gets to. What I need is in my pockets, just a little bit, that's all.

The bathroom is cramped, with chipped black and white tile and a smudged mirror. I sit on the toilet lid, and place everything in an ordered line on the counter next to me. Spoon, H, lighter, needle. A little mix of water, flick of the lighter, make it sizzle. It's too late to question because a belt is around my arm and the needle is already in and the hit packs such a punch, it, it . . .

House sparrow, *Passer domesticus* . . . very social birds that live in colonies called flocks . . . *down and down I go* . . . they are carnivores by nature but mostly eat moths and other small insects . . . *I'm not scared of moving on* . . . a male sparrow is responsible for building the nest and will use it as an excuse to attract a female. She'll help him if she's interested in mating . . . I don't blame myself. *I don't blame myself. I* . . . both parents take care of the eggs and chicks and young birds are ready to leave the nest fifteen days after birth . . .

Pounding on the door. "Finn, what are you doing in there? Jacking off?" My eyes flick open, and I survey my surroundings. I'm on the floor with drool on my face—I must have fallen off the toilet. More pounding. Peter.

"What are you talking about, man?" I call out, quickly untying the belt around my arm.

"You've been in there for like a half an hour. Are you okay?"

It's been that long? It's feeling like one heartbeat to me. I scramble to shove everything—the needle, the spoon, the left-over foil—back in my pocket, to cinch my belt where it belongs around my waist.

"I'm fine. Just feeling a little sick. Must have been those nachos."

"Are you sure?" he asks worriedly. Goddammit, Peter, why do you have to be so nice?

"My stomach has been bothering me lately. Like, I might have ulcers or something," I groan for effect. "Gonna go to the doctor next week, get this shit checked out." The lies slide right out—their delivery is effortless.

"Oh," Peter says. Now there is suspicion in his voice. I hear him backing away from the door.

When I walk into Peter's room, Taylor eyes me. I make

sure my sleeve covers my arm, of course it does, I'm just being paranoid. The fact that I blacked out unnerves me, but I'm not going to dwell on it. I don't want to be a downer while everyone passes around indigo (God, that name has caught on). They offer me some, but I refuse, making up some excuse about wanting to stay clean. Why is it becoming so easy to lie?

They all take their hit of indigo at the same time. Taylor's fingers twitch; her bubblegum-pink nails are fluorescent under the yellowish light of Peter's room. Peter's head is tilted up toward the ceiling, his mouth open like he's trying to catch snowflakes, his eyelids fluttering, he looks so happy, he's a kid again. Bryce's shoulders are shrugged so high they're reaching his ears, and he's laughing without sound. I'm many worlds away from them, my foggy brain, slack jaw, sweaty palms. My high seems impotent in comparison. When they return, it will be a storm of chatter and excitement, their happiness will be palpable, and I will be jealous. I consider going back into the bathroom for more, and it takes all my willpower to restrain myself.

Peter comes out of his memory first, and Taylor is right behind him, but it's Bryce who has my attention. He raises his hands up in the air, he's cheering, and then suddenly his T-shirt appears damp. I'm thinking it has to be sweat. But does sweat come on *that* fast? Taylor's eyes widen because she sees it too, and Peter is laughing because, well, just because. I touch Bryce's arm and feel the wetness on my fingers, and Bryce is in shock, but it's happy shock, thrilled shock, he's jumping up and down, saying one thing over and over again.

We won! We won! We won!

Peter falls to the ground, cracking up, his arms around Taylor's legs. Soon she's on the floor too, in hysterics. Bryce is looking down at himself, at the dabs of liquid in the palm of his hand that appear clear in color, but if it hits the light just right, there's almost a reddish tinge. But then again, I'm not as lucid as I could be right now.

"Dude," Bryce says, holding out his hand so I can see better. I raise my eyebrows. He licks the water on him and whispers again, *we won*. What is Bryce tasting? Why does he look so thunderstruck?

"Your memory," I say to Bryce. I have to know. "What was it?"

Peter and Taylor are tickling each other now on the bed, and I yell at them to pipe down. They listen for about a half second, then they're at it again.

Bryce smiles, licks the palm of his hand once again, excitedly. Taylor cheers with her hands raised, and Peter tickles her armpit, eliciting a squeal from her that's so high-pitched we all cover our ears.

Bryce squeezes my arm. and I try not to wince from the pain of it. "Do you remember when we were on the baseball team in middle school? We were playing against the Spartans, and I hit a home run that won us the game? Do you remember that?" His words are hurried; he's almost stuttering. I vaguely recall this.

"You were never good at baseball, but that day you were," I say slowly, dredging up the memory of the game from hundreds of almost equally unmemorable ones.

"I was on fire. Even the coach—he finally called me by my last name. Nauset. Like he did with the rest of you," Bryce says. "After I won the game, you all ran toward me, even the others from the dugout. Picked me up." Bryce squeezes his eyes shut, trying hard to see it clearly again. "Picked me up and dumped cherry Gatorade on my head."

Gatorade.

Holy moly and then more moly. I have to sit down—but the others, the idea of magic occurring right here, right now—gives them boundless energy. Bryce joins Peter and Taylor playfully wrestling on the floor, yelping, their breath raspy and ecstatic, until they get this grand idea to roll down the gradual slope of Bryce's backyard. They haven't quite registered the insanity of what we've all witnessed; they're flying so high it's hard to watch, but I follow them outside and watch them anyway. Peter's yelling something about a cut on his skin, "It just appeared out of nowhere! Spontaneous boo-boo!" I'm not sure what Taylor brought back from her own indigo trip, but I've never seen her so giddy and elated either.

The stars are smudged across the sky, and a single cloud swipes against the moon and moves on. Taylor tumbles first, then Peter, then Bryce, roll, roll, roll, down the hill, I'm surprised they're moving so fast, or maybe it's my brain that can't keep up. Their bodies crush the grass, bringing up the scent of lawnmowers. I sit down at the top of the hill, light up, take a hit, and exhale, the smoke thick around me. I'm the moon and it's the cloud about to blot me out. Even if I were to try indigo again, I know I wouldn't be coming back from it thrilled about the world and my friends. Maybe I deserve the blackout, the bathroom floor, the drool on my face, while being barred from their manic joy. I don't feel like myself, and they don't seem to care that I'm up here and they're down there, captivated by wonder and the potential for different dimensions; a multitude of them. It's like I'm not even here.

FRIDAY, APRIL 26

CHAPTER TWENTY-FOUR

A TEXTBOOK IS NEXT TO ME ON THE BED, BECAUSE I PROMISE I'M GOING TO GET TO MY HOMEWORK, I *NEED* TO GET TO IT EVEN ON A FRIDAY NIGHT, BECAUSE I'M ALMOST FAILING HISTORY AND MATH. However, at present, I hold a new glass bowl in my hands. The colors on this one are of the female cardinal variety, grays, muted reds, and tans. Perfect match with my tattoo. I close my eyes and let the high seep in and go about its wonderful business.

My sister bursts into our bedroom. I reluctantly open my eyes. Her face is red, the color of the male cardinal variety. She pinches my shoulder, way too hard.

"Ow, you little—"

She makes a grating noise with her mouth closed. "Guess who called me today, Phineas? Just *guess*," she says.

"I don't know. Barack Obama?" I say, picking up the weed clumps that fell to the floor.

She pauses, clenching her jaw. "You're so funny I can't even stand it." She hits me on the shoulder; I look at her appalled. "*Harvard. Harvard* called me. Asking me about student loans. Telling me the housing options available, because I didn't specify on the online form. I'm not going there, Phineas. I'm going to community college. I told you. You can't hijack my life like this."

Her nostrils are flared, and she gets all angry teacher on me, shaking her finger. Maybe what I did was wrong in her mind, but I know she'll thank me later. When she's older with a six-bedroom house, four-car garage, and two practical but pricey sedans, she'll take me aside and say, Phineas, you were right. You're a pain in the ass, but *right*.

"You're going," I say. "I know you want to. And I'm taking care of it. Just relax and enjoy your time there, and let me worry about financing your education."

She lunges toward me and yells, "Stop telling me what to do! I've had it with this brother-knows-best crap. You've been doing it since *forever*, and I'm sick of it. I'm sick of *you*. You don't think I'm smart enough to make my own decisions?"

I sit on the edge of the bed and calmly set the bowl on the nightstand. Her lips are turning pale. I take her arm and pull her down so she's seated next to me.

"Of course you're smart enough," I say gently. "You're smart enough for anything."

She massages her temples and takes a deep breath, just like her counselor told her to do.

"You've been certified out-of-control lately. Peter said—"

Fucking Peter. One moment he's on my side, the next moment he's telling Faith I'm the devil. It's not like he's the straightest edge in the world—and I think that might be part of it. He's got one foot in the chaos of my world, and the other foot in the order of Faith's. How he does not flip-flop between the two? "What did he tell you now? That I'm a horrible person and murdered a litter of kittens?"

Groaning, she readjusts her eye patch. "He knows you were

170

shooting up, but you *lied*. Typical addict behavior. Lying, not thinking you did anything wrong, oh, it's just recreational, blah, blah, blah."

"Faith, I'm letting loose because of all the pressure."

Her face twists up. "What pressure? Is your life that bad?"

I ignore this. "Is that why you told Stacey about me? Thought you could use her for a mini-intervention?"

She looks shocked. "That was all her idea, bud."

"But you were talking about me. Talking behind my back. So not cool, sis." I shake my head and squeeze my lids shut. It still pains me to think that my sister would discuss my business with Stacey, with anyone, rather than come to me first. Where's the kinship? The loyalty?

"Yeah, I was talking about you. You're my twin brother. My favorite person in the world . . . and I think you need help. Like rehab. Before it gets worse." As her face flushes, she continues. "I was looking into outpatient programs around here, there's this one in Albany that looks promising—"

"Faith," I say, more forceful than I want. My history textbook falls to the floor. I try to make my voice sound steady, less defensive. "I'm fine. Do you hear me? I could stop right now if I wanted. It wouldn't be a big deal."

"Right," she says, shaking her head. "Just like you could stop dealing that new crap that everyone's talking about. Indigo this, indigo that. I'm not going to be financed by your drug money. You look terrible, by the way. Strung out."

I fight against exasperation. "Thanks. I'll keep that in mind."

"Let me make my own decisions, Phineas." She pauses, pins me with her beautiful eye. "You can't buy away your guilt."

This is the first time she's said something like this. I'm

171

frozen. Or wilting. Or both. My high from a few minutes ago plummets and shatters, and it's like waking up not knowing whose bed you're in. Buy away my guilt? I mean, how dare she even bring that up—the very act of mentioning it affirms that I *am* to blame, for *that* day, for many days.

"That's not what I'm trying—"

She stops me by holding up her hand. "Then whatever you are doing, *stop it*. Live *your* life. Fix your own, instead of trying to fix *mine*. I've proven to be a pretty capable person, don't you think? One eye and all?"

Normally her self-confidence and self-reliance wouldn't bother me, but today I don't think I can take it. I've tried to pretend I've got enough confidence to go around, to go around twice, but Faith knows my act. It used to be charming, even endearing. Soon, however, it'll be pitiful, and Faith will see it as such. That can never happen. Faith can't ever pity me. If I could only make her understand.

"I just want the best for you. You deserve the best," I say.

Her expression grows mournful. "What do *you* deserve, then?"

"The world and puppies," I say, hoping for a laugh and an immediate end to this conversation. I get neither.

"Come on, Finn, seriously."

"I don't know!" I yell. Faith flinches, and I quietly apologize; the last thing I want to do is alarm her, to scare her like I did with Taylor. What I don't say is that when I think about it, when I really, truly think about it, it becomes not a matter of what I deserve, but of what I've got coming to me.

Faith stands up. She fetches her lip gloss, changes into her "going out" eye patch (lined with rhinestones), checks her face in the mirror, and throws on a black blazer.

"Where are you going?" I ask.

"Hanging out with Stacey and a few friends at Peter's." She swipes her brush through her hair one final time, then throws it on her bed.

"Oh," I say, thrown by her response. Peter's? I knew nothing of this gathering, and I'm *always* invited. Am I being punished for bad behavior? Excluded on purpose? Faith shrugs as if she hears my thoughts.

When Faith leaves, I look through the bedroom window and watch her hop into Stacey's car—a powder-blue Prius— and immediately they're throwing their heads back, laughing, I can hear them from inside the trailer. Probably laughing at me, at the drugs and desperation, the supposed lack of motivation. Prosophobia my ass.

SATURDAY, APRIL 27

CHAPTER TWENTY-FIVE

THE SUN'S SERIOUS BUSINESS THIS MORNING, HEATING UP THE GRAVESTONES SO MUCH THEY'RE TOO HOT TO TOUCH. I'm waiting for Orah on the bench next to the mausoleum, I have my pocket bird book, and binoculars around my neck; I puff on a cigarette. The day is almost filled with promise.

Orah's coming around the bend. She's taking it slow, up the hill, her head bent to the ground, her old feet stepping carefully. I think about running down there and taking her arm, steadying her a bit, but I know pride when I see it.

"Phineas," she says when she's finally reached me, extending her hand. It's a firm handshake, one that's strong but not trying too hard. The best kind.

"Only my sister calls me that. Finn is good."

"I think I'll call you whatever I like, thank you very much."

"Um, okay then," I say, stubbing out my cigarette. Now I see where Stacey gets her stubbornness.

She hikes up her elastic waistband pants and sits next to me on the bench, revealing light-pink socks she probably got as a six-pack at Walmart. I wonder how close she is with Stacey. I wonder if they've ever talked about me in the morning room.

"Indigo's been selling like crazy. It's already gone." I hope that this comment will prove to her how trustworthy I am, how right I was, and prompt her to give me another bagful, but it doesn't. Her face is angled away from me.

"Indigo. Is that what you're calling it?"

Her voice is neutral, and I want to fill in the silence, get some enthusiasm going. "Yeah, the name has really been catching on. I saw your indigo buntings print, and it seemed way appropriate. Is that your favorite of Audubon's?" I know I'm talking too much, but I can't stop.

"It's one of my favorites. I like how the female bird is so self-assured in that one."

"Me too," I say, not able to hide the passion in my voice.

"I also have Audubon's snowy owls," she says, squinting in the sun. Her voice seems to be warming up just a bit.

"You do? That's a good one as well." In that picture there are two owls—male and female—perched on separate branches, against that backdrop of a thunder-ripe sky. Their yellow eyes assault, question, challenge you, and even though the female's left eye is barely there, the picture is a thousand stares tearing into you at once.

Orah studies me. First she scans my tattoo, then the holes in my earlobes from earrings I never put in, then the simple silver band I wear on my forefinger. Faith gave it to me for my birthday one year—she said it gave me a hint of sophistication and class. I thought it just looked cool.

"What?" I ask, addressing her examination. It's the only way to get what I want. *And*, it's a beautiful day, and I'm pretty comfortable on this bench, in spite of her inspection. The fact that she loves Audubon's snowy owls helps too. The woman's got good taste.

"I'm just looking at you and your ornamentation. Tell me about your tattoo." She points to it and frowns—not meanly, just out of concentration.

I go on automatic with the explanation, holding out my forearm so she can take a decent gander. "Female cardinal. Beautiful, understated, powerful. Just like the kind of women I respect, the kind of girl I hope to be with."

Orah leans back away from me. "Oh, now, Phineas, what is the *real* meaning behind it?"

"Huh?" I say, alarmed. Did I just get called out? "I like birds, that's all. You know that."

She looks at me and waits, still not buying it. I bounce my knee, and I sigh, surrendering to the fact that even my best charm isn't going to slide with this lady. Fine, I think, I'll play nice.

I grudgingly begin, "When my sister was in the hospital . . . because of something stupid I did . . . anyway, there was a light-red and gray female cardinal that landed on the windowsill of her room. It would come every day, without fail, during the time she was there. At first I didn't think she was seeing it, she wasn't talking much and—and they had her so hopped up on meds she barely knew right from left. But it was like . . . the bird knew to be patient . . . so she kept coming back, roughly around the same time every day, you know? Perched right there, watching, singing a song or two. The first time Faith saw it, she moved her hand toward the window. *Phineas*, she said, *that bird's got a crush on you.* First words out of her in days."

I laugh softly, swiping the back of my hand across my eyes. I realize that this is the first time I'm telling someone, besides my sister, the real reason why I got the tattoo. The slingshot of emotions hitting me right now, all I can say is, *um* wow, and *um* embarrassing, yet Orah's not even commenting on it, not staring me down—she isn't even looking at me, and I feel so damn grateful for that. Like, this lady *gets it*.

"Did you think it was a sign?" Orah asks, finally accepting my answer.

I shrug. "Signs are like believing in horoscopes. You can always squeeze out some kind of relevance."

Orah nods. "Yes, but I think it's more than that. Signs are real. They are all around—it's just up to you to interpret them."

I have a response right away. "Then it's not really about the sign itself, but about the interpretation," I say. "It's bogus. I used to think that seeing this one bird—an albino sparrow—was a sign of some serious good luck, only because it was such a rare sighting. Everything that happened afterward was just . . . it was just life . . . bad or good or boring. There's no rhyme or reason to it, and I think it's kind of a waste of time, constantly trying to read a future you aren't ever going to know."

Orah seems to consider this. Maybe I would have told her something different if the blowout hadn't happened with Stacey. Maybe I would have told her, like I'd told Stacey, that bird sighting *was* good luck. But now I'm starting to believe that the sparrow was an albatross, telling me I've got to start watching my back.

"The right interpretation of a sign isn't the important thing," Orah says. "It's the paying attention. It's the noticing. These days people are running too fast to really *see*. Me included. I have to tell myself to slow it down, or else. It's a game to keep myself in check—how fast are you going today on a scale of one to ten? Anything above an eight isn't sustainable on a daily basis for *anyone*. And an old lady like me? I need twos and threes, or I'm in trouble."

Her side of the bench is all sun, mine is all shade. Is this supposed to mean something too? I rest my elbow on the back of the bench. A robin is standing watch in the grass. I guess I never really viewed life that way—an exercise in paying attention—and that we may have a personal responsibility to see a rose and take a giant whiff.

"I paid attention to that cardinal, I'll tell you that much," I say. "It would look at me, and I swore in her eyes there was something human. A soul trapped in her body, but not really trapped, you know? You can't really be trapped when you can fly." There hasn't been a day I haven't thought about that cardinal; my tattoo, my sister, and how we both want to take flight from D-Town, maybe from ourselves—the tattoo is a daily reminder.

Her eyes shift back and forth, like the carriage of a typewriter. She's probably thinking, wow, this kid is batshit, what have I gotten myself into?

"Souls are everywhere," she says softly.

"Like your husband?" I ask. She doesn't respond right away. Maybe it is too blunt of a question.

But she looks pleased to answer it. "Oh yes, he's here right now, enjoying the conversation, like me. I talk to myself sometimes—Stacey must think I'm off my rocker—but it's really him I'm talking to. No shame in that, no shame, I say. Things change, we adapt. That's all we can do."

"What was your husband like?" I ask. She seems surprised. And pleased. People must have stopped asking her that a long time ago.

"He was my person," she says, looking down at her gold wedding band. "The one, no doubt about that. Strong and silent type. Loyal and caring. It's as if he was tagged with my name as soon as he set foot on earth. We met when I worked at a hospital in Worcester. He was the head administrator; I was a lowly nurse. My nurse's uniform must have been flattering back then, all that attention he showered on me was rather embarrassing. At first." She winks at me; I smile. This is kind of like shooting the shit with Nurse Caven, but better. Conversation is nice, and maybe I'll be getting something out of it.

We have a good view of the whole front end of the cemetery and the road that runs next to it. There are no cars in sight—there usually aren't so early on a Saturday morning. This puts me at ease. This is my venture and my venture alone.

She's not paying attention to any of her surroundings, just me and the sound of her own voice. "Our good times were miraculous. We had a spell of rough times too—like all marriages do. He lost his job after I had quit mine to raise our daughter. Those years were trying. Jobs were scarce and money was tight and there were times when all we ate were bananas, eggs, and rice."

"Why don't you want to bank off your product?" I ask, finally taking the opportunity to bring the conversation back around to why we're here, or at least why I'm here. "I mean, you don't seem to be hurting now, but you could make a killing."

"I told you, I want it out of my life. My son-in-law moving here with my granddaughter . . . this is a new beginning, and I want it to be pure. That's all I want to say about that for now," she says curtly.

"Okay," I say, raising my hands. "Didn't mean to hit a nerve."

"You're not hitting a nerve, honey, you're just getting at the truth, and sometimes it's too much to handle, especially on a sunny day like this."

I bow my head in agreement, fingering the pages of the travel-size bird book in my hoodie pocket. The smoothness of it soothes me to no end. It's a form of protection, it's thick enough to be bulletproof, it's a good-luck charm because of the heron on its cover. Herons are good omens when you see them. Why? They are self-reliant and are hyperaware of the world around them. People who see herons in their dreams are good at dealing with others and make good leaders. I've never dreamed of one. I should.

"Come with me," Orah says, standing and walking up the path into the older part of the cemetery that disappears in the woods. I'm following along, as the path gets steeper and steeper and then slopes down sharply again, a few gravestones scattered here and there, some still upright, while others are laid out on the ground, broken, chipped, even tagged, oh the blasphemy.

I've never been this deep into the cemetery before because the bird watching isn't as good among the heavy cover of branches and leaves. Orah knows exactly where to step, what turns to take, even though there is no clear path. The forest thickens, it's getting all Sleepy Hollow in here as we make our way down a somewhat treacherous incline, infested by tree roots and slate.

At the bottom of the incline, Orah disappears behind a large patch of tall grass. I follow. When I reach her through the thicket, I look up to see a ledge about twenty feet high. I didn't even know the drop-off existed. I see her take a key from her back pocket and use it to open a metal door in the middle of a stone wall that I wouldn't have noticed just passing through. It looks like the wall was shoved into the earth of the ledge.

"What is this?" I ask, as she pushes the door open. Dust puffs up around her ankles. She tucks the key back into her pocket.

"The crypt of my ancestors," she says. "They built it and died and got buried here. Come in. I'm assuming they built it into the ledge so it would be as inconspicuous as possible." She gestures me inside; I pause at the entrance.

I try to catch a glimpse beyond her, but it's too dark to see anything. I can't imagine how it must look in there, how it must *smell*. "Uh-uh. I'm not going in."

"Suit yourself. You might want to see what's in here, however." She smirks; she's so damn *tickled* by my hesitation.

I groan and press on behind her. Damp, cool, suffocating. I have no idea what I'm getting myself into, but I'd be stupid not to see this through. The deep dark bandages itself around us, mummifying me. I've been to some rough locales throughout my years of drug dealing, but I've never heard of anyone hiding their drugs inside a tomb. Though I'm sort of impressed, I'll admit there is a small part of me that is nervous, maybe a little scared. Why is it here, among the dead? Is this yet another sign?

Suddenly, there's light. Praise be. Orah has pulled out a battery-powered lamp from behind God knows what. There are two stone coffins, or more accurately there are two *sarcophagi*, one on either side of us, but they're not sealed off. The lids are gone, and the bodies are exposed, so exposed, bones at all different kinds of angles, they aren't bodies, they're just a bunch of sticks rigged together. Good *God*. I'm surprised it doesn't stink of death and decay. It doesn't smell like anything but dirt.

"Phineas, are you okay?" Orah asks.

"Yeah, yeah. I'm fine," I say, bending over, clasping my hands around my knees, trying to catch my breath. The ringing in my ears is a siren's wail. It's okay, I'm a weakling, but Orah can see me this way, I guess I don't mind. Because it's not just the bodies that are bringing me to my knees, man, it's the *flowers*.

Flowers.

Everywhere.

Their point of origin is the skeletons. They're bursting directly from the bones like souls finally released, and these souls are stunning, like roses, but with more petals, bigger heads, shinier, silkier, heavier. And their blue color—what is there to say? In the barely-lit dark they seem to glow from within and change shades: there's an almost blackish purple, oh wait, a blueberry blue, nope, it's got to be dark denim, on second thought it's lapis lazuli. Each variation of blue is a different word of a different language reciting a sonnet, singing a lyric, exclaiming a truth. True blue, citizens of D-Town! The flowers rise up from the dead and climb up the dirt walls of the crypt and hang from the ceiling, their vines snaking across surfaces, their leaves heart-shaped with long, curly tendrils. They make their way down the other side of the wall and onto the ground where their heavy-petaled heads gaze upwards.

"What is this?" I say, touching a petal. It immediately disintegrates upon contact. I try to pick up the pieces, but there is nothing to pick up.

Orah raises her eyebrows. "This is indigo."

CHAPTER TWENTY-SIX

IN THE DANK ATMOSPHERE OF THE CRYPT, ORAH TELLS
ME ABOUT THE FLOWER THAT HAS NO NAME, EVEN
AFTER YEARS OF RESEARCH IN TRYING TO IDENTIFY IT.
She urges me to never tell a soul—not Stacey, not her father,
not Faith—about this place, to never utter a word, because it
is the only location on earth where indigo—in all its delicate
glory—is protected from the outside elements.

"How the heck are these flowers growing without sunlight?" I ask.

"It's part of the magic. They're fueled by the dead." The
idea of this gives me the creeps, but at the same time it's a
damn good representation of the circle of life. We die; we are
born again.

"So you just came across it here and decided to snort it up
your nose? That makes no sense."

"It wasn't like that at all," she says. There's a small bench up
against the wall where she sits. She pats the empty space next
to her. Why not take a load off? If she's not weirded out by this
place, I'm not going to let it get to me either.

She continues after I sit. "When my daughter died—
Stacey's mother—I was in a terrible state of mind. I thought

God had already taken too much away from me when he took my husband at such a young age. But then he went and took my daughter too." Her sadness is palpable. It seems like the flowers are shimmering different versions of blue in response to her emotions. If Faith were here, she'd compare their petals to mood rings.

"Stacey told me she died of a virus." I sense that she might want to tell me more about this.

"You know how we realized something was really wrong?" she asks.

I shake my head, and I'm more than curious to know. It hits me—the yearning to learn about Stacey and what has shaped her into the person she is today.

"It started out with the flu. But then Page's fingernails began to turn a shade of blue and so did her toenails. We thought that they were bruises until the whites of her eyes turned a pale blue. The doctors couldn't figure it out. They ran test after test and couldn't figure it out. Everyone was baffled. No one knew what to do."

"Talk about inconclusive," I say, looking at my own chewed-to-the-quick fingernails.

"The closer she got to death, the darker blue the whites of her eyes became, to the point where you could barely see where the blue disease ended and the black pupil began. It scared Stacey. Billy tried to be brave, but all he wanted was his daddy."

"Poor kids," I say, but the comment falls flat. What do I know about kids? About families in general? About what it's like to want to be with your daddy?

"The more I thought of it, the more I wondered if it was something in our genetic makeup. I'd heard over and over again from my mother about the Klaski blood being 'contaminated.'

There was a story about an infection on a farm of my great-grandparents in the Adirondacks. Who knows, maybe something was contracted from the animals." Her voice sounds tired, and she falls silent.

But I want to know everything now that she'd started. "So you think that the virus was passed down—like through DNA or something?"

"It's one possibility." She straightens up, summoning up the strength to continue. I know this is a hard story to tell. But I know she wants to tell it. Maybe she needs to.

"I was there holding Page's hand the day that she died. The hospital room was dark; it was past two in the morning. She opened her eyes, squeezed my hand, and said, *Everyone is right about seeing things before you die. My memories are flashing before me. All my best ones.*"

I know I've just heard the story of her daughter's death, and there's part of me that feels sad for Orah and for Stacey, but I can't help but get a little revved up by how the story connects with indigo. Indigo makes you see your favorite memories, like what Page was seeing. Page, who was turning blue, the color of indigo, and dying. So did that mean that when you take a hit of indigo, you have to die a little to see the memories?

Orah breaks my train of thought. "After Page died, I couldn't visit her grave. I just couldn't. No mother should have to experience her child dying before her. She was only twenty-seven when she passed . . ."

"Life isn't for the faint of heart," I say. I immediately feel stupid for trotting out this cliché. Luckily Orah doesn't seem to notice.

She sighs, and her expression is one of tired melancholy. "Finally, I found the courage and went to her grave. It's next to where my husband's is and where mine will be. I was there by myself. I had to be alone, this first time, with my grief."

She pauses. I know there's more and, I admit, I'm eager for it, even though I know I'm being kind of morbid. "I showed up at the cemetery, around this time, early morning. What I saw was a shock. It literally brought me to my knees."

"The flowers," I say.

"They were so blue in the sunlight. They didn't look real—they looked like they were made of glass—almost transparent in the light. I started to cry just thinking I wanted to die and be put in the ground next to my daughter. But when my tears hit the petals, the blue turned different shades. I watched, almost enchanted, and for the first time since Page had died, I saw the beauty of life. The flowers were showing me life could change with a single tear. Hopelessness may surround you, but then you see a bird you like, things shift, and you start to feel different. Different in a way that you can look at what's ahead of you in a new way. So when the flowers were changing, they were speaking to me, and telling me that it was going to be okay, if even just for a moment."

I am drinking in her words. She had wanted to die, and then the flowers gave her hope. Page had died, but something about her death, maybe her DNA, and the blue disease mixed with the earth, gave birth to a new form of life. Death to life. To hope. To rebirth.

"I reached out and touched the flowers," Orah continued, "and they disintegrated. Their residue dusted her grave, made it blue-toned. I said good-bye to my daughter again that day and kissed the top of her grave. The stone was sweet-tasting. I licked my lips, which were even sweeter. The taste seemed like a gift. A gift from Page. The flowers had grown from her bones, and were so strong their roots sprouted through the cracks in the coffin, and pushed through the ground. How do I know this? I've seen the way the flowers behave in this crypt and how fast they grow. Nature is powerful. It will always fight to make itself known. These flowers were an extension of her. Why wouldn't I want her to be part of me forever? I grabbed one in my palm and ate the petals even as they turned to powder."

"And you had a flashback when you ate the flower? A memory?"

"Oh yes, a very lovely, heavenly one at that." I don't ask her what her memory was. I could tell it was private, and I didn't want to know. Some things aren't meant to be shared.

"It was such an intense experience it became addicting. I went back and back until all the flowers were gone, and they didn't grow back. That's when I started to do some research."

Now her tone has changed. She's leaving behind the personal memories and is moving to a new part of the story, the part that she knows is going to be about me and what I'm looking for. I know she knows this, because she looks at me out of the corner of her eye, clearly amused by how captivated I am. Well listen here, Mother Goose, Faith and I were never read bedtime stories as kids, so there's a lot of catching up to do.

"I spent the next year trying to track down gravesites of my relatives."

I'm sure she pauses here for effect. She's playing with me now. What an old lady. I imagine Stacey being like her in fifty or sixty years.

"What did you find?" I ask, because I know she's going to make me beg for it.

"There's an old Klaski graveyard at an abandoned farm. Those gravestones are the oldest I've ever seen in our family, dating back to my great-great-grandparents."

"Were the flowers there?"

"Not many. I think indigo needs to be protected and can only survive outside for so long. There were a few plants, but the petals were not that deep blue, and the experience they gave was barely anything. But I'm convinced that's where the flower began because that's supposedly where the virus started, at least according to what my grandmother told me long ago."

"Anywhere else?" I prompt. I'm beginning to hope that the indigo is growing all over the area.

"Don't get ahead of yourself. This is the only indigo place you'll ever need. Believe it or not, this crypt was the hardest to find. No one knows it's back here, it's so old."

"And there's so much of it." I look around again. It's hard to believe anything could live in this gloom, but the flowers are everywhere.

"No snow, no wind, no drought. Just dark and dank, like a grave. This is the only place I visit, and I've been coming here for years. The flowers just keep blooming."

Forgive me for salivating at this fact. Endless supply. An endless opportunity for cash. I could finance Faith's education, no doubt, on this. I could finance her freaking *life*. And the idea of indigo potential on the farm where it all began? I bet those old bones would grow an indigo even more divine.

"You know what I learned throughout this whole experience, Phineas?"

I set the fantasy of my future life aside. "Do tell."

"We are not put on this earth to be happy all the time. I don't think trying to be happy is the secret to life."

It certainly isn't what my life is, that's for sure. "Then what is? Be sad and suffer?"

"No, no. It's not about trying to be anything. Happiness is not something that can be attained and once attained, that's it. It's an ongoing project."

She's losing me now. We're into Buddha Zen land, not where I want to be. I try to bring her back. "Okay, but what does it have to do with this?" I gesture around us to the flowers that seem to have gotten bigger, bursting with more life the longer we're in here.

"You have to find the bright spots. The little moments. Hold onto them for however long they last, and when they're gone, pay tribute by remembering. The memories can restore us, history can teach us, and the fact that happiness isn't all the time makes us appreciate it more. Life is hard. Tragedy befalls us every day. But there's always going to be a bright spot, no matter how big or how small. We will always have something to look forward to, and we will always have bright spots to remember."

Thoughts of the deals I'll make, the money I'll make, disappear. I am only listening to her voice, her advice, and what seems like a truth I haven't digested before. This woman, she should speak to the masses. I'm sad I never had a grandmother like this. I could have used a dose of this philosophy way back when.

"I'm going to be ruminating *the crap* out of this, Orah. For a long while."

"I hope it will help you." I hope so too.

———

I spend the next hour learning how to harvest indigo, per Orah's instructions. She reiterates how gentle I have to be, but my hands are big and clumsy, my feet unsteady. Bull in a china shop? More like a T. rex. It's safe to say that I'm not a natural. Because of my ineptitude and overall shakiness, I do wonder if I'm suffering mild withdrawal from H, from coke, from the pills I've been taking. When I run through all the drugs I've done within the past weeks to keep my energy up, to bring my anxiety down, it's a long-ass list that no one should be proud of, unless you want to win an accolade for recklessness.

"No, Phineas, you aren't doing it right," she says, holding up a ziplock bag. "Bring the bag as close as possible to the flower, then give the petals a gentle touch so they disintegrate right into the bag. Use delicacy."

I pay special attention to her movements, not wanting to waste one mote of indigo to the stale air. It's *crazy* hard. It takes a lot of practice to capture just one of the flowers in a bag, and I'm starting to get frustrated and annoyed she's so good at it. Her technique is expert, her fingers are deft. It could be the nurse in her. Or it could be the addict.

I'm calculating how much all this indigo is worth. I've been selling grams for fifty dollars a pop, easy. So far, the indigo I've harvested in my hands right now would be worth hundreds, hell yeah, and Orah's bag is probably worth thousands. Cha-ching. This whole crypt is a legit gold mine, I'm talking hundreds of thousands of dollars, I'm talking I could be a millionaire by the time I turn eighteen. There's only one way to celebrate this, yet I've left all my feel-good paraphernalia at home, save for my pack of cigarettes.

After a while, she takes a break to wipe her hands on her black pants, leaving streaks of blue powder, to roll her shoulders back. My muscles are sore from all the concentrated movements, all the focus in general. I haven't wanted to use throughout this whole visit, but now I do. My body is screaming for it. If I don't get out of this place soon, man, I'm going to be hurting.

I consider dipping my finger into one of the quart-sized bags I've filled, taking a taste, maybe I'd have a good memory again, but the risk is too much. You'd have to put a gun to my head before I relive the worst memory of my life. My sister on the floor bleeding, sharp plastic lodged in her eye, my father sobbing . . .

"Are you okay, Phineas?" Orah asks.

"I'm fine. Just getting claustrophobic, I guess."

She looks at me doubtfully. "We should leave now," she says. "It's not healthy for us to stay in here for very long . . . the drug is in the air, eventually it will absorb into your skin, and you'll be hallucinating before you know it."

I nod, relieved, fishing through my pockets for my cigarettes and a lighter. But when I pull out the lighter, Orah slaps it from my hands.

I throw her a look of outrage. "Hey, lay off," I say, scrambling to pick up the lighter, which she kicks to the front of the tomb with her black sneaker before I can grab it. She clamps her hand down on my shoulder.

"I failed to mention that indigo is *incredibly* flammable," she says fiercely. "If you light up in here, you'll blow up this whole ledge. You can't even smoke it."

"Really?" I say, turning my attitude down a notch. "Sorry." I'm going to have to spread around the black box warning. It would really hurt business if someone got hurt.

We leave the crypt and Orah locks up, and aren't we a sight, hair, face, clothes all coated with fine, blue-ish powder that glistens impressively in the sun. Indigo in her purse, indigo under my sweatshirt. On the trek back we're quiet, the dust slowly disappears, we're us again. When we arrive at her minivan, I open the door for her, she settles in.

"Hey listen," I say, arm over the door. "Thanks. For this opportunity, you know?"

Orah places her hand on my forearm. Her palm is soft and her fingers are strong. She smiles warmly, like she actually cares about me. "You're a good boy," she says.

"Oh." I let out a nervous laugh. "Sure. Okay."

On the car ride home, Orah's sage advice on happiness is needling me. Maybe it really can't be attained. Maybe I'm going to be running around in circles for the rest of my life trying to find satisfaction, my *fill*, when there is none with permanence to be found. But whatever, I can't deny the thrill of a new beginning coursing through me, on high voltage. The possibilities. All that indigo waiting to be turned into money, more money than I've ever had. Indigo. The new drug of the century, and my empire to rule.

TUESDAY, MAY 7

CHAPTER TWENTY-SEVEN

MY CUSTOMER BASE SKYROCKETS AFTER I VISIT THE CRYPT WITH ORAH. I've got kids I've never seen before buying from me at a Taco Bell downtown, in the parking lot of Walmart; Jesus, I did a drop in front of a toy store with a life-sized teddy bear in the window. People are coming out of the cracks in droves.

The money I'm making is out of this world, and the space underneath the floor panels is starting to fill up. If I keep going at this rate, I'm going to need another hiding spot.

One thing is for sure. Magic is going down. I pretty much have all of D-Town High indigo'd up and loving life. Everyone at school is brighter, happier, and energized, even looking better. Eyes are sparkling, voices are less confrontational. The quietest student starts participating in class, and the wiseass sitting in the back stops harassing the girls in the front. Teachers see the transformation and wonder if their lessons are finally changing lives. Too bad they don't know that it's me. *Me.* I'm making the world go round, and people won't stop raving about how indigo makes them feel.

Check this out:

A girl in third period English says to me, "I'm seeing for

the first time. Really seeing. Like I'm leaving Plato's cave, into the light I go. I *know* you know what I'm talking about, Finn. I haven't forgotten about that speech of yours on Socrates. Well, here's to your brain on Socrates and indigo. Hand in hand, my friend."

"Man, I feel like I just rode a rainbow, made out with a supermodel, and won an Olympic gold medal. And I haven't even left my couch today," says some stoner guy who thinks he's friends with me, but I can never remember his name.

This one from the shyest girl in my grade shatters my heart a little: "I've stopped cutting myself. I was a little girl again in my memory, and it made me want to go back to that innocence. I want to. I really do. And now I can."

It's a flood of appreciation washing over me, and it feels good. I'm helping them. All these kids who used to be depressed and withdrawn are now coming alive, and everyone's living the best version of themselves. The guys are congratulating me like I've been elected governor of New York, and the girls are coming on to me so much, I feel full, full with their big eyes and low-cut shirts, gluttonous from their soft hungry voices and soft shiny hair.

But it's not all sunshine and rainbows. I've got Faith and Stacey giving me the cold shoulder like it's their full-time job. I can't tell if they know what I'm up to, how deep I am in dealing indigo, or if they're choosing to ignore it. Whatever they're thinking, I'll show them I know what I'm doing.

After school I end up in the library for a deal with some freshman who is desperate for indigo. I pass him a book on World War II with a gram tucked between its pages and give him a wink. That should tide him over for a while. As I make my way back through the maze of book stacks, I come upon my sister and Stacey at one of the circular tables by a window overlooking the back fields of our school. It's probably the prettiest spot in D-Town High, and the two prettiest girls are monopolizing it. I consider taking another way out of the library to bypass them; I don't want them to question my presence here, since the library isn't really my joint. I'm no bibliophobe, but the forced quiet of the library spooks me. On second thought, though, Stacey's looking too good to pass up, in a purple dress with puffy sleeves, and maybe I can work on softening my sister.

I strut over there after choosing a book on tropical birds I don't already have. It doesn't bother me that Faith and Stacey will see me with it. Maybe the nerdiness factor will help.

Faith's got her head buried in *Jane Eyre*, and Stacey's writing notes from a Western Civilization textbook in a college-ruled notebook. The closer I get, I see doodles of flowers in the margins of the page. It's so girly and wonderful.

My sister looks up first. "What are you doing here?" she asks with a hard expression on her face. Her hair is curly today; her face paler than usual. She hasn't spoken to me about her anxiety lately, but I sense it close—she's jumpy and tense.

How could I think approaching them is a good idea, especially with how my date ended with Stacey? And Faith won't even tell me if she's taken back her acceptance to Harvard.

"I needed a new book on birds," I say as proudly as I can, but it comes off sounding smug if anything. Stacey hasn't given me one glance.

"Bully for you," Faith says. They go back to their school work, and I'm left standing around like an idiot.

Stacey finally looks up. "You made quite the impression on Mimi when you came over."

I'm startled by this. Is Orah talking about me? Is she breaking her own rule and blowing our cover for whatever reason?

"He tends to have that effect on people," Faith says irritably.

Stacey isn't discouraged by my sister's instant bad mood. "Mimi and I were talking last night, and she mentioned you. *The young man in the morning room.*"

This thrills me to no end, because I don't sense any contempt in her voice. Orah hasn't mentioned the indigo. I should have more faith in the old lady. This chat is going better than I thought it would. That disaster of a date seems years away now, even though it was just weeks. Maybe it wasn't even as bad as I remember.

"That's got a nice ring to it," I say. *The young man in the morning room.* "I've been told before that the air changes when I walk into a room. I mean, doesn't the library feel different to you right now? Like more awesome?"

Faith's annoyance doubles; she knows I'm acting like I'm the shit because I'm nervous. "Don't get all cocky, her Mimi brought you up in conversation because you like Audubon and so does she."

"It's amazing what one common factor can do," Stacey says.

Faith muses on Stacey's comment and says suddenly, without bitterness, "Phineas has always liked Audubon, ever since he learned about him in elementary school. One of the teachers showed a few of his prints as part of a lesson on animals, reptiles, and birds. She gave him photocopies because he was so jazzed about it. Which ones were they again?"

Talking about me and Audubon loosens her up. At one point when we were kids, Faith looked at the photocopies just as much as me. She liked the postures of the birds and would try to mimic them—an impossible task—to make me laugh. And would she ever.

"The great blue heron, the wild turkey, the roseate spoon-bill, and the cardinal," I say. There were more, but those are the most famous ones the teacher shared with us. I remember my excitement turning quickly into passion. The more pictures I saw, the more devout I became.

"Of course the cardinal. Male and female," Faith says.

I shake my head, almost in reverence. The Audubon cardinals demand respect. Whenever I look at them, even if it's on the computer, a hush settles around me, a quiet cool. The assuredness of the male is shown in his upturned beak; the emotional intelligence of the female is in her graceful yet relaxed stance.

"The pictures were all in black and white. Imagine if they had been in color," I say, aware that the tropical bird book under my arm is sticking to my skin. I hope they don't notice how sweaty I am.

"I've only seen you excited like that a few times."

"What were the other times?" Stacey asks, clearly into it.

Faith and I lock eyes, and it seems important. It's the first time in a while that we're actually seeing each other, remembering how things used to be between us. I know we're simultaneously scanning our past, so connected, finding the bright spots, as Orah called them.

"Whenever he rants and raves about facts he knows," Faith says.

"Like your oration on frogs?" Stacey asks. "You should be a teacher."

Generally I get nasty when people tell me what I should do. But this time, it's different because it's coming out of Stacey's mouth, and because I don't necessarily hate the idea.

"What can I say? I'm a font of worthless knowledge."

Stacey smiles, and I know I'm ahead of where I was before this conversation began. So before this goes sour, and because I know at some point it will, I announce my exit. Plus, I have more people who are after indigo today. "Things to do, people to see," I say. Faith makes a noise in the back of her throat and returns to her reading.

"Enjoy the book," Stacey says, waving good-bye.

A teacher, huh? I think to myself. Like the world would really trust me with our future generation.

SATURDAY, MAY 11

CHAPTER TWENTY-EIGHT

I HEAD BACK OUT TO THE CEMETERY ON SATURDAY MORNING, AT THE DESIGNATED UNGODLY HOUR ORAH AND I PLANNED OVER THE PHONE. The calls for indigo are nonstop, and I don't want to be running low any time soon. This is all I'm hearing lately: *Can I get a gram for the party tonight? Man, I'm so hungover I need a bump. I'll meet you in front of the D-Town Diner. You better be holding.* Yeah, yeah, yeah, I say to them, slow your roll, you'll get it when you get it. I'm probably popping too many pills to stay calm throughout my increasingly hectic days.

Why isn't Orah asking me for any of the profits? I still can't believe she just wants to spend time with me and that's payment enough.

Bryce has pretty much dropped out of the dealing scene because he's afraid of getting arrested again. Peter, though at first eager to make money, is now backing away from the business venture. He says he's trying to get clean for his first semester of college, but I don't doubt Faith has something to do with it and how he wants to sober up for her, even though they're not together. That's all to say the burden of selling indigo is on me now, because I don't trust any of the others to do this kind of volume of work. But that also means more money for Faith.

Orah and I shuffle around the crypt, harvesting indigo, the battery-operated lamp illuminating the tombs of the dead. There is Horvath E. Klaski, who died at sea, and Lily P. Klaski, who passed away during childbirth at age nineteen. Orah and I talk to them, asking them how they're holding up and if they're taking care of our indigo. Saying things like, how are your old bones today? Cranky, satisfied, somber?

"You're losing weight," Orah says with her back turned to me. She harvests indigo fast and effortlessly, as I still struggle to collect the fine powder into a bag. "Your face looks hawkish. You're high right now, aren't you?"

I stop plucking flowers. "Why would you think that?"

"Your eyes are red, and you're being clumsy."

In truth, I *am* high, but she doesn't need to know that. I snorted a line before I headed over because my energy level was waning. A quick fix is what I needed.

"It's been a long week. And it's probably allergies. Springtime? Come on. The pollen's out of control. Been having to take Claritin, you know?"

Her hands are on her hips, face tilted up to the ceiling of the crypt. "Why do addicts make up elaborate lies?"

"I don't know, you tell me. At least *I'm* not addicted to this stuff," I say, holding up my bag of indigo. Then I realize it's probably not a smart idea to antagonize my supplier. "Anyway, did you know that the color indigo means certain things?" I say quickly to change the subject. I'm not discouraged that she doesn't respond to my question. "Indigo, on the positive side of the spectrum, means perception, intuition, and the higher mind. The color stimulates right-brain activity and creative thinking and helps with spatial skills."

"Where are you getting this information?"

"The Internet is a glorious thing. On the more negative side of the spectrum, the color indigo means addiction. Can you believe that? *Addiction*."

Orah purses her lips. "I know exactly what you're doing, Phineas, you and your tactics of distraction."

I place one of the backpacks to the side. Don't want either of us tripping on it and making a mess. Precious cargo we have here, and next to the dead no less.

"What do you want from me, Orah?"

She sighs. "Why do you do it, Phineas?"

"Do what?"

"Marijuana, cocaine, whatever else you do."

The dirt scratches against the soles of my sneakers when I shift my weight. Nobody has ever really asked me why. This is the last thing I feel like going into right now, but with Orah, I guess it's okay, she's judging me, and that makes her a hypocrite. And strangely enough, her being a hypocrite is a relief. Young people, midlife people, old people—can never really figure out their shit.

"I don't know, I just do. It feels good. I want to feel good. Who doesn't? You do indigo, it's the same thing." I consider telling her that the reason why I'm not addicted to it is because I'm the only person on the entire planet who had a bad trip from it. I haven't heard about anyone else suffering. It still seems so unfair, but at least it's benefitting me in other ways.

Her eyes narrow; down, down go the corners of her mouth. "That's why you're helping me to get rid of it. Don't you see? Stacey and her father moved in with me, and now life is different. I want it to be different. I want to prove to them I'm different. I didn't think an old lady like me could turn over a new leaf, but here I am."

"And here *I* am," I say.

"Indeed you are. My Billy left a while ago. Stacey's father claims he doesn't know where he went. Stacey won't tell me anything either. I know it's drug related. I know he's an addict too. He was tempted by indigo because of catching me doing it. It probably is what opened him up to other drugs."

I hear the self-blame in her tone, and it's heartbreaking to hear. I know guilt. I've been in its dragon mouth too many times.

Surprisingly, she continues. "Billy and I used to go up to the lake house south of here that Jimmy and I built with our bare hands. I wish you could have seen it. Big windows in front with unobstructed views of the water. Those windows had to be twelve feet high. Maybe more. My, life was good back then. Too bad I had to sell it eventually. It was just too much to keep up." The lamplight flickers, and I notice the beauty of the flowers again. They are almost Stacey beautiful. Almost.

"It was good even when we didn't have much. There was this one month when all we ate were bananas and eggs. Did I mention that before? For a whole month . . ." She leans up against a wall that isn't fully covered with indigo, though when she leans back, a puff of powder surrounds her. She shuts her eyes.

I watch her closely. She needs a break from all this talking. "Faith and I used to sneak into the cafeteria after lunchtime and take all the leftovers when the lunch lady was cleaning up with her earphones in. We'd take anything. Brussels sprouts, wrinkled green beans, congealed spaghetti, you name it. Mom and Pop weren't known for their stellar culinary capabilities."

I'm not sure if she's paying attention to me, because her head is sagging to the side and her eyes are still closed. I rest my hand on her shoulder. "Hey, are you okay? You want to go outside?"

"I'm fine, Billy—I mean Phineas—thank you very much," she says, a little winded. "I'm a nurse, I know if I'm okay or not. Worked with the mentally ill and saw how they were treated like second-class citizens. I used to tell stories to Billy about my time there. Scared the holy bejesus out of him."

I'm evaluating her, from the top of her hair down to her butt-ugly shoes. She doesn't look okay. But I continue along like nothing's up. "What kinds of stories?" I ask. I remember back to my date with Stacey when she told me about Orah's patient who made clocks.

There is liveliness in Orah's demeanor again, and I start working while she talks. "I once was strangled by a man who thought I was a demon. It took three attendants to get him off me."

"No joke?"

"None whatsoever. When Billy and I were up at the lake house together, he'd make me tell him stories like that, over and over again. Told them so much he started telling them back to me—better, in fact. Boy, he has an imagination, that one. We'd just stand by the water, skipping stones and swapping stories."

"Sounds like a lucky kid," I say with sincerity, sealing up one of the bags. I try to blink the sting of the air out of my eyes. "I used to tell my sister stories. You know, when she was upset . . . well . . . not really stories, but facts. Like I can run through a list of bird facts faster than you would believe. I also know a lot about other animals too, like cheetahs. I went through a phase where I was kind of obsessed with them. Faith would calm right down when I'd start telling her how fast cheetahs can run and how they can't roar. They can purr loudly, but not roar."

Orah lets out a short laugh. "Well, isn't that interesting. Seems like you know a lot about a lot."

"I pride myself on it."

This tidbit about cheetahs and other felines I shared with Faith while she was in the hospital. She wanted me by her bedside every day, and I made sure to read up and memorize as much as I could about animals she liked when I wasn't at the hospital. Very rarely would I have to refer to my notebook densely filled with handwritten information—I knew everything by heart. However, if I did have to take a peek, Faith would give me a sly smile, and I would exclaim, "Oh come on! How am I supposed to easily remember that hyenas originated in the jungles of Miocene Eurasia 22 million years ago?"

Orah's mouth is parted, body angled forward to speak. Her voice is softer than usual. "There was a woman at the hospital with schizophrenia who would run around her room in circles until she passed out. The only way that I could get her to stop was to sit in the middle of the room and read her nursery rhymes. She'd circle around me, a frantic duck-duck-goose, but eventually she would stop, climb into bed, and suck her thumb."

"God, how old was she?" I ask. It was kind of reassuring that there were people out there maybe more messed up than my parents.

"Forty-eight. Yep." She nods. "Look at those wide eyes of yours. You can't make these things up if you tried. There was another man who kept crystals of different shapes and sizes hanging from dental floss in his window. They would catch the light and flash different colors. They would flash rainbows.

He told me that each one held a different kind of energy, from happiness to sadness, from humor to dread. I asked him why he kept the crystals with the negative energy. He said it was a reminder. A reminder that life is a spectrum from the good to the bad—like the spectrum in the colors of the rainbow. You can never stay fixed forever, you walk, run, jump, crawl on red, orange, yellow, et cetera, and everything in between throughout your time on earth. *Everything* changes. *Nothing* ever stands still." She looks at me pointedly.

"It's like those bright spots you were talking about. They are there on the spectrum of things," I say, comforted by this thought. Orah nods, and I know that she feels comforted too— yes, by this knowledge, and probably by the fact that I listen to her, I digest what she has to say.

"He gave me one of those crystals before he was discharged—a beautiful round one—but he wouldn't tell me what kind of energy it held. I had to decide for myself."

"So what did you decide?"

"I decided it was hope," she says, pausing. "I gave it to Billy. When he was going through a hard time. But I'd be quite surprised if he still has it . . . after what I did to him."

She bends over and leans on her knees, whispering to herself, "Isn't that right, Billy, isn't that right, Billy . . ." Sweat is standing out on her forehead, matting down her hair.

I go to her, reach out my arms, I don't know what the hell I'm doing, supporting her, comforting her, just showing her I'm here, but she pushes me back like I'm bum-rushing her, like I'm some bully, like I'm worthless with the worst intentions.

"Whoa, sorry, I'm just trying to help," I say, hating the hurt I hear in my voice.

Orah's not listening to me. She's saying Billy's name again

and again, and she is now only present in some faraway place that is all past, past, past.

"Why don't we go outside?" I offer, thinking she might be hallucinating, maybe even having a bad trip like I did—we have been in the crypt for a long time.

She jerks her head up to glare at me. "Don't tell me what to do, child. You are in no place to order me around. You should be worrying about yourself, because *frankly*, you should be doing more. One day you're going to wake up and regret not turning your life around sooner." She shakes her finger at me. I'm not sure if she's talking to me, or if she's thinking I'm Billy.

I blurt out, stung, "Says the woman who's helping me deal drugs." I wait for her to respond, and then, when she doesn't, I shrug. "You know what? I don't care. I don't know where this is coming from, and *frankly*," I say, eyeing her down, "just because you couldn't control your grandson doesn't mean you can control *me*."

Orah snaps out of whatever state she was in, trance, fugue, delusion, and says, "We've harvested enough. I want to go."

Fine. Just as well. I'm sick of hearing about what I *should* be doing, what I *should* strive for, I can't stand that word, God, I can't stand all the shoulds. I *shouldn't* be doing anything except what I'm doing in this moment. Indigo is my everywhere, my everything, my *now*.

She grabs a backpack and shoves into it bags and bags of indigo. I do the same with my two packs. We don't look at each other, we don't say anything. I do a rough estimate of how much indigo we have. I'm thinking twenty-five thousand dollars conservatively. Why do I feel like it's not enough?

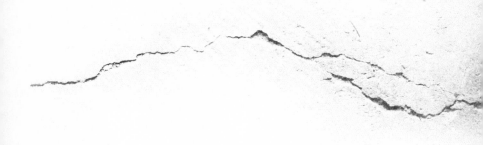

CHAPTER TWENTY-NINE

SHE CLICKS THE LAMP OFF, I OPEN THE CRYPT DOOR, AND WE'RE BATHED BY LATE-MORNING LIGHT AND BLESSED BY FRESH AIR. Orah is unable to fit the key into the lock because her hands are shaking so bad. I approach her like she's a skittish deer, goddamn Bambi, gently take the key out of her clammy hands and lock it up. It's quiet, I hear a squirrel skitter by. We walk up the incline, leaving the ledge behind, but before we get into the main section of the cemetery, there are other noises causing bad vibes to jingle up and down my spine.

The path is blocked up ahead.

Four big guys with beefy arms are coming toward us. One of them is smiling grandly, like he's cheated death, and he's here to spit all over it. Mike. Fucking Mike. I should have known—given my strained relationship with a bitch called karma—that he would appear at the worst time.

Orah grabs my arm. I push her behind me and tell her to stay still. Of course she doesn't. Of course she's yammering on about how we should have been more discreet, we should have come even earlier, we should just get rid of the rest of the indigo and be done with it. Should, should, should, should.

Meanwhile, my heart's working so hard it's weeping. If anything happens to her . . .

I tell her to go, I try nudging her away from me, but she stays attached. Really? She trusts me as her protector?

Mike's smile is vast. His three friends, ones I don't recognize, are as tight as slingshots, ready to launch, all different heights yet bulked up with steroid-fueled muscles. One of them—the tallest—wears a black rosary around his neck that bounces against his chest when he moves. Mike is limping from my workmanship, but this does not make him any less intimidating—in fact, he looks even more like a monster, lurching along, out for blood.

My blood.

"Hey guys," I say. "Visiting the dead?"

"Yeah," Mike says, a yard or two away from me now, he's a stop sign in his XXL red shirt. "The *almost* dead. We've been tailing you long enough." His eyes bore into mine as his men flank him. The rosary wearer is to his left, and to his right stands a man with a black bandana and another with silver rings on both thumbs. Orah sucks in a powerful gasp, I whisper to her, *it's okay, you'll be okay, I'm going to handle this.*

Then Mike flicks his chin, and Silver Rings is dragging Orah away from me, a robotic reaction to complement his emotionless face. Before I can launch a hit, she's digging her heels into the earth, she's pawing at him with useless effort, and without a thought I'm tackling Bandana and Rosary, who have conveniently made an impressive wall between me and her. I pull at their clothing, latch onto the rosary that doesn't break, *Godspeed* indeed, my strength initially overpowers them, punching what I can punch, shoulders, chests, jaws, aiming kicks, scratching, you name it. I got Bandana's ear pinched between my fingers, and I think I scratched Rosary's cheek. Still, it's not working. They're like stones, they can't feel a thing. And soon they've got me. Bandana body slams me down with ease, crushes my spine with a foot, his sweat not even close to being broke. My brain jostles against my skull. They don't see that she's just an old woman? Mike is chuckling at my tendon-popping struggle, my immobility. That stupid smile of his. He lights up a cigar.

As I'm down, Rosary tries to yank the two backpacks from me. I roll on the ground out of the way, and he smiles as if thinking, aw, isn't that cute, this kid's *so brave.* Then his dark eyes deaden, and he looks over at Silver Rings, who starts squeezing Orah's neck so hard she's turning purple and her eyes are bulging out of her head. I use my remaining strength to throw myself toward her, but Bandana's nimble and has me pinned again quick.

"Let her go!" I yell. I shout until I'm hoarse, and the whole time, in the back of my head I'm apologizing to her, over and over again.

"You give us the product, and we let grandma live," Bandana says, not looking into my eyes but over my head, like empty air holds more importance. Mike's standing there, leaning against a tree with casual interest.

"Leave her out of this," I say, barely able to make out the words. "Leave her alone." I'm out of breath, and my vision is cramped. I can only see her face, her terrified eyes, and how a silver-ringed hand is squished against her mouth to discourage her from screaming. He squeezes her harder.

"Here," I say, heaving the bags filled with indigo at them. "Now let her go."

He releases Orah, who collapses to the ground, her hands up to her throat, her mouth open, gasping, gulping for air. They let me scramble to her. She pushes me away, fucking A, then gives me this desperate, relieved look that breaks me in two.

But Mike and his friends aren't going anywhere. This isn't over yet.

I start praying to the dead. Help us. Horvath and Lily from the crypt aren't listening, and the others are silent too. The birds are singing *what did you expect? What did you expect? What did you expect?*

"So here's the infamous indigo," Mike says, yanking out a ziplock bag and lifting it up to the sky. It sparkles. It dazzles. "Yes, this is definitely not Early's stock. I think they're calling Early's stuff 'flower' down in the city. I like the name *indigo* so much better." He throws the bag over to Rosary, gestures for him to test it out, and the dude snorts up without any reluctance; Mike's got these suckers on automated response. Indigo hits, his eyes roll back, he leans up against a tree and slides down to a squat. The crucifix bobs against his stomach.

"So the question is, where is the rest?" Mike asks, waving his cigar-holding hand toward the three confiscated backpacks.

"There isn't any left," Orah rasps.

"Bullshit."

She looks sternly at him. "I don't tell fibs, young man."

My arm is around her as she holds onto her neck, all I'm thinking is how much of a warrior she is. I scan her face, her skin, I think she's all right—but how do I know? Mike shoots her an icy glare and then starts cackling. His guys join in. He stops. They stop.

"Is grandma running the show?" Mike asks, scratching his chin—it's the first time he doesn't look indifferent.

Orah twists away from me, gets up, and starts to walk back toward the crypt, only slightly unsteady on her feet. I scramble after her, calling her name, because for a second I actually think she's going to show them. That would be ridiculous, after her stressing constantly that the crypt must be a secret. Mike pauses with slight disbelief, then yells for Silver Rings and Bandana to follow her. Bandana grabs her arm, but she shakes him off. I think I hear her say something like, "Keep your paws to yourself."

"Where's she going?" Silver Rings asks, his sweat a reflection on the bridge of his nose.

"I'm taking you to our harvesting spot," she calls out without looking over her shoulder.

We all follow her. Rosary is still tripping, eyelids aflutter, lips twitching. I'm not sure what to expect, but I'm really hoping Orah has a plan. Mike is behind me, and before I can make some comment like stop checking out my ass, he locks his hand around my upper arm and kicks the bottom of my shin, right where there's more bone than muscle. It takes all my strength not to fall over. Bile rises in my throat.

"You know you did some serious damage to my foot," Mike says. He pulls a Buck knife out of his pocket. My Buck knife. "Does this look familiar?" He runs the knife along the line of my jaw, then slides it down underneath my Adam's apple; it's the sound of a way-too-close shave. Sweat is immediately dripping from my temples.

"Go ahead," I say. "Kill me. Slit my throat." And for a second, I mean it.

Bandana points toward Orah. She's reached a clearing in the woods where power lines are running down a long slope of rolling grass that changes color depending on the direction of the wind. Light green to the left, dark green to the right. Orah is looking down on what appears to be a picked-over garden.

There are plants I recognize—tomato plants, zucchini, and basil—and others that I don't. Some look like ferns, others look like pot plants, but I know they're not, and there's some kind of flower that's red and meaty.

"So is this where you grow?" Mike asks. He starts laughing. "You remind me of my noni," he says, pleased, almost nostalgic. "Tough-ass bitch she was. But man, did she have a green thumb."

We all approach the garden. "The ground isn't ripe for growing anymore. We harvested the last of it," Orah says, motioning to an almost entirely bare patch of dirt. Mike crouches down next to it and smiles sweetly.

"There's only one way to prove that this is a genuine grow spot," he says to me. "Isn't that right? After your visit, I had my guys scope out the situation of this new drug. They came out with some pretty interesting intel from a source who happens to be connected with your competition. They found out the drug they call *flower* grows off the bones of the dead."

I'm feeling pounding in my ears. How the hell do they know that?

Mouth a tight line, Orah nods sharply, very businesslike.

"Dig then, if you don't believe me," she says. I hate to admit it, but she's got more balls than me.

He roars with laughter. "You got some fight in you. I'll give you that." He sinks his chubby fingers into the earth, chunks of dirt flying over his shoulders, the few remaining plants ripped, murdered and quartered. He's not finding the buried treasure. He gives her the evilest of eyes. I try to tear away from Bandana, but no there's no use, he's just too strong.

"It's there, and that's the gods' honest truth," she says, crossing her hand over her heart.

"Don't you realize you just stole like twenty-five thousand dollars' worth of indigo?" I yell. "Isn't that enough, man?"

Mike ignores me. A noise rumbles in the back of his throat while he digs into the ground again, and I'm shaking because though *I* might deserve to die, *she* doesn't. A grunt, a hiss, an intake of breath from Mike. His hand comes up with a bone. Is that a femur?

"Well whaddya know?" He wipes it off on his shirt, holds it up to the sky. "I guess this lady ain't pulling my chain, after all." When he stands up, he carries the bone over his shoulder.

"Nice doing business with you."

But they still don't leave. Mike's just standing there, antagonizing me with his eyes, and clutches his fingers tight around the bone. Silver Rings looks smug, Bandana is smirking. Then: a swing and a hit against the back of my head. *Clunk*. Seeing stars is an understatement. Meteor showers before I even hit the ground.

The last thing I hear is, "What did I tell you, Flynn? This shit is mine. *Mine*."

———

Everything smarts. Body parts I didn't think I had are screaming in agony and the side of my face is pounding like a subwoofer. At first I don't know where I am, at first I think I partied a little too hard and that I'm in for the hangovers of hangovers.

"Finn. Phineas," she's calling my name. Reality hits. And reality pretty much sucks.

I'm on the ground with my hands over my head as a shield way too late. Orah is bending over me, hand on my shoulder. Orah, one tough cookie, thank God she's alive.

"Should I take you to the hospital?" I say, each syllable an ice pick to the head.

"You're the one who needs a medic," she says. "I'm fine. Just a few bumps and bruises."

"Yeah right," I say, finally turning my head and looking up at her. Bad idea. I almost pass out again. "We're going. I'll drive you there." The aftershock of fear has blanched her lips, reddened her cheeks, purpled the skin under her eyes. Whoever invented emotions must have been a big fan of paint by number. I want to reach up, but my *everything* is weak, and I feel like a fool.

Her expression softens. "Not necessary. Let me look at you," she says, crouching down. She places a shaky hand on my cheek, arctic fingertips, a chill that bites. Goddamn, I feel so bad, no one should have to go through something like this, she was probably a breath away from a heart attack.

"I'm sorry," I say, croaking, but those words are rarely enough. In this case, they don't even get me a quarter of the way to everything's okay. But she's looking at me with sympathy, like this was some scuffle on the playground, and a Band-Aid's enough to patch it all up.

"You know the bone in the garden over there came from a deer?" she says, smiling weakly. "Bones work like Miracle-Gro. There are more of them in the soil, I'll tell you that much—it took me a whole day to fertilize it." She sits on her knees on the ground next to me, brushing the hair away from her face. "The garden was a way for me to be all by myself, instead of out in the open in my yard. Nice stretch of land here, just enough sunlight. My family knows about the flower, and about my addiction to it. But nobody knows about *this place*, not Dan, not even Billy. I hope those men don't go snooping back there anymore. If they do, what if they eventually find the crypt?"

There's that harsh tone and look I was expecting; a smack-down of accusation. We both sit there, me uncomfortable, her who knows? Then there's the surprising fact that Stacey and company know that indigo is Orah's kryptonite. I assumed they didn't know about it, didn't even know the flower existed. Have they done an intervention? Or have they given up on her?

"I'm sorry." I'm a ball of shame. "I wasn't expecting Mike to follow us out here." But when I think about it, I really did. I just forgot for a while because of my laser focus on my *plan*. My thinking process is all crosshatched and zigzagged and making no flipping sense. Am I blind because of greed? Or because of all the poison in my system? I should have stopped the whole thing before we got to this point. Oh, Finn, you have reached a whole new level of stupid. You've compromised the location of the crypt, you nearly got Orah killed, all because you need a drug that will get Faith out of here.

I listen to the wind swoosh and whisper (shhhh, keep quiet now) through the leaves. I'm only seeing blackbirds around here, no color, no variation.

"How am I going to pay for my sister's education?" I ask myself this, not realizing I'm speaking out loud. My anger at the situation is coming up full force, but it's Orah who explodes.

"Is that all you're thinking about?" she yells, slapping her hand on the ground. "We're done. Consider this *over*."

I sit up, and my head swims, unnerved by her watery, power-packed eyes. "What do you mean this is over? We just *began*. I mean, I can talk to Mike, and we can come to an agreement." God, the words sound so lame coming out, I know, I don't mean to be so damn . . .

"These young men don't seem to be the diplomatic type," she says flatly.

The muscles in my chest contract. I want to kill them for laying a hand on her, for ruining this endeavor. My throat is burning, my body limp, one big flat tire, time to pull this clunker off the road. I struggle to my feet, more shooting stars galore, and help her up too. I'm bitter, toward Mike, toward her, toward myself, toward the stupid blue sky and the long-armed trees.

"You don't have to be involved anymore," I say.

She looks at me straight on. "That wasn't our deal. Don't you see? This arrangement is for both of us. For me it's about watching indigo slowly vanish . . . I need that to start over again, even though at one time it helped me start over again after Page's death. And you—"

"What about me?" I challenge.

"Apart from the money, you mean? You don't mind my company. You don't mind the talking. The stories."

This comment jars me because it's so true. "I'll still hang out with you," I say, then wince at my word choice. Who uses the word "hang out" under these circumstances?

"Hang out?" That grin, man, that grin isn't anything to smile about. "Hang *out*? It's only a matter of time before my son-in-law catches us. Now that the word is out . . . I didn't realize this put us in harm's way. I thought you'd sell it quick enough that it wouldn't even matter. And to think you'd want to continue now, after what happened?"

"I guess you underestimated indigo. And you underestimated *me*." I know I sound cold, but she doesn't get it, she just doesn't.

She slinks away from me, *slinks*, that's the only verb to describe it, as if she doesn't want to brush up against me, contaminated Finn, as if she wants to slide right past the unraveling seam. I walk after her, but it only seems right that we don't walk side by side, that I'm stuck behind, following, because what a dick move it is to argue against her, say, hey grandma, let's put you in danger even more by continuing this. Even as my head pulses with pain. Even as my knuckles leak with blood. You're a sick puppy, Finn. Sick. Yet continue I want, I want it so bad, we were onto something, we *were*, we are, and those stories, the magic, man, wouldn't *you* have a hard time letting go?

MONDAY, MAY 20

CHAPTER THIRTY

THOUGH DAYS HAVE PASSED, I'M STILL SHAKEN UP BY THE MIKE ENCOUNTER. What's going to happen now? Nothing good seems to be a trend of late. As I walk down the hallway at school—with no indigo to sell—I'm trying to ignore the vibes coming from indigo users. The forgetfulness and general haziness. The quietest girl—who was so vibrant a week ago—isn't talking anymore in class; it seems like no one is talking anymore. Everyone is floating through the world between hits. I'm beginning to notice that Bryce is more out of it than usual too—always forgetting his keys, misplacing his hat, staring into space for long periods of time . . . I guess paradise wouldn't be paradise if you could go there all the time. I thought I was helping everyone, but I don't know anymore. Maybe I was helping them to forget everything except what was in the past, in the pursuit of Faith's future and mine. As they float through, I'm tempted to float along with them, do a line of coke, pop another pill, catch whatever wave I can to escape.

I'm in front of my locker when I feel fingers clamp down on my arm. I turn around and see Stacey who looks like the perfect definition of pissed off—figures she would ace at being angry. I'm kind of enthused just her being around me, though this disgusts me, getting all worked up even when she wants to tear my balls off. I'm a pig of the highest order. She slams me into my locker, her green *I will cut you* eyes up in my face, I've never had a girl be so aggressive and mean it for real. Except maybe Faith.

"Can I help you?" I ask, half smirking, half smiling. I've been told this is a good look for me. She's totally not buying it. She reaches into her pocket and slams something against my chest. It slides down my shirt, and I catch it before it hits the ground. A baggie of indigo. Fuck me. Of course this was going to happen.

"Where'd you get this?" I ask. An instant shot of sweaty and uncomfortable.

"It doesn't matter," she says, smacking my chest again. I step to the side, away from her unpredictable hands.

"Whoa, whoa, I haven't done anything wrong," I say, cramming the indigo into my back pocket.

All of a sudden her face crumples. This is the only time—besides the pig incident—I've seen her tough façade break. I want to take her into my arms and put her back together again. Of course this was going to happen sooner or later, and I should have planned for an indisputable rationalization. *My sister, she needs my help; Orah, she needs a friend; and me, I like the rush of dealing drugs. The headiness of potential danger. Plus I was going to stop, I swear.* It all sounds so grandly lame and worn out, even in my head.

"*Indigo*, Finn. At first when it hit the school, I thought it was the other strain called flower circulating around . . . and then I take a close look at this—the deeper blue color? Nothing looks like that, besides what we have in our family. Everyone thinks it's the best thing ever, right?" She's breathing hard through her nose, and it's not unattractive, not in the least.

I'm bowled over by the fact she knows about flower. Orah had told me that Stacey was aware of her addiction of indigo, but this is making me wonder what else Stacey knows.

"Things are complicated, I can explain."

She groans. Students move around her, barely glancing, they don't want their ogling too obvious. She's still a hot topic these days. New girl. Out of everyone's league. You can look but you can't touch.

She wrenches me by the wrist—*ouch*—to a semiprivate area underneath the stairway where some rather shady business has gone down. Groping, dealing, cheating, all that good stuff. Never made an indigo drop there, though, too conspicuous. But here's Stacey, in the shadow of the staircase, pulling something from her backpack. A bright-red wallet. Fumbling around inside it. She slides out a rectangle and slaps it into my hand.

"Look," she says, as if my life depends on it.

In my hand is a picture of a guy, maybe around my age, maybe a little older. Good-looking dude, I guess, if you want to go there, green eyes, light brown hair, all-knowing smirk kind of like mine, with a ghastly scar on the left side of his face. Spreading from his forehead to his cheek down to his neck— *waaaaay* worse than mine. I know without looking too hard that it's a burn scar, and that similarity hurts.

"This is Billy," she says, accentuating his name, pointing at the photo in my hand. "My *brother*. Mimi's grandson."

"Why—"

"Don't even," she says, holding her hand up to shush me. "Don't even say a word. The reason why he is the way he is? Because of this drug you're peddling. The reason why he isn't

a part of our family anymore? Because of this drug you're peddling. The reason why my whole family is in danger? Because
of this drug you're peddling." Stacey impatiently swipes a tear
off her face; she's clearly repulsed at herself for getting this
upset. I wish I could embrace her. I wish I could understand.

"What happened to him?" I ask, but she's not listening.

"I don't think you're working with Billy—he's in a place
where he won't be found. Where he doesn't *want* to be found.
The only explanation is that you're working with Mimi. I know
she uses indigo—or used to. We *all* know she does even though
we don't talk about it. I just didn't think she was going to partner up for a business venture." She throws her hands up in the
air with exasperation. "She's not in her right mind, obviously.
Want to know why? *Because of this drug you're peddling.* Years
of abuse and she thinks that it's a good idea to team up with
you, without thinking of the consequences. She doesn't *think*.
She *can't* think. Indigo screws with your head. Just like every
other drug out there. It tempts, it thrills, it feasts. She's on
her way down, Finn. My brother's already there. Looks like
you're following."

I'm not doing indigo, I think, though I'm doing everything
else under the sun. Obviously I don't say this. Also, her comment about indigo screwing with your head? Immediate guilt
rips through me when I think of the students' recent behavior.

"Oh, and how about this," she continues, her cheeks
flushed. "A year ago an associate of a drug kingpin caught Billy
dosing up on indigo. Billy was working at a pizza place in the
city backed by said criminal and was stupid enough to get high
on his break—not that he knew he was collecting his paychecks
from a gangster. The gangster's associate thought he saw a
piece of paper appear out of nowhere, right in front of Billy as

he was flying high . . . that magic that goes along with it, you know? The associate grabbed it and realized that it was a lottery ticket. He realized that the drug was going to be a gold mine. It goes without saying that the drug king found out about the powder, and that's when the trouble for my family began."

"Orah never told me about this. And you're talking about Early, right?"

She steps back, surprised, assessing me, assessing what she should tell me next. "Orah isn't aware of the gang ties. And yes, it's Early. And you need to hear the whole story so you understand how royally you fucked up."

"Sure, okay," I say quietly. I want to hear everything, I have to hear everything. This is my chance to learn about the notorious Early—finally.

Stacey looks at her hands, strong and steady, doctor's hands. "Early and his people were up my family's ass. Late-night phone calls, letters, drive-bys and dead animals on our front doorstep, until my dad got scared, and my dad doesn't scare easily. So he and Billy took them to a cemetery plot outside of New York where Billy was growing the flower, and they taught Early how to grow the flowers on Early's own property. My dad figured that if Early could grow his own supply of indigo, he wouldn't bother us again."

"But I thought indigo was only from Klaski DNA?" I ask. I'm confused, this is too much to take in, the mob growing its own indigo because Stacey's dad showed them a new cemetery—another site for indigo?

"When Billy was fourteen, he saw Orah snorting it. He wouldn't leave her alone about it until she finally gave in and told him she'd gotten it from our mother's gravesite. I guess he figured out it had to do with the bones, or Orah told him. I don't know. But we didn't live with Orah then, so he dug up the roots of some of the plants of Mom's gravesite and took them home with him. He experimented planting it on the gravesites of this cemetery outside the city. The little roots manage to seep into the tiniest cracks of the coffins. The bones nourished them and the flowers grew, although they weren't as strong as the ones from our mother's grave. By the time he was our age, he was addicted. Now that he's twenty, you can imagine that he's not in the best shape. The drug seems okay at first, it makes you happy, but then it turns against you, just like any drug."

Okay, she clearly knew a lot more than Orah. So I ask her what had been weighing on my mind ever since I encountered indigo. "So do you think the virus or whatever causes the Klaskis to die is what is in indigo and what makes it so powerful?"

My question calms her down. Now we're into the realm of science, her realm.

"Maybe. Or maybe everyone has the virus, and it's just lying dormant. Ever heard of the insanity virus? Scientists theorize that we all have a virus that leads to schizophrenia, and it could be triggered by something like the flu. So it could be that our family just has a really virulent strain of it for some reason, and it actually kills us and causes the flowers to grow."

"But the lottery ticket that appeared when Billy tripped out?" And Bryce's Gatorade? I don't tell her about the smell of pinecones on my hands.

She jumps on this, excited. "Science is fact-based; researchers haven't even begun to think about the metaphysical. That's what I want to do when I'm a doctor, to see what else exists out there that we don't understand yet."

Is this an alternate universe I've found myself in? She doesn't want to clobber me anymore, she wants to actually talk to me, about her past, her future.

She sighs, and goes back to her story. "My dad didn't interfere when Early ran his flower game in the city, and he left us alone. But Billy disappeared, and my dad felt we should move here with Orah, and maybe help save one person in the family. It seemed like it was over, we were done with it. But now things are going to change if Early catches wind of indigo in D-Town. He considers this drug to be his, no matter whose bones it came from. You're in danger, Finn." She swallows, I freeze.

This is an overload of information for me to process. I knew I was in danger when it came to Mike—but she's really driving the point home that there are bigger issues at play here. Mike's business is beans in comparison to Early's enterprise.

"I didn't know. I—"

She interrupts. "I shouldn't be aware of all this, but I put the pieces together from what Billy and my father told me. Mimi doesn't know, has no clue about all the crap my dad went through in the city. We *all* wanted to shield her, even though she started it all by telling Billy about the drug."

I'm feeling a little defensive now. Orah is my pal, my partner. I don't want her to be the reason for all of this. She just wanted to get rid of the stuff, to start over. I'm the one who fucked up, not her. I open my mouth to say this, but Stacey jumps in.

"She's not thinking. What she's doing with you, it's just because she wants Billy back. She wants a grandson again. She thinks you're him. I mean she knows you're not, not all the time. But it's like you're filling a hole in her. I love her, but it's crazy what she's doing."

I'm shaken now. Is Orah doing all this because she wants to think I'm someone else? She doesn't really care about me? Now I feel like I'm wrong about everything. All I can do is try to fix this.

"I have contacts, I can make a deal with Early. We'll come to an agreement. The city is one territory—why would he care about D-Town?"

Stacey laughs. It's harsh, it grinds, there's so much strength behind it, so much—

Stacey-ness.

"Make a deal? Who are you? You can't make a deal with Early. He's straight-up OG. Original gangster. He'll want control of the better strain right away. He'll want it all. He'll have no reason to negotiate with you. You have no clout."

It's sinking in. This isn't a Mike we're talking about. This is an Al Capone. I'm fucked.

She's nodding, seeing the panic break out on my face. "I feel so stupid that I didn't figure out it was you and Orah sooner. I heard about people using it in school, I saw them using it, but I thought the gangster's version had managed to work its way up from the city to here. And then this morning, when I took a look at this—" She lifts up the bag of indigo. "I knew that wasn't the case. This is what Orah uses. And now you're dealing it."

At this point she's glaring at me again. I knew it had to come back around to this, but I'm feeling ashamed and defensive. "You don't know . . ." I start.

She shoots a look of contempt at me that shuts me up fast. "Every particle of me wants to rat you out to my father. That it's *you* who started this mess. But Mimi is involved too, and that makes it more complicated. She can't be tied up in this."

I think about Mike, about how Orah must have hidden the bruises on her neck somehow when she went home. She's *already* tied up in this. "I swear to you, I'll make it right," I say firmly, testosterone surging. And I mean it too. I'll take the heat, because I can figure this out. That's what I do, that's my thing. I'd save her before I'd save myself, I really would.

With bitterness she says, "You're *so* naïve, Finn. I know you've got some major issues, Faith has told me a lot. And I'm not saying that I'm a model case in good mental health. But *you* resorted to drugs. Mimi and Billy—*they* resorted to drugs. You know what *I* resorted to? *Nothing.* I resorted to *living.* To *dealing* with it. To accepting that there is no perfect remedy. You've got to wade through the shit, face the world. Cowards. That's what you all are. Fucking cowards."

She's right. I feel evil, fit for hell, but there's part of me that wants sympathy too, that wants a pat on the back for trying to do something good with all this bad.

"Me dealing indigo?" I whisper. "It isn't for me. It's for Faith."

"She doesn't want your help. At least not like this." She almost spits it.

"You don't know anything about my sister," I snap. *I'm* the one who held my sister's hand while we waited for the ambulance, who sat with her in the hospital day after day.

She smiles tightly. "I know that Faith had a panic attack last night. Peter and I thought we were going to have to bring her to the hospital. You know what we'd been talking about? *You.* We were talking about what a mess you are and that Faith feels hopeless about how to help you."

It takes effort to think of a rebuttal for this. It takes effort to think. People talking behind my back, my sister and

Peter—now Stacey. The three of them are ganging up on me, and there's nothing I can do about it. All I'm feeling is betrayal. Betrayal and loss.

Stacey plows on. She's relentless, she wants nothing left of me. "I can't believe I went on a date with you. I can't believe I thought that this," she says, gesturing at the space between us, "would work."

I wince. "Give me another chance."

"It's too late."

The bell rings for class, startling me. She's getting ready to leave. This is it. So I say the only words I can think of, the ones that I mean.

"I'm sorry," I say. She shrugs and walks away. They don't mean anything to her.

And now there really is nothing left. She hates me. Faith hates me, and so does Peter. I've endangered Orah. I've gotten involved with a drug kingpin. The classroom I'm supposed to be in I've already passed, and I'm reaching for the keys to my car, wanting nothing more than to get home, shoot up, shut my eyes, shut myself down for a while. Besides, I know what I have to do. Just like I told Stacey, I have to find Early.

CHAPTER THIRTY-ONE

I COME OUT OF MY HAZE WHEN FAITH GETS HOME FROM SCHOOL. She throws her bag and jacket on the bed, and as she goes back out to the bathroom, I rummage through the bag trying to find her iPhone. I've got a plan. Can't find the phone, though. I scoop through books, papers, eye shadow—tons of eye shadow—*no, no, no. Grrrrr.* Her jacket. Pawing through her pockets. Got it. I hear the toilet flush. Goddammit.

The first thing I see is a text from Peter:

R u coming over? I can't stop thinking about u.

I take a moment to collect myself because first, I don't like thinking about my sister with other dudes, and second, it's *Peter.* Origami crane-making, sporadic stoner, highly attuned and intuitive Peter. Not that I think there's anything wrong with him, or them together for that matter. That's not the point. He didn't tell me, she didn't tell me. All this shit they're hiding from me; I'm getting sick of it. What else is she not telling me? I grab the two oxys I have in my pocket and pop them in my mouth. *Aaaah.* The warmth. The relief. It feels like home.

I hear Faith coming out of the bathroom. I scroll through her contacts, see Jason's name and number, and fire off a quick text to him:

D-Town Diner. 9 pm tonight.

He's going to piss himself when he sees it's Faith sending the message. It grosses me out, thinking about the thrilled look on his face when he gets the text, but I don't dwell on it. I delete my sent message and delete Jason's insanely fast response (*ok . . . c u soon*), sneak her cell phone back into her pocket, and throw myself back on my bed just as she comes in. She stands there in the middle of the floor, eyeing me. I sit up and wait for some kind of snarky comment or scolding about my behavior—Stacey has probably already told her about the shit storm I've gotten myself in with indigo and gangsters. Or maybe she doesn't want to involve Faith and is keeping it under wraps. Who knows?

The eye patch Faith wears today is suitable for school—it's black with sparkly purple around the edge— but not at home where she likes to be comfortable. There's a sky blue one that she likes, the texture of satin, and that's the one she's reaching for now after she sets the books on her desk. I can sometimes gauge her mood by her eye patch—today I'm coming up with nothing.

"Stacey hates me," I say, curious of her reaction.

Faith snickers as she looks at herself in the mirror, straightening the patch. I know she doesn't look at herself out of vanity—I think she's searching for something in her reflection, maybe she's checking on her anxiety to see if it's receding or if it's pushing through. She doesn't think I notice her deer-in-headlights look in the school hallway or the worry that hits her face for a split second when she hears Pop's voice. The anxiety attack she had at Peter's is just going to lead to more. I wonder if he took care of her. I wonder if he knew what to do in the first place.

"She has every right to," she says to me in the mirror.

I collapse on my bed. My comforter feels like a dream, and my body is light, ghostlike, a flame's flicker away from good night. Go ahead Faith, talk your head off.

She's right on cue. "Do you remember when we were twelve, and you just discovered alcohol? You and Bryce would steal liquor from Bryce's grandparents every Saturday, and they would never notice?"

"What's your point?" I mumble, barely knowing the language that's coming out of my mouth. Her smile is distant, not meant for me. Or at least not the now me.

"You used to hide the bottles underneath your bed before you got smart and started putting your stash underneath the floorboards."

She pulls her fingers through her long hair. My disjointed memories of those days still feel close—the first time I got drunk was on rum and Cokes at Peter's house: lots of laughing about nothing, stumbling into furniture, rough-housing until we broke a lamp and two glasses. I puked so much the next morning I popped blood vessels underneath my eyes. I wait, floating, for her to continue.

"You were so mad when you found all your liquor gone one day after school. And when you went back to the grandparents' house, they had locked up their liquor cabinet."

I nod languidly, remembering all of this, even through the haze of my all-encompassing, knockout OC high.

"I was so pissed, dude. Anyway, you got drunk with me, a few times. Hello, selective memory." My arm's up for a moment, gesticulating, but then it collapses with a *thunk*. Lead bones, lead brain, I think to myself, or rather, I not-think.

She closes her eye, and her face is a mixture of sadness and disappointment. "*I* was the one who got rid of your alcohol, Phineas. I was the one who made up a story when I ran into Bryce's grandparents at the grocery store that they should lock up all their cabinets because there had been burglaries around their neighborhood. You know how gullible they were."

I sit up, too fast, I see stars by the time I'm upright.

"*You*," I say, barely feeling my lips from the high. "*You* told Stacey I'm dealing indigo." It's staggering I'm not even mad. Thank you OC.

Faith nibbles a finger. "Well, she pretty much knew but yeah, I did. She asked if it was you, and I told her, because maybe she'll get through to you since I can't."

I don't say anything, and she hovers over me. "You know what? Forget it. You are totally zonked right now." Tired disappointment is in her voice.

There is silence as I let this marinate. Then I start to laugh. "You bet I am, sister. I don't even fucking care. Go ahead, sabotage my relationships. Sabotage *me*." Another wave of laughter erupts from me. "How did you know it was me?" I ask. I cup my hand over my mouth. It does nothing to quell the giggles.

"Peter told me." She crosses her arms over her chest and leans back against the wall next to her bed, facing me.

"Peter!" I exclaim in complete hysterics, cackling until my gut hurts. She narrows her eye and examines me. Do I tell her I know about her and Peter? I decide against it because I'm tired, and frankly, I just don't care. Those two can ride off into the sunset together on their high and mighty horses. Orah asks me why I do drugs? For shit like this. For what I can't handle and for which I need a buffer, and what better buffer is there than an instant cushion of oblivion?

"I'll admit I've seen the things that indigo can do. Or

231

maybe it's because I've heard about its magic. It could be the power of suggestion," Faith says, her tone turning serious. "I witnessed Peter dosed up on indigo . . . afterward he started talking all this nonsense, didn't make a lick of sense. I'm glad he's laying off the stuff now."

"You've been hanging out with him a lot, haven't you?" I ask, I can't resist. Maybe she'll tell me without any prompting.

She brushes me off and continues, "It was nighttime, but I swear a scratch appeared out of nowhere on his hand that wasn't there before. The rest of the day, he wasn't all there. Saying all this weird shit about some chick—he dropped a name. Nancy, or something like that. The cut started to bleed. *Bleed*." Her breath is a gust from her half-open mouth. "Indigo is border-line evil, brother. That's some voodoo nastiness right there. You're spreading it, and it's only going to come back to you in the worst of ways."

If only she knew it already was. I sigh. My high, my fickle friend, isn't going to last very long, I can already see the front edge of it backing away, and I imagine myself holding a gun up to its face. Don't you dare move. Not until I tell you to.

"Nancy," I say, fidgeting with my comforter. "That was his babysitter. When we were like nine, she was the first girl we ever got a hard-on for." Even though the scratch probably hurt him, his crush on Nancy was enough to cancel out any pain. I can see why this is one of his favorite memories. The comfort of being taken care of. The simplicity of being a kid again.

"That's gross." She makes a face.

"Well, whatever. I can handle the situation. I'm handling it as we speak."

Suddenly she's grabbing at my arm, pulling my sleeve up. "Just like you're handling that?" she says, pointing at the track marks. I didn't think they looked that bad. I mean, they really don't, and the light's kind of bright in our room, and there are only a few slight bruises. I vow to myself, here and now, that I won't be doing H for a very long time.

Instead of yelling and screaming and calling the cops and thirty rehab facilities, she sits next to me and presses down the knuckle of my forefinger, so my finger is straight, just like she used to do when we were little, to get me to pay attention. *Pay attention, Phineas.* She used to do it during long car rides when she liked the way the autumn trees looked. Or when we'd hear Mom and Pop fight. Or when we're out with friends, and I'm acting up. The pressure right now is hard and unrelenting. I'm surprised by the solidness of her hand. I tell her with my eyes, you don't understand, you don't get the deep, dark, black, crypt coffin that's made its home inside me, digging its roots deep into my core. She tells me with her eye that she *does* know, but she won't accept this is how it has to be, because we're so alike and that should carry me past the crypt and past the core straight to the other side, the Faith side, to a color of the rainbow where I'll sit and wait for the next color and the next and the next. That spectrum that Orah was talking about. I think to myself: just let me do this thing, ride this out, Faith. She nods, I nod, we're twins, we get it. She's not going to give up on me just yet, but she also knows there is only so much she can do to help her beyond-damaged brother. As if to tell me this, she won't let up on my knuckle, she keeps holding it down, harder and harder until we're both red in the face, eyes locked, minds locked on all these things, the things we don't say.

CHAPTER THIRTY-TWO

THE D-TOWN QUEEN DINER IS KNOWN FOR SERVING UP GREASE WITH A SIDE OF FRIES. Jason loves it there, and I know for a fact he goes every week to gorge on cheeseburgers and milk shakes. My bird watching to his binge-fest. I've known this about him for a while, and he never gains weight. Some time has passed since I kicked the crap out of him, so I might have more luck pumping him for information about Early now than I did before.

When I arrive five minutes before nine o'clock, he's looking about 80 percent Neanderthal, give or take. Scrawnier, scruffier, straggly black hair down to his chin, clothes that look more like rags. Whatever state of mind he's in might work for me or against me, I'm not sure, but I have to make things right. He's balls deep in texting on his iPhone, so it gives me a chance to plunk right down in the booth next to him so he can't get out. It takes him a second to turn and realize that Faith didn't decide he's the love of her life.

"Fuck. You," he says, trying to get up to leave.

"Sit the fuck down," I say. He's halfway standing when I slam him back to his seat. "I want to help you." I have him *so* trapped, unless he wants to hop over the table and cause a scene.

"No, you want *me* to help *you*," he says, eyes hardening, "I need to get in touch with Early. I have an inkling that you know how I can."

"I'm not doing this," he says, attempting to push me out of the way, but I'm parked and not going anywhere.

I clasp my hands together on the sticky table, all professional-like, putting on my serious voice. I'll have to tell Jason what I know, so he can help me out with what I don't know.

"I've come to several conclusions. This guy Early is slinging shit-imitation indigo I guess they're calling flower down in the city. He's going to find out that Mike is selling the premium stuff that's from the more potent strain. *Stolen*, mind you, from me. Early isn't going to believe that Mike grew indigo himself, once he starts asking questions, trust me. He'll make Mike tell him about yours truly and how *I* was the one selling it first, even though I'm not anymore. Mike tapped me out."

I don't tell him that I *could* still sell indigo if I wanted to. And I do have to be careful about selling it in the future, so he doesn't discover that I'm in fact *not* tapped out. Orah gave me the key to the crypt, and there is plenty left. I'm still determined to make money for Faith for college; I could also help her expand her eye patch business. The potential is there. I need to tell Early that there's a way we can split the indigo trade before he tries to assassinate me or something. I'm not sure how I'm going to convince him of this—at least not yet anyway, but I can improvise, I can surely think of something.

It's not going to be easy. I'm well aware that Early will ask why my product's got more punch. He's going to want to see the crypt and every other site where the Klaski indigo grows. Then what am I going to do? How am I going to find out the locations without getting Orah and her family involved?

Jason chomps down on a burger that's surely gone cold and soggy. Limp lettuce reminds me of Pop's middle-of-the-night bologna sandwich. I steal a French fry and shove it in my mouth. Jason stink-eyes me.

I have to be careful of what I reveal and what I don't reveal in this conversation. The effect of the oxys died down hours ago, so I'm sobered up, mind clear, ready to do some interrogative work on Jason and un-cluster this cluster fuck.

"If Early catches wind of Mike's connection to indigo, he'll kill him," I say, figuring Jason'll do what he can to save Mike.

"Early," he says. "You for real? How do you know what Early's gonna do?" He's got a thousand crumpled up napkins around his plate and crumbs on his mouth. Not his finest moment.

"I have my sources. I need to talk to him. Negotiate."

"Bullshit. You're going to negotiate for no one else besides yourself."

"And you're lucky that I'm trying to help out your old bro by giving him a heads up on my plan to contact Early. After ganking my shit and assaulting . . . my . . . friend," I trail off.

That word . . . friend . . . it's so . . . it doesn't even cover it. After the Mike fiasco, Orah and I sat across from each other at another diner in another town. We both refused to go to the hospital, instead deciding upon coffee (me) and Earl Grey tea (her) as the cure. Our conversation was lighthearted, about her family (mostly Billy before drugs), about the subjects I like in school (English and biology), and the dialogue was such that I could be myself, be normal, be all right. We both forgot about the preceding events and sank into the rhythm of our chatter. Midday morning clouds parted by the time we left.

Jason's mouth is full, food bulging out his cheeks. "That's right, Mikey told me about that. Shit, dude, you into geriatrics now?"

"Blow me," I say, popping another fry in my mouth. It's deliciously disgusting. "You can't go choke-holding an old lady like that. Don't you people have any manners? Any respect?"

"Dude, don't even *talk* to me about choke-holding," he says, rolling his eyes. I slide in closer to the window, locking him into his space even more. He scowls. All he can do is sip on his milk shake like a fucking toddler.

"Let's not get off topic here. Early."

Jason slams down his milk shake and picks up his phone. "You're going to be sorry you ever came here." He starts dialing, but I'm kung-fu fast and have his phone in my hands right quick.

Jason pounds his fists on the table, the silverware shakes, the milk shake in his cup sloshes. Everyone glares at us. It's dark outside, but the windows are reflecting the light from the dessert case, the fluorescents over the counter seating, the other diners' faces are in various stages of annoyance.

"Come on, man," Jason says quietly. His black hair grazes over his eyes.

I smirk. "Are you getting sick of me yet?"

"Yet? I was sick of you the day you came out of your mom's skank-afied vagina." A piece of food flings from his mouth.

I do an eye-roll scoff and pull out a paper lunch bag from my backpack. I'm not sure if the timing is right for this move, but I don't want to jerk around any longer than I have to. In it is two hundred dollars' worth of heroin. Indigo is becoming like currency now—I was able to trade some for H, an arrangement my dealer, Carter, was psyched about. He's not a stand-up dude, but he knows an opportunity when he sees it. Plus he's got street cred. He lives in D-Town Heights, and everyone knows to stay out of his way.

"This is for you. I know how much you like this stuff, especially the kind that Carter sells." I cross my arms over my chest. He peeks into the bag, and though he's trying to guard his reaction, I see the shock over the amount and the white-hot yearning for it, a yearning I'm having myself but trying not to show either—shoulders no longer slumped, still frowning but not as tightly. He's entranced.

He tucks the H next to him, but his fingers stay latched around the rolled-up edges of the bag. I choose the cleanest used napkin I can find on the table to wipe the grease off my hands. Jason has the gall to call to the waitress.

"Hey, what's it going to take to get my check around here?" he asks, two fingers up high.

"Man, listen, I just need to know how to reach him," I say. "That's it. Then we're done."

Jason pauses, then he starts to crack up, in one of those silent but full-bodied laughs, when you don't know if someone might be choking or having a heart attack.

He gathers himself. "*You* don't find Early," he says, knocking his knuckles on the table. "Early finds *you*."

"Oh God," I say, rubbing my temples. "Could you *be* any more dramatic?" The waitress waddles to the table, slaps down the bill. Jason checks out her forty-year-old ass as she leaves. Christ, I think, as a waitress, Mom must deal with this punk-ass behavior on the regular. No wonder she wants to stay on the couch her entire life.

"You don't get it, dude." Jason says. "Early's always looking to grow his business. I know that indigo is new, and it's not even having an effect on his profits, but it will eventually, and he'll do anything to prevent that. It's not just the city, he wants the whole state."

Jason goes on to say that as it stands now, Mike and Early have an understanding to stay out of each other's way—Mike supplies weed for much of New York State, Early supplies the harder stuff that manages to make its way up to D-Town: heroin, cocaine, meth. Mike never wanted to get into the heavier stuff—until his crop started failing, and I introduced him to indigo.

Jason continues. "Rumors are going around that Early is killing people so he can fertilize the ground with their bones so the flowers will grow. Mike heard about how he tortured a nark who was working with the DEA. Hung him up by a meat hook and chopped off pieces of him, one by one, like some tribal shit. This isn't just some dude trying to get paid off, man, he's the real deal." He takes a huge bite of his hamburger and looks out the window, chewing aggressively.

"I am becoming more and more aware of that fact, trust me." And I am. I don't even want any of those disgusting fries anymore. They're looking like bones, and the ketchup oozing from Jason's mouth is looking like blood.

After some coaxing, I finally get more information, and unless Jason is feeding me BS, I'm getting an ultradose of in-over-my-head. Early—birth name Mario Coletti—is apparently this supernatural g-force of a person who will fuck you up just by blinking. He started off his stellar career by stealing cars when he was fourteen and holding a person for ransom when he was fifteen. When he was sixteen, he killed a man for not paying the hundred-dollar debt that was due to him. That's how he earned his name—nobody's late with Early. *Boy, oh boy.* When he wasn't killing anyone, he worked at his cousin's pizza joint in Queens, a front for drug trafficking and other illegal shenanigans. This must have been the pizza place that employed Billy when he was discovered taking a line of indigo.

I'm not that shocked I haven't heard of Early before. I deal weed, which means I only deal with Mike's guys. The harder stuff, well, I didn't start using until this year, and Carter is a freelancer and real hush-hush about his supplier.

"So if Mike knows that Early is pretty much a madman, then what's *his* plan? What does he want to do with the indigo he stole from me?"

Jason wipes his mouth with the back of his hand. "He wants to talk to Early about partnering up with indigo distribution. Why do you want to talk to him?"

Huh, that was my plan.

Mike has no idea that the bone in Orah's garden was a deer bone. He doesn't know about the crypt or the Klaski history or the other potential indigo sites. He doesn't know that it's the Klaski bones that make my version so much better.

I nail him down with my eyes. "Never mind about that. Just tell me where I can find him."

"Whatever, it's your funeral. If you do find him, he's not going to talk to you."

I make a sour face. Jason sighs. "Fine. He owns Ti's Pizzeria and Café, on Bank Street in Schenectady. Good luck finding him there—I've heard he spends most of the time in the city. He wants to keep a low profile. People don't know him, they just know *of* him."

The waitress comes by again for the check. He doesn't tip her well. He shoves his wallet in his back pocket, scrawny arm all tracked up, causing me to self-consciously check my own.

Luckily I was with it enough today to wear long sleeves. I slide out of the booth to let him get out. I chuck over his phone that I confiscated, then throw down some more change for the waitress.

"You decide to pursue this, you'll be dead in a week," Jason says. The door chimes its obnoxious noise as he leaves.

I got what I came to get. Early's whereabouts. Now I need to refine my plan—and there isn't any room for mistakes.

TUESDAY, MAY 21

CHAPTER THIRTY-THREE

IT'S TUESDAY NIGHT, WHICH IS LIKE, THE MOST INNOCUOUS NIGHT EVER. Who does anything of real importance on a Tuesday night? Come on. Well apparently *this* guy does, because as I'm pumping gas in my car, a middle-aged hot chick is about to approach me, looking all *Friday* night, in tight jeans, V-neck T-shirt, and done-up blond hair. Then it's like she changes her mind because she turns around, walks toward a silver Jetta. I shrug my shoulders and check the pump. Whoops, there she goes, facing me a second time, scrunching up her face, narrowing her eyes, trying to decide. I raise my eyebrows.

Finally she comes over and says, "Hey, I know you."

"Yeah?"

"Finn. You must be Finn. I recognize you from hanging around my son. Spencer? You're the one with the bird tattoo." She's closer now, and I get a whiff of lilac perfume or lotion or some other girly varietal. Fucking Spencer, really? This kid's so lame he makes Jason look like a superhero.

"That would be me," I say, leaning against the side of my car. "And your name is?" I reach out my hand for a shake; her fingers are soft and way too breakable.

"Claire," she says, pearly whites not disappointing in the parking lot light. She shifts her weight, I notice her sandals are silver, a style a little too young for a mom, but maybe that's the point.

"So this may sound a little odd, but my son, he won't stop talking about this . . . I don't know what it is . . . maybe an herb? This holistic remedy that's been going around at the high school. I have to admit . . . I tried some . . . and it's . . . wonderful." Her breath catches in her throat, and she touches my car with the tips of her manicured fingernails. Pale pink. Real classy.

"Herb, huh?" I say. "That's what your son told you? And he dropped my name?"

Her face pops a deep crimson. "No, he didn't give away your name, but I've seen you with him, seen you with the other boys when I drop him off at school . . . and well, you look—"

"I look like what, now?" I feel my own blush of shame rising up, but I've got claws to swat it down.

"Oh no, no, that's not what I meant. I'm simply just asking around. Do you have any clue about it?" She brings her hand up to her collarbones, where she fidgets with a heart charm on a thin, gold-chained necklace.

A jet stream of brilliance flows through me, an idea, though inchoate, is beginning to solidify.

"I might have a clue," I say, but nothing more. I want to make her squirm, but the truth is, I can tell she's the type of lady who's been squirming most of her life.

"It's just," she says, still fiddling with that chain. "Well, I've noticed the difference, in Spencer. Even myself, after one try." Her voice is getting stronger the more she talks. "It's been a rough time, for me, and for my family . . ."

"I'm sorry to hear that," I say, leaning, crossing my ankle over my sneaker.

Then it's all happening so quick, she yanks my hand to her chest where I'm expecting to feel boob, but all I'm feeling is flat. The material of her shirt is silky, and her chest is warm. But it's her stance that tears me a new one. Unapologetic. Proud. Our eyes meet, tangle up, and I fight against the internal sting of it. She's telling me how it is, by saying nothing at all. I don't want to hug her, I want to *embrace* her, *envelop* her, give her what pathetic strength I have, maybe she can make something out of it.

She releases me. "The surgery was painful, and the chemo is horrendous. Medical marijuana is hard to get, and I don't want to get addicted to pain pills," she says, brushing a lock of blonde hair—that I now assume must be a wig—from her face. I nod, I got heartstrings, they've been *thoroughly* pulled.

"How 'bout this," I say. It's all coming together, all the pieces in this jigsaw are falling into place. "You get all your friends together, and we'll have a party. An indigo party. Order pizza, drink some wine. Is this sounding reasonable?" I ask. I'm hoping so, because the party will be my way of contacting Early, while at the same time profiting from a bunch of ladies who need an escape from life. Will it work? Am I being too rash?

She has to ruminate on it for a minute (just as I am); I see her scrolling through her contacts in her head. I can tell she's in the mindset of full speed ahead. No time to waste.

I reassure her. "It'll be spiritual, you and your best friends, a bonding moment, better than therapy. You've been through hell. I get it." I look at her with sympathetic eyes (but not too sympathetic) and reach out to touch her necklace, I can't believe I'm doing it until after I'm doing it. I'm not laying game, I'm really not, but it feels like a button that should be pushed. She looks down at the pavement, then at me, and nudges me away.

"Friday afternoon," she says. "Three o'clock. Bring enough. There's a lot of pain to go around."

I shake her hand with both of mine. Strength in those manicured fingers. She gives me her address and number. When she walks to her car, her initial nervousness is past tense, her posture is straight, strong, steel. This is the benefit of hope: sometimes you inherit that don't-fuck-with-me swagger.

CHAPTER THIRTY-FOUR

I'M IN MY CAR, AT MEADOW LANE PARK BY MYSELF, GETTING BAKED. The conversation with Spencer's hot mom is an hour behind me, and I'm going over my plan, but my mind keeps wandering. I can't believe it's the end of May. Graduation is at the end of June, and I'm really hoping that the teachers will be sick of me enough or so vulnerable to my charms that they'll give me passing grades. It's dark and quiet here, just me and the crickets—exactly what I need. My mind's too loud. I have Mike to worry about if he hears I'm dealing indigo to a bunch of ladies on Friday. I have Early to worry about, who might be killing me before I get in touch with him. Faith, who deserves the world and more, is a millimeter away from giving up on me. Stacey probably thinks I'd be better off dead. Though I haven't seen her since the Mike incident, Orah is the only one who doesn't seem to judge me—even when I put her in danger. But she's also the one who's most oblivious.

The pot smoke is dense around me; I can barely see out the windows. I'm not experiencing the high like I used to. My joints are aching, and my arms and legs are so out of whack that my head's too big and my feet are too small, Humpty Dumpty sat on a wall. I want to send myself toppling over the edge, just for a little while. For a few hours tonight, I need to shut down.

When I make the phone call to score some heroin, my hook-up Carter doesn't answer. This is not cool. I need something *now*. I know that he lives in D-Town Heights; he's invited me out to his place before. I don't think he'd mind if I dropped by. I'm giving him business—how could he mind? Before I start my car up, I attempt convincing myself to not go through with it. I remind myself of the aftereffects of heroin, and how I want to lay down and die when the euphoria is over and done with. I remind myself that the tracks on my arms are getting worse, and I should probably start shooting up between my toes so no one will suspect. I remind myself of my sister, and her reaction if she found out how desperate I am for a fix right now.

My keen persuasion tactics work on everyone else besides myself. As I drive out of the park, my tires crunch against the gravel parking lot and kick up sharp pebbles in their wake.

Carter's apartment is on Fourth Street, the top floor of a nondescript six-story block of a building. White siding, bars on the windows, one bare bush that has lost its nerve. It's nearing eleven o'clock, not the best time to be here, but it'll just be a quick in and out. As I ring the buzzer, Faith is calling my cell phone. I pick it up.

"Where are you?" she asks.

"I'm at Walmart," I say. "Needed a new pair of pants."

She lets out a *hmmph*. "Where are you *really*, Phineas?"

"I told you, sis. I'll be home in a little while. I had to go to the Walmart in Glenville because the Rotterdam Walmart didn't have my size in these specific jeans I want. Probably won't have them here either, but I just thought I'd check." I'm not sure why I'm weaving this tale, but I go with it, what's got to come out will come out.

"I need you here," she says adamantly. "Dad's acting up, my car isn't working, and nobody's around to take me somewhere else." Well, where's your savior Peter, I think. Let him come rescue you, damsel that you are.

"That dumb car," I say. "I *told* you I've got money to fix it. Why don't you just let me—"

She heaves out an exasperated sigh. "That's not the point, dumbass." I look at the paint-chipped white door before me and listen to my sister's ragged breathing. It softens me, and I start to feel bad. This is your chance to back out, take advantage of this rope to pull you out while you can.

But I don't. It's just too hard.

"Okay, I'll be there as soon as I can. What's he up to?"

"He took out the Jack Daniels." She's moving around, doing something, it's jostling the phone so I can barely hear her. "He's starting to talk about the past, you know, and it's moving into fucked-up territory. The no-going-back zone."

"Where's Mom?" I ask, knowing that it's a stupid question, knowing that her whereabouts aren't going to make a difference in this situation. Last time Pop drank Jack and talked about the past he head-butted the wall in the living room and left a skull-shaped imprint. He didn't do anything to repair it until I couldn't take it anymore and patched the wall up myself. There were strands of hair stuck to the jagged edges and small streaks of blood, nothing heavy-duty, but enough to think, oh yeah, that's just Pop's head breaking open.

"Mom's in the bedroom, ignoring him," Faith says with a break in her words. I hear her swallowing back tears. "Will you just forget about your stupid pants and get here?"

"Just give me a few minutes," I say gently.

That's all I need, just a few minutes, and then I'll be there for her. I'll *always* be there for her. I peer up at the top window of the building, in fact I peer up at all the windows—not a single light seems to be on. Is this a trick? Have I been set up? I pat down my pockets, to make sure I've got the money to buy.

"How many minutes?" she asks, her voice sounding like she's ten.

"Not long. It's going to be all right, okay?" I say this as encouragement for myself too—it's too quiet around here for comfort.

"If you're in Glenville, it will take eighteen minutes for you to get home," she says.

"I won't be late. Just hang in there. I'll see you soon."

I end the call, ring for the dude to let me up, and wait a stupid amount of time before he finally buzzes me in. I've got to get to Faith. I don't have much time to do what I've got to do. I'm checking out the clock on my phone, figuring that I'll be a few minutes late. Maybe she won't notice. *Of course she will, Finn, she notices everything.* By the time I'm walking up the stairs, I'm shaking, from the thought of Pop, to Faith, to the need for a fix.

A good brother would just leave, say fuck this.

The hallways are littered with empty soda bottles and beer cans, broken furniture, a baby carriage that looks like it's been dragged through the River Styx. Cigarette smoke and grease from cooking aren't just in the air, they *are* the air. There's spray paint on the wall and the only words I can recognize are "suck a dong 4 life."

I knock on a busted-up door on the top floor; someone opens it right away. A strung-out girl in her early twenties is chewing gum in my face; it's cinnamon, it does nothing to hide the smell, the dirty, sweaty smell of her.

"I'm looking for Carter." She opens the door wider and says nothing. I step in, answering her silence.

It's a one-room apartment with barely any furniture, save for a black leather couch that looks way too expensive for its surroundings. Small kitchen with just a microwave and a sink. Minifridge. Flat-screen television that's already driving me nuts because it's crooked on the wall. Three guys on the couch, four on the floor, Ms. Strung Out the only female and *take advantage* is written all over her. Bongs of varying sizes, thickly stained, beaners scattered about. Burned foil, empty bags of potato chips, canisters of shoestring potato sticks, Dunkin Donuts coffee cups. But what strikes me the most are these gallon-sized bags of . . .

"Are those poppy seeds?" I ask, pointing at the filled plastic bags. Carter is in the middle of the couch, smoking a blunt. He's a skinny mother-effer, olive complexion, rat tail (hello, 1989), but I don't let his looks deceive me. He can tussle; he's a quick son of a bitch. At a bar in Saratoga Springs, I saw him take six-foot-seven Kevin down for the count over a ten-dollar bet.

"My man, Finn. What're you doing here?" He isn't smiling, but he doesn't look altogether pissed that I'm here.

"I tried calling, but you weren't picking up. I'm looking to buy."

It's not like I've never been to a place like this—I have, many times—but there's something darker at work here, and it's like I stepped into the brain of some drug-addled, sociopathic freak. The most frightening thing is that I'm hypnotized by what I see—the vibe and people are wretched and slimy, the light is dim, the space is tight; it's the perfect place to use. Faith is calling for me, but this place is calling for me too, saying *Finn, you know you kind of like it here, you know you kind of belong here, so give in. Just for a few minutes.*

Carter disrupts my thought process. "PST," he says, pointing at a jug on the table, filled with turd-color liquid. "Poppy seed tea. Opium, get you done up right."

"Oh yeah?" I say, but what I really want to communicate to him is that I don't care, and that if he could just send me on my way with a little fix-me-up, then all will be well. But then I start focusing on the empty packaging of the poppy seeds thrown to the floor, sixty-five-ounce Ocean Spray bottles with just the dregs fermenting at the bottom. It's disgusting. It's cheap and desperate. If I want poppy seeds, I'll call Martha Stewart. Yet I can't look away. I want what they're having.

Carter pushes his friend off the couch, the friend plunks down, outraged and amused at the same time. He's got a stoner laugh that's more a cough.

"You chill out, sit down, homie, stay awhile," Carter says, clearing his throat. "Hook me up with that indigo shwag and maybe I got something for you. I like how we made that deal last time. H for I. A *hi* for a *high*. How 'bout that?" The dude he just pushed off the couch explodes with laughter. I flash the guy a look. It's not that funny, dude.

"Nah, brother, I'm not looking to trade tonight. Got nothing on me anyhow." I tap my pockets to make the point. If only I kept a little indigo in my car, then this wouldn't be a problem. It's too bad I store it halfway across town in Tupperware and ziplock bags in the crypt. I figure right now, with Early around and Mike, it's too dangerous to have any on me for more than an hour.

Carter smiles slightly, motions to the empty seat next to him. I stay put. "All my friends here want to partake. They're crazy for it. Go home and get some. We got *all* night."

There are knots in my stomach an expert Boy Scout couldn't tie. I just wanted this one simple thing. I need to go, but I can't leave without something. Forehead sweat, palm sweat, back sweat taking over. Faith's waiting for me. Why are there so many unpaired shoes and sneakers on the floor? Jeans and boxers scrunched in the corner; a belt at my feet. The air in here is bitter and suffocating and no amount of window opening is going to air this joint out.

"I . . . I . . ." I can't catch any of my words. "I'll pay you double for the H. Don't be holding out."

The desperation colors my voice, I'm starting to pick up shit from the floor, looking for some dope, turning over the grocery bags filled with empties, scanning the countertops, tabletops, anything, everything, *goddamn* what do I have to do around here to get a little happy?

In the meantime a voice is telling me, *this is what it's come to. You're rooting through garbage like a homeless person.*

One of Carter's friends gets up, pushes me with all the weight he's got, which isn't a lot. I've seen him around town, only rides a dirt bike, never seen the kid in a car.

"Stop messing with my stuff," he yells. "We don't got nothing for you." Acne-ridden, punk motherfucker. My rage becomes center stage, it's like, *right* there.

I swing, sail a good crack into his face, and it's a solid hit, I tell you, a jab that's felt across the room, into middle America for God's sake. Carter signals him to back off when he tries coming at me for more, and I want more; the anger is still there, taunting me, doing its devil dance on my shoulder, expert tap shuffling, step, ball, change. Three guys are standing up, closing in on me, and this is the last thing I want right now, I just need to leave. Should have listened to the other shoulder.

"I'm sorry," I say. Hands up. Surrendering. "I'll give you some bills, and I'll be out of your way." I'm feeling around my back pocket for my wallet. Check the time on my phone. My phone is blowing up with texts from Faith. Where r u?!?! You should b here by now!!! It's already been fifteen minutes since I walked into this hellhole.

"Nah," Carter says. All it takes is the flick of his eyes for his guys to sit back down. "Let's start over, okay? I want us on good terms. I have an idea you'll like."

"All right," I say. I just need something. Anything.

"Hey Lisa," he says to Ms. Strung Out. "Why don't you give our friend Finn here some of that tea as a peace offering?"

She hands me a water bottle filled with that rank concoction, but how can I trust her when the tattoos on her wrists look like misspelled words?

"Taste some, honey. Just brewed. It's an intense batch, too, dark seeds, that earthy stank. *So good.* Like nothing else. Won't you?"

"I'm not trying that. It looks nasty." I smell the stench so hard I can taste it without drinking. I'm staring into the fluid, its diarrhea brown mesmerizing.

"Trust me, dude, just push through the first couple sips, and you'll be as right as rain," Carter says smoothly. And I give in. If I can't get high on H, I guess I'll have to get high on something else. I don't care anymore what it is. I know Faith is waiting for me, but she's such a smart girl, she'll figure out what to do. She's Pop's favorite anyway.

"Cheers," I say, raising the drink.

Bottoms up. I swig it down, drinking almost half in one gulp, that's some poison . . . holy hell it hits quick, my stomach assaulted but my body warm, tingling, going, going, gone.

Pain? What pain? Guilt? As if.

"Amazing, right?" the chick says, snatching back the bottle. "You can make that yourself. Just soak a pound or two of seeds in water, strain them out, and voilà!" She giggles, and the sound I can bite into like a lime; I can hold it in my teeth and feel the acidic fizz.

"Yeah," I say, dreamily, immediately wanting another swig, it's premium vampire blood, certified, funk-ified. I've got to sit down for a spell, take this in, man, though I can't see my pupils dilating, I *hear* their expansion, creaking, groaning, settling like a door in an antique home. *Fuck.* I don't even have to ask, and Strung Out is giving me more, and why the hell has no one told me about opium? Just a sip, just one sip and it's amen hallelujah.

At some point I'm lying on the floor while everyone else is getting baked; I'm on this separate island, in a field of poppies, red, pink, orange, joy, life, love, you don't know the parts that hurt because they don't hurt any more. I think the chick is asking if I'm all right, she's wondering if I drank too much of it, you know, you can die from this shit, she says, my brother's friend . . . yeah, yeah, yeah, I'm just going to lie here for a few more minutes and get a grasp on the situation. Then get in my car and . . . Faith. *Oh Lord.* I fumble around for my phone, find that it's already in my hand, and discover ten more texts from her. I jerk up, blazed out of my gourd, anybody got some water, I ask, but no one's listening, I might as well not be there, ghost Finn, just passing through, *boo!* I pull myself up, trip over the poppy seed bags, Christ, how many are there? Make sure I got my keys, and nod to Carter who nods back. Ms. Strung Out walks me to the door, real guest-of-honor treatment, she kisses me on the cheek, and twiddles her fingers in a cutesy, blitzed, barely there *bye-bye.*

CHAPTER THIRTY-FIVE

IT'S A QUARTER PAST TWO BY THE TIME I GET HOME, AN HOUR LATER THAN I PROMISED. I can't remember the drive home. All the lights are out in the trailer. Pop is snoring on the couch, empty bottle of Jack tipped over on the floor, cigarette butts and ash everywhere but in the ashtray. In our room I slide off my shoes.

"Faith," I say. She's in her bed, on her side, got her back to me, covers pulled up to her ears.

No answer.

"Sister. I'm sorry. I got caught up. Ran into Max, he had this problem with his car—funny how you're having car trouble too—and I had to help him out. Jumped his car, that didn't work, had to call some other peeps . . . things seem okay, here, right? Are you okay?"

Still no answer.

I sit on the edge of her bed. She moves closer to the wall, away from me. That obvious disgust of hers guts me.

"I don't understand," she says, voice muffled against the blankets.

"You don't understand what?" But I do.

She waits, then shifts over on her other side. The dim lights from the other trailers seep into the room through the blinds and onto the sheets of her bed.

"I don't understand," she repeats. I'm wrong. There's no disgust in her voice, no anger. Just distance. "If you just want to go and use, then use. Don't make shit up. Just say you're going to do it, then do it. Knock yourself out. But the story about the pants at Walmart? Max and his car? That's where it gets disturbing. I don't recognize you anymore. We share the same genes but it's like you're a totally different species."

There is sadness on her face, and in her eye, which is fine, I get it, but what I can't stand is pity coming through.

"I'm the *same*," I insist.

"No, you're not. You're a liar and a user." She says it. She's made it true.

It's time to change tactics. "Pop didn't do anything crazy, did he? Is Mom okay?"

Faith answers with no tone in her voice. "Even if he did, it's too late for you to do anything about it, isn't it?" She flips over onto her back now. Someone in another trailer is banging around pots and pans to fix a late-night snack. One of those little shit dogs yaps. The poppy seed tea high is dead and gone, and the itch to get even higher is superiorly powerful; it's a sharp-nailed finger tapping my shoulder.

"I apologize," I say, smoothing down the covers. "Are you . . . did anything . . . how are you? Do you want me to get you one of your lorazepams?"

Faith just squeezes her eye shut. Not a word between us for a while; the dog continues to bark and the smell of fried potatoes is wafting through our open window.

Finally she breaks the quiet. Her voice is different now, not mad at me, no pity, not about me at all in fact. "I'm not going to

Harvard. I rescinded my acceptance."

"No!" I exclaim, kicking the bed with my heel, unwilling to come to terms with this. I know this was bound to happen, and maybe I'm stupid to be this upset, but this makes it official. This makes her officially stupid. Life is about goals, isn't it? If anything, life is about goals for people like Faith. And now here she goes pissing it all away. What am I going to do now? What goal do I have, now that she won't let me help her?

"No," I say again. "Faith, you're being totally unreasonable. I—"

"I counted your money tonight," she says softly.

"You did *what*?"

She sits up now, legs scrunched so her knees meet her chin; she's a tiny ball, a miniature version of Faith. She never grew as tall as me, hence her stupid arsenal of high heels.

A mixture of anger and embarrassment is bubbling up inside me. "It might not look like a lot. But more is coming in, I promise. Please, Faith, *please*." I'm desperate, almost whining. I don't think anyone has ever wanted to give this bad. I don't think anyone has ever felt this bad about not being able to give. Contradictory thoughts ping-ponging back and forth: wanting to provide for my sister equals selling indigo, but keeping Stacey and Orah out of danger equals not selling it. Now I understand the meaning of *you can't have everything*.

She looks at me like she knows how pathetic I am.

"Did you know that if I had a million dollars right there, all in one-hundred dollar bills, it would only weigh twenty pounds?" I ask.

"Shut up, Phineas. There's no one around to impress. I know how much you have: $8,027. How long did it take you to make that?"

I hesitate. I don't know what the right answer is, so I go for the truth. "About a month."

"That much in a month?" She looks scared. "You say it's not a lot, but it is. That's a lot for such a short amount of time. That's too much for this to be safe."

"Why are you fighting me on this? All of it is yours. *You. My family.* Let me provide."

She just shakes her head. Disappointment, disgust, done. I get up and collapse on my own bed and steeple my hands together, yet there is nothing reverent about it. Recently I looked up Orah's name, thinking it sounded religious. Orah with an "h" means light, Orah without an "h" means pray. Faith is faith, and Phineas means the mouth of a snake. Enough said, right?

Faith says out of nowhere, "You know why things are different between you and Peter now?"

I look over. I don't want to hear, but I know I have to. It's like penance, punishment for everything I've done wrong.

"He can't trust you. He says to me, how do you know when an addict is lying?" She pauses. "The moment he opens his mouth."

"I'm not an addict," I immediately say.

That's when she starts laughing, really yucking it up. *I'm not an addict, I'm not an addict, I'm not one, goddamn . . .* In the back of my mind I hear Mom saying *you and your declarations . . .* and Pop saying he'll quit drinking every other week. Yellow outside light is streaked across Faith's face, illuminating the scar tissue around her eye. She never wears an eye patch to bed. The skin is wrinkled, old sea captain textured, weathered, withered, yet the rest of her is a stun gun of vibrancy; potent spirit. A forever shut eye, yet still all-seeing. Sometimes it's the damage that gives us wisdom. I hate her damage. I hate that it's mine too.

She finally stops cackling. "Do you *hear* yourself? I don't know what to do with you anymore. And I'm starting to think maybe the reason why I want to stick around D-Town is so I can be with you when you fall."

Wow. That comment would bring down any kite at any height. And the thing is, I don't have shit to say.

A tidal wave rolls through me, and I don't know what I'm doing. I stomp out of the bedroom into the living room— where Pop is no longer sleeping—and suddenly I've got a thing called a rain stick in my hands. Mom bought it when she was in her Zen phase, it's leaning against the wall and calling out my name. When you turn it upside down it produces the sound of rain pouring in a forest, but tonight it's more than that—it's torrential and cyclonic—it feels good in my hands, and good to swing too, and the first box I hit has a little bit of give, but just enough solidness that the impact is satisfying, and that's all it takes, another shot, and down go more boxes, down goes the junk, packages burst and break, plastic and glass and Styrofoam peanuts fly, and all the while the rain stick is playing its sweet swishing, plinking song. Chaos, crash, I crash, pop of cardboard and plastic, turning round and round, sweat flying, scratches on my arms from the sharp corners of the boxes, Mom and Pop rushing in, Pop grabbing my arms and yanking them behind my back. I'm yelling something, he's talking calmly, *calmly*, what's he doing with all that serenity? Finn, he says, get a hold of yourself, there's nothing to be upset about. Mom's being violent and volatile, slapping me on the chest, saying how *dare* you, how dare you Finn, you have no right, these are *my* things, it's *my* collection.

"Trish, calm down. It's nothing that can't be fixed," Pop says, wisdom is everything he's about right now.

"No one gets it, do they?" she says, wild-eyed and breathless, her fingers clutching the collar of her robe. "No one does. I try to explain, but you wouldn't understand, would you?" She lurches forward again, her nails out to scratch, but she misses.

"You're not helping," Pop says as he tows me away from her, I resist and struggle, because it's a fight for the sake of fighting. He's still strong, I'll give him that.

Why is *he* helping? Why's he on my side? Mom backs off, and I'm released, but his palm is pressed against my chest as my back is up against the wall. The rain stick drops and makes a final cascading *whoosh*. Forgot I was still holding it. Pop tells me to sit down.

He lets me move away from the wall, and my body drops onto the couch, I clasp my head in my hands, I'm not crying, I swear I'm not, and before Mom can come at me again, it's no secret that stubbornness runs in our blood, Pop hauls her into the kitchen area, talks her down, and hands over a couple pills that will do her in for the night. I thought this QVC shit was only important to her up to the moment it arrives in the mail, but I guess not. She likes the graveyard of junk. She wants to hold onto the bones, her beloved inanimate objects, dead things, numb things. She moves with zombie gait into her bedroom. Faith appears, watching me. I should apologize, she knows I should, and that's why she waits. When I don't say those words, those *simple* words, her whole face changes—I've never seen her look so tired and well past her seventeen years. She backs away and disappears down the hall.

It takes us—me and Pop—a while to pick up the pieces (back in their coffins they go). When we're done he puts a hand on his hip and says, "Okay?" and I say, "Okay," and I think it's the best question-and-answer exchange we've ever had as father and son. I sit on the couch until six in the morning, the rain stick back in my hands, still hearing the cloudburst even though I'm not swinging.

FRIDAY, MAY 24

CHAPTER THIRTY-SIX

"OKAY, LADIES, I'D LIKE TO INTRODUCE YOU TO THE CURE FOR ALL YOUR WOES," I ANNOUNCE.

Oooos and *aaaaahs* all around. I'm sitting in Claire Longwood's living room surrounded by an overabundance of floral print on the wallpaper, curtains, throw pillows, and blankets. I've never seen so many goddamn sunflowers in my life. There are fifteen women in the room, *fifteen*, all in their forties and fifties, all wearing too much makeup and too-tight clothes, all wishing they were my age again. Well, here I am, ladies, and I've come to give you back your youth.

Orah calls them the indigo-go girls.

I've done my homework on each one of them, even after Claire and I had a reassuring talk that they would keep this little shindig to themselves. Amazing what you can find online. Claire is a stay-at-home mom with gobs of money and runs marathons to fund oncology research. Her husband is a financial advisor, and we all know without too much digging that her son is kind of a loser. But still, thank you to Spencer, for making this afternoon possible. There is a secretary who works at an insurance company, a hairdresser who styled my sister's prom "up-don't" (as Faith liked to call it), and a waitress who works at the D-Town Diner. Then there's the mayor's wife. When I found out she was going to be in attendance, I was *this close* to backing out of the deal, but Claire said she's cool. Says nobody takes the woman seriously, and it's no secret she likes her pills and martinis. I'm concerned that the mixture of perfumes in the room might set off the carbon monoxide alarm.

I present to them a giant basket, overflowing with grams of indigo carefully tucked away in adorable jewelry boxes, tied lovingly by Orah and me with colorful ribbons. Who knew I was an arts and crafts buff? I didn't quite love the fact that I was in Hallmark for an hour trying to convince the cashier to let me buy in bulk those jewelry boxes you get with earrings or some shit. But it seemed worth it, to view them spread out in a neat line across Orah's hardwood floor, waiting to be filled with the D-Town's finest.

We prepared them all in the morning room when we knew Stacey was in school and her father was on call. Orah was pleased too, I could tell by the way she tilted her head when I tied the last bow.

She said to me, "One of my patients liked wrapping presents so much I'd give him random things to wrap. Paper plates, toilet paper rolls, forks and spoons. One time he giftwrapped his shoes and presented them to me. It was very sweet. I taught him a class on the art of gift wrapping. I've never seen a person so passionate about folding paper in my entire life."

"Obviously you haven't met my friend Peter," I said. Then I told her about his origami obsession. I'm sure she sensed from me an air of sadness. Peter. I couldn't remember the last time we hung out, just him and me.

The morning room that day with Orah was how a space should be—uncluttered, functional, and nice. Just really nice. And now here I am in a living room murdered by sunflower wallpaper.

I pick up one of the boxes from the basket, and the bow bounces delightfully as I set it on the coffee table. Inside the box, bagged indigo is nestled in tissue paper that matches the color of the ribbon. This is some top-shelf work, if I say so myself.

"You see this?" I point at the green bow. The ladies all sit around me, a captive audience on the couch and on chairs with seat cushions. I'm squeezed in between the waitress and the hairdresser. Claire made sure the place is set up right, complete with crudités on the coffee table next to champagne glasses and Asti. The pizza delivery is on its way.

"Green means success. You're going to relive a tremendous moment in your life of great achievement." I wave my hand in the air with a flourish. They seem to appreciate the theatrics.

The hairdresser keeps touching my knee, like she and I are sharing some secret, and she's reminding me of it. Her mane is that unnatural shade of red where it's almost purple, but I can dig it. Kudos for being bold. I go on.

"This one here—this blue one—means clarity." I hold up the box, so they all can see. "You'll experience a time in your life where you and the world are best friends. And here . . ." I point to the red ribbon. "I think you all know what this one means. Love. Passion. Lust." I say the words slow and soft.

I go through the other colors, yellow is happiness, purple is power, orange is energy. I'm under their skin, I know this, but not under Rory's, the mayor's wife, who looks about half in the bag on white wine. Her brown eyes are cold and unwavering and not buying any of my bullshit, or so I think.

I get up and sit (throw the petunia-printed seat cushion

aside) next to the lady who's a bank teller, no ring on her finger, no lipstick on her mouth, quite unlike the others. I place the red-ribboned box in her hands and close my own around them. Her skin is cold against mine, but she doesn't shrink away from me.

"I think you should try this one first," I say. "You're in for a ride. An *amazing* ride." I squeeze her hands; her shoulders tense up, maybe I'm taking this too far, but no, no, she's still with me.

"I hope so," she says shyly.

"It's church. Sacred. Like seeing God. No. More than that. It's like kissing Him. Isn't that right, Claire? Want to testify?"

She nods with kind eyes; she thinks I'm kind of charming. Today a tiny gold wishbone adorns the gold chain around her neck.

"You all know I haven't been myself this past year." She squeezes her lips together, but she isn't about to cry, she's too hard for that shit.

The hairdresser takes her hand and whispers, "It's all right, honey. We're all here. We'll always be here."

"*This*," she says, looking down at the box in her palm, "does *not* make me weak."

The declaration. It floors me. The chills are giving me all they've got.

Murmurings, yes, of course, they all agree, and the support I feel, the support isn't like anything I've felt in a while, these heavily perfumed, unassuming women rally around Claire, holding shit down, *for real*, their will titanium, their loyalty as sure as my eyes are brown.

"You do crazy stuff, you know, when you face death and all," she continues. "I spied on Spencer doing indigo." She smiles back at me gently. "He's never looked so happy, at least not since he's been a teen. That's when they turn, you know?"

They all nod in agreement. I pretend I don't hear this comment, like teenagers are zombies or something. Maybe we are. I keep my head bowed out of respect, like I'm praying.

She closes her eyes. "So I tried it. Thought, hey, what do I have to lose? Sniffed it right up my nose, like I saw him do. I mean, how crazy do you have to be? But I was. And I don't regret it *at all* . . . I . . . I relived a memory . . ." She opens her eyes and brings the back of her hand up to her nose, takes a deep breath in.

"My father. He would take us out on his boat, taught us how to sail . . ." she shakes her downturned head. The room is quieter than an indigo crypt. "My dad, he was a hard-ass. Barking orders at me and my brother, and would never let me take the reins because he always thought my brother did things better. Better grades, better athlete, better looking . . ." She smiles to herself. "Anyway, one day we were out sailing by Martha's Vineyard, and Brian was goofing off. I was doing all the work, and doing it well. My father was sneaking glances at me, I could see how proud he was . . . he took me aside when the waves got calm, and the sun was straight above our heads, and said, 'Ya done good, kid.' Pressed his rough hand up to my cheek. He'd never given me that much affection before."

She has her hand to cheek, we *all* have our hands in that position, even me, goddamn, it's like we're all feeling the bob of the boat.

"I came out of my memory, hair smelling like the sea, fingers hurting from the ropes of the jib." She throws her head back and laughs. "Nothing short of a miracle."

There is a moment of reverence, quiet, a peace that doesn't come around often.

Then they all start talking at once. How much is it? Are there any bad side effects? Will my husband know? How long does it last? What if I don't have any good memories? Rory isn't saying anything, but she's holding the box with the blue ribbon, and pressing her finger against one of the corners, frowning.

The doorbell rings.

"Pizza," I announce. I pull my billfold out of my pocket along with a box I made special after I left Orah's, tied with a silver ribbon. A Hispanic kid wearing a "Ti's Pizzeria" T-shirt tries to shove three pizza boxes in my arms, but I motion for him to place them on the side table next to the door.

I wave some cash in front of him and say, "Come on in for a second, I've got a favor to ask you." He looks surprised and hesitates. I gently take him by the shoulder and guide him inside.

The ladies are talking among themselves, opening up their boxes, putting them up to the light, smelling the indigo, touching it, not quite ready to fully dive in. For a second I admire Claire, the woman is glowing like it's her job, happiness emanating from every inch of her. My stomach cinches in a knot, a benign one, feels like I might be doing something good, for once. Or maybe I should remember what's happening to kids at school because of indigo. One thing I should remind myself of: it will all go to hell the moment I start thinking it won't.

"What is it, man?" the kid says, all nervous. He's my age, maybe a little younger. "I've got five other deliveries to make."

"I know," I say, handing him a hundred dollar bill. His eyes widen, slightly. "You see this," I say, gesturing at the room. "It's an indigo party. Take a good look. You've heard of indigo, right?"

The kid acknowledges me straight on. He knows about it. He has to know, red-eyed, sunken-cheeked kid like him.

"Here," I say, pressing a gram into his hand to sweeten the deal. "For your troubles. Because *this* I'd like you to give to your boss. Mr. Mario Coletti."

That's when I hand over the special box with the silver ribbon, containing a short message inside (wrapped around a small bag of indigo) asking for a meeting to discuss indigo distribution and a possible compromise. Nothing threatening, wholly respectful. I included the number of the new burner phone I bought. I know that this is exactly what Jason told me *not* to do, but I'm a firm believer in discussion, dialogue, and working shit out. Anyone's capable of that.

"What do you want?" he asks. He regards the gram with disbelief and undeniable yearning. *Need.* I'm goddamn Santa Claus here.

"I told you. Mr. Coletti will want to see it. It's in your best interest not to be *late* in delivering it to him." I accentuate my words carefully. I pray that this is going to work, that even if Early has talked to Mike already he'll want to talk with me too. But I don't know this yet. I have no idea what's going on behind the scenes and that doesn't jive well with me. I'm taking control of the situation—at least I'm doing something. The kid starts to stammer and backs away from me.

"He's never been to the shop, what if I can't—" I pull him toward me, a firm hand on his upper arm. Rail thin, this one.

I say close to his face, "Well that's not my problem, is it? Make sure he gets it. And make sure you say it's from me, okay? It's Finn. Phineas Walt."

His hands are shaking as he pockets the money, the gram, and the special box. I push him toward the door. "I don't want nothin' to do with this." Yet the indigo in his pocket he can't stop touching, making sure that it's still there.

I shut the door on his face and turn to the ladies, who don't have any interest in eating. They're asking more questions, so I go through the prices, just throwing numbers out there, *ridiculous* numbers, and they all want five or six boxes, one of each color, and it's so out of control I have to go to my car and dig into my backup reserve. When I return, I give out what everyone wants, and silence falls over the room. They all look to me.

"How do we do this?" Rory asks. Her voice is surprisingly high. I was expecting a husky, radio-talk-show voice.

"Forgive me, ladies." I apologetically place my hand over my heart. "As Claire described, you can snort it, or you can dip your finger in and give it a taste. *Never* smoke it. It hits faster through the nose." I pour them each a glass of champagne and then show them how it's done: I cut a line with a razor blade on a hardcover book on the coffee table, and bring a rolled-up one hundred dollar bill (just for the wow factor) to my nose. I don't snort; they ask me why. I tell them *someone* has to be the responsible one. Laughter. They ask me to stay put, just stay through their hallucinatory trip down memory lane, and Claire insists.

Cheers. They clink glasses; they jump in. I hold my breath. Watching them takes that very breath away.

CHAPTER THIRTY-SEVEN

THEY ALL LOOK TEN YEARS YOUNGER IN AN INSTANT, CHEEKS A BRIGHTER SHADE, CLOSED EYELIDS A SOFT PEARLY PINK. But something changes; with a single tick of the grandfather clock in the corner a darkness, a dark feeling, an evil spirit, what have you, swoops in and takes me over. I don't get it: just a few minutes ago, I was flying high on the excitement of making contact with Early and looking forward to the ladies flying high on indigo. How did this darkness transpire so quickly? It seems that my life is one big back-and-forth mood swing, unpredictable and mercurial. I'm not sure what's real anymore—is there anything or anyone reliable out there? The high of the eight-ball of coke in my pocket—now *that* I can consider a loyal friend. The women are all swooning, unaware of the night-black aura, there without reason. I'm desperate to yank them back to reality, pull them from the past. Maybe the foreboding I feel is isolation from the women's experiences, or maybe Faith got it right—indigo is some voodoo shit.

Rory comes out of her memory first. She throws her head back, lets out a long exhale that ends with a sweet-sounding giggle, and claps her hand over her mouth with embarrassment. Her reaction relaxes me a notch. Something prompts her to check the pockets in her dress, and when she does, she exclaims in utter shock.

"What? . . . Wait, why?" she asks me, dumbfounded, gazing down at a small amount of sand in her palm. The dark shadow in the room seems to lift as Rory brushes off her hands, her wedding ring blinging all over the place in the afternoon light.

I approach her. "You need some water? You hungry?" I point to the pizza. "Just want to make sure you're feeling all right."

She's up on her high-heeled shoes, giggling to herself, expression on her face that could mean a number of things: (a) she's blitzed out of her mind, (b) she's kind of lost it, (c) she's flirting with me, or (d) all of the above. This is not good— I don't much like multiple choice tests. There's no time to think because she's taking my hand with her long fingers with rougher skin than I expected. She's got a post-trip charge so intense I can feel its electric fuzz around her.

I say to Rory, hey, what's going on? Where we going? This is all happening way too fast, and it's probably a terrible idea. Everyone loses their shit a little after giving indigo a go. Mike acted all wonky, his mind was frayed, his senses were jumbled, Faith said Peter was talking nonsense, and just think of Bryce being so whacked-out after the Gatorade incident. But indigo isn't running through my bloodstream, so what's my excuse? I follow her anyway.

Rory senses my reluctance, and smiles a single choice smile, pushing me down a hall and into a bedroom, a really big, nice, suburban bedroom with billowing drapes and a king-size bed. Hold up now, I didn't ask for this. Not looking to get laid. Not looking to get laid by a middle-age mayor's wife. Shit. This isn't her house, but she knows it well. The carpet is thick, expensive looking. She backs me up toward the bed.

"You're a liar," she says as she pounces, so I fall against the thick comforter. Her irises are a darker brown than mine; her nose comes to a sharp point. She tears off my shirt, bites my chest, holy eager beaver. I make a noise through my clenched teeth and try to get my act together.

"Why do you say that?" I ask, trying to push her off me and trying to fight against my dick that's giving orders like a drill sergeant. It's too bad that every guy's got a Mrs. Robinson fantasy. Consequences. Think of the consequences. I can't, my body's on overload, and her hand is squeezing me where it counts. I pull her head down so that her lips meet mine. Her tongue is surprisingly cool. It's not too late to back out. You should probably back out, Finn. Like *now*. I try to think about the shadow I felt in the living room, even though her mouth is all over me, and she's grinding against my junk.

"You said that I would have clarity," she says, her voice raspy. She's yanking off her black dress to reveal a pink lacy bra. I notice she tied the blue ribbon around her wrist, her wrist that I grab and twist, I'm on top of her now. The bed groans under our weight, and her breath is hot against my cheek.

"You did have clarity," I say caressing the side of her waist, running my tongue up her neck. "I didn't promise the clarity would last."

She smirks, she kisses me, and I feel her hard, probably personally-trained body against mine. I've never done it with an older woman. It's already feeling different. Darker. Angrier. Or maybe it's just her.

"I relived the first time I met my husband," she says, dragging her teeth along my shoulder, which sends jolts down my spine. I'm searching for a scent, every girl has a scent, but hers is absent, and that's a scent itself.

"He was so nice in the beginning. So charming. Like you." She touches my nose and then pulls off my pants. Then it's a mad rush to undo the rest of our clothes, there's ripping involved, tossing, pulling, pressing against each other, tangled tongues, hot skin, and her teeth, all the time.

She continues murmuring, "When I met him I had cut my foot on a piece of glass when I was walking on the beach. He was the first to come help me. He wrapped my foot with his beach towel. I had sand in my pockets for days." She swipes her short hair out of her face and goes in for another tongue-heavy kiss.

"We should stop," I try to say though it comes out garbled; I don't really mean it. My mouth is still filled with hers. Is she doing this because of the drug or because I'm so damn irresistible? I'd like to wager on the latter, but no, you douche, it's the drug and middle-age rebellion. Indigo makes you temporarily loony bin–worthy, and there's no red Corvette around for her to buy.

"You're cute, kid. Now shut up."

There's joy, on her face, all over her, she's drenched in it, and she starts to laugh, and it's contagious, a pretty laugh that flutters, butterfly style. I shouldn't be so worried, this is just a fling, and indigo is fun and darkness doesn't exist in this room.

Our bodies move against each other, as the sunshine streams through a gap in the floral-printed curtains, and her mouth tastes sweeter, and her body turns softer. Her eyes widen as I'm about to slide off her underwear, when I feel big, heavy hands on my back.

I'm thrown on the ground, pants around my ankles, shock, shock, and more shock.

And then even *more*.

Because Stacey's *dad*, Sergeant Braggs, is standing over me, screaming in my face, teeth surprisingly white, screaming at Rory who's covering herself up with a pillow, and she's saying, Dan, Dan, Dan, I didn't mean to do it, I don't know, I'm sorry, I'm sorry—

He's off duty, but I see he's packing heat, and by the way, *WTF?* I have no idea what's going on, and he's yelling, she's turning crybaby, and his green eyes are scorched with fury. Pointing at me, pointing at her, it's mass chaos and confusing as all get-out.

"I know exactly what came over you, that *drug* came over you, and him . . . *him.*" He barges forward into my face. "I should arrest you right here," he says, out of breath, inhaling aggressively through his nose. By then my boxers are back up, but I'm floundering on the ground, fish-out-of-water Finn, dragging my pants over my legs, they seem to have shrunk about twenty sizes.

Rory follows suit and fumbles to put on her bra, hiding behind the other side of the bed. Modesty kicks in at the weird-est times.

"You can't arrest me on account of indigo," I say, trying to find my T-shirt, patting the bed behind me without break-ing sight from him. He's bigger than I remember. Tanned, built, a quintessential cop. "It's not even registered as an ille-gal drug."

Dan wrenches me by my upper arm toward him and searches me. Fuckity fuck fuck. He finds the eight ball of coke in my back pocket, something I thought I'd need, I wanted to have my fun as the ladies had theirs.

"I could throw you in jail right now," Dan says, waving the bag in front of me, a cocaine pendulum, his face twisted with repulsion. "Or kick the living shit out of you." But he does neither.

He runs his eyes over Rory, the how-could-you glare bearing down on her. I see him trying to pull himself together, hands close to his sides, mouth a tight line, shoulders no longer scrunched up. So . . . they're lovers.

"Dan?" Rory says, quivering mouth, watery eyes. Oh, thank God, there's my shirt. I tug it on as quickly as I can. She pleads with him to stay, to talk it through, let's be adults about this, yeah sure.

He glares at her, disgusted. "Not right now. I can't talk to you right now. I can't *look* at you right now." He squeezes the bridge of his nose that looks like it's been broken more than once.

"You're coming with me," Dan says, pointing at the space between my eyes.

I scoff. "I'm not going *anywhere* with you. I could totally expose you, say that you're fucking the mayor's wife. Ruin your career, man, in a heartbeat." I bump my fist two times against my chest. *Thump, thump*, my heart says. *Dumb, dumb*, my mind says, but it's too late to take back the threat of blackmail.

Intake of breath from them both. She's fuming, Dan's hands are clenched so hard I bet his fingernails are drawing blood, he's looking at me, looking at her, the vertical creases of her aging chest now visible in unforgiving light.

"I'm sure Stacey wouldn't be thrilled if she knew. And the mayor . . . sheesh," I say, wondering why I don't just shut up.

"Punk," he says, grabbing me toward him and then slamming me into the wall, forearm pressed against my Adam's apple. Hard to breath, am I really going to jail? I try to remember the law, but it varies county by county. I'm hoping I'll just get probation and be stuck with community service. He draws back from me and picks up Rory's dress and holds it out with his thumb and forefinger. Contaminated, radioactive.

"Get dressed," he barks as she grabs the dress from him. Then he turns to me. "You. My car. *Now.*" Rory's murmuring his name. He tells her shut the hell up, this is unbelievable, a kid? A dumb, cokehead, good-for-nothing *kid*?

Then Dan pushes me out of the room, his huge paw clamped around my neck. When I glance behind me, I see Rory standing in the door frame, clutching her dress close to her chest, biting her lips that were bitten by me.

As we pass through the living room, the women are flying so high they barely notice us. My foreboding was on the mark. The darkness isn't creeping in, the darkness is already here, and has been for a while. My predicament with Faith, my conundrum with Mike and Early, and now my fuck-up with Dan—it's all intertwined and very real, and I'm unable to neatly package each situation, tie it with a bow and hope for the best. There's no compartmentalizing. Indigo is turning from dark blue to a night without stars, a tar-black raven, the blackest of black ribbons.

CHAPTER THIRTY-EIGHT

WE DRIVE FOR WHAT SEEMS LIKE EONS IN DAN'S BLACK JEEP CHEROKEE OUT TO THE BACK ROADS WHERE IT'S NOT DAMMERTOWN, IT'S JUST *GODDAMN* COUNTRY TOWN, COWS, PASTURES, SILOS, HAYSTACKS THAT ARE SO PART OF THE LANDSCAPE THEY MIGHT AS WELL BE TREES. Dan says nothing, I say nothing, I'm not sure if I'm supposed to out-silence him or what. Part of me wants to rage against all of it; another part of me wants to behave because of Stacey. Play nice with Daddy. Like that would really make much of a difference anyway. I'm thinking about the backpack full of money from the party—I'll have to pick that up later. I'm wondering if my message will be delivered to Early loud and clear. Finally I can't take it anymore.

"We taking the long way to the police station or what?" I ask finally. He looks at me; his emerald eyes are like Stacey's—eyelashes way too lush. "I don't want to cause any more—"

He slaps me on the arm and snaps, "Shut up and listen. You have done nothing but make a mess. And you're quite good at drawing attention to yourself. It only took me over-hearing someone at the diner talk about an indigo party to find you."

I scrunch myself down low on the seat. The interior of the car looks brand new, but judging by the mileage it most certainly is not. He has a few CDs visible in the storage compartment between us. Tupac and Guns N' Roses. Celine Dion and Jimmy Buffet. Um, okay. No comment.

"It's all coming together for me now," he says. "I don't understand why my mother-in-law is helping you, but she must have taken a shining . . . you do look a little like my son." He taps his finger on his chin, mulling over how much to share with douchebag Finn. I wonder if he knows I'm in love with his daughter.

"How could I be so stupid? When he asked me about it, I didn't think for a second that my mother-in-law was your drug supplier."

"Who are you referring to, when you say 'he'?" I ask. "Are you talking about Mario Coletti?"

His face twitches at the name, prompts him to squeal over to the side of the road and turn off the car; I'm fully expecting him to ax murder me. I'm not sure if there is a way to finesse this situation, I'm not sure that my mouth is going to be my ally this time. At Claire's house I felt like a king; now I feel like a punk-ass bitch.

Dan's shoulders are bigger than the width of the seat. When he shifts his weight, the car moves under it. "Yes, Mario Coletti. I thought for a second it was Billy, but it's not. It never occurred to me it was Orah. I really thought she'd quit her habit since we moved here. I don't even know where she's getting it from. You know what? I don't even *want* to know." Dan looks down at his hands, trying to collect himself. So he really isn't aware of the crypt. He then eyeballs me. "How dare you put *my entire family* in danger?"

And how dare I almost fuck his mistress. And be in love with his daughter. Wow, the points are stacked up against me. I start constructing my most stellar argument in my head, I consider telling him that I've got something worked out, I have a message out to Early, but he interrupts me before I begin.

"I could put quite the case against you," he says flatly. "I'd start with this coke ball, but I know that it won't take me long to find more evidence to put you away for a while. I've got the mayor's wife, who can convince him of anything. I'm backed by a team that is just as passionate as me to get rid of the drug problem around here. Now you're on our list." His palms rub the top of the steering wheel.

But he's not saying he's going to do this, only that he could. "What do you want from me?" I ask.

His *I will fuck you up* expression is a blast in my face. "Stop. Dealing. Indigo. You're done." He slashes the air with a flat hand. "With all of it—your dirt weed, coke, whatever else you got your stinking hands on. Done."

I consider telling him off just on principle, I got some beef, some words. However, I feel like a kid again, Pop scolding me, bullying me, treating me like I'm of the lowest caste. My blood is boiling hot and rancid, not at Dan, but from my stupidity. I actually thought that I would be successful. Competent. Pop was right. I'm nothing. But part of me wants to do what he says, to stop, to get out of this.

"Do you hear me? Everything is taken care of. All you need to do is *stop*," he demands. Loud and clear. There's a shift in my brain. Wait—wait just a minute.

"Everything is taken care of?" I ask, anxious, not quite believing.

He eyes me, green grass irises of passion and toughness,

his energy gritted up from years of battle against the drug war. There isn't an ounce of Stacey in him, besides the intense green of his stare; how can such grace come from such a brute?

"Yes. That is why you need to stop dealing, or I'll throw your ass in jail."

"What do you mean everything is taken care of?" I repeat, panic coursing through my body, my fingers clamped around my knees.

Dan considers me, gauging what to disclose. "Early—Mario—and I have a relationship, and this is a delicate relationship that has taken years to forge, years of bargaining to stay out of each other's business. We struck an agreement about the drug a while back, and he agreed to stop harassing my family. But then one of his guys came to me less than a week ago about this new strain called indigo. It came out of left field. I thought I had solved that problem long ago. I told him I would find the dealer and scare him away. First I figured it was another distributor—a weed grower in Vermont—but I can't make the connection to him. I had never thought it was *you* until I saw you with . . . Rory." He can barely say her name.

Early, Mike, and Dan are all connected, and Orah is drawn in by default. And now Finn, idiot of the century, is added to the mix. Aren't we one big, happy family?

"Why are you looking so pale?" Dan asks. "I'll tell Mario this is over. You'll drop it, Finn, leave it alone. Start fresh."

"I—" is all I can muster. I highly doubt that it'll be that simple. I'm at a loss on whether or not I tell him I reached out to Early. On the one hand, I could tell him, have him tell Early I'm out of the game, and it's all over. Everyone is safe. On the other hand, how do I help Faith?

The evening is closing in, the sun is low, murmuring its good-bye with light pinks and purples. *Freaking. Out.*

"It'll be okay, Finn." Dan saying my name makes an undeniable impact. Some people just know how to say names right, with a firmness, with authority. I respect that. Though I don't like how it makes me feel two inches tall.

But he doesn't know. The note I sent to Early could be interpreted as a threat. I just threatened a *gangster*. There was no reason to talk to Early in the first place, and there was no reason to work out a compromise, because he and Dan had already done so only days ago. I could have shut my mouth and bowed out of the indigo business gracefully, and Early would never have known about me. Dammit, Jason, for once in your life you were right. Now the note's going to draw attention. It's going to look like I called Early out.

I don't tell Dan this. It's my instinct that saying something is only going to make the situation more complicated, because that's what happens when I open my damn mouth. Dan drops me off at the trailer without a good-bye, without a word. There aren't any lights on inside. Coming home to a dark, empty house reminds me too much of a crypt visit. Don't need to see any bones to know that ghosts are near.

THURSDAY, MAY 30

CHAPTER THIRTY-NINE

I CARRY OUT A TRAY HOLDING A TEAPOT, CUPS AND SAUCERS, CREAMER AND SUGAR BOWL, MINIATURE SPOONS TOO, ALL MATCHING WITH RED AND YELLOW ROSES. Orah and I sit in the morning room, and I pour hers first. This time we're both having chamomile. What a sight I must be, big hands, little cups. Smoker's voice, silver clicking against porcelain. Don't feel like a girl, not even close, but I pour without a tremble and set the cup down without spillage. I'm surprised, considering what I put in my body and my current state of mind. I left school early, around eleven a.m. so I could be here—with her. It was the only thing I could think to do to calm myself down after the horrible string of events. It's good to be in a quiet house; it's good to be in a room that was made for sun to sweep through. Dan's at work; Bryce was the one who dropped me off here—I don't want anyone seeing my car parked at the Braggs'. I need to see Orah, but I don't want to bring any more trouble to her.

"People can make tea out of poppy seeds and get high off it," I tell her. She doesn't look that surprised. Seriously, nothing fazes this woman. If I told her I just gave birth, she'd be like, oh, is that so?

"Sorry I don't have any poppy seeds to offer you. I could dig up a bagel in the pantry though," she says, chuckling.

"It's nothing to joke about," I say. "It's true."

"When was the last time the truth wasn't something to joke about?" Her response is quick and deadpan.

I smile all over the place, not hiding it, it's the first time in a while my teeth have seen so much air. I'm beyond worry right now—I just want to be here, forgetting. I reassure myself: Early might not even take the bait, he might not even get the message, kind of counting on that actually—that delivery kid didn't look like an ace at anything or like he wanted anything to do with Early. He was downright scared that I even mentioned him.

"Billy and I used to have teatime," Orah says, taking a sip. The steam moistens the tip of her nose. "Up at the lake house, we tried all different kinds. Blueberry, raspberry, vanilla honey, passion fruit, green tea, black tea, yippee—"

"Indeed," I say.

We clink our teacups together as we sit on the same blue sofa, the one with the lion's feet. It faces the window; the books are on all sides of us, and they feel like friends.

"I never drank tea before I met you," I said.

"Well, good then," she says, setting her tea cup down gently. "I try to be useful. Tea can be relaxing, and Billy—he, well he was *such* a worrywart. That boy . . ." She shakes her head and smiles down at her feet.

"There's a name for the fear of everything," I say, sipping, it burns my tongue, but I drink it anyway. A little bit of pain hurts no one, plus it's tea, and it's comforting and gentle, pretty much like nothing in my life right now.

"What's the name?" she asks, clasping her hands in her lap. Right now she seems to be the only person who seems genuinely interested in what I've got to say. Like what I say actually matters, and she's picking up what I'm putting down, because what I'm putting down isn't half bad.

"Panophobia," I reply. She nods and presses her lips together so they disappear. She takes a breath, a story-mode anticipatory one.

"So I'd help him—through his fears, you know? He and Stacey are so different. Stacey's a doer and a worker, she'll get rid of her anxiety by doing more homework than she has to, studying harder than she needs. Billy's an analyzer, to the point where it becomes debilitating. It would really eat away at his confidence, seeing his sister excel in school while he barely squeaked by. I told him that he could find his own way of coping—he loves to read, so I'd give him a bunch of Louis L'Amour paperbacks. He was crazy for those westerns. I always saw a writer in him and suggested he get a journal and write out all his emotions, even if they didn't make sense."

"Did that idea go over well?" I ask doubtfully. It's the kind of advice that would make me go crazy.

"Not at first. He thought having a journal showed weakness. Teenaged girls aren't the only ones with diaries, I told him. I bought a leather-bound notebook that was as masculine as it gets. He used it too. Very discreetly."

"Sounds like you guys were friends or something," I say, after a little bit of silence.

She sighs. "Oh, as adults, we're not made to be your friends, Phineas. We pretend we know better than you, and sometimes we do and sometimes we don't. Maybe for a while I stepped in as the mother figure for Billy, since Page had passed when he was so young. Every boy needs a mother, and maybe Billy saw me as a calming force. Storytellers like myself tend to be that way—and Billy was a listener, was he ever, so he took it all in. The stories were an escape. Those worth telling always have some kind of message to relay."

I nod my head in agreement. That's how I feel about Orah. Her stories calm me, take me out of the story of my own life, which, as it stands right now, is all types of black-colored birds: grackle, ashy storm petrel, Brandt's cormorant, Eurasian jackdaw—each name harsh and choppy, each wing a black slash against thunderous sky.

"I'm not really close with my parents," I say. "They're not around a lot. Mom's always working at the restaurant, and Pop's checked out. I don't really care, you know? They can go and have their fantasies and regrets, but I really don't give a shit."

She nods slowly. "You've got some anger in you."

"Aren't you perceptive," I say, leaning back on the couch. I play with a pull in the fabric.

"There's a way to let it go, I think."

Let it go, right. Wouldn't that be nice, having these balloons of emotions we could release, ah, good-bye angry red balloon, I feel so much better! I grit my teeth and blurt out, "But what if you have every goddamn right to be mad, and it would be goddamn disrespectful to yourself and the rest of human existence *not* to be mad about it?"

I trust Orah enough to tell her about how Faith lost her eye, but I don't trust myself to keep my shit together long enough to tell it. So I don't.

And I don't know why she's smiling tightly, but she is, and it's doing nothing but pissing me off until I see that smiling is just the beginning of another story. I think it's going to be an important one.

"We were up at the lake house, one weekend. Now, how old was Billy . . . he was around eleven years old, that's right. Took him up there, and it rained all day, so we played cards and drank iced tea and read magazines. *Reader's Digest.* We would read the joke sections out loud. Some of them were a hoot."

"Nice," I say, calming down. "I like those too."

I take another sip of tea, and my body relaxes again. I see why the Brits like their afternoon tea; it slows time down. Taking out a tea set and rushing through that shit isn't going to fly. What person have you seen hurrying it up with tea? Can't speed up boiling, steeping takes a while, don't want to pour quickly, cream and sugar can get complicated especially when you've got someone like Orah who likes both in different proportions. It's a party, but it's a take-your-time party, the world isn't going anywhere, so sip and stay awhile.

Orah's looking at me over the rim of her cup, eyes lit up, like she knows my thoughts.

"It was late at night. Billy was sleeping on the couch. Loved it in the living room because of the large windows that overlooked the lake. When I say large, I mean *gigantic.* Don't see windows like that anymore." She had told me about the windows before; the woman is getting more forgetful. I'm not sure how much of her behavior has to do with getting older and how much of it has to do with the effects of indigo. The day we packaged up the drug for the indigo-go girls, she seemed completely with it, and then some.

Her voice lowers. "I had taken more indigo than I should have. I was looking out those windows, standing next to the couch Billy was sleeping on, when I came out of it. I had a steaming cup of tea in my hands, suddenly. I don't know where it had come from. It frightened me and I dropped the mug, big mug it was, and it spilled all over Billy. His face, his neck. He woke up screaming."

"God, Orah, I—" She silences me with a slight motion of her hand.

"After the hospital and the healing, he didn't talk to me. He was so angry with me. Hated me. Especially when I told him I was . . . high. Dan didn't let him come visit me, not that I was expecting Billy to *want* to visit. So it was just me, and I was fine with it, but I was—I was *angry*. Like nothing else. And that's hard. Knowing that Billy probably won't ever forgive me."

"Orah," I say, placing a hand on her shoulder. Oh, how I can relate. It's a relief that life is a disaster for all of us. "You didn't mean it. It was an accident."

"Come on now, I shouldn't have been using around a child. I shouldn't have been using at all."

"I know about guilt," I say.

"I know you do. That scar of yours," she says, gesturing to it, like she knows all about it. But she doesn't. I turn my face so she can only see my profile. The skin of my scar always feels twenty times hotter than the rest.

"I'm strong because of it. You don't fuck with me. People know that. You don't fuck with me," I repeat. I'm getting all worked up again. My hands are grasping the edge of the couch, holding on so tight, like it's the only thing between me and a sixty-foot drop. Orah places her hand on top of mine, and I flash a don't-you-dare look, but she isn't scared of me, she'll be taking my dares and calling my bluffs all day long. The pressure she puts on my knuckles, it kind of reminds me of Faith, what she used to do to get me to pay attention. *Look. Listen. See, goddammit.* Orah's trying to get me there too, or maybe she's also doing it for herself, who knows, things are never just about you. That's why there are two cups in a tea set. You can't do this shit alone.

"Hi," a voice comes from the doorway. It's Stacey. Great. Grand. The last time I saw her was in the school hallway when she told me about the evils of indigo in her family. Her light-pink button-down blouse looks delicate and soft. I glance at the time—should have left an hour ago to avoid seeing her after school let out. How did I lose track of time? Her eyes flit over Orah's hand on mine, before I'm able to slide away.

"What are you doing here?" she asks, irritation in her voice. I'm assuming she heard that last part of our conversation about my scar, and it's humiliating. She's not supposed to see that side of me.

"I'll go," I say.

"He was here to see you," Orah says, lying. It's awkward city, because Stacey's not moving and neither am I, and Orah's just sitting there. We're all set on pause. I don't think Orah is aware that Stacey and Dan know about our indigo arrangement.

Stacey breaks the silence. "I've never heard you tell that story before. I heard it from Dad and Billy, but not you." She sets her backpack down and waits for a response. The sunlight through the window dashes across her white sneakers. She doesn't seem altogether pissed. At least I got that going for me.

Orah gently smiles up at her. "I guess I thought you had heard it enough times."

"Actually no. We never wanted to talk about it. And now Finn hears it?"

I raise my hands. "I don't want to cause any problems—"

Orah cuts me off. "I brought it up."

"It's fine," Stacey says. "I just wasn't expecting Finn back here . . . bonding. And such."

Trust me, I want to say, I wasn't expecting it either. It's probably pathetic and definitely bizarre that I've never felt so open with a woman—an elderly one at that—besides my sister.

Orah stands up and brushes off her pants. She turns to Stacey. "Your father won't be home until late. I'll make salmon for us. We can talk. How does that sound?"

With some hesitance Stacey says, "All right. Sure."

It's not the most enthusiastic response, but Orah seems satisfied. "I'll leave you two alone to chat," she says. "You still do that these days, right? Or is texting your only mode of communication?"

Stacey smirks; I look up at the ceiling, avoiding all eye contact. I'm not sure I want Orah to leave. But leave she does, and it's just me and Stacey. I get up and make a move toward the door.

She steps in front of my path. "Let's go for a walk," she says.

Oh boy, here we go. "I didn't mean to cause any trouble. Orah and I aren't doing anything, you know, drug-related," I say quietly. "It's just—"

"She enjoys your company. Come on," she says, touching my wrist lightly.

CHAPTER FORTY

STACEY'S WOODS OUT BACK AREN'T HALF BAD, NOT AS DARK AND PINE-TREED AS WHAT'S BEHIND THE TRAILER PARK, BUT IT SMELLS GOOD, AND THERE'S A FIELD OF WILDFLOWERS WITH TRAMPLED PATHS WINDING THROUGH. Sparrows flit across our path; they are known to like the company of humans. A bunch of purple knotweed and Brown-Eyed Susans, Queen Anne's lace and milkweed. I pick a sprig of lavender and tuck it behind my ear as we trudge through, colors popping so hard, each flower bud an exclamation. I keep walking in front of her, thinking I know where I'm going, looking like I do, might as well be the inventor of goddamn GPS. Confidence is the key in this life. Bullshit until it's no longer bullshit.

"Did you know that lavender comes from the same family as mint? And it's a great deterrent of mice and mosquitoes?" I ask. I figure if I ramble on about something, I'll avoid the inevitable. She's going to bitch me out, and that's okay, I can't think of a time in the past month where I didn't deserve it.

"No," she says. She's not amused, but she's not dismissive either.

"Yeah, it was also used in Egyptian times during the

mummification process. Don't ask me how. You'd have to consult the experts about that," I say, turning around, walking backward so that I'm facing her.

"How do you know all these facts?" she asks. Her pink sleeves are see-through with the sun hitting her from behind; there's the delicate outline of her arm, there's the elegant curve of her shoulder.

"Oh, well," I say, shrugging, peering up at the late afternoon sky. "I used to always read those amazing fact books when I was a kid. Amazing facts about foxes, amazing facts about zebras, you get what I mean. The first one I ever had was amazing facts about ants."

"Ants?" Her quizzical expression murders me. It really does.

"Yep." I'm on edge; I try to squelch the feeling with a hard swallow. "I bet you didn't know this: ants are capable of carrying objects fifty times their own body weight."

"I knew that," she says, unimpressed. She uproots a piece of switch grass and casts it away. All right, smarty-pants, you want game, I got game. I stop dead in my tracks; she almost runs into my chest.

"Hey, watch it," she says, pushing on my shoulder with the heel of her hand, but she doesn't look at me.

A warmish wind ruffles the bottom of my T-shirt, whips her hair north, east, south, west. "The total biomass of all ants on earth is roughly equal to the total biomass of all people on earth."

"Impossible," she says, yanking up another piece of grass.

"Scientists have estimated that there are at least 1.5 million ants on the planet for every human being. Suck on that, sweetheart," I say, grinning.

She looks slightly annoyed.

"I knew you didn't know that one." I snatch the grass out of her hand and throw it into the field.

"It's a good one," she grudgingly admits. "Now sit. I want to talk to you."

I don't expect the tug on my wrist. I don't expect to be so *close* to her, I'm talking face-freckle close. We sit crossed-legged, our knees almost touching—the path is just wide enough. Her ankle bone peeks out from under the cuff of her pants, and it's so pale and vulnerable, God, it's kind of dangerous, such beauty exposed to the elements.

"I'm not going to tell Mimi I know about your arrangement. I'm pretty sure Dad told you to stop selling."

"I'm taking care of this situation." This is not a lie. She doesn't need to know about how exactly I'm taking care of it. To be honest, I don't know what I'm going to do at this point. Will Early contact me? It's been almost a week since I gave the pizza boy the box of indigo. Will Dan find a way to mitigate the situation? Will I have to give up on my plan to help my sister? No. That's not an option.

"I hope so. I want this to be resolved by the time I go to Stanford. I want it to be a distant memory I don't have to worry about."

"It will be," I say.

She doesn't look convinced. "I want to trust you." She pauses. "And I don't want to like you. But I do."

Do I apologize? Do I jump up and down with joy? I think for once I'll just sit still and let her talk. But she doesn't say anything right away, so we watch hyper sparrows dart around us.

Finally she speaks. "I used to come out here as a kid, when we'd visit Mimi."

"Oh?" I say, wanting her to talk more about it.

She sighs heavily. "I didn't visit Mimi for a long time after Billy's accident. Mostly Dad came here to check up on her, to make sure she was okay, but even he wanted to keep his distance. For a while she didn't use indigo, and I think Dad's visits helped. She knew that if she behaved—for lack of a better word—we might come back into her life. But then she'd fall off the wagon. She'd get that cloudy look in her eyes and get confused for no reason. She'd think my grandfather was still alive. I hated being around her when she was like that. Lately I'd say she's using less than before. I feel like you might have something to do with it."

"She's turning over a new leaf ever since you guys moved in with her."

"I noticed that." I could bring up that the origin of my partnership with Orah was precisely to get rid of indigo once and for all, but I don't want this conversation to be about me. I'm sick of me. I focus on some trampled white petals—probably of a hibiscus. She smiles to herself, tucks a strand of hair behind her ear.

"Mimi came out here with me one day when I first moved here," she says. "The whole walk we bickered; she was convinced there was some red flower growing in the field when I knew for a fact there wasn't. We arrived right here, where you and I are. Or close to it, anyway. And . . ." she pauses. "And then she started telling me about my mom. I was only a year old when she died, so she feels like a ghost to me. She told me about how good my mom was as a first-grade teacher—always the kids' favorite. She told me how she made dried flower arrangements in a way that they always looked better than fresh flowers. She told me about how she'd read classic literature out loud when she was pregnant with Billy and me—*Pride and Prejudice, Anna Karenina, Wuthering Heights.*"

"You were bound for intelligence."

She scoffs, shaking her head.

I ask, "So after, it was better between the two of you?"

"Not so much better, but different," she says. "Then different eventually turned into a little better. I see she's changed. We talk more. I want to hear what she has to say."

"Glacial progress is better than no progress at all," I say.

"I can tell she loves you," she says. She briefly touches my knee. I feel something akin to electrocution. "When I saw the two of you together back there—"

"God, how long were you listening in?"

"Long enough. Long enough to know that there is more to your relationship than selling drugs. And to know that it's not altogether a bad thing. I wish Billy could see her like this—coherent and healthy. If he hadn't run away and moved here with us instead, he would have given her a chance. I know he would—even in the years he wouldn't go see her, he still talked about her. He'd talk about her stories as a nurse."

"Have you talked to Billy?" I ask. For some reason I want to know this dude's okay. Scar brothers, or something lame like that. Has he found it in his heart to forgive Orah? Or forgive himself for not forgiving her?

Stacey pulls at the flowers around her. Her fingers will be stained green.

"I know where he is." Her voice is whispery, secretive, as if someone's listening in. She looks up over the horizon of weeds. All I see is sky and wisps and dashes of clouds.

"Where?" I ask before I can stop myself. I'm not sure she'll tell me. But she does.

"You know that farm where we think the flower first grew? Where we think the virus started?"

"Yeah." Now this is getting interesting.

"That's where. No one else knows. Not even my dad," she says. "Orah told us the location a long time ago. She was high, we were just little kids, and she talked and talked about where the farm is and how it's no longer in use. It's just land forgotten and wasting away. But she was so specific about it Billy was able to find it. I don't think she thought we would ever remember."

"And no one knows but you?"

She nods, biting her lip. "He's staying in the farmhouse, even though it has no heat or electricity or running water. But it's the only place where he wants to be. The only place he feels safe because no one knows about it. God, you must think we're a family of freaks."

"Trust me," I say, covering the top of her hand with mine, "you're not."

I wait for her to pull back, retreat. Wait for it, wait for it . . . but there is just the type of inhale you make before a statement—that's happening. Clearing of the throat—that's happening too. Yet everything is so still. Until she snags the lavender sprig behind my ear that I had forgotten about. I reach out to take it back, hey, I say, get your own, her laughter could inspire a rose to bloom . . . I don't deserve this, a moment of such beauty and purity and preciousness. The sparrows have settled, as if they know better than to disrupt. And then, miraculously, it gets better. She grasps my forearm, I bring my hand up to her cheek, her eyes lift to meet mine. Good God, my heart. Ablaze. Our lips brush against each other softly, the quietest sound in the world, the swaying grass knows of it, the wildflowers do too.

SUNDAY, JUNE 2

CHAPTER FORTY-ONE

EVERYONE IN DAMMERTOWN IS AT CHURCH EXCEPT FOR MY PARENTS, WHO ARE WORKING, MY SISTER, WHO'S PROBABLY AT PETER'S, AND ME AND MY BUZZ. Sometimes I like to think of my high as a person or an animal. A little kid endlessly jumping on a trampoline. A cat lazing in the sun. It's never too early for cocaine.

I decide it's a fantastic idea to clean out my drawers and then rearrange the organizational system under my bed. I can do spring cleaning at the beginning of June, right? My shirts in Tupperware boxes are folded all wrong. Mismatched socks are the worst. My boxers are not in the order they should be in. Prints on top, solids on the bottom. It should be the other way around, obviously. I spend the next thirty minutes folding.

I'm starting to smell exhaust from an engine. It's ruining the purity of my organizational overhaul, ruining the soaring high that's giving me these housewife need-to-clean urges. I pull the curtain aside, peek outside. The windows of a Lincoln Town Car are tinted too dark to see anything. Another line is waiting for me on the nightstand, so I do it, and it goes through me hard. A zap, a boom to the middle of my chest, electricity whizzing through the folds of my brain. I walk out of the trailer with my fists balled at my side. This car doesn't belong here; it's the kind of car you see important white dudes slink out of in front of big shiny buildings. And then it dawns on me, my charged-up brain is just registering the situation and what it means.

The driver's side window slides down.

"Get in," a middle-age man says. He's got a bulbous nose and forearms as thick as my legs.

"Who are you?" I ask. Stupid question. My voice is one big prepubescent squeak.

He cocks his head to the side. "Who the fuck do you think I am?"

I am not prepared for this. I'm *so* not prepared for this. No knife, no cell phone, no right mind, no defense but surrender, and all I can say is that my socks and boxers are folded correctly.

He's aiming a gun at my stomach. Holy shit of all shit. The black paint of the car, the shiny tint of the windows. Sun beating down on both, showing my dumbass, weak-ass reflection. Sloppy clothes, sloppy hair, unshowered and greasy. I feel out of control. My head isn't on straight. I've got to get my head on straight.

"Okay," I say, putting my hands up. Immediately I feel even more idiotic because he's laughing, almost giggling, because I'm such a fake. A fraud. I should have never asked Jason about Early. Should never have thought I could tango with people like this.

"Put your hands down, kid. I'm not the police," he says, chuckling through his words.

I reach for the backseat door.

"Front seat," he says, flicking his gun.

We drive to the outskirts of Dammertown and then even farther. The interior of the car is all beige leather, the seats are soft and would be a great reward to my ass, if I didn't think I was going to be murdered at any second. The new car smell is so prominent, it's a separate feature of the car altogether, like the dashboard GPS or the tinted glass that hides the backseat or the Bose stereo system.

I can't help but see out of the corner of my eye that his forearms are so *big*. Popeye-massive, no joke. I take notice of my own. I should have lifted more weights. Joined the track team. Of course his nose looks like it's been broken seventy-five times. Of course he holds the silence so long, so well, that I don't dare to interrupt it.

We drive over potholes on a country road, see cows lying down; Orah says that means rain is coming in. Despite that, the sun is high and almighty and I think, no way, this can't be happening on such a picture-perfect day. Yet stress and panic don't even describe what I feel, nope, it feels more like the strongest fist in the world, the damn fist of a *god*, is squeezing my insides.

I hear the tinted window between the front and backseat open. When I crane my head around, I see only the flash of an old man, he's got to be *at least* eighty years old, Orah-age, before the driver hits me in the face with the butt of the gun. I'm surprised I'm not down for the count. I hold my nose to catch the blood, which has already dribbled down my shirt. The cocaine has left my body, got shocked right out, the high ran away kicking and screaming.

"Don't turn around, kid. You'll speak when you're spoken to," the driver says.

"Okay, okay," I say, pulling up my shirt to wipe my nose. My eyes are stinging, my joints are rattled.

A voice from the backseat says, "I hear you want to speak with me." It's a surprisingly normal voice—no grit, no rasp, not the slightest bit sinister. Sounds like a regular dude with kids and a two-car garage. Friendly. Neighborly. I don't know what I was expecting.

"Yeah," I say, through the material of my shirt. I try to get my act together, but that's kind of difficult when you're gushing blood and on the edge of blacking out. *Don't pass out, please consciousness stay with me* . . .

"I'm getting old," Early says plainly. I don't know where this is going, but I'm feeling a senior citizen diatribe coming on, that weighty kind of air strung with pearls of wisdom. The familiarity of it is Orah's fault.

"But we all share the same fate, and that's the beauty of it, you know. All of us so different but ultimately headed in the same direction. We should revel in that. We should count our blessings that there is a beginning and an end, and we should cherish our time on earth more because of it. If our time on earth went on forever, life would be watered down and there would be no drive or motivation to build. To *create*. Doesn't that sound terrifying?"

Now I hear his barely there Italian accent, mixed with a New York City tinge, and a gentleness that you would think contradicts both. But it doesn't. What do I say to his commentary? He's dropping philosophy left and right, but the point is completely lost upon me. And usually I get the point before it's halfway explained. Usually I'm the one *making* the point.

"I asked you a question," Early says. The threat in his voice is feather-light, but I hear it as loud as a train whistle. "Isn't that thought terrifying?"

"Yes," I say carefully.

"I think about that when I contemplate death. It's like that 'would you rather' game my grandchildren play. I'd take death over forever in an instant."

I really don't want to answer another question. The relief sinks so deep inside me when he doesn't ask one and goes on with his monologue fit for Shakespeare.

"What is the character of a man who thinks too much about the future? It took me a long time to let go of things I can't control. Fate is fate. Destiny is a living, breathing thing like you and me. There is nothing we can do about this creature. All we can do is take the present, the *now*, by the balls and hope that it doesn't turn on us." He sighs; I smell him. Piney cologne with an old furniture stink underneath. I hear him shift. How his clothes scratch against the leather. He taps something against the floor, and I can't tell if it's his foot or something else. "But I find myself dwelling upon the past. Are you a man who looks back?"

I don't risk any hesitation this time. "No."

"A one-word-answer man. I can respect that. Brevity can say so much." I listen to a swishing, perhaps it's his hands rubbing against the seat. "I reminisce on my roots. The fine nostalgia of it, the time when I was a young man—your age—just starting out fresh with that solid gait and a confidence surer than sure, but behind it all was a fierce anticipation of the world and the yearning to sink my teeth into it. That *drive* I was talking about." He makes a sound with his mouth, wet, repulsive, he's tasting the flavor of his words. "You can't move ahead without knowing your roots. Understanding the foundation of your life and how you can stack your wins up, one by one. Sometimes it all falls apart, sometimes the mortar doesn't hold. Then death mocks you, and you have two choices: give up or start all over again."

"Listen," I say, mustering up the courage to speak. "I was hoping we could—" All it takes is the menacing glare of the driver to get me to shut up. Doesn't even have to say anything.

"Yes, the foundation of things. The beginning. Roots," Early continues, as if unaware I'd said anything. "I asked Dan Braggs about the history of indigo—as you call it—when we had our talk just a few days ago. He didn't know a lot about it—didn't *want* to know a lot about it. He had no desire for the knowledge of its roots. I let it go for the time being. But Orah . . ."

The sound of her name out of his mouth is blasphemy, as if someone took a giant dump on the altar of a church. I want to scream out *don't you dare say her name*, and the effort to hold back is reddening my face. My nails are dug into my palms hard.

"I wasn't aware of Orah until Mike Frye told me he saw an elderly woman and a teenager with indigo. It was a comment made—with minimal coercion I assure you—while investigating who was selling a more powerful strain than mine. Do you want to know how I found out about indigo in the first place? My granddaughter. Just recently I was over at her parents' house and saw a bag of it in her room—it had that same look as my product, but even more beautifully colored. After questioning her and then trying it myself, I knew it was going to be a problem for my business. She didn't know who had sold it; she had gotten it from a friend. After that, everything came together so quickly—I talked with Dan, then chatted with Mike after he reached out to me, and then you and me? We found each other. I'm glad to know that indigo is so new to the streets that it's made no impact on my sales—yet. I'm nipping this in the bud." He pauses, taking a thin breath. "In terms of Orah Klaski, however, I thought, she's an old dog like me. A seasoned woman involved in a business that depends on growth would know the foundation from which success burgeons."

"Leave her out—"

"Please," he interrupts quietly, darkly. "Just a few hours ago, I paid her a visit at home while everyone was at church. Dammertown must be a spiritual place. As a spiritual man, I can appreciate that."

My reaction is faster than my wits. I punch the glove compartment, not caring that the driver sledge-hammers me back against the seat with his meaty forearm and then presses against my throat to restrain me. "What did you do to her?" I croak out.

"I had a discussion with her, just as I'm having with you." He waits to continue so his message sinks in. "I asked her a simple question: where did indigo begin? I want to know everything about it, how it all started, and why your indigo is so much better than the flowers that grow in my fields. After only a little bit of persuasion, she started to mention the Adirondacks. She mentioned telling stories about it to her grandchildren. I don't think she was quite in her right mind at that point, but it sparked my interest. I haven't been able to stop thinking about it since. Unfortunately, before she could say any more, she vomited, slurred her speech, and then passed out. I believe it was a stroke. Poor, poor woman. That is a harsh ending for her," he says somberly.

I'm rambling on about something, I'm not sure what I'm spouting, I swat at whatever is near me, I'm trying to climb past the partition so I can get my hands on Early, who is looking at me like a disappointed father with a disappointing son. Cold metal is against my head again. It's amazing how hard the barrel feels pushing into my skull, and how soft I am against it.

302

I slump back into my seat, tears streaming down my face, combining with blood from my nose to make trails of pink.

"Give him a break, Leo. Let him mourn the loss of his friend. You'd consider her a friend, wouldn't you?" Early asks.

"I consider her family," I say simply.

"I am sorry for your loss. I can promise you that I didn't touch her, didn't hurt her. Just very bad timing." He leans in close to my ear. "Now *you* wouldn't happen to know where the origin of indigo is, would you?"

"No," I say. "That's the God's honest truth."

I could tell him where the crypt is, couldn't I? Then they'd leave the farm alone. And Billy. If they were to find him at the original indigo site then he's in trouble—we all are. If only he hadn't been caught snorting indigo by one of Early's guys. Stupid. Freaking. Addict. How can I keep Early away from at least one member of Stacey's family?

I'm unable to take the thinking any further because Leo suddenly plummets his elbow into my throat. I pitch forward, holding onto my neck, while I raggedly inhale for breath that's playing hard to get.

"I don't believe you," I hear Early say, somewhere in the midst of the ringing in my ears. I'm suffocating, my windpipe has probably collapsed. I bend myself forward even more, toward the floor mat. Finally the oxygen decides to make an arrival. The ringing subsides. I think it's okay to sit up.

"I have no reason to lie to you," I rasp. "If I knew, you bet your ass I'd be there myself."

I feel something sharp graze the side of my neck. When the knife pierces skin I let out a loud groan. He's slit my neck. I slap a hand around my throat in case my head falls off, I wait for darkness, the sweet relief, the gushing blood. It never comes.

Dread. Panic. Worse than a timonous bird. I'm calling out to the powers of improvisation to get me out of this bind. "I'll offer you all the indigo I have. Pounds and pounds of it. Let me bring it to you," I say, grasping for straws. "Then I'll find you the origin of it. My shit should tide you over till then. And I already told Dan I'd stop dealing. Everything."

Early's laughter is grating and unnerving. It goes on and on, prickling me like fields and fields of dried grass against my bare ankles. But now I'm jacked up something fierce just thinking about Orah and how he must have treated her. He probably didn't even flinch when she fell to the floor.

"Look at me," Early says.

I answer the demand. I can't believe my eyes when I fully view this squinty old man with a straw hat, blue band around it, khaki pants and a white, short-sleeved, button-down shirt. He holds a cane with a smudged brass handle that looks sturdier than him.

"You're in way over your head, kid."

I ignore this. "Do we have a deal?" I ask.

Early scratches his tanned cheek, cranks his mouth off to the side. It's not grotesque, it's the look of a pensive man, a man who wins and wins and wins. I didn't think it was possible to sweat this hard. I try to look confident without saying a thing, but it's too late for that. Early and I eyeball each other, yet he's been staring people down since the beginning of time, and I've barely earned my staring stripes. Don't even need to say I look away first. All the while I'm shrieking in my head, Orah, Orah, you can't be gone, you were, you were, no, you *are*—

"Tonight," Early says. Then stops. "I want you and the rest of the indigo in this same spot at two in the morning. And I want more information on the origin. I'm not letting this go." I make note of where I am. There are a few dilapidated shacks along the treeline used as hunting cabins a long time ago. There is a moose crossing sign up ahead. This is where it's all going to happen.

Leo yanks the door open and pushes me out of the car. He squeals away, dirt and pebbles kicking up in my face, it's all I'm tasting, and even so, I feel like I got off easy. I watch the red taillights disappear around a corner that leads into the woods and eventually toward western New York. And here I go, sprinting then running then limping back into Dammertown, which is ten miles away, ten long miles to get real cozy with questions all the walking in the world won't answer.

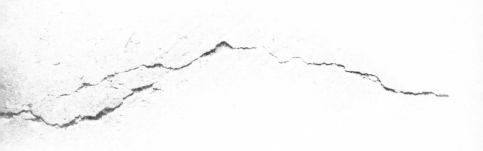

CHAPTER FORTY-TWO

DO I BOOK IT TO STACEY'S HOUSE OR TO THE TRAILER OR STRAIGHT TO THE HOSPITAL TO SEE ORAH? By the time I'm nearing D-Town, I decide to use my final strength to make a run for home, grab my cell phone, and jump into my car with the salt-sting of sweat in my eyes. I know there is blood on my face and neck, but there's no time to clean up. I'm dialing numbers, Stacey, Dan, their house, the hospital, no one's picking up, I'm thinking I'll choose the hospital, Dan and Stacey would have already left church and discovered her. I don't want to think any further than that. I'm so out of breath my whole face is numb, my legs are achy as all get-out, my thoughts are stumbling over themselves to catch up and register what is now beyond a dilemma.

Ellis Hospital isn't the easiest place for me to visit. When I pull up in the parking lot, the memory of my sister's accident crashes down on me: me and Pop in the ambulance holding each of her hands, me reciting bird facts in alphabetical order, Mom rushing through the wide automatic hospital doors still wearing her waitress's apron. We sat in the waiting area after they took her in, a room that Dante should add as a tenth circle of hell. Screaming child, quiet crying, antiseptic smell that doesn't "anti" anything, television stuck on the same channel.

Busting through the door, I storm right up to the main desk where a nurse sits wearing pink hospital scrubs, hair slicked back in a tight ponytail. I tell her I'm looking for Orah, Orah Klaski. Is she here? What did they do with her? A man being pushed in a wheelchair glides past me, and there's a slight breeze from the brisk roll. The smell of its metal reminds me of swing sets. I say I'm her grandson, and it doesn't feel like a lie. When she tells me Orah's in intensive care, I demand her to repeat it, until I believe Orah *is*, and not *was*. I sigh with relief, she's still alive, thank *God*, a new burst of verve surges through me because she's going to pull out of this, champion her way into the light and through her nineties, wouldn't be surprised if the tough broad would live to see one hundred.

"Floor four, east wing," she says. I don't even bother waiting for the elevator, I lunge up the stairs, taking two steps at a time, pound the door open with the heel of my palm. I walk down the hall, it's hushed, none of the noise of the ER. I reach the east wing, and there's a waiting room where I immediately see the back of Stacey's head. Dan sees me and in a second he's up and moving my way. Stacey whips her head around, her hair is frizzy and spectacular, her frown I fully expect.

"How is she?" I say to him. I'm so on the edge I don't care that I'm grabbing his shirt sleeves and repeating the question over and over. Sweat stains galore under my armpits, but this is me not giving a fuck, because I would sweat out my guts to change the course of events.

"Hey." He coaxes me to sit down. "What the hell happened to you?" he asks, pointing at the blood and grime on me.

I shake my head. "Orah?" is all I can say.

"She's alive. We won't know the damage until she comes out of it," he says.

I bow my head. "That's good, that's really good." I knead my hands together, let the water drain from my eyes and splat on the linoleum. Stacey's bottom lip is trembling, she looks away, swiping a knuckle over her cheekbone. It isn't right, this thing called death, even though Early says it's the reason we live, well sure dude, death's great, go have your bro-mance with it. I'll stay on this side of living, thank you very much.

Dan sits next to me on the sagging polyfoam couch and puts a hand on my shoulder.

"He paid me a visit this morning. Early," I say.

"What?" The weight of his hand on my back abruptly vanishes. He tugs me away from the room, into the light-pink hallway. I give a quick last look at Stacey; once I tell Dan what I have to tell him, I might not ever be allowed near Stacey again.

I clear my throat, fist against my mouth, wondering how to begin.

"I sent him a message. At that party at Claire's house. I wanted to talk to him, and I thought I could work something out."

"You did *what*?"

"I know, I know," I say, nodding, my fingers fanning out in front of me as if to hold off the anger that's already building up in him. "I did it before you and I had our talk in the car. I didn't know, okay? I thought that maybe the message wouldn't be delivered and all this would blow over, I really did. That's why I didn't tell you. I didn't think he would actually—" Dan's jaw is tensing, though it doesn't dissuade me to continue. "He showed up at my place, took me for a drive asking about the origin of indigo, and of course I don't know where it is, and he said *you* didn't know, and that he'd just been to visit Orah—"

Dan grabs my wrist, it takes all my willpower not to yelp.

"He hurt her?" he growled.

"No, at least he said he didn't." I try to wrench my arm away from him, but he's on it like a pit bull. "She said there was a place in the Adirondacks," I say quickly. The strain from my ten-mile trek is catching up—I might vomit from exhaustion. "But then she had a stroke, and that's everything she told him. I swear." I didn't think it was possible, but Dan squeezes me harder, finally eliciting the yelp I was holding back. "I made a deal with him. I said I would give him the rest of the indigo I had and that I would try to find the origin of it. I don't know why I said that, I panicked, I can deliver the first thing but not—"

My wrist is liberated, but not without a slam against the wall. A nurse speed-walking down the corridor cranks her head back, but decides we're not worth breaking her pace.

"There's more indigo?" Dan asks.

"A crypt that only Orah knows about. Well, and me." There's no use in hiding the fact from Dan at this point. "In the D-Town Cemetery."

He frowns. "Apparently Orah knows a lot of things. She never told me about her ancestor's farm in the Adirondacks. I should have been more aware of how far the flower went back in her family. I should have known that this whole situation was running much deeper than I anticipated. My son is lost because of it and now Orah . . ." He rakes his fingers through his dark hair and turns his back to me.

The air changes, becomes denser, *readjusts*, and I don't need to look to know that Stacey is there listening. Our gazes meet; we are aware that the knowledge of Billy's whereabouts is dangerous. We are the only two people on the planet who know. She doesn't want to betray him, but Early won't stop until he finds the farm. Her mouth parts, there are jewels of sweat on her forehead. Is she scared that I'm going to expose her brother?

"I'm meeting Early tonight," I say, so she doesn't have to speak. Stacey steps back, bites down on her bottom lip. "Two a.m. on Old County Road, going west, that stretch of road with those abandoned hunting cabins? There's a moose-crossing sign right there. I'll give him the indigo, we can talk it out. I don't doubt my skills of persuasion, okay? I'm still alive, aren't I?"

Stacey mumbles under her breath, I'm sure it's a derisive comment, it's got the tone to go along with *stupid* or *imbecile* or *downright prick*.

"You won't be after tonight. It's a guarantee. Once he knows he's not getting anything out of you, you're of no use to him, you're only a hindrance. I'm coming with you tonight—"

"Daddy, no," Stacey says, the first words she's spoken since I arrived.

Dan continues, "You harvest what's left and pick me up. The only way to come to an agreement is if we're all there. He might not welcome my presence, but . . ."

"Daddy," Stacey says again.

"I'll be fine," he says to her, but he's still looking at me.

"Or he might send someone in his place," I say.

"Then I guess that's the risk we're going to have to take." He's as tired and strung out as I am and not hiding it very well, as I am. "God, Finn, why didn't you just tell—"

"Hey," I say, not wanting to interrupt Dan, but I have to because I see Jason scoot by us. He's not looking so hot. I grab him by the back of the shirt.

"What the fuck are you doing here?" My tone comes out way too harsh. He faces me head-on, and instantly I feel bad because of the expression on his face. Poor bastard's been crying.

"Seriously, bro. You better step off," he says, a ferocity in his energy that has never been there before, out of hibernation here he comes. For the first time, he intimidates *me*. I throw my hands up in the air between us, stepping backward.

"Okay, okay, man. I'm not looking for a fight." I don't think I'd be physically capable of one anyway. Jason's head is down, he's about to leave. "What happened?"

"I told Mike to leave the indigo alone, not to sell that shit, we all warned him about Early, but he didn't listen, said he could work it out with Early, and now Victoria is in surgery." He swallows. "They fucked her up pretty good. If only he had been home . . ."

Jason chokes up, puts his hands over his face. Dan stays quiet and takes a position at Stacey's side. I don't think Jason realizes who Dan is, and *what* he is—the grief just keeps him talking, talking, and talking.

"She's like family to me, Finn, and you know how much Mike loves her. Borderline obsession. He's going to be on a rampage, but I tell him, I say, these guys aren't people you want to mess around with. But I know he's not listening. He's not going to let it go, not when Victoria was . . ." He chokes up again.

Ever noticed the flavor of anger in your mouth? The bitterness starts in the back of your throat and migrates to the tip of your tongue until metal is the only thing you taste. It's where I'm at right now. I'm pretty sure Mike's ten steps ahead of that.

"Stay out of it, you two. It's being taken care of," Dan says, off to the side.

Jason flicks his eyes toward Dan and then back to me. He's just registering that Stacey's dad is the cop who arrested me after the pig's head fiasco, but instead of freaking out about it, he shuts his eyes in resignation.

"Whatever, man. If you want to use what I said about my brother against me, go right ahead."

"We've got bigger problems," Dan says.

"Yeah. Right. I got to get going," Jason says, trudging away. Dan murmurs to Stacey about how he's going to smooth things out, make it right again, but I'm finding it hard to believe that any of us are coming out of this unscathed. Or even alive.

CHAPTER FORTY-THREE

THE FACT THAT DAN AND STACEY EVEN ALLOW ME TO SEE ORAH IS BEYOND ALL COMPREHENSION. Maybe the image of me and Orah in the morning room is an imprint on Stacey's heart. Or maybe they are both too exhausted to argue. The nurse allows us only a few minutes with her. If my heart was wrecked before, it's good and destroyed the moment I see her hooked up to machines, with an oxygen mask covering her face, and surrounded by tubes and beeps and other equipment I don't understand. Stacey collapses in a chair and gently takes Orah's limp hand. I take the liberty to follow suit on the other side because Dan doesn't approach her, and he doesn't stop me. He squeezes his eyes shut and presses the back of his hand underneath his nose. After a silent few seconds, he excuses himself, mumbling something about making phone calls.

Looking at Orah as still as stone is unnerving, because I guess I never *really* looked at her before. I know she has hazel eyes. I know she has a weird mole on her jawline. Her hair, of course, I know. But I never noticed that her hands are surprisingly smooth and not too wrinkly. No liver spots, no creepy veins that fork all over the place. In them I see youth, I see her teenaged self. I start talking to her like she can hear me:

"Orah, seriously, you've got to be doing this now? We have so many teatimes to hit up, we got the morning room, which is pretty much no good without you. I'll make sure that I get the Earl Grey you like, the tea in the blue box and not the gray box—you can see why I got that confused, right? The *Birds of America* book is getting pretty worn down, but that doesn't mean I'm not treating it with respect. I read that goddamn thing every night like scripture, pray to a different bird every night, pray for my sister, pray for your granddaughter, pray for you, you know? To let go of your guilt and the anger toward yourself? I'm not going to lie, I pray for myself sometimes, that's probably selfish, but I pray that each of the birds I see will take away a little bit of the stuff in me that makes me . . . off, a little off, I know I am . . . and eventually I'll be free. The birds will take away my fear, my sadness, my weakness midflight, and drop them like seeds for a different species of wildflowers."

I hear Stacey crying, but I keep going. I have to talk, to get Orah to listen.

"I want that for you," I continue. "Your wildflowers will grow too, just as mine will, and I'm seeing purple for you—maybe lavender . . . yeah, that seems right—and I'm imagining some yellow ones for me. Maybe like buttercups; you can put those up to your chin, and they reflect their yellow, it like, becomes a part of your skin. I wouldn't mind that, making a kind of thumbprint on some people, here and there, because, because . . . you know . . . Orah . . . you know, you've made your thumbprint on me—and I don't need a stupid flower to go reminding me of it."

A sharp intake of breath, so serious it changes the pressure in the room. Stacey.

"Fuck you, Finn," she says, sniffling, hiccupping her breaths, clogged nose. "Fuck you."

I slowly pull the chair away from the bed, because I know that Orah is her family, really her family, and she needs her privacy, and I have no business being here, and I'm the one who—

"Don't you *dare* leave," she says, getting up and coming around to my chair, her shoulders scrunched and tense. I brace myself for the slap. I'm going to take it like a man; I sit up straight and give her my whole face to do as she pleases. Her shadow umbrellas me, moving closer. There is anger, but there is also fear, and I think that's what makes her crumple against me and onto my lap, makes her mold her body against mine so I'm cradling her as she sobs into my chest. I hold her tight. I try to be strong. Footsteps scuff behind me; I feel Dan's presence in the door frame. My chin grazes the top of Stacey's head, and I stroke her hair until she gets quiet, until the crying and shaking has subsided, and her chest expands with breath and mine constricts, and then we switch, and Orah is somewhere between our heartbeats, fighting.

Dan and I talk out in the hospital parking lot about the meet-up tonight. He wants me to pick him up with the remaining indigo from the crypt, we'll go to the place on Old County Road, and then he'll tell them it was all my fault. I'm an impulsive, shoot-before-he-aims cretin, and I didn't know what I was doing, and I didn't realize the territory I was encroaching upon, blah, blah, blah. We'll guarantee that Early can have all the indigo, as long as we can walk away unharmed. It seems so simple. It seems *too* simple.

The parking lot is spookily quiet. Stacey is still in the waiting room, per Dan's orders; I can't help but peer up at the hospital windows to catch an impossible glimpse of her.

"He's still going to want to know where the origin is," I say. "In the Adirondacks."

"I don't know where this place is. Orah didn't talk to me a lot about her family—for a while she didn't talk to me a lot about anything." He pauses. I'm not sure now is the time to tell him that Billy is in the Adirondacks and that Stacey didn't spill the truth to her father in order to protect her brother. I decide I'll keep my mouth shut until I talk to Stacey—if I even have the chance.

"Why didn't Orah ever tell you about it?"

Dan's getting clearly aggravated. "I didn't want to talk to her about certain aspects of her life—her addiction, her family history of sickness. I don't dwell on the past. I like *now*. I like moving forward. And Early? We'll have to find a way to tide him over so he's not so focused on the origin site. You have an impressive amount of indigo, don't you?"

"Yes," I say. And it used to be all mine. There goes my promise to Faith; now it's just a matter of staying alive. How did I get to this point? In the beginning it was all so harmless. "If he hasn't figured it out by now, we'll tell him that it's the Klaski DNA that creates the best high off the drug. We can give him the list of Klaski gravesites."

We both pause on this; all the Klaski graves are now bound to be desecrated by Early's crew. There is a special place in hell for people who grave-rob. What about people who facilitate the grave robbing?

But Dan is thinking two steps ahead. "That should hold him off for a while. I'm in the process of building up a strong case against him on other charges, and the PD supports this every step of the way. I might be able to arrest him before he comes after us for more."

"Ulterior motive," I say.

"Always," he answers.

"What about Stacey?" I'm fidgeting, biting the skin around my nails. I'm overly trying to hide my emotions and doing a terrible job.

He nods, he's already thought of this, *duh*. "I've got a guy who knows a little bit about what's going on. He'll watch over her until I return."

"What about my family?" I ask, a quivering in my voice. I'm weirdly freaking out, not just about Faith of course, but even about Mom and Pop. He's sensing it.

"I can have another of my guys check on them too."

I nod, but without much conviction.

"We have to have faith that this is going to work," Dan says. "We have to go into this situation with all the confidence in the world."

His eyes flit across the parking lot. He tells me to harvest quickly, go straight home, lay low until it's time. How could I not feel a deep premonition when the painfully blue sky darkens with clouds? How could I not think planning this out at a hospital isn't an omen? The best thing to do is get in my car and drive to the crypt. And with that thought, I almost laugh. Great, I think; the omens keep stacking up.

CHAPTER FORTY-FOUR

I CAN BARELY WALK STRAIGHT TO THE CRYPT AND I'M NOT EVEN THAT HIGH, JUST TOKED UP ENOUGH TO SCARE AWAY SOME OF THE NERVES. The trees and ferns and bumps all the same, the landscape on an everlasting loop. When I come across Orah's garden that she played off to Mike as the grow site, I know I still have a ways to go. Eventually I find the tall grass that hides the opening of the crypt. I dig the key out of my pocket and unlock the door. I'm instantly dowsed in drug dust, crypt dust, *other world* dust and the darkness enfolds me even though I'm not fully in. I feel for the lamp in the corner of the space and power it on. What I see before me is one giant NO.

No. Just *no*.

There is no indigo. All the flowers are gone. Just the vines with their spiraling tendrils are left, completely stripped and ravaged. Someone didn't come in here to harvest; someone came in here to destroy. And of course there are the bones, bigger now that they are exposed and abandoned. I've never seen a skull before, and the indigo had covered it up so well that it never dawned on me that oh yeah, that's a human head that was once filled with a brain, firing off thoughts and impulses, electrical currents of reasoning or lack thereof.

As the shock sinks in, I want to tear out my hair, gouge out my eyes, pull out my tongue, and I would do it, I really would, if I thought it would bring indigo back, but no, silly Finn, you actually thought this plan would work? Silly nilly. *Stupid. Fucking. Idiot.* The room turns around me, but it's me who's swaying, I feel for the wall for support and slide down it to the hard-packed ground, queasy, all tremors, no breath.

Who did this? Only Orah and I are aware of this place. Even Dan didn't want to know; he told me to just go get the stuff.

I almost want to laugh. Howl. Except for the part of me that wants to climb in with the skeletons. I pat down my pockets, feeling the slight relief that I had the foresight to bring it, maybe I knew this was going to happen and that I would need a little something to keep the peace. *Ha.* Like I'm at war with myself, and this needle is a pen to sign the treaty. At least I've still got my humor, and that's saying a lot in a shit storm. I'm shaking my head, wow, just wow, they should *at least* make a low-budget film out of this. I take out my lighter, got everything lined up, wait, *wait*, what was it that Orah said? *Orah says a lotta shit*, I answer out loud, giggling. Oh yeah, damn, this place will spontaneously combust if I dare light up in here . . . but . . . but . . . it'd be a great way to go out, you know, go out with a bang, a *crypt*-bang, bones shattering, the remnants of indigo dust gracing the air, floating up, up, up. Me, in pieces too, I would intermingle with the Klaskis and it'd be one big party, raise the roof. I bite my lip and concentrate on my thumb on the Bic's flint wheel, imagining myself flicking it. The flame would swallow me at breakneck speed, and I'm almost sure it would barely hurt.

But why would I do that when heroin is much more pleasant? I don't even remember crawling outside, I don't even remember the needle going in, I just know the slump and the wave and the roll and the oh, oh, oh. The *no* experienced before is replaced with a *yes*; my head teeters on my neck, my limbs feel separate from my body and as soon as the apex hits, I'm needing more. More yes. Less no. Again. Slump, wave, roll, oh—if the sweetest dream could be liquid, that's what is gushing through every passage, tunnel, crevice in my body, a dream that overflows and spills and coats me with an internal glaze, my brain eats the dream, my heart is the clock that paces it, and my eyes that possess my soul grasp and catch hold. But only for a blink.

It's not enough. What's that? More yes! Less no! I'm supposed to . . . Dan . . . again. Again. A—

— — —

A crow. So close. Even in the dark I see its terrible eyes. What do you see, friend? Wasted lump of a person. Utterly useless. The truer than true epitome of fuck-up-edness. It takes all my effort just to move my head, but when I do the stink of vomit assaults me. I'm not exactly sure where I am or what I'm doing here and I get the sense that I'm lucky to be forming thoughts, even lucky to be alive. I try sitting up, but it's too much movement, I try wiping off my shirt, but there's too much stickiness. I strain to pull it over my head. At least I can do that. Plants are damp around me and then here it comes, the realization of where I am and *why*. Indigo gone. Bargaining chip gone. The will to problem-solve is gone too, and that's no good, because usually I'm a pro at it. If I don't have that, then who am I? Rock fucking bottom, that's where you are, homeboy. I drag my hand down my face and somehow I know that my skin has a green pallor, the green of an almost-OD. What have I done? I study the crow, still next to me, it's watching and then pecking; hopping to the side yet not leaving, it wants to witness me, the hot mess that I am, a guy who screws up everything and everybody within a twenty-mile radius.

What time is it? The moon is a faceless clock. Finally I'm able to push myself up, paw around for my cell phone until I find it in my backpack, where the indigo should be by now. Holy shit. It's already one in the morning. My life is good and over. There's no point in telling myself to take deep breaths and calm down. I don't think my heart can take the sprint it's running, I'm close to blacking out again. I should already be at Dan's right now, already going west on Old County Road. *No one's late for Early.* Shit. I've got calls, voice mails, texts, everyone in my life coming at me from different angles, Dan, Stacey, Faith, Bryce, Peter, fee-fi-fo-fum, I'm *done*. What the hell am I going to do? How am I going to explain this? I wonder if this is Orah's doing. A little heads up would have been nice.

My mind goes on default mode, crows, yeah, crows, I know a lot about them, I'm pulling myself to my feet as I think of the facts, like how they recognize faces, that they have the biggest brain-to-body ratio among bird species. When a crow is unable to crack a nut for food, it drops it on a highway so a car can run it over—studies show they've learned to drop nuts under smaller cars so the meat inside isn't completely obliterated. If a crow is dying, a bunch of other crows attack it to death, hence the reason a group of crows is called a murder. Ruthless creatures they are, intelligent suckers, loving to pick and pluck at tendons and bones.

This gives me a last-minute idea. I don't have much time.

I never thought my car could push close to one hundred, but there it goes, engine groaning, body creaking, I'm riding the clunker like a thoroughbred horse. Good thing I had a clean shirt in the trunk. I arrive at Dan's house in record time, disaster written all over me.

"Where the fuck have you been?" he asks, getting into the passenger seat. My stench, my eyes, my everything assault him. "You've been using. All the times you could have used, you choose tonight to do it? God, Finn, you're risking our lives here, don't you understand that?"

"I do, I do." I clench my jaw, preparing myself for more Dan-sized fury. "There's one other kink that you should know about."

"What now?" He presses the back of his skull against the headrest.

"When I went to the crypt, all the indigo was gone. Completely gone." I'm leaning over the steering wheel, an old man hunch, having a hard time seeing the lines of the road. The probability that I murdered half of my functioning brain cells is high and the will to persevere, the will to even *live*, is bottoming out.

"You're kidding me, right?" he asks, fuming.

"I think Orah may have—"

He puts his head in his hands and groans long and loudly.

I say quickly, "But I have a contingency plan. Get my pack from the backseat."

He rustles around in the back and brings the bag to the front, unzipping it with annoyance. He pulls out a femur bone from the crypt and other bones too. I tried to pack up as many as I could, without thinking of the blasphemy I was committing to Orah's relatives. The pact that I made about never sharing the crypt has to be broken—I have no choice. Would the ghosts of the Klaskis past understand?

"This is the proof that Early needs so he can grow the better strain. We tell him where the crypt is, we say the crypt is the origin."

"He'll want to know why the flowers in the crypt are gone."

"We can just tell him that it is between harvests, and that indigo grows back quick." Dan looks doubtful, but he knows we'll just have to cross that bridge when we get there. I go on. "We'll make up some excuse about how Orah got confused about the origin being in the Adirondacks, you know, because she was having a stroke and not thinking straight." In my periphery I see Dan mulling it through, or maybe he's just astounded by my major league stupidity. "Don't you see? This'll work. We don't have the indigo, but we've got the bones, and that's the crucial element to this whole thing."

The bones are in Dan's hands. When I stole them from the crypt I was astonished at their surprising smoothness and light weight. Dan regards them with disgust and sadness, until resignation spreads over his face. He returns them to the bag and places it at his feet, then wipes his hands on his pants.

Without any inflection he says, "I guess it will have to do."

CHAPTER FORTY-FIVE

OLD COUNTY ROAD AT TWO IN THE MORNING IS DESERTED. No one comes out here because there's jack shit around, no farms or houses for the next fifteen miles, a few shacks are set back in the woods, hunting cabins that aren't used anymore. At last I see the moose-crossing sign and start to slow down.

Soon there are two cars behind us, one with its lights flicking on and off. It's the same Lincoln Town Car sedan from earlier today, and the other is a Humvee-sized SUV, silver, tinted out, rims blinging in the moonlight. I pull off to the side of the road, palms slick with sweat, as the car inches up behind us. I reach for the door handle—Dan motions me to stay put. Even through the shut windows I hear the orchestra of crickets, I see the light-show of fireflies, and it makes the road lonelier because there are so many of them and so few of us. A growling in my stomach, rancid taste in my mouth. Vomiting again is definitely in order. After several minutes, the driver-side door of the sedan opens, and Leo approaches my car with a graceful gait for such a huge man. I knew he was monstrous but I didn't realize the extent of it as he strolls toward us. Once he's at the window, he directs me to roll it down. His eyes flit from me to

Dan. It takes all my willpower not to vomit all over him.

"We were hoping Dan would join us," he says. "Get out of the car."

Dan raises his eyebrows and isn't surprised when we both are searched. With my legs spread apart, I can't help the quaking of my knees, I can't stop the rivers of sweat trailing down my back, can't ignore the fact that I got no knife, no lighter, no nothing. Of course Dan takes it like a champ, and I envy his steadiness from police training or years of experience or his wonder-boy genes. Leo turns us around, his expression expectant.

"We have something better than indigo for you," Dan says.

Leo makes a face. "What are you telling me?"

Dan turns to me. I'm more versed when it comes to indigo history based on what I've learned from Orah and Stacey—knowledge that he chose to ignore.

I start in. "I think you're underestimating the importance of the bones to grow indigo," I say. "I'd stop focusing on the origin if I were you, and on the bones. I've got some in a bag in the car. They're from Orah's ancestors. They make the best indigo, the strongest. You can start your own crop from these, instead of using the bones of random people. To sweeten the deal, we'll give you a crypt in the D-Town Cemetery. It's protected and hidden, there are more Klaski bones in there, and it's all you're ever going to need for a nice setup."

He signals for me to get the backpack out of the car. I do it slowly, my movements almost comical, so Leo doesn't think I'm up to any funny business. There's a lump in my throat the size of a fist.

"This is not what we asked for. We want the location of the original indigo site. You said that you would tell us." He takes the backpack of the remains anyway. "Why weren't we aware of this in the beginning—of the Klaski bones being the important part, and this crypt you speak of?"

"Because I wasn't aware of it," Dan says. "The drug was ruining my family, turning them into addicts. I didn't want to know about it. Finn's the one who found out about it and told me. This is a good deal for you. Everything related to indigo is yours now."

Leo smiles but it doesn't reach his eyes. Dull and flat. He runs his hand over his close-cropped hair. Then he stalks back to the sedan with the bag of bones and opens the back door. Dan gives me a reassuring look. He hasn't stated his full case yet. There's still time.

Another of Early's thugs climbs out of the SUV, dragging someone along, with a gun to her head.

Stacey.

My Stacey. Dan's Stacey. That's when we both yell *Noooooo*, it's our instinct to run to her, and we do, but Leo sees this coming and shoots at the ground before us. One bullet sprays fragments of road in our eyes. My breath feels jagged going in and out of my throat, I wipe dirt and debris out of my eyes and hair. Dan's trying to bargain, talking a talk that is just jumbled words and desperate promises . . . *we'll do whatever you want, I'll talk to my people in the NYPD about easing up on you, we'll give you every site where indigo grows best . . .* while Stacey whimpers with dirt-stained tears. Her hair's a mess, there's a shadow under her eye that might be a bruise, Jesus Christ, these people, monsters, how could they even *think* about causing her harm? Dan is nowhere near his steady disposition right now, hands waving, running his mouth at mach speed, not sure what he's saying as I step back, feeling oddly removed from the situation. I'm colossally powerless.

Leo's just standing there, no expression on his face, while Dan is continuing to negotiate, persuade, convince, and failing miserably. The guy who's holding Stacey has his sights on me, wide stance, gun at his side. His hair is crow black and he has one of those butt chins. Early slides out of the car—which is still running with the headlights on—cane first, his demeanor somber, sympathy all over his face. He nudges Leo out of the way and places a decrepit hand on Dan's shoulder. A frail dude Early is, cane looking like the only bone keeping him upright, khaki pants baggy on his stick legs, still wearing that straw hat I saw before. He smiles at me sadly, like he really feels bad about the course of events.

"Charles," he says to the goon holding Stacey. "You may let her go."

Charles pushes Stacey against the car so she doesn't move. She slumps to the ground; they tied her hands behind her back with rope.

My anger, my powerlessness, my panic all collide inside me, and the most awful birds come to the forefront of my mind. Vultures. Their piss is so powerful it destroys bacteria in the filth they trudge through. Cassowaries. They have a five-inch-long claw and a kick powerful enough to kill a man. This is the exact force I need but will never have.

"The whole family attended," Early says, looking around with what might pass for a smile. "I like this. It's exactly what I envisioned. It's a roundtable to discuss our beloved indigo. The problem is, I don't want it to be *ours*. I want it to be *mine*. I like the sound of that much better."

Early squats in front of Stacey, slowly, painstakingly, as he uses his cane for support. He places a crooked finger underneath her chin, forcing her to tip her face up to meet his gaze. Her bottom lip trembles, and he studies her, tilting his head to see her from all angles. I want to kill him.

"Leo and Charles have done their best to get Stacey to disclose the origin of indigo." He pats her cheek. "She says she knows nothing. But I know she's lying, based on what Orah told me when she rambled on about telling her grandchildren about the Adirondacks." He looks up at the clear night sky wistfully. "You must wonder why I seem so obsessed with this. It's because as my life nears its end, I want to know how this beautiful drug began. To be in the midst of its true, original spirit is all I ask for."

How did he know Dan would be here and that he should take Stacey? And what the hell did Early's goons do to her? She's half in shock, half crying. It's not right, I've got to do something, someone's got to take action around here, all Dan's doing is talking and talking and no one's listening. A shudder runs through me and I fling myself in Stacey's direction. I end up with my arm twisted against my back—I howl something awful—and Charles' gun against my head. Leo points his at Dan. Checkmate.

Early nods at Charles, who lets go of my arm. I should shut up, keep my mouth closed, but I can't help it, I have to try to get him to see things my way. "The Adirondacks don't matter," I say, not liking the desperation in my voice. "The bones matter. That's the key. *They're* the only thing that matters." I'm repeating myself. There's no use.

Early ignores me. He walks slowly over to Dan, clacking his cane on the pavement. "I should have asked Billy about it when I had a chance. But he's gone, isn't he? Gone into hiding? Let's see if we can't pull something out of Stacey."

Early lifts his cane and cracks it over Dan's head. He doesn't go down, tough bastard, but falls to his knees, dizzy and ashen, holding his hand up to his temple.

Stacey screams.

Early asks, "Stacey, I think you're holding back information from me, aren't you? Why don't you tell me, sweetheart, or there will be more of this." He nods to Charles. Uh oh. Charles splits my forehead open with the butt of his gun. I grunt as I crumple to the road. I'm not sure how much more of this my brain can take.

"What do you say, Stacey?" Early asks gently. "Do you want to keep seeing your father get hurt?"

Stacey just stares, too stunned to say anything; she's sunk into a state of *cannot compute*.

"They'll both be dead and gone if you don't speak."

Charles has a gun on me again, what's new, and Leo has pulled out a knife from somewhere and is holding it against Dan's neck.

"Okay—okay . . ." she says slowly, swallowing. "I'll show you where. There's no way you could find it on your own . . . it's too far out of the way. Just leave them alone."

I look at Dan. He's completely confused. He has no idea if she's lying or if there really is an origin. Soon he'll realize she isn't lying and he'll find out where Billy has been the whole time. If he's allowed to live. Without rhyme or reason, he's shoved and kicked in the face by Leo. Kicked over and over again. A grimace of pain, a moan, then a sickening crunch. Stacey screams. *Daddy, Daddy, Daddy. Stop, please stop, I told you, I'll give you what you want, he doesn't know, just leave him alone.* I'm up next, I'm sure of it, I wonder if I'll feel my broken skull before I'm lost to the dark.

"Thank you for cooperating," Early says. "But I'm afraid you'll have to come alone. I respect your father too much to bring him along."

Stacey says quickly, "Finn has to come. He's the only one who knows how to harvest it properly." This girl does not cease to amaze me. How the hell does she know about the intricacy of harvesting? "I bet you don't know how to do it without losing half of it. I bet your guys here have never done it before. The indigo flowers are more delicate than the flowers you grow."

Early considers me, frowning. "Charles, tie him up too and put him in the trunk. You follow us in the SUV." Charles does as he's told, and soon I'm hog-tied and squeezed in the trunk as the lid slams over my head. There's barely enough oxygen, and I've got no cell phone—the two essentials right now for survival. I have no idea what they're doing with Dan. However, I now have the chance to protect Stacey. I would die for her if she asked. But I'd really rather save her. I just have no idea how this is going to play out and I have no plan. Who is Finn without a plan?

"We'll have plenty of time to get to know each other, Stacey, won't we?" Early says. It's the last voice I hear before the car engine starts. The car ride goes like this: pass out, hit a bump, wake up, sheer agony, repeat.

CHAPTER FORTY-SIX

A CREAK OF THE TRUNK. An onslaught of sunlight. I'm lugged out, still tied up, fully hungover from my heroin withdrawal, woozy, and positive that I have a concussion.

"Where's Stacey?" I ask.

Leo answers me with a grunt. I'm being dragged to a clearing in the woods with giant pines on all sides. Smack in the middle of the clearing is a run-down, small, two-story farmhouse with white paint peeling off in ribbons. Moss grows on the roof, and one of the front windows is sealed off with plywood, its blue shutters askew. Leo continues to pull me closer to the house, until I see Early, Stacey, and Charles (and no Dan) standing before a grave that abuts the side of the house where a birch tree stands crooked yet tall. They are awestruck, as am I, once I see the flowers encircling several tombstones and the immediate area, snaking up the side of the house in vines that fork and travel their way to the roof. Indigo. I've never seen so much of it before, even in the crypt, and in the sunlight its blue is sublime and three-dimensional, and if a color could walk and talk, this one would fly. Billy must be taking good care of them. We are frozen in church-worthy silence, stupefied and dismantled from the miraculous sight.

It's Early who breaks the stillness. "Let's start," he says, turning to me. I dart my eyes quickly at Stacey, then back to Early. They untie my hands, and then train their guns on me. I take stock around me—there's no place to go anyway. East Bumblefuck is where we are.

"We're going to need bags. Garbage bags, given the amount of it," I say. Early nods, beaming with satisfaction and joy. Stacey's wrists are no longer tied, yet Charles has his fingers tight around her upper arm, so she might as well be. She pipes up.

"I know where the garbage bags are," she says. Early nods and Stacey and Charles disappear through the front door. I wonder if Billy is there, and if Stacey is going to warn him. I know something is going to happen. Probably something not good.

Early pats me on the back.

"Good show," he says. "I knew that you were going to be useful." It isn't lost on me that he's using past tense.

A few moments later, I hear Stacey scream. I don't care that Leo has a gun at my head, I run. This is Stacey we're talking about. Inside, she's hunched over a body on a couch—a body of a guy with a scar, just a guy like me—sobbing hysterically. She's slapping his face, squeezing his sides, trying to awaken him even though it's clear it's way too late for that. Needles and other drug paraphernalia are scattered across a coffee table, and a thick belt is still tight around his arm. I don't need to look closer to know that this is Billy. We can all smell that he's been dead for a little while now. I place the back of my hand up to my mouth and look away, my stomach clenching from Stacey's sorrow and the foul odor.

Charles is about to pull her away from the couch when Early says from the doorway, "Let her mourn in peace."

Leo, who had followed me in, now starts rummaging around in the small, open kitchen for garbage bags. It doesn't take long for him to locate a box of them. Stacey moans, placing her cheek on Billy's shoulder, arms limp at her sides. He's a tall lanky kid, wearing Converse sneakers and a black zip-up hoodie. His scar is much more severe than mine, though with the same texture of puckered skin and pearly shininess.

I can't look at the body of someone who could easily be me any longer and I turn around. The open room is sparsely furnished and surprisingly tidy, and the windows are all decorated with the same sheer white curtains. A small, hand-woven rug is underneath the coffee table, its multi-colored pattern dizzying. Billy lived here and here was cozy. I wonder if he thought so. I wonder if he even noticed at all. I have a momentary memory of myself waking up in the woods next to the crypt, a pile of vomit at my side, one crow, soon to be a murder, waiting for my ending.

Leo clamps his hand on my wrist and says, "Come along now. We've got work to do."

Leo and I take garbage bags and begin. I tenderly touch each petal, watching it disintegrate into the plastic, as Leo massacres a batch of it, not understanding the meaning of delicate. Early watches the abomination and wobbles toward us, yelling at him to stop. I still hear Stacey. She is outside now, weeping. For the next twenty minutes or so, I harvest by myself quietly, with Leo guarding me, Charles guarding Stacey's distress, and Early standing in the shade observing us all. I see a break in the trees, and in the distance there are fences in disrepair and a crumbling foundation that could have been a barn. My mind is racing, trying to devise a plan. But I can't. Thirsty. Hot. Headache. Almost passing out. Up close, the indigo petals shimmer, or maybe that's my vision blurring in the blazing brightness of the morning.

Think, Finn, *think*. I'm throwing quick glances at the gravestones, I spy a name etched out in granite, it starts with a K. These are the Klaskis. I bet they never knew they were going to cause such a mess.

There is only one thing that I can think to do. It is outrageous. And it terrifies me just as much as the men who hover over us. I had told myself *never* again, because going back is a form of torture, it is all-encompassing suffering. After the last time I snorted indigo, the memory lingered for days, and my palms still tingled from the shards of plastic and metal from what could have been Faith's sunglasses. I'm shuddering at the thought and it doesn't go unnoticed.

"What's his deal?" Charles asks, pointing at me. "He looks like he's going to piss himself."

I wave him off. "I'm fine. Think I have a concussion, that's all."

Leo chuckles at that, proud that he delivered the blow to my forehead. I wish I had never been introduced to indigo, I wish I wasn't such a greedy, cocky good-for-nothing bastard whose eyes are forever bigger than his stomach.

There is a one in a million chance this could work, but what other choice do I have? How real was the Gatorade on Bryce's skin and the sand in Rory's palm? I think that a trip would bring me back to a bad memory, and I think my bad memories could supply me with something to use against them, possibly a weapon. Without analyzing the consequences too

much, because I never really do, I take a handful of indigo powder, bring it up to my nose and huff it so hard I lurch backward.

"What the—" I hear Leo say.

I'm plummeting, falling, sinking . . . it feels different this
time, disastrous, heart-stopping, and the regret, oh the weight
of it . . .

CHAPTER FORTY-SEVEN

THE CONCRETE AROUND OUR TRAILER IS SCORCHING HOT. My feet are bare, a magnifying glass is in my hand, and *Amazing Facts about Ants* is on the ground next to me. Mom's inside drinking red wine before lunch, but I'm too young to understand that this isn't normal. I'm eleven years old and beginning to recognize other things, however, like the squishy feeling I get when I see Rose Madison and her unkempt blonde curls, or the anxiousness I experience when Pop is listening to Led Zeppelin too loud. Lately I react to the sound of ice tinkling against glass and the slamming door. But at least there's the front yard, visible from the other trailers, where I feel safest—besides when I'm not at home.

Though I think ants are cool—and boy, do I know a lot about them, let me tell you—I've just discovered what a magnifying glass and direct sunlight can accomplish. That pinpoint of illumination I fix upon the ant's back, poor sucker, bull's-eye, here we go, it takes no time at all to make life stop. The morbid curiosity fuels me, I'm supersaturated with fascination, I can't stop. At this stage in my life, I know the word *addiction*, and I think I might have it. I've heard people call Pop an alcoholic, I've heard Mom's name paired with "pill popper," and that's okay I think, because Rose's mom is a "whore," and Peter's dad is a "womanizer." I wonder what I am. Murderer of ants. The Formica butcher.

It's the big carpenter ants that are the best to kill, because you can see the smoke trailing off them, and one time, there was a split-second spark, and then drop dead Fred. I feel a mixture of remorse and sadness, but the excitement of it wins over both. I don't consider myself a serial killer or anything, I'm not into chopping up cats and dogs, but this is something I'm not going to go bragging about to my friends. Or Faith.

I'm so mesmerized by my experimentation that I don't hear Pop pulling up and getting out of his truck. Dust puffs up and a shadow falls on me. I whip around to face him.

"What the fuck you doing?" His voice is lethal, and I smell his alcohol breath from here. There's something else too—he's got that look in his eye and slackening of expression that tells me he hasn't just been drinking booze. He's standing above me, hands on his hips—a newly appointed sheriff stance. It's not like him to start bullying me in the afternoon; he usually saves that for the night hours. I toss the magnifying glass aside, too late for him not to notice, and snatch up my ants book, a shield against my chest.

"I—I . . ."

"You what? Huh?" he says, slapping me on my forearm. "I—I . . ." He's mocking me. Always mocking me. Am I really this lame? Maybe I am. I'm still a runt at this age, limbs skinny as twigs, floppy hair. A special brand of dorkhood that the strong love to attack, and my pop, he's a big dude, over six feet, lifts weights with his buddies after work. Then drinks. Plays cards. Doesn't come home until late when Mom is passed out on the couch.

"I'm going inside," I say, but Pop signals me to stay where I am.

"Frying ants, are you?" I'm taken aback because his voice sounds soft now, kind of nice. I nod, silent with confusion. "Is that what's going on here?"

"It's cool," I say, hugging my book closer to me.

Pop plops himself down on the steps next to me, the magnifying glass between his hands—didn't see him pick it up. Yesterday he watched cartoons with me and laughed. He's been nicer lately, after Faith's accident. I didn't even know he liked cartoons.

"I used to do this when I was your age, believe it or not." He brings the glass up to his eye, then breathes on it, rubs off the smudges on his yellow shirt. Hands it over to me.

"You did?" I ask. The magnifying glass is warm—from the ants, from my father's handling, from the high June sun. I never took note of his thinning hair and reflective, exposed scalp until now, when I have an impulsive, horrendous thought of shining the magnifying glass upon him. Would his remaining hair light up in flames? Or would his skin start smoking first?

"Yep, I sure did," he says, leaning back, fishing out a cigarette pack from one pocket, Zippo lighter in the other. The smoke curls between us in a matter of seconds; he takes a contemplative pull, furrowing his brow. I never really had a full conversation with Pop before. We juggle around questions and one-word answers. *How was school today?* Good. *Can I come with you to the dump?* Sure. *Your mother's being a bitch, right?* Okay.

It's a script that's worked for us so far, but today I sense Pop wants more.

"I've got some homework," I say, because I really do, and engaging in dialogue is the last thing I want to do with Pop. I check my cheap Mickey Mouse watch, hoping that Faith will come home soon. She's at a friend's house—and my heart sinks knowing she'll probably be there all day and into the evening. Pop and Mom are being more lax with her after the accident, and I suspect they have a hard time just being around her now. She's making herself more and more scarce. Every time I think of it, I miss her and the piece that she lost.

"You don't want to sit out here with your old dad?"

"No, that's not it, it's just—"

"What, you're too good for me now?" he snarls. My thoughts are weaving back and forth, do I stay, or do I run away? The fact that Mom's inside makes no difference. When he starts up, there isn't anything she can do, so nothing she does.

"No, Pop. My room's a mess, I got to clean it up before Faith comes home, you know?"

"You said you had homework."

"Well, that too. I have both things to do," I say nervously. He eyes me something harsh, but I stare straight ahead. What do they say about bears? Or maybe it's rabid dogs? Don't look at them straight on, or they'll rip out your throat.

"What's that you got there?" he asks, tearing the ant book away from me. I wince, not because he hurt me, but because I really think of the book as a line of defense. Now there's nothing between me and him but air and the savvy I don't have.

"Give it here," I say weakly, reaching for it. He blocks me with his muscular shoulder, cradles the open book in his arm, and takes a long drag from his cigarette. He's actually reading it. Never seen Pop read a damn thing besides magazines and car manuals.

"You think you know a lot?" he asks.

"I know a lot about ants," I say, ready to pay tribute to the book and its world of knowledge, I'm all for unleashing *amazing* facts, it's one of the things I do best. "Did you know that ants—"

"Shut up," Pop says, hitting me in the stomach with the book. I hunch over in pain, I'm not expecting this, I didn't say anything disrespectful, Jesus. There's a pounding in my ears, and I'm ashamed that lately my fear intensifies so quickly and abrupt. Pop's eyes home in on me, unblinking, then he grins. I should be used to him being volatile, unpredictable, but I'm not. I never will be.

Without saying anything, I get up to go inside. The screen door whines as I open it, and there's Mom eating popcorn in her designated spot watching her designated show: The Home Shopping Network. A half-empty bottle of wine sits on the end table. She barely acknowledges me. The solace of my room calls.

I hear Pop yell, *Don't you walk away from me, son,* cranking the screen door open, tripping over the threshold, causing a few boxes to teeter on their stacks. I walk past the kitchen briskly, but not briskly enough. Pop catches my wrist, the callouses from lifting weights scratch against my skin, and without any reservation, he slams me against the wall in the hallway. Picture frames clatter with the vibration of impact as I try to not make a sound. This time a box does fall. I think I hear Mom say *leave him alone,* but I can't be sure because of her thick, sloppy slur. I barely remember him fumbling through his pocket, I barely remember hearing my mother's laborious attempt to stand up, but I *do* remember to the minute detail the flick of his lighter and the power of his forearm across my chest. He's so strong I hear the flimsy walls of our trailer creak,

I'm hoping that the drywall will cave in and that the roof will collapse on both of us.

"Don't ever walk away from me," he repeats, his viper eyes meeting mine, a splatter of his spit across my face. The alcohol stench is so concentrated it stings. "I could squash you like *an ant*."

He raises the lit Zippo to my chin, I strain against the wall, twist my neck to avoid the heat, try to wrench away from him with the strength of my legs, but he's stomped and ground his feet on top of mine. When I squirm, that only makes him angrier, makes him dig his elbow and fist against my torso, and that's when the real pain starts. With the flick of his lighter the flame licks from my neck to the side of my face, and I hear the feathery hairs sizzle, smell the burning of it and now my flesh, my skin is burning, burning, my mouth is closed but I'm shrieking in my throat, and he's laughing in his. The flame goes out but does nothing to relieve the pain. Mom appears in the hallway, she says, "Cut it out, you two." As if we're rough-housing and this is a playful challenge between father and son. Pop's not listening, lights it up again for another moment or two, and the agony lasts forever. My skin must be melting like wax; he's burning me to the bone. The flame goes out, yet the heat has already burrowed in my ear canal, reaching my brain to fry all gray matter.

"Mom," I say hoarsely. "Mom." She drops her wineglass; it breaks into large pieces. The flame's back on and he's out for the kill, torment and torture. I'm on the verge of fainting. Witch burning. Tarred and feathered. A thousand lashes. I'm done. That's when he lets me go. As if he knows the line to the exact millimeter. I double over with my hands on my knees and dry heave. Placing my palm to the side of my face twists me up in hellish agony, the stickiness against my fingers horrid, the smell of burned flesh pungent. Mom and Pop stand in silence, watching.

Still bent over, I spy a glass shard at my feet, curved and pointy. I grab it and catapult myself at him, arm raised, white-hot and unthinking with rage. Shock sparks over his face and in a flash he shields himself with his arm. A slash against his skin, immediate gash of blood, I gasp, fighting the urge to apologize. Then he slaps the shard out of my hand and I turn and run.

Hop on my bike, slamming down on the hard seat hurts my balls, but I almost welcome the pain as a distraction from the mother of all hurt. I'm not afraid of the damage done, I'm not concerned with how it looks. The thing that scared me the most was the curve of his lips in the faintest of smiles and her standing there, watching.

CHAPTER FORTY-EIGHT

I COME OUT OF IT STRANGELY ECSTATIC, OR MAYBE IT'S JUST THE RELIEF OF LEAVING IT BEHIND. The first thing I'm aware of is the heat on my cheek and neck. The other worst memory of all time sticks to me, tattoo permanent. All these years I've pushed it back, and now it's here, front and center, star of the show. I want to kick, punch, scream, it's not fair, it's not fair, yet despite the tantrum, the damage, it changed me. Maybe I'm changed once more for experiencing it twice. The blisters took a few hours to bubble up from my face—they were big yellow bulges that popped eventually without me touching them. It took weeks to heal: flaps of skin after the blisters burst, then pus, next the scab, red graduating to purple. Second-degree burns, the doctor said. We lied about the cause. Pop apologized for a month straight and went to one session of therapy. I got hit sometimes in the years after, but it was never as bad as being burned.

Then before I can touch my face to confirm if the heat is really there—if I'm reburned, phoenix'd, born again—Leo tackles me to the ground, grappling to gain control of my legs, hands, and arms, and Charles's gun is pointed at my head. No superhuman strength, it's just me, Phineas, nothing to write home about. But adrenaline enables me to wiggle my hands from his grasp and desperately pat the ground around me, dig into my pockets, hoping to find a weapon from my memory. What about the lighter? The glass shard? Nothing. This whole scheme was pointless, like all the rest. I should have known that this world wasn't meant for magic. I'm groping for everything, anything, but it's just grass, dirt, and more grass. And the heat on my cheek. Leo's got me pinned now, panting with effort. I'm reeling. Fuck. *Fuck*.

Then everything happens fast and at once. Early barks an order, points with his cane, Leo jerks up off of me, and Charles is sprinting to the house. Stacey is nowhere to be found—my spontaneous indigo hit was distraction enough to give her a window of opportunity to escape, good, that's my girl, but soon I realize that she's *not* escaping, instead she's *staying*, and through the window I see her setting the curtains on fire with a cheap yellow lighter, probably Billy's. The flimsy material flares up right quick, done and *done*. She stands in the middle of the room, and the fire rages on all sides of her, murky black smoke, pumpkin orange, she isn't meant to be the phoenix . . .

I imagine her taking one beat to say her farewell to Billy before the couch goes up in flames.

Charles bursts into the house after her, but she's already out the back door, calling my name, saying, *Finn, do it, Finn*, running toward the woods. Stacey's escape is enough of a distraction to snatch up an open bag of indigo I've just harvested and throw it toward the fire-breathing window with the blaze of curtain lashing out like a tongue. The bag hits the ledge and indigo puffs everywhere, covering Leo, who is just registering what happened. His shock is a trophy. I bound toward the woods after Stacey, nothing is happening, why is nothing happening, dear *God*, I'll do anything, I'll stop all bad behavior, I'll give you my soul for you to clean up, spic-and-span, just please, oh *please* . . .

I hear Stacey's feet slapping against the ground just ahead— An earth-shattering crack.

A gust of wind against my back. An explosion that knocks me off my feet, sending me tumbling, tumbling, sharp branches, layer of pine needles, back against bark. Stacey immediately halts. Don't stop, but I only think it, because my tongue is a boulder and the words aren't coming, don't stop, Stacey, run until you can't anymore, I don't know the status of the others, but I'll be your last line of defense if it kills me.

The smoke engulfs the forest and the crackling is so loud I expect to hear *timber!* and the deafening break of falling trees. There is a rumbling sound too, I'm not sure where it's coming from, and I'm too confused and paralyzed to run away. I roll over, groaning, I don't think I've broken anything, but the tinnitus in my ears isn't letting up. I've never been so disoriented. I can only see the outline of tree trunks in the dense fog of smoke. Another smaller burst of explosion, then the smoke clears, but only temporarily.

During that brief opening I see a figure limping toward me.

———

"Where are you, Finn?" Stacey shouts, she wants to locate my voice, me. Smoke is all I'm seeing, coughing is all I'm doing. Instinctively, I know to stay silent. There are several noises happening simultaneously: the gushing breath of fire, a distant whir of a motor, and the nearby crunch of twigs against footfall. The gray cloud slowly dissipates, revealing more trees and the outline of a man who struggles to stay upright. Early appears out of the backdrop of blankness, clutching his cane-turned-crutch. He somehow survived the blowback of the explosion—maybe he had seen it coming. He points a gun at me from ten feet away.

"Get on your knees," he says. I'm so delirious that I'm already there without argument, and I don't want to run because at least I can keep Early occupied and away from Stacey. I have enough dignity to not break eye contact with him, my golden-brown irises to his watery, non-colored ones. His hat must have blown off in the explosion, and it's the first time that I've seen his whole face, and I'm taken aback by a full head of gray hair. He calls out, "Stacey, you better come here and witness this. Or should I spare his life for your own?"

"Stacey, get away from here," I holler.

"I knew this was going to be a messy ending," Early says, coughing, though his gun remains steady. "I recognize so much of myself in you. Smooth talking, egotistical. *Machismo.* A leader of your pack. Yet you understand the elderly, our compulsion to reminisce and share whatever measly wisdom we may have. You learn from our stories, Finn, don't you?"

My eyes sting from the smoke and I'm overwhelmed with tears. I want to scream in his face, *Don't talk to me about your stories! Yours are useless, empty things. Orah's stories are bursting with color, they are peacock feathers, a kaleidoscope of high-octane blues and greens and purples. They are life. Yours are death. And now she's dying because of you.*

I don't answer Early. I'm no longer afraid of his questions.

"You should pause in this moment." He waves his hand in the air. "Take time to enjoy the clarity before death, take inventory of what you have accomplished, what you have begun.

Finn, what have you accomplished?"

I hear footsteps. "Get out of here, Stacey!" I yell. I ready myself for my last move. I can take this guy out, go for the hit, steal the gun, end this once and for all. My determination is powerful and relentless, and in all my life I've never felt a decision so resolute.

He snickers. "I admire your bravery, son," he says, reading my taut stance, my tightening fists. "But *you* must end with indigo. You've destroyed it, where it all began—and—and—it was so divine, so *pure* . . ."

When Stacey appears next to me, I flash her a look of outrage; she answers with a frown. She should be at a safe distance by now. But no, always the stubborn one. This wordless exchange pleases Early—he smiles with delight, he'd probably clap his hands if they weren't otherwise occupied.

He tightens his finger on the trigger, I scream for Stacey to get down as I throw myself at him. I wait for the point of impact, I squeeze my eyes shut, and there is forever in the moment between *now* and *then*. Snapshots of the past flash over the back of my eyelids: Faith and me in a fort with a kitten, the yard sale, the female cardinal at the window. Me defending her honor when the first—and last—kid made fun of her eye patch. Amazing facts books, binoculars, bird-watching, blitzed out of my mind. The time I got drunk and ran up and down the trailer park butt-ass naked. Dropping acid in the park. Waking up not knowing who I am. Stacey walking into the sub shop, my heart stopping. Rising from the dead, next to the dead, knowing full well I was lucky. And Orah. Drinking tea together in the morning room, utterly myself.

The three seconds of forever have passed. There's a vicious-sounding pop. I don't even make contact with Early, because he's already on the ground, and I'm about to stumble over him, baffled, befuddled. Smoke lifting, almost clear. And I'm seeing that Early is dead, blood blooms from his skull, someone killed him, and that someone wasn't me. I kick the gun away from him and jerk around, scanning the area.

Stacey is covering her head, lying on her stomach behind me, trembling.

"Are you okay?" I ask, scrambling to her, pulling her up into my arms. She looks around, sees Early's body and nods. Face splotchy and dirty, but otherwise okay. Thank God, I think, looking up at the sky.

The smoke has traveled beyond us and someone appears from behind a tree. I'm up on my feet going after the gun without hesitation. It's not Leo or Charles, however.

It's Mike Frye. Mike with a still-smoking gun, a couple of his guys flanking him. He barely acknowledges me when he approaches Early's body and stands over him for a painful but necessary length of time. Stacey leans against a tree trunk, and I step backward, giving Mike space. He clears his throat and hacks, tightens his mouth in a pucker and pummels a gob of spit in Early's face.

"You killed my Victoria," he says quietly, voice cracking. He crumples to his knees and brings his head to the ground. I get the sense that he's praying and mourning, but not exactly falling apart—that will come later. His hand and Early's hand are inches apart and that seems to be what he wants: to feel with all his senses a life diminishing and a black heart silenced. The cane has been thrown off to the side in the chaos, and it's one of Mike's guys who picks it up, considering it. My sights are then set on Stacey, whose posture changes, who leaps up and starts running back toward the house. I almost call out

348

in panic, until I see Dan limping to meet her, arms stretched wide, tears of relief and gratitude smeared down his cheeks. That tough motherfucker.

Mike stands up and brushes himself off, signaling to his guys to take care of Early's body. I understand that the cane will be a souvenir.

"How did you find us?"

Mike scratches the side of his nose, such a casual gesture for the given situation. "Dan went to the hospital to ask your old lady Orah for directions to this place. He knew about what Early did to my . . . my Victoria."

"Orah woke up?" I ask, my voice cracking. Dan nods as he squeezes Stacey into a hug. Yes, I think; there was some justice done today. Orah is alive. She woke up from the blank nightmare of a coma, and the relief of that is unmatched.

"Seems like everyone was at the hospital," Mike says. "Dan saw me, Jason, and a few of my guys and told us what was going down. He thought he might need backup." He tilts his head up to Dan, the biggest thank-you he's going to get out of him. Early's body is being dragged away, probably to be thrown into the long-burning fire of the house, along with the bodies of Leo and Charles. So appropriate—Early's end where indigo began.

There is an awkward pause between me and Mike as we stand facing each other. It's not every day that an enemy saves your life. There's also a perfect opportunity to take the blame out on me to complete the blood bath. They have the guns, and we're weakened and maxed out. Maybe he considers it; I am part of the series of events, you might even say I was its origin, but that's where it gets fuzzy, so I'm not going to linger on that too much. But—but . . . there's tension between us spiked with anguish spiked with deep-set loathing spiked with what else? A tacit understanding? An unspoken commonality? A blood bond? With that said, I'm spent, he's spent, I just want to go home and make peace with everything leading up to this moment. Indigo and I? Not exactly soul mates. Oil and water. Black and blue. Heaven and earth. Now thinking of it, we were only meant to be a match made in hell. I want to tell Orah that I'm sorry it took so long for me to realize that.

"I don't expect that we'll get in each other's way anytime soon," Mike says. It's the perfect statement. It is exactly right. I nod, open my mouth to speak, but decide against it.

CHAPTER FORTY-NINE

THE FUNERAL IS HELD AT THE D-TOWN CEMETERY NEXT TO JIMMY'S GRAVE, AMONG THE BIRDS I'VE BEEN SPYING ON FOR YEARS, NOT TOO FAR AWAY FROM THE CRYPT WHERE THIS ALL BEGAN. A few weeks have passed since the incident in the Adirondacks, and though there have been some aftereffects to deal with, I have no desire to look back and consider how I could have done things differently. Fuck you, indigo, but thank you too.

It's a simple gravestone of dark gray granite, with Billy's full name, William Edward Braggs, and the dates of his birth and death. Too short of a range, barely a wingspan.

As we form a circle around the gravesite, I take stock of the cast of characters that have made up my life in the past few months. Some physically here, others not, doesn't matter because there are spirits wherever we go. Stacey's hand squeezes mine. The bottom of her dress brushes against my pants, a sound that reminds me of our wildflower field in the wind.

I found out from Jason that Mike has moved, nobody knows where, which is probably a good thing. Though he does have friends in the police force, he didn't want to take any chances, even with no evidence found to connect him with Early's death.

If he wants to get into supplying again, he'll have to build up from the ashes.

Dan stands closest to the grave. He has taken a leave of absence from the D-Town PD, which is just what he needed in order to spend more time with his family and to help mend what's left of it. I know part of his sabbatical is a result of his less-than-ethical approach to drug enforcement, but with his clout and connections with respected people (including the clueless Dammertown mayor) who can vouch for him, I know his career is nowhere near to being over. I'm sure there are a shit ton of enforcement who are silently applauding him for playing a role in Early's takedown.

Stacey is a quiet version of herself now. This may be a temporary version, or it may be a new version to stay; whatever the case, she's with me a lot. We go on walks, eat lunch together in the cafeteria, I drive her home from school. She's still attending Stanford in the fall. In those times when she thinks I'm not looking at her (though I *am* looking, *always* looking), I recognize the aching strain of guilt in her eyes—*I could have visited him, I could have loved him more, I could have been a better sister*—I see all this, I *feel* all this, but it's something that she's going to have to work through herself. You can duke it out with regret, sadness, even *emptiness*, and you should fight in true gladiator fashion, but don't go expecting life to take it easy on you because you've won a few. It will never be *easy*. That's the point.

When others look at my face, do they see the underneath of my underneath? It's ego on top of ego on top of distrust of the world and myself; it's sadness and anger and boo-hoo everything is *so hard*. Yet embedded in it all, I feel a tiny seed beginning to take root. I'm going to let it grow. I'm going to wait and see how much light it'll find. Our graduation is just around the bend and yes, I'll be walking across the stage, thank you very much. Maybe there will be another stage to walk across in the future. I'm not ruling out the possibility. Faith's still going to D-Town Community College and I'm coming to terms with that. By making money (not enough) and trying to control her life (as mine spiraled out)—I wanted nothing more than for her to forgive me. The truth of the matter is, she had already done so years before, when a female cardinal perched on the hospital window and showed us hope.

And Orah. Oh, Orah . . . there are still so many stories for her to tell me. I want to hear about her greatest memory, and I don't want to know if that's what she experienced during her first indigo trip. I want to hear more about her husband and her time as a nurse. Have I earned these stories? It's too early to tell, but I've got time. She stands next to me now, holding my other hand, with her good ear toward me—the stroke took away her hearing in her right ear, the doctors said it was a miracle it didn't take anything else. That is no consolation for her now that her grandson is dead with no final words spoken between them. Closure is not something that should be taken for granted. I used to think of it as a word for separated couples who needed "closure" to move on and love another. Closure for Orah, I would imagine, is twenty thousand leagues deeper than that, more than *I'm sorry* and *it's okay*, more than her destroying all the indigo in the crypt—which led to the destruction of the rest—though that might be coming close.

Stacey walks up to the gravestone. Her tears sparkle in the light, though it's an overcast day with low, cushion-like clouds. She takes something out of her pocket and holds it up for everyone to view.

I can't tell what it is at first, but I know it's important because there is a sharp intake of breath from Orah; there is a Herculean grip of her fingers. Then I see. It's the circular crystal Orah gave Billy, the touchstone of positive energy, the representation of the rainbow spectrum of life. When it hits the light just right, it dazzles with a riot of colors despite the cloudy, washed-out day. Red to indigo and back again.

She places the crystal on top of Billy's grave and walks back. I inhale—hadn't even known I'd stopped breathing—and the inhale tastes blessed, it's there, it's goddamn holy water, and aren't I lucky that there's more to drink? Stacey's back to holding my hand, and I feel honored that she graces me with it, I feel honored that Orah is still holding on to me too. Faith is tearing up, but her eye is bright (*Think bright, Phineas*) and on me, like she's kind of proud that I'm her brother, her eternal fraternal twin. So it's like, these women, *man*, I don't know, for a second they have the ability to fly, they could at a moment's notice jump up and soar and say, see you, fuckers, I've got places to be—and you'd think—or maybe the *old* me would think—I'm the anchor that holds them to the ground, the weight, the burden, but that's not really it. I'm just not ready, I hold onto them because I'm scared, I'm so fucking scared, and they know it and accept it and will wait for *me* to let go. They are the subtle red to my fire-engine hue. They will be the ones to teach me to fly.

ACKNOWLEDGMENTS

Enormous amounts of thanks to the following people who helped make this story fly:

Rubin Pfeffer, an amazing agent who was the best navigator and cheerleader in finding a home for this book. Not many people have his wisdom of the industry, steadiness, and overall loveliness.

Alix Reid, a kick-ass editor who knows how to whip a story into shape and make characters come alive on the page. She beams with passion, encouragement, and positivity. What an editorial superhero!

The team at Carolrhoda Lab—I'm so honored to be on your list.

Lesléa Newman, mentor, pal, and inspiration. I am grateful to know you, your generosity, and warm spirit. I still have your marked-up manuscripts and use your brilliant writing exercises!

Writing group buddies Cal Armistead, Karen Jersild, Pauline Briere, and Chris Daly whose critique over wine and snacks was always spot-on. A special shout-out to Cal, for her comments on multiple manuscripts, her insights on life, and OOB.

The Stonecoast MFA program and its instructors—a life-changing graduate experience by the sea.

Devon Sprague, who was my first writing compadre in graduate school and now a lifelong friend. May we always bond over Stephen King and Margaret Mitchell.

Lisa Yelon and her keen eye for young adult literature and intelligent writing advice.

My family—Kiki, Mark, David, Paul, Barb, Kathy, Rachel, Sam, Louis, and Lina for their love, humor, and support.

Allison Chou, for the impromptu photo at the Lawn on D, first shot, done and done.

Mr. Pekar, my high school English teacher, who told me I'd get published one day and that he better be in the acknowledgments.

Millie, who was the inspiration behind the character Orah. May you rest in peace and forever be looking out from your cabin on Lake Champlain.

My grandparents, who are always with me in spirit when I write about birds.

ABOUT THE AUTHOR

Kara Storti knew she wanted to be a writer when she decided to skip her junior prom to attend the Bread Loaf Writers' Conference in Middlebury, Vermont. In the years following, she spent most of her free time writing short stories, novellas, and poems, and composing pop songs. In 2006 she graduated from the University of Southern Maine with an MFA in Creative Writing, where she fell in love with writing novels for young adults. Kara has been a singer, songwriter, pianist, and flautist since she was a child and has performed throughout the world. She grew up in upstate New York in a place not unlike Dammertown and now resides in Cambridge, Massachusetts. *Tripping Back Blue* is Kara's first book.